AFRICAN-AMERICAN *Classics*

Graphic Classics® Volume Twenty-Two

2011

Edited by Tom Pomplun

and Lance Tooks

EUREKA PRODUCTIONS

8778 Oak Grove Road, Mount Horeb, Wisconsin 53572

www.graphicclassics.com

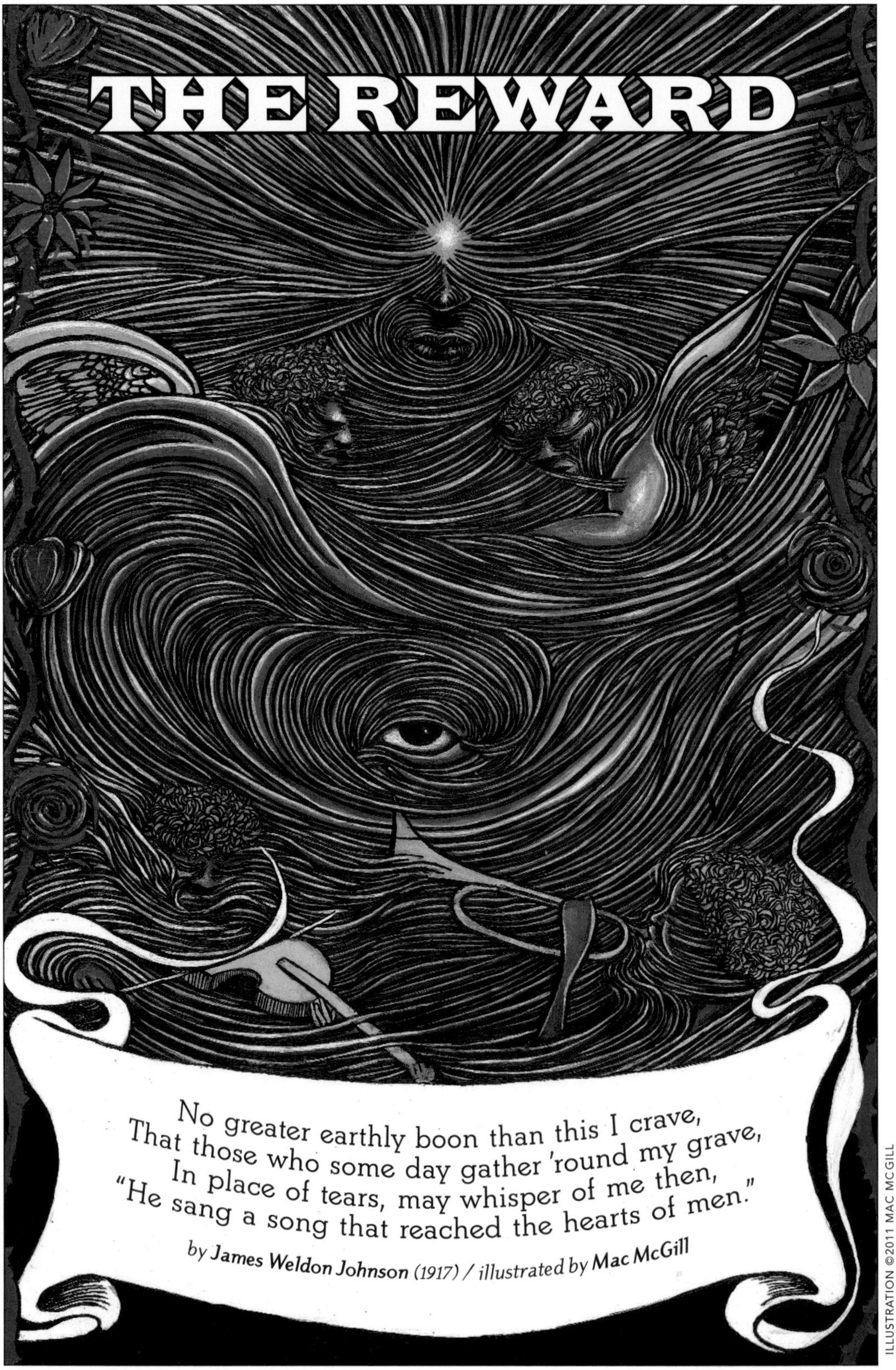
THE REWARD
No greater earthly boon than this I crave,
That those who some day gather 'round my grave,
In place of tears, may whisper of me then,
"He sang a song that reached the hearts of men."
by James Weldon Johnson (1917) / illustrated by Mac McGill

Graphic Classics®
Volume Twenty-Two

Cover illustration by Afua Richardson / Back cover illustration by Jimmie Robinson

African-American Classics: Graphic Classics Volume Twenty-Two / ISBN 978-0-9825630-4-5 is published by Eureka Productions. Price US $17.95, CAN $22.50. Available from Eureka Productions, 8778 Oak Grove Road, Mount Horeb, WI 53572. Tom Pomplun, designer and publisher, tom@graphicclassics.com. Lance Tooks, co-editor. Eileen Fitzgerald, editorial assistant. Compilation and all original works ©2011 Eureka Productions. Graphic Classics is a registered trademark of Eureka Productions. For ordering information and previews of upcoming volumes visit the Graphic Classics website at http://www.graphicclassics.com. Printed in Canada.

TWO AMERICANS

BY FLORENCE LEWIS BENTLEY (1921) / ADAPTED BY ALEX SIMMONS
ILLUSTRATED BY TREVOR VON EEDEN / COLOR BY ADRIAN JOHNSON

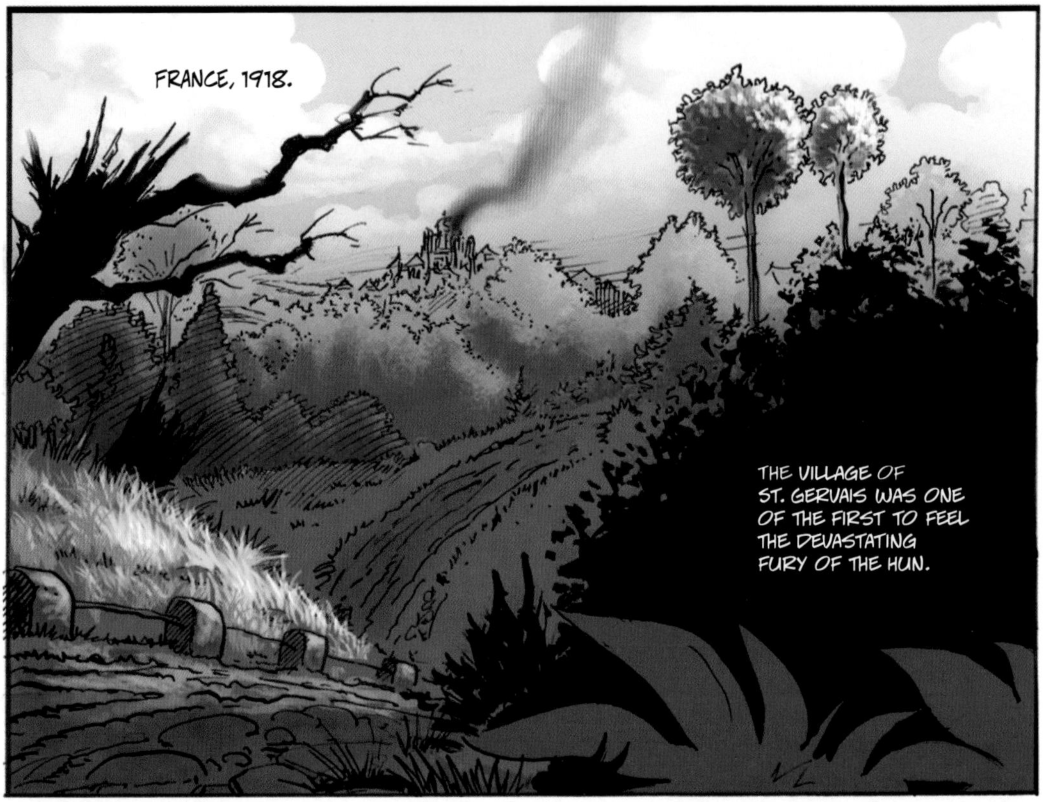
FRANCE, 1918.
THE VILLAGE OF ST. GERVAIS WAS ONE OF THE FIRST TO FEEL THE DEVASTATING FURY OF THE HUN.

AND FOR MANY MONTHS IT HAD LAIN DESERTED AND DESOLATE. BUT AFTER TWO YEARS OF EXILE MANY OF HER PEOPLE HAD STRAGGLED BACK. PATIENTLY THEY REPAIRED AND REBUILT; AND NOW ST. GERVAIS...

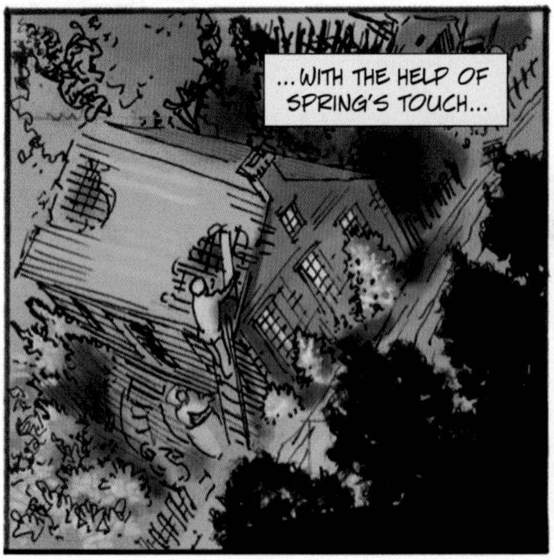
...WITH THE HELP OF SPRING'S TOUCH...

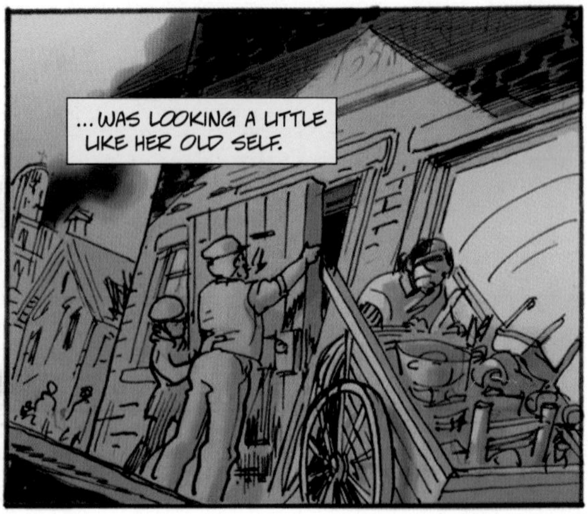
...WAS LOOKING A LITTLE LIKE HER OLD SELF.

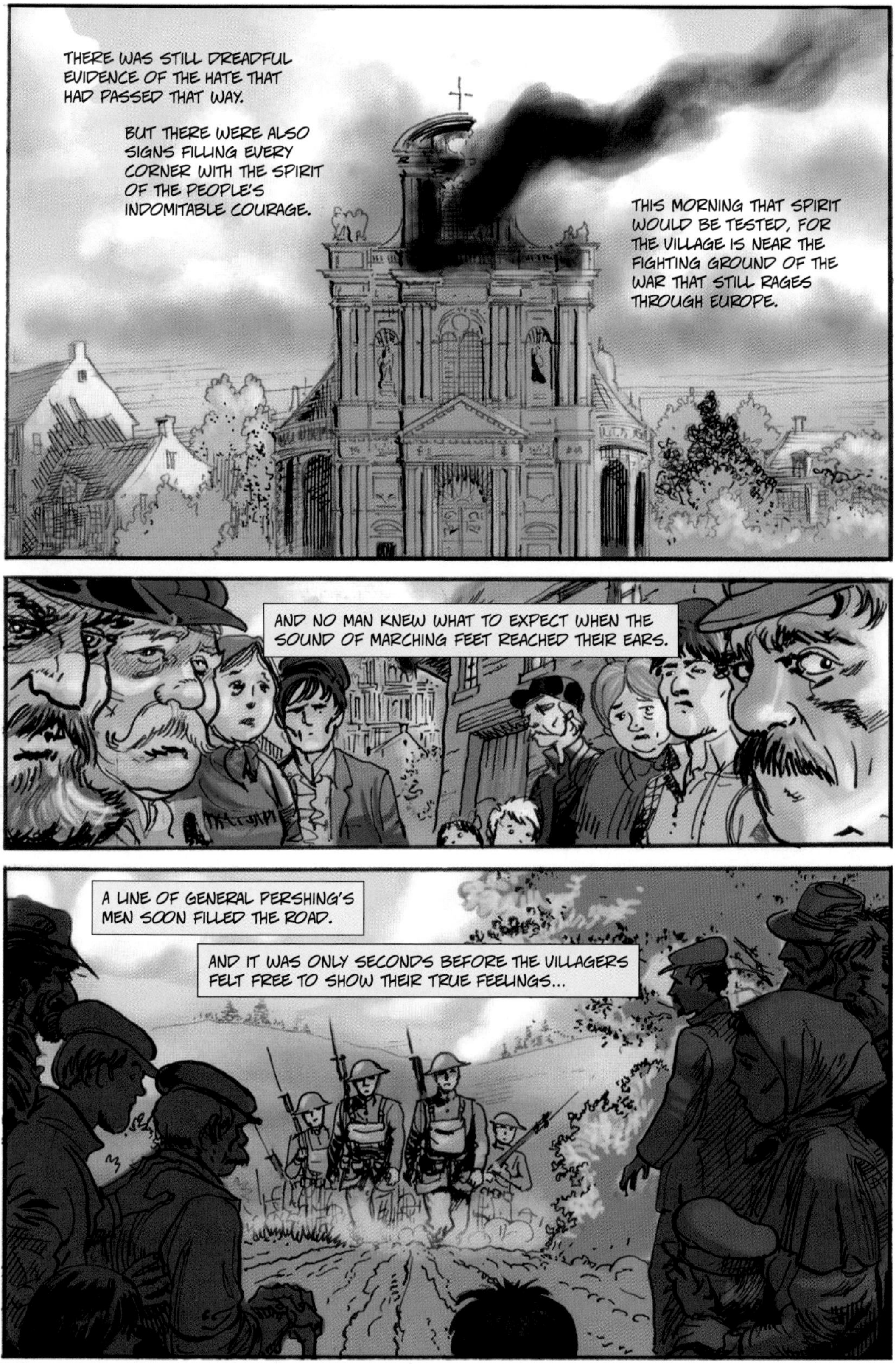
THERE WAS STILL DREADFUL EVIDENCE OF THE HATE THAT HAD PASSED THAT WAY.
BUT THERE WERE ALSO SIGNS FILLING EVERY CORNER WITH THE SPIRIT OF THE PEOPLE'S INDOMITABLE COURAGE.
THIS MORNING THAT SPIRIT WOULD BE TESTED, FOR THE VILLAGE IS NEAR THE FIGHTING GROUND OF THE WAR THAT STILL RAGES THROUGH EUROPE.
AND NO MAN KNEW WHAT TO EXPECT WHEN THE SOUND OF MARCHING FEET REACHED THEIR EARS.
A LINE OF GENERAL PERSHING'S MEN SOON FILLED THE ROAD.
AND IT WAS ONLY SECONDS BEFORE THE VILLAGERS FELT FREE TO SHOW THEIR TRUE FEELINGS...

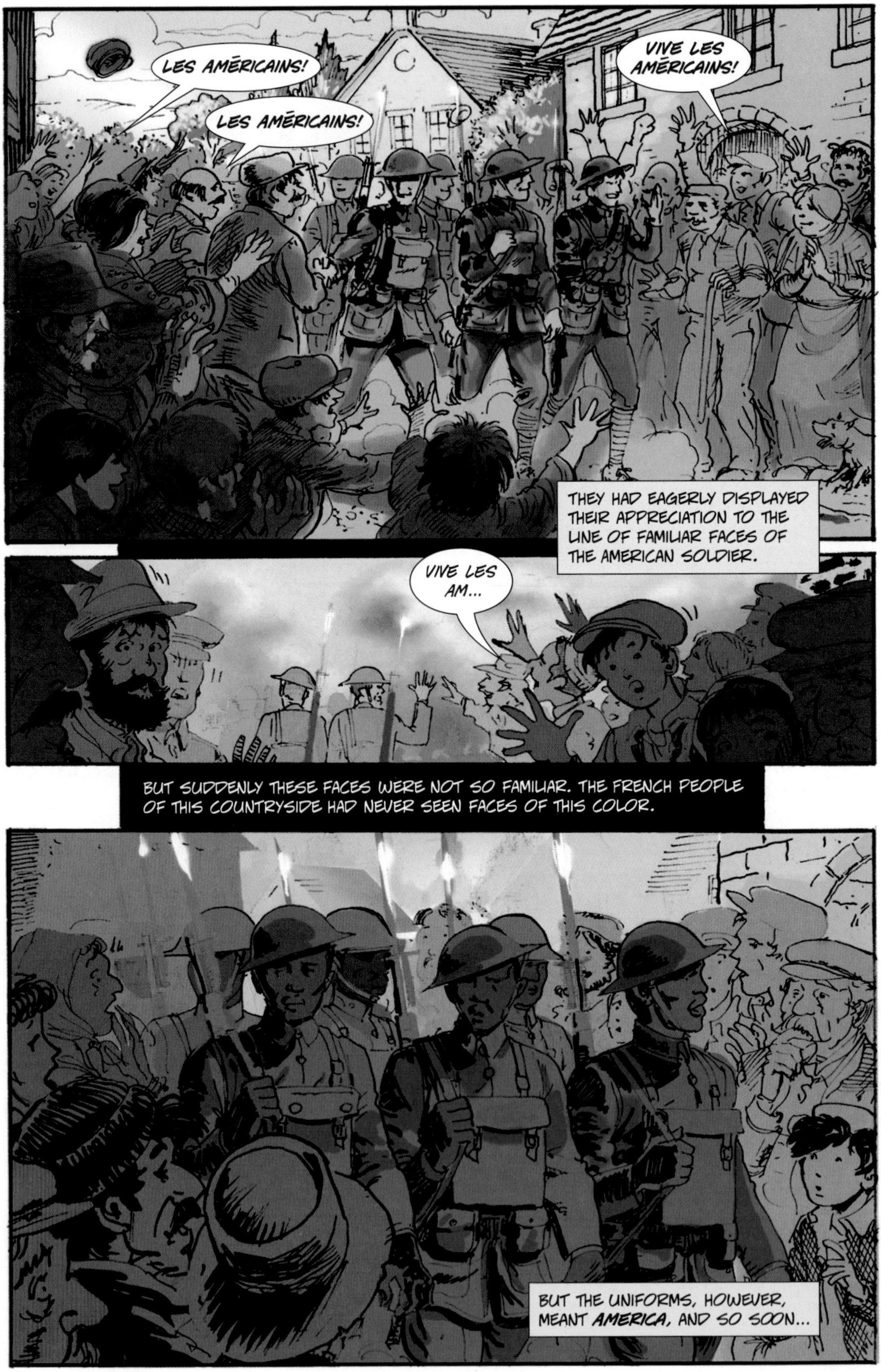
LES AMÉRICAINS!
LES AMÉRICAINS!
VIVE LES AMÉRICAINS!
THEY HAD EAGERLY DISPLAYED THEIR APPRECIATION TO THE LINE OF FAMILIAR FACES OF THE AMERICAN SOLDIER.
VIVE LES AM...
BUT SUDDENLY THESE FACES WERE NOT SO FAMILIAR. THE FRENCH PEOPLE OF THIS COUNTRYSIDE HAD NEVER SEEN FACES OF THIS COLOR.
BUT THE UNIFORMS, HOWEVER, MEANT ***AMERICA***, AND SO SOON...

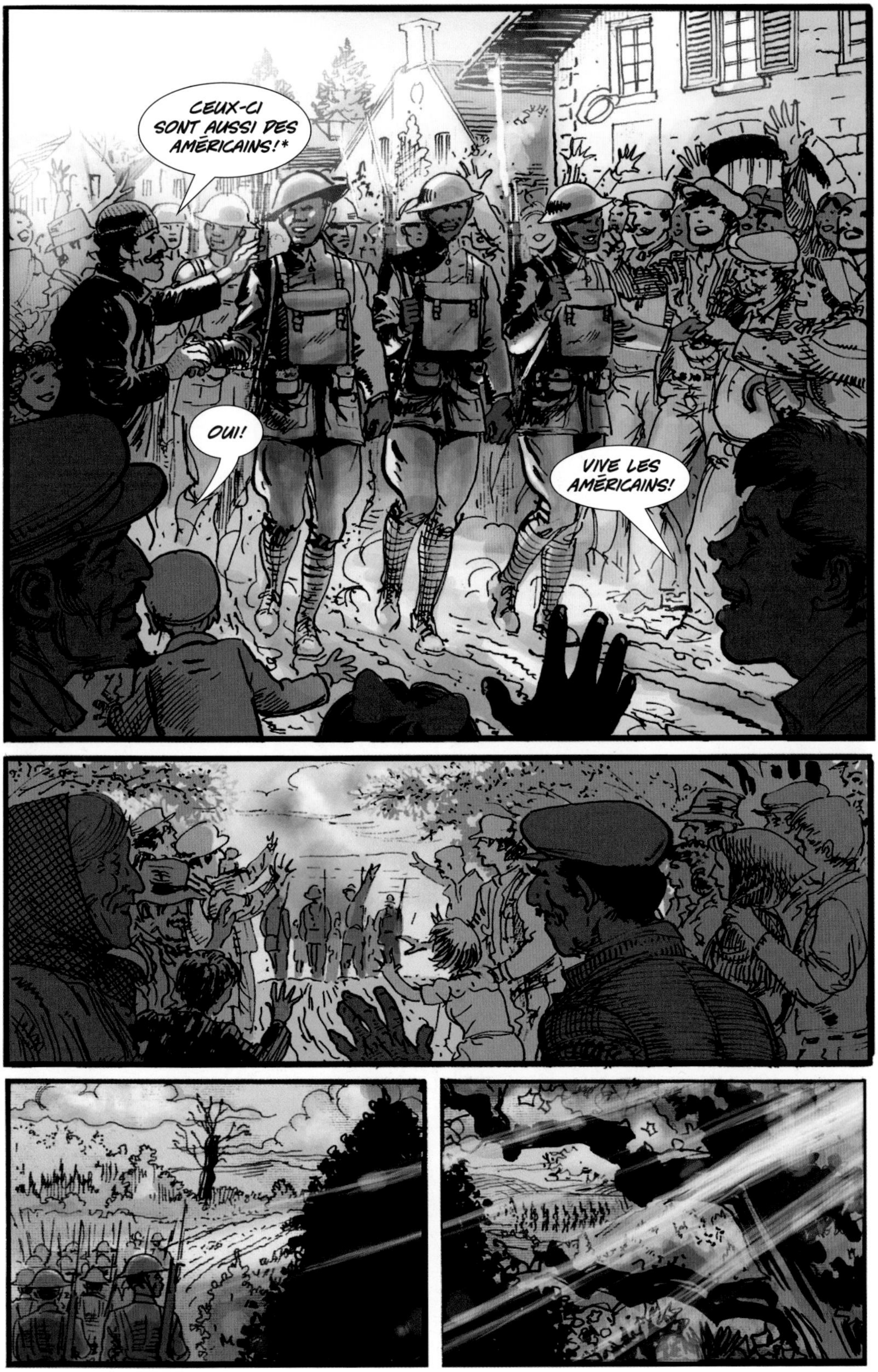
CEUX-CI SONT AUSSI DES AMÉRICAINS!*
OUI!
VIVE LES AMÉRICAINS!

* These are Americans, too!

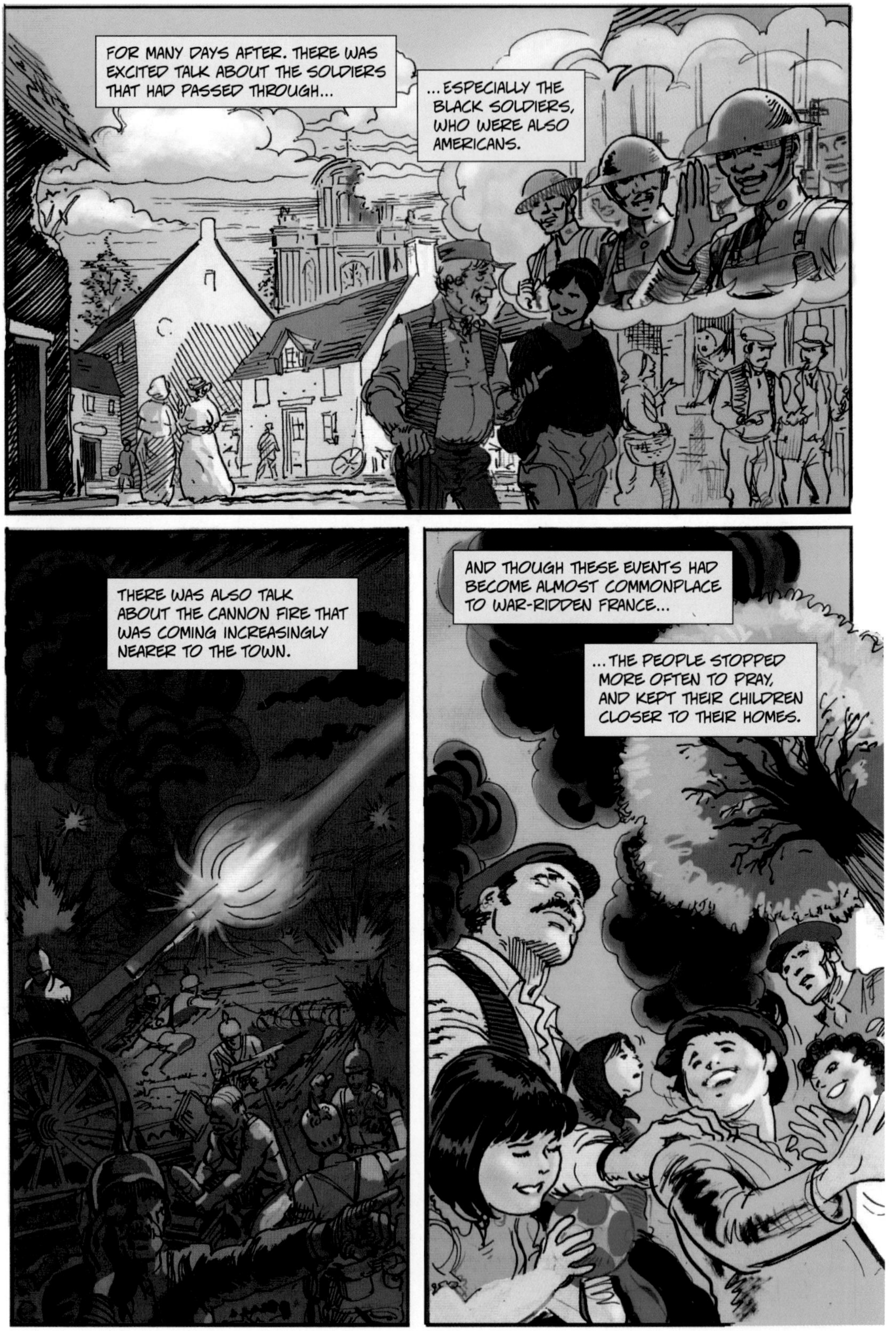
FOR MANY DAYS AFTER. THERE WAS EXCITED TALK ABOUT THE SOLDIERS THAT HAD PASSED THROUGH...
...ESPECIALLY THE BLACK SOLDIERS, WHO WERE ALSO AMERICANS.
THERE WAS ALSO TALK ABOUT THE CANNON FIRE THAT WAS COMING INCREASINGLY NEARER TO THE TOWN.
AND THOUGH THESE EVENTS HAD BECOME ALMOST COMMONPLACE TO WAR-RIDDEN FRANCE...
...THE PEOPLE STOPPED MORE OFTEN TO PRAY, AND KEPT THEIR CHILDREN CLOSER TO THEIR HOMES.

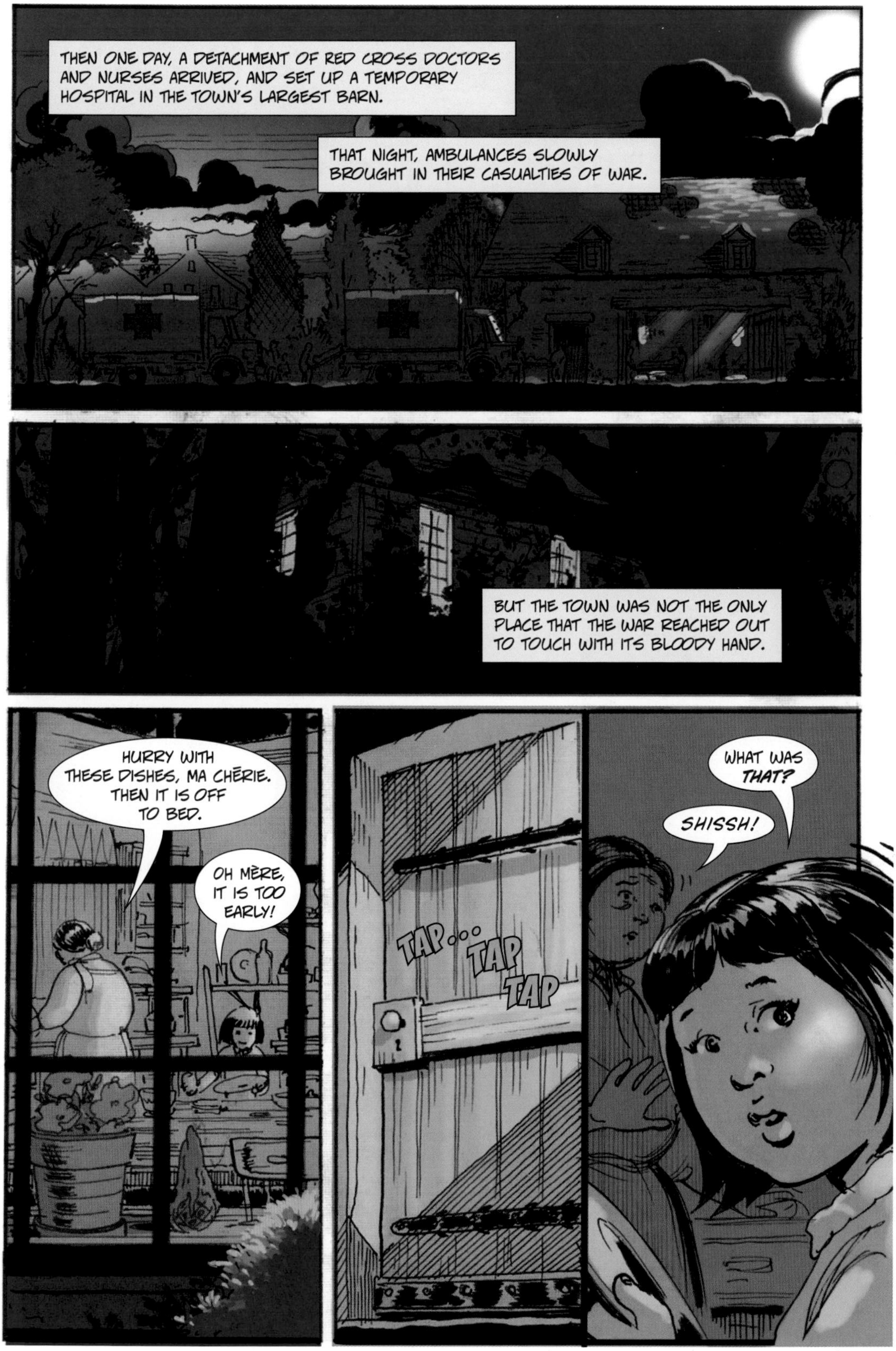
THEN ONE DAY, A DETACHMENT OF RED CROSS DOCTORS AND NURSES ARRIVED, AND SET UP A TEMPORARY HOSPITAL IN THE TOWN'S LARGEST BARN.
THAT NIGHT, AMBULANCES SLOWLY BROUGHT IN THEIR CASUALTIES OF WAR.
BUT THE TOWN WAS NOT THE ONLY PLACE THAT THE WAR REACHED OUT TO TOUCH WITH ITS BLOODY HAND.
HURRY WITH THESE DISHES, MA CHÉRIE. THEN IT IS OFF TO BED.
OH MÈRE, IT IS TOO EARLY!
TAP... TAP TAP
WHAT WAS *THAT?*
SHISSH!

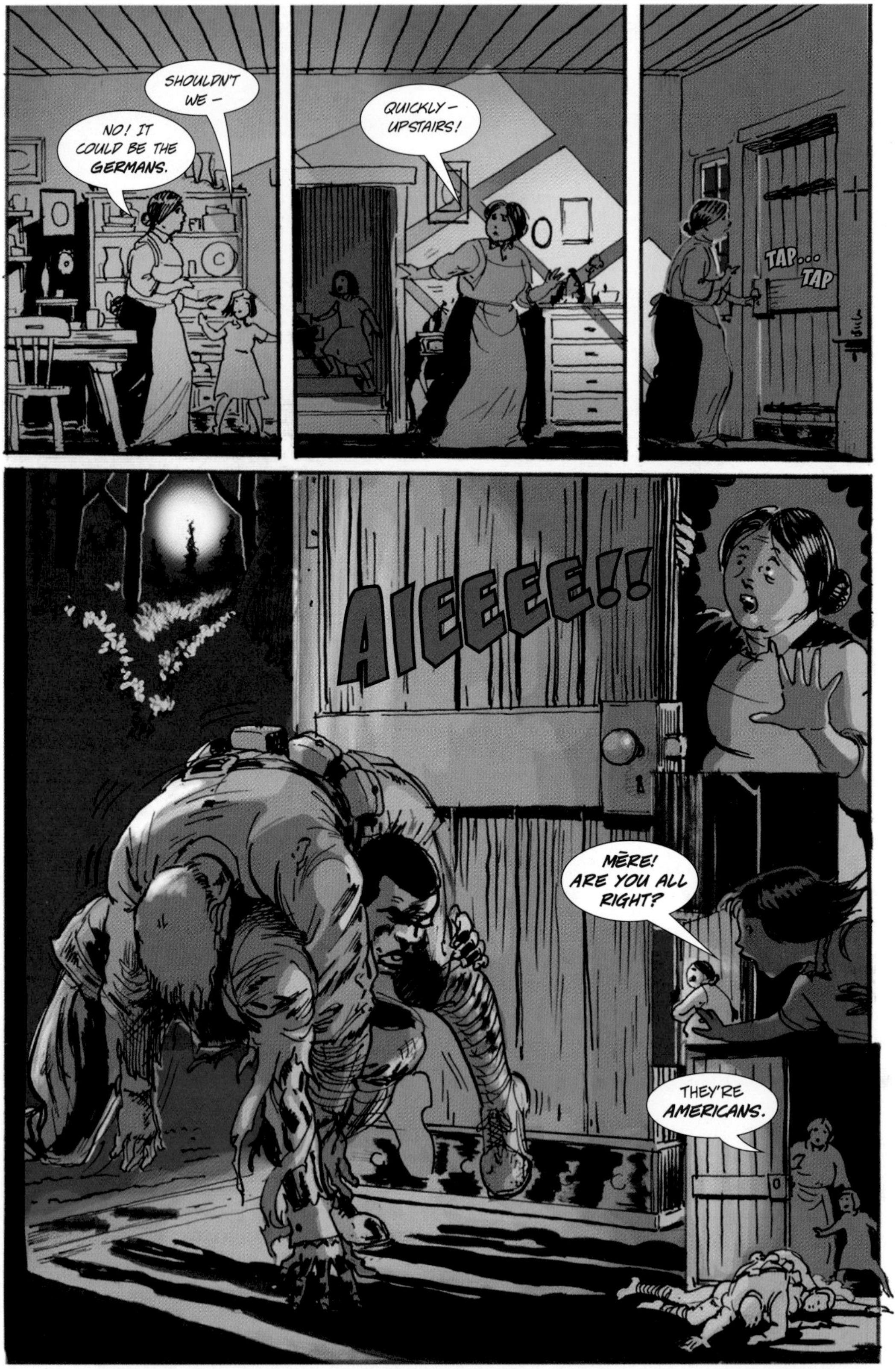
SHOULDN'T WE –
NO! IT COULD BE THE GERMANS.
QUICKLY – UPSTAIRS!
TAP... TAP
AIEEEE!!
MÈRE! ARE YOU ALL RIGHT?
THEY'RE AMERICANS.

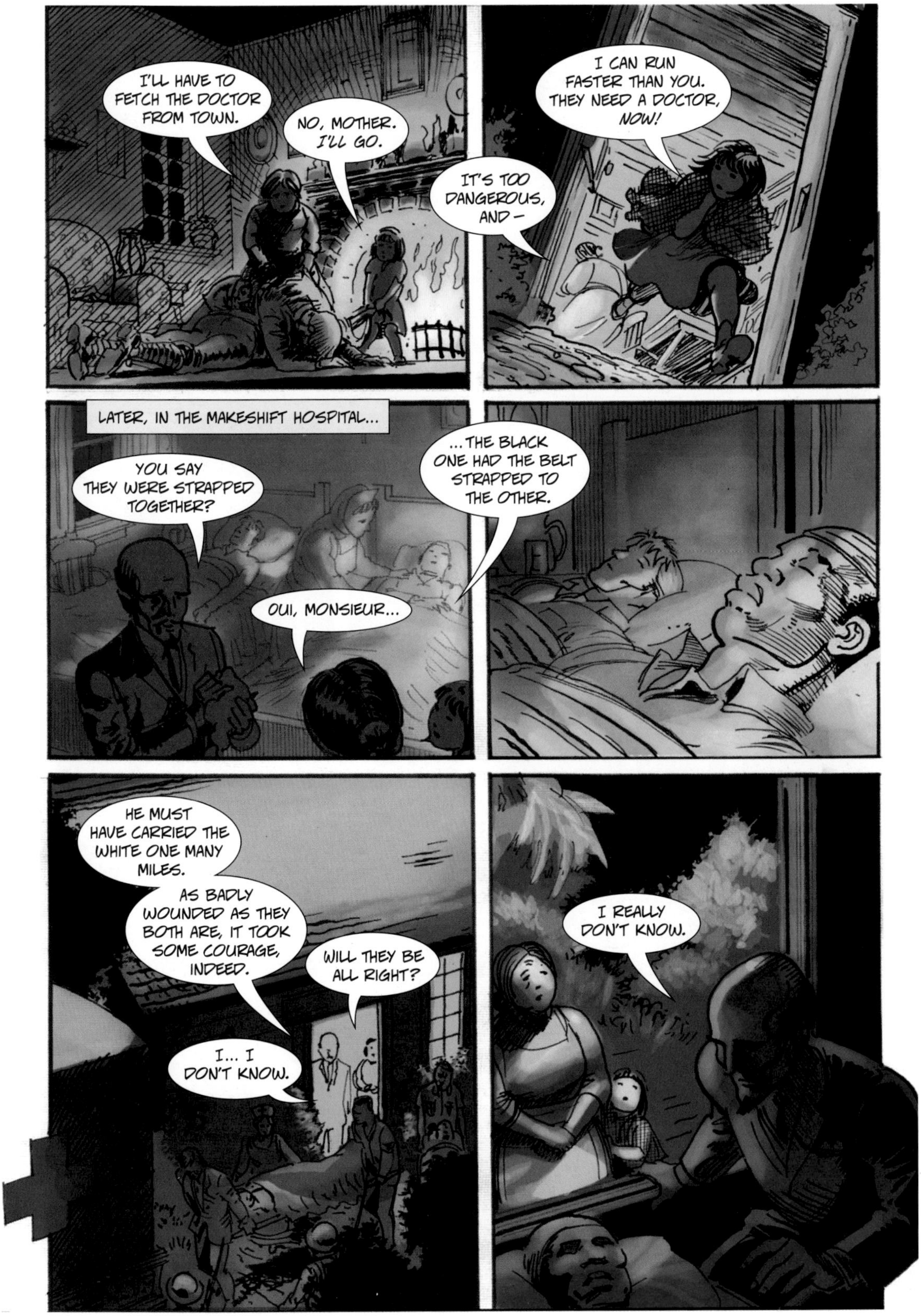
I'LL HAVE TO FETCH THE DOCTOR FROM TOWN.
NO, MOTHER. I'LL GO.
IT'S TOO DANGEROUS, AND –
I CAN RUN FASTER THAN YOU. THEY NEED A DOCTOR, NOW!
LATER, IN THE MAKESHIFT HOSPITAL...
YOU SAY THEY WERE STRAPPED TOGETHER?
OUI, MONSIEUR...
...THE BLACK ONE HAD THE BELT STRAPPED TO THE OTHER.
HE MUST HAVE CARRIED THE WHITE ONE MANY MILES.
AS BADLY WOUNDED AS THEY BOTH ARE, IT TOOK SOME COURAGE, INDEED.
WILL THEY BE ALL RIGHT?
I... I DON'T KNOW.
I REALLY DON'T KNOW.

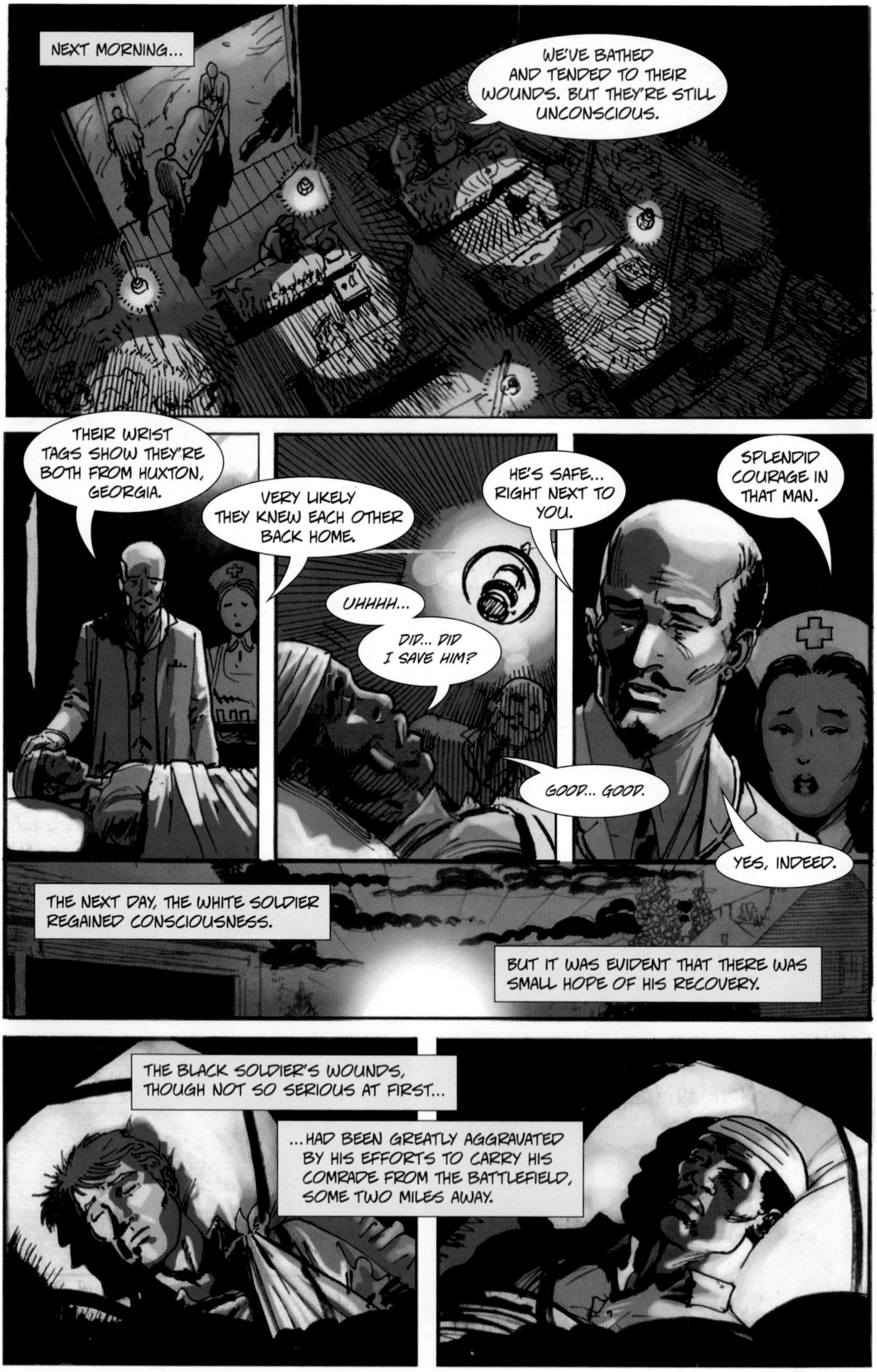
NEXT MORNING...
WE'VE BATHED AND TENDED TO THEIR WOUNDS. BUT THEY'RE STILL UNCONSCIOUS.
THEIR WRIST TAGS SHOW THEY'RE BOTH FROM HUXTON, GEORGIA.
VERY LIKELY THEY KNEW EACH OTHER BACK HOME.
UHHHH...
DID... DID I SAVE HIM?
HE'S SAFE... RIGHT NEXT TO YOU.
SPLENDID COURAGE IN THAT MAN.
GOOD... GOOD.
YES, INDEED.
THE NEXT DAY, THE WHITE SOLDIER REGAINED CONSCIOUSNESS.
BUT IT WAS EVIDENT THAT THERE WAS SMALL HOPE OF HIS RECOVERY.
THE BLACK SOLDIER'S WOUNDS, THOUGH NOT SO SERIOUS AT FIRST...
...HAD BEEN GREATLY AGGRAVATED BY HIS EFFORTS TO CARRY HIS COMRADE FROM THE BATTLEFIELD, SOME TWO MILES AWAY.

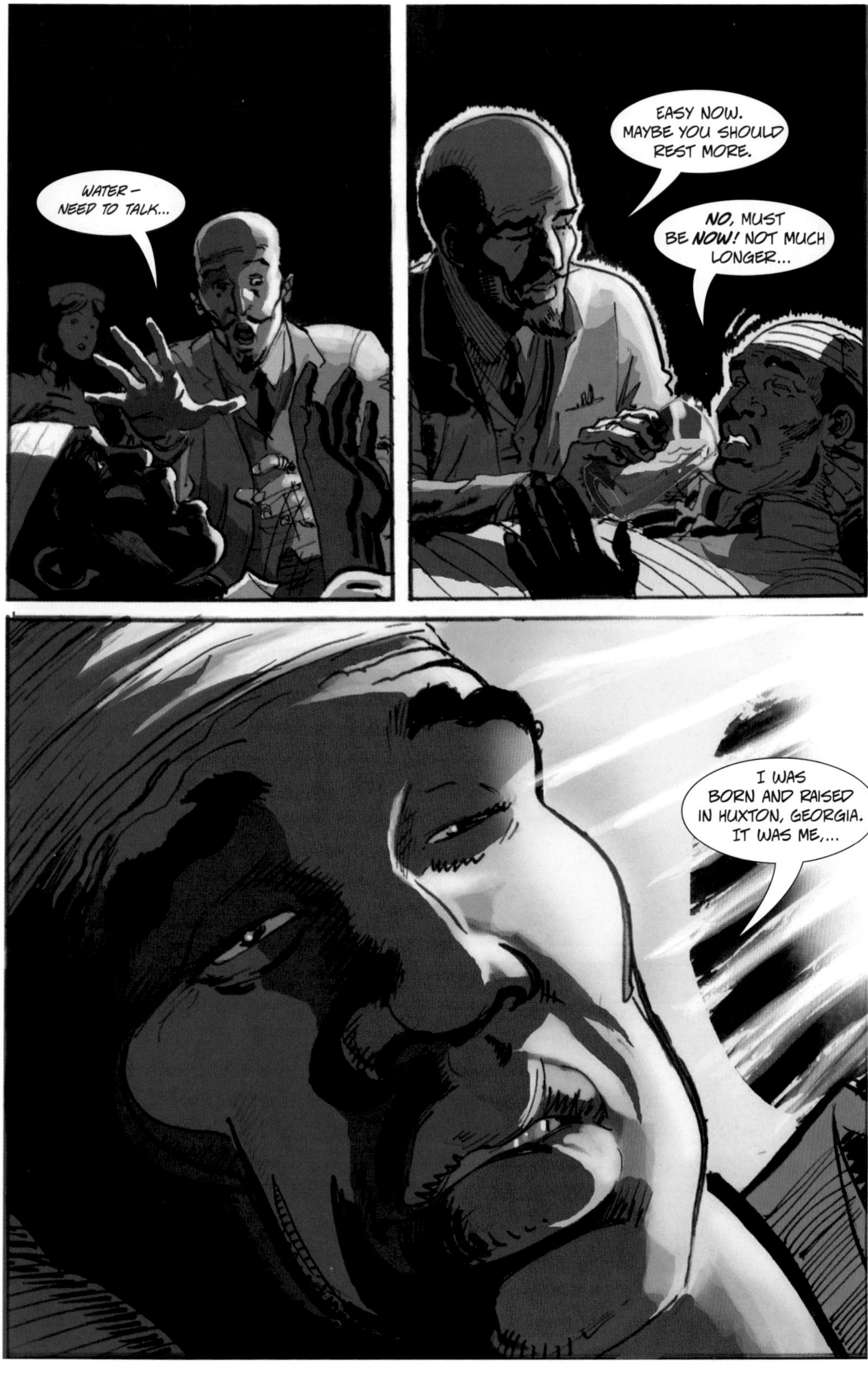
WATER—
NEED TO TALK...
EASY NOW. MAYBE YOU SHOULD REST MORE.
NO, MUST BE NOW! NOT MUCH LONGER...
I WAS BORN AND RAISED IN HUXTON, GEORGIA. IT WAS ME,...

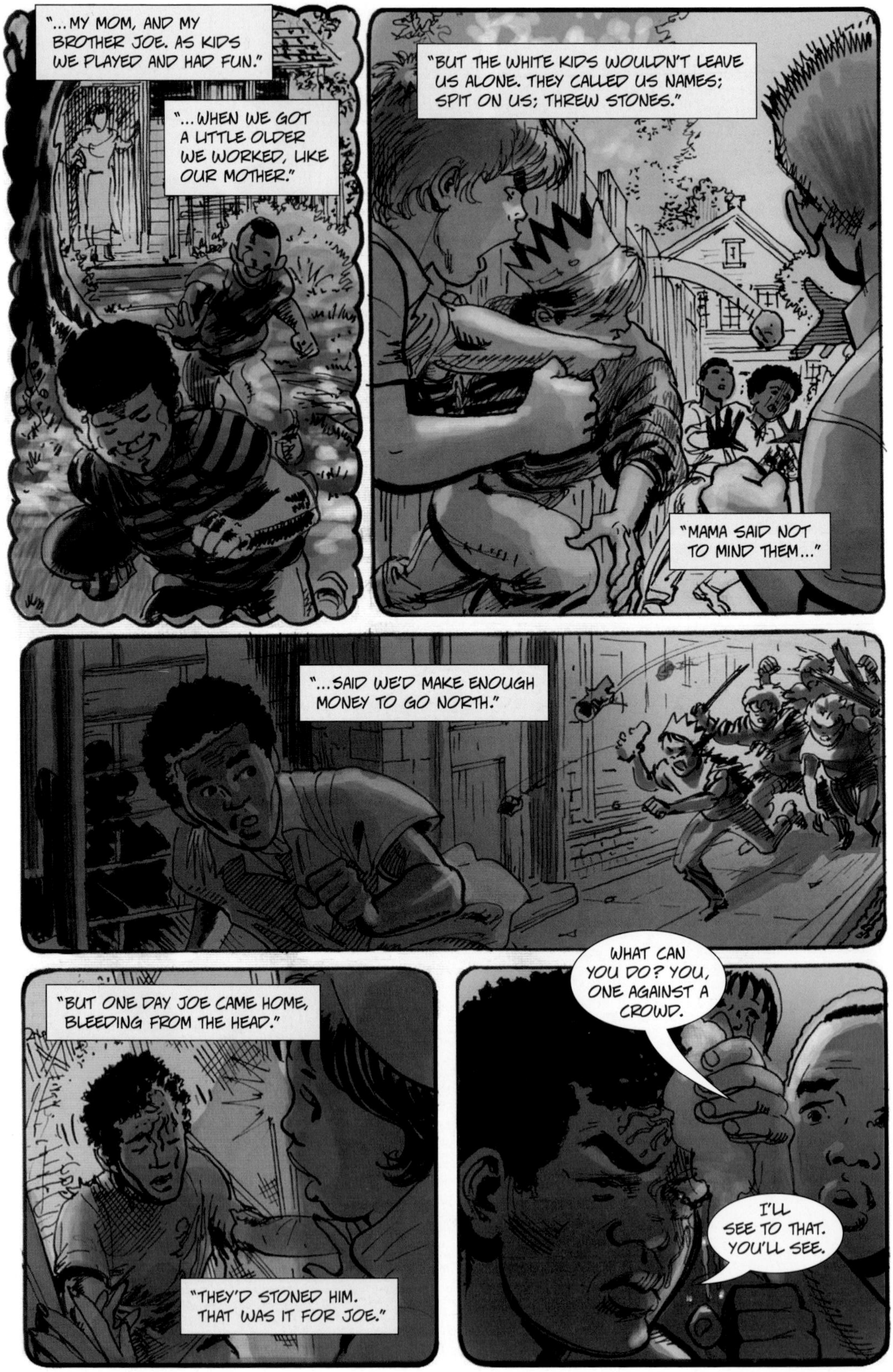
"...MY MOM, AND MY BROTHER JOE. AS KIDS WE PLAYED AND HAD FUN."
"...WHEN WE GOT A LITTLE OLDER WE WORKED, LIKE OUR MOTHER."
"BUT THE WHITE KIDS WOULDN'T LEAVE US ALONE. THEY CALLED US NAMES; SPIT ON US; THREW STONES."
"MAMA SAID NOT TO MIND THEM..."
"...SAID WE'D MAKE ENOUGH MONEY TO GO NORTH."
"BUT ONE DAY JOE CAME HOME, BLEEDING FROM THE HEAD."
"THEY'D STONED HIM. THAT WAS IT FOR JOE."
WHAT CAN YOU DO? YOU, ONE AGAINST A CROWD.
I'LL SEE TO THAT. YOU'LL SEE.

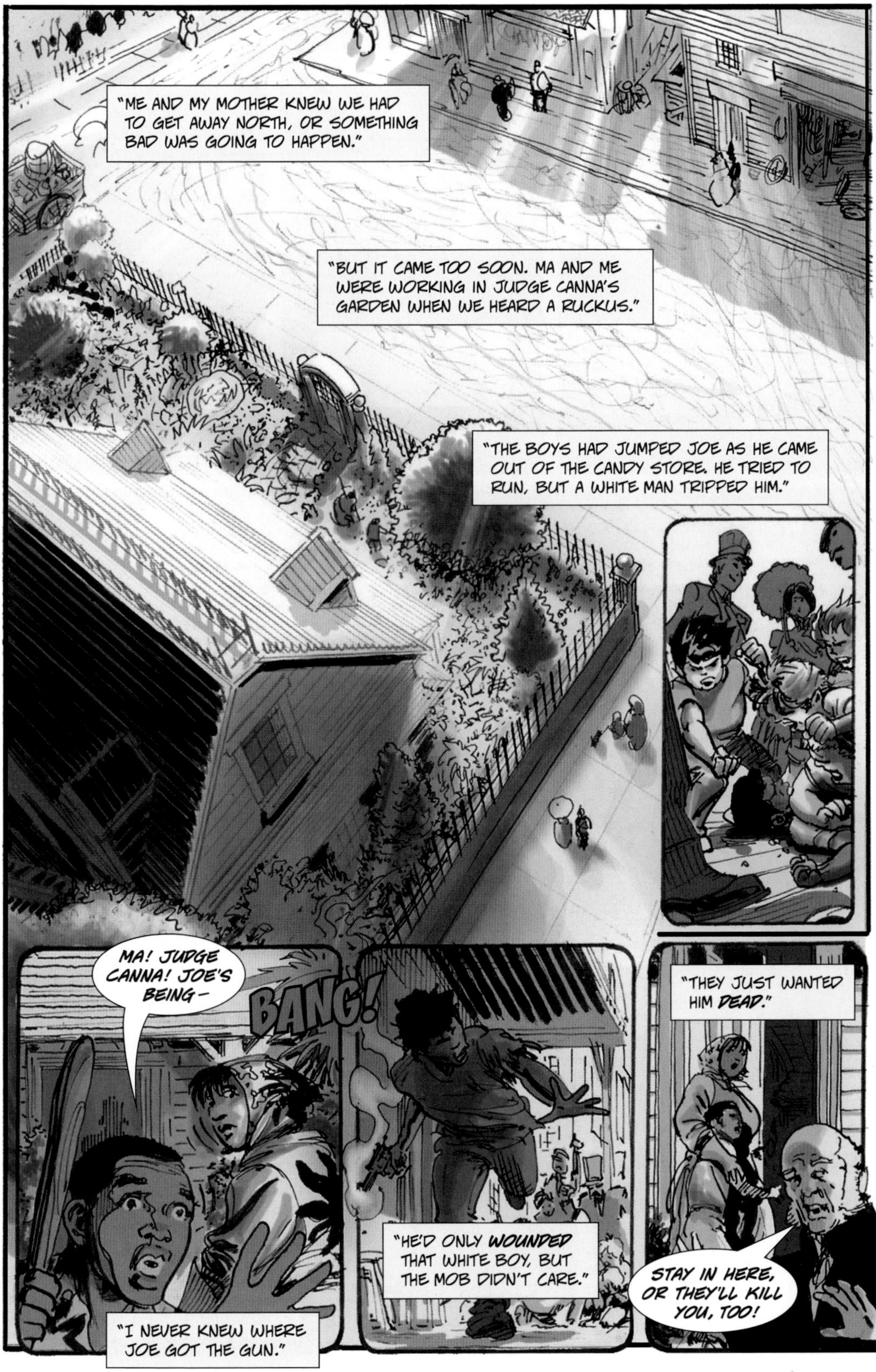
"ME AND MY MOTHER KNEW WE HAD TO GET AWAY NORTH, OR SOMETHING BAD WAS GOING TO HAPPEN."
"BUT IT CAME TOO SOON. MA AND ME WERE WORKING IN JUDGE CANNA'S GARDEN WHEN WE HEARD A RUCKUS."
"THE BOYS HAD JUMPED JOE AS HE CAME OUT OF THE CANDY STORE. HE TRIED TO RUN, BUT A WHITE MAN TRIPPED HIM."
MA! JUDGE CANNA! JOE'S BEING—
"I NEVER KNEW WHERE JOE GOT THE GUN."
BANG!
"HE'D ONLY WOUNDED THAT WHITE BOY, BUT THE MOB DIDN'T CARE."
"THEY JUST WANTED HIM DEAD."
STAY IN HERE, OR THEY'LL KILL YOU, TOO!

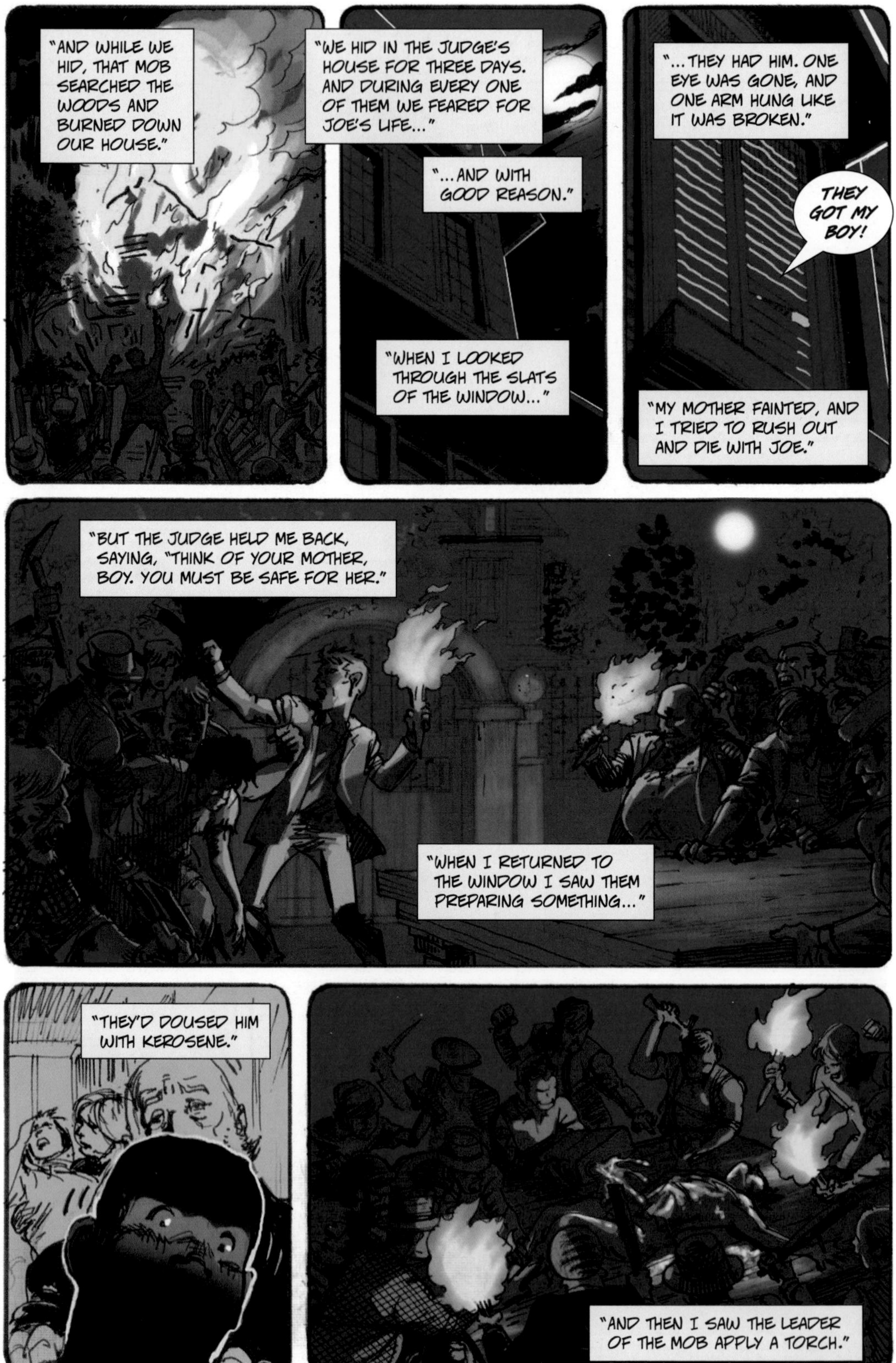
"AND WHILE WE HID, THAT MOB SEARCHED THE WOODS AND BURNED DOWN OUR HOUSE."
"WE HID IN THE JUDGE'S HOUSE FOR THREE DAYS. AND DURING EVERY ONE OF THEM WE FEARED FOR JOE'S LIFE..."
"...AND WITH GOOD REASON."
"WHEN I LOOKED THROUGH THE SLATS OF THE WINDOW..."
"...THEY HAD HIM. ONE EYE WAS GONE, AND ONE ARM HUNG LIKE IT WAS BROKEN."
THEY GOT MY BOY!
"MY MOTHER FAINTED, AND I TRIED TO RUSH OUT AND DIE WITH JOE."
"BUT THE JUDGE HELD ME BACK, SAYING, "THINK OF YOUR MOTHER, BOY. YOU MUST BE SAFE FOR HER."
"WHEN I RETURNED TO THE WINDOW I SAW THEM PREPARING SOMETHING..."
"THEY'D DOUSED HIM WITH KEROSENE."
"AND THEN I SAW THE LEADER OF THE MOB APPLY A TORCH."

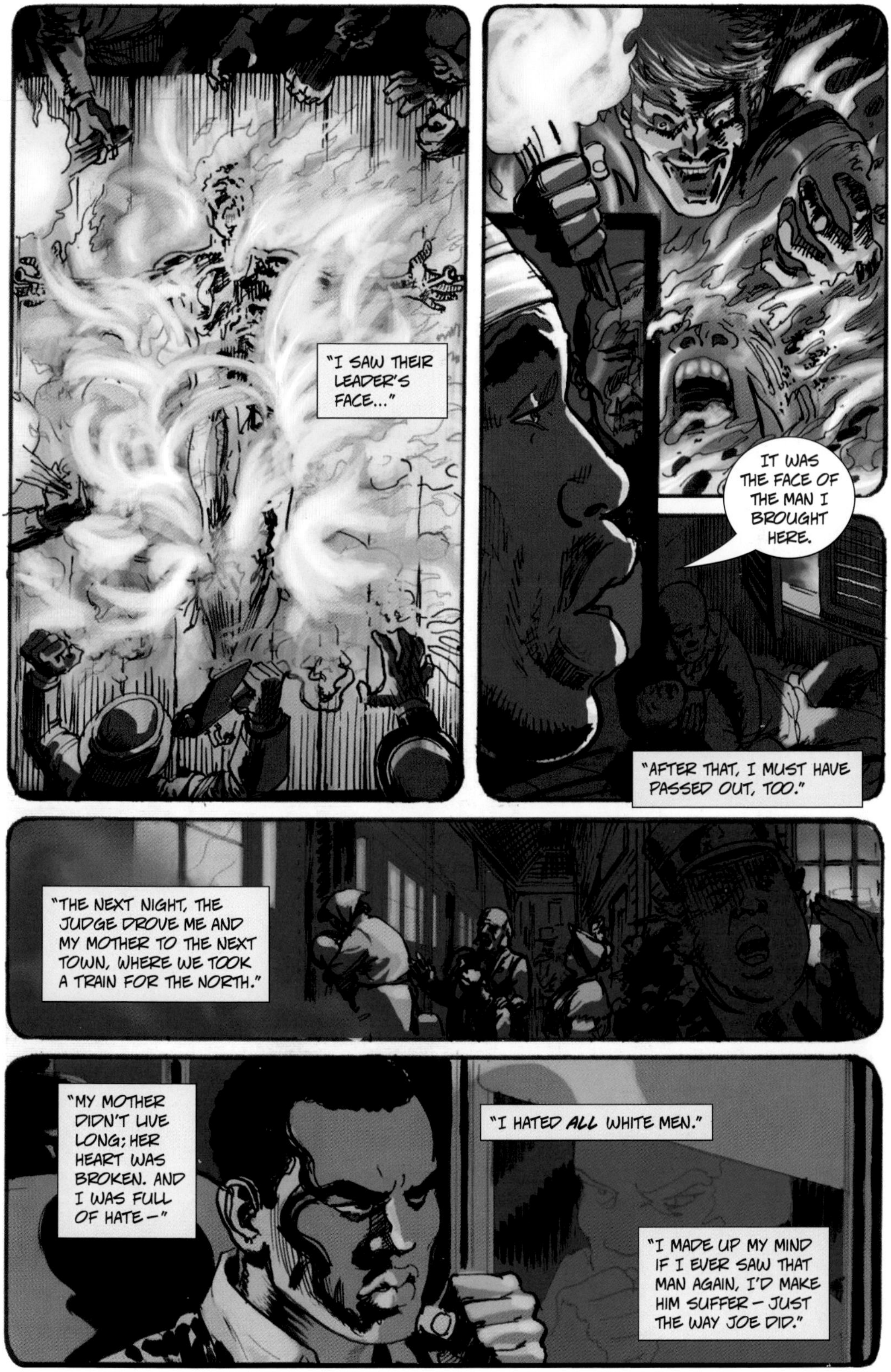
"I SAW THEIR LEADER'S FACE..."
IT WAS THE FACE OF THE MAN I BROUGHT HERE.
"AFTER THAT, I MUST HAVE PASSED OUT, TOO."
"THE NEXT NIGHT, THE JUDGE DROVE ME AND MY MOTHER TO THE NEXT TOWN, WHERE WE TOOK A TRAIN FOR THE NORTH."
"MY MOTHER DIDN'T LIVE LONG; HER HEART WAS BROKEN. AND I WAS FULL OF HATE–"
"I HATED ***ALL*** WHITE MEN."
"I MADE UP MY MIND IF I EVER SAW THAT MAN AGAIN, I'D MAKE HIM SUFFER– JUST THE WAY JOE DID."

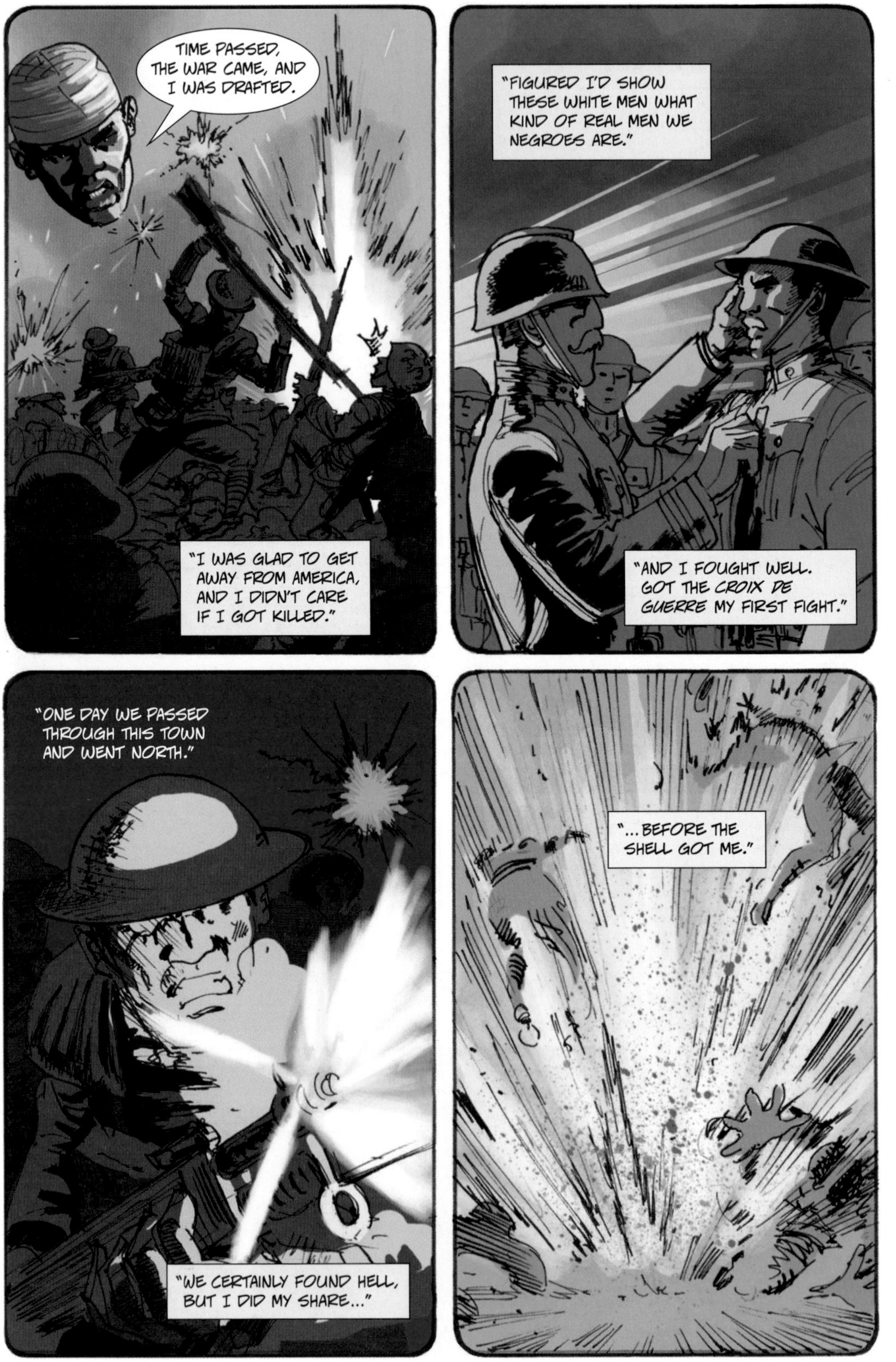
TIME PASSED, THE WAR CAME, AND I WAS DRAFTED.
"I WAS GLAD TO GET AWAY FROM AMERICA, AND I DIDN'T CARE IF I GOT KILLED."
"FIGURED I'D SHOW THESE WHITE MEN WHAT KIND OF REAL MEN WE NEGROES ARE."
"AND I FOUGHT WELL. GOT THE CROIX DE GUERRE MY FIRST FIGHT."
"ONE DAY WE PASSED THROUGH THIS TOWN AND WENT NORTH."
"WE CERTAINLY FOUND HELL, BUT I DID MY SHARE..."
"...BEFORE THE SHELL GOT ME."

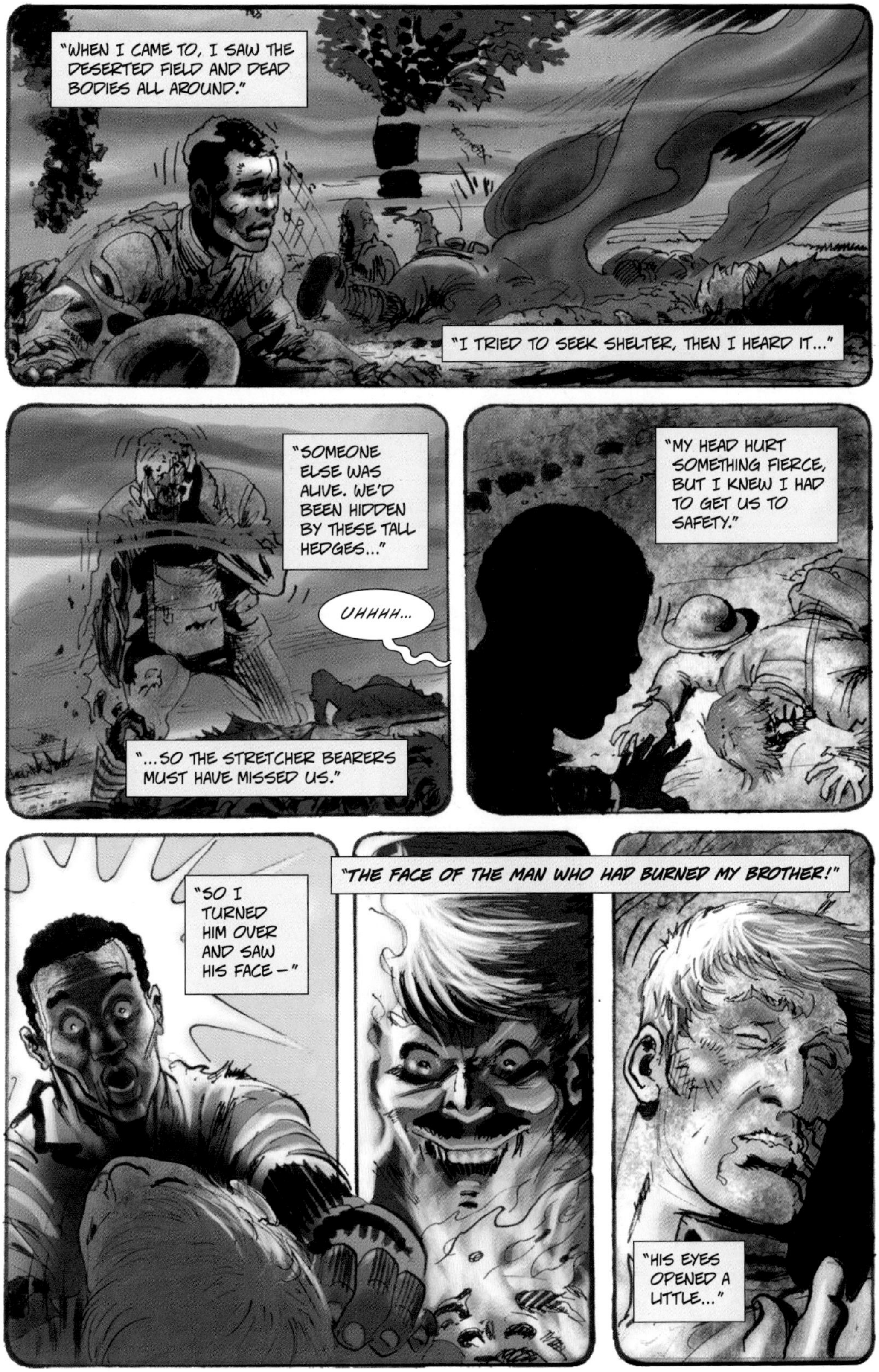
"WHEN I CAME TO, I SAW THE DESERTED FIELD AND DEAD BODIES ALL AROUND."
"I TRIED TO SEEK SHELTER, THEN I HEARD IT..."
"SOMEONE ELSE WAS ALIVE. WE'D BEEN HIDDEN BY THESE TALL HEDGES..."
UHHHH...
"...SO THE STRETCHER BEARERS MUST HAVE MISSED US."
"MY HEAD HURT SOMETHING FIERCE, BUT I KNEW I HAD TO GET US TO SAFETY."
"SO I TURNED HIM OVER AND SAW HIS FACE—"
"THE FACE OF THE MAN WHO HAD BURNED MY BROTHER!"
"HIS EYES OPENED A LITTLE..."

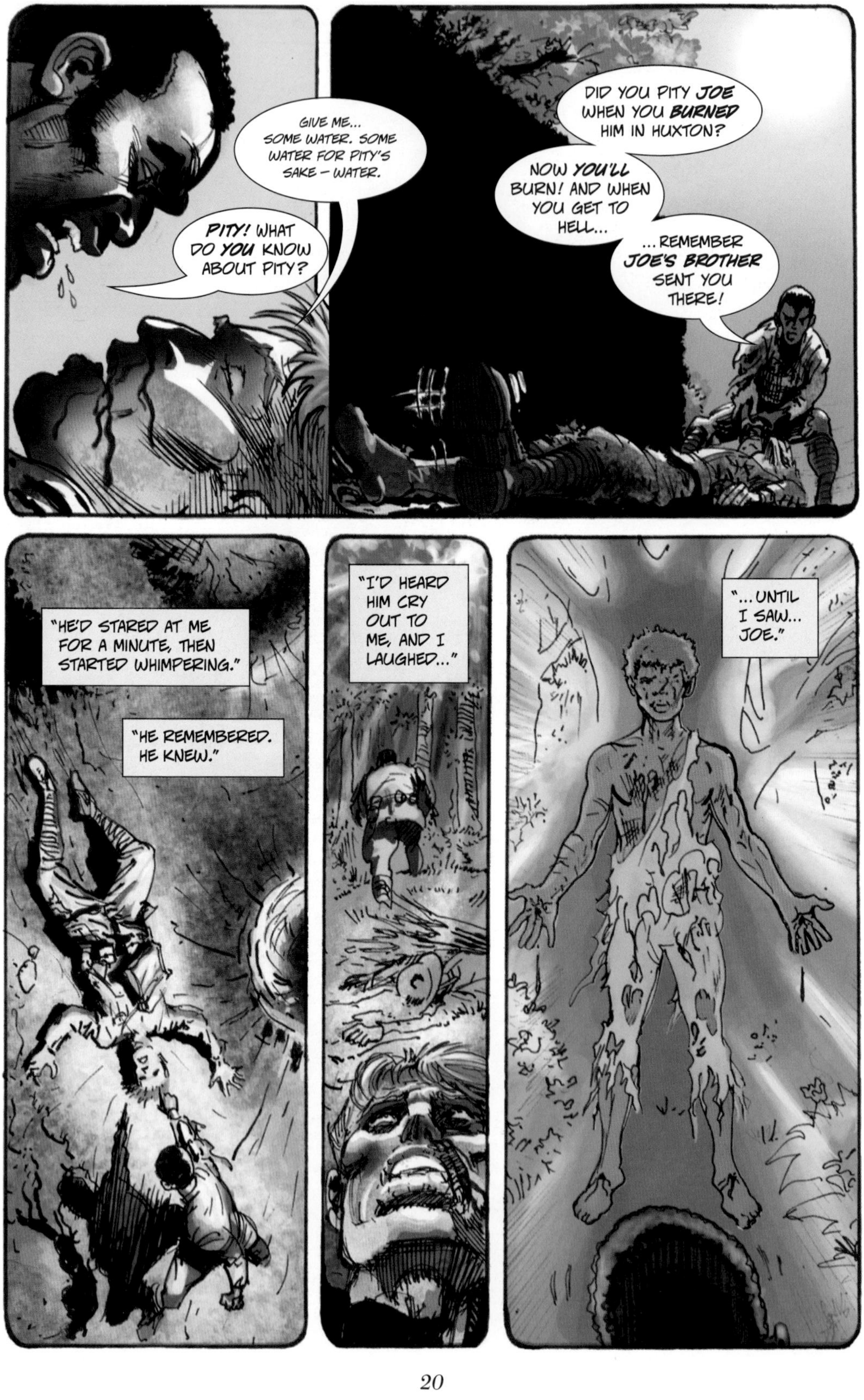
GIVE ME... SOME WATER. SOME WATER FOR PITY'S SAKE – WATER.
PITY! WHAT DO YOU KNOW ABOUT PITY?
DID YOU PITY JOE WHEN YOU BURNED HIM IN HUXTON?
NOW YOU'LL BURN! AND WHEN YOU GET TO HELL...
...REMEMBER JOE'S BROTHER SENT YOU THERE!
"HE'D STARED AT ME FOR A MINUTE, THEN STARTED WHIMPERING."
"HE REMEMBERED. HE KNEW."
"I'D HEARD HIM CRY OUT TO ME, AND I LAUGHED..."
"...UNTIL I SAW... JOE."

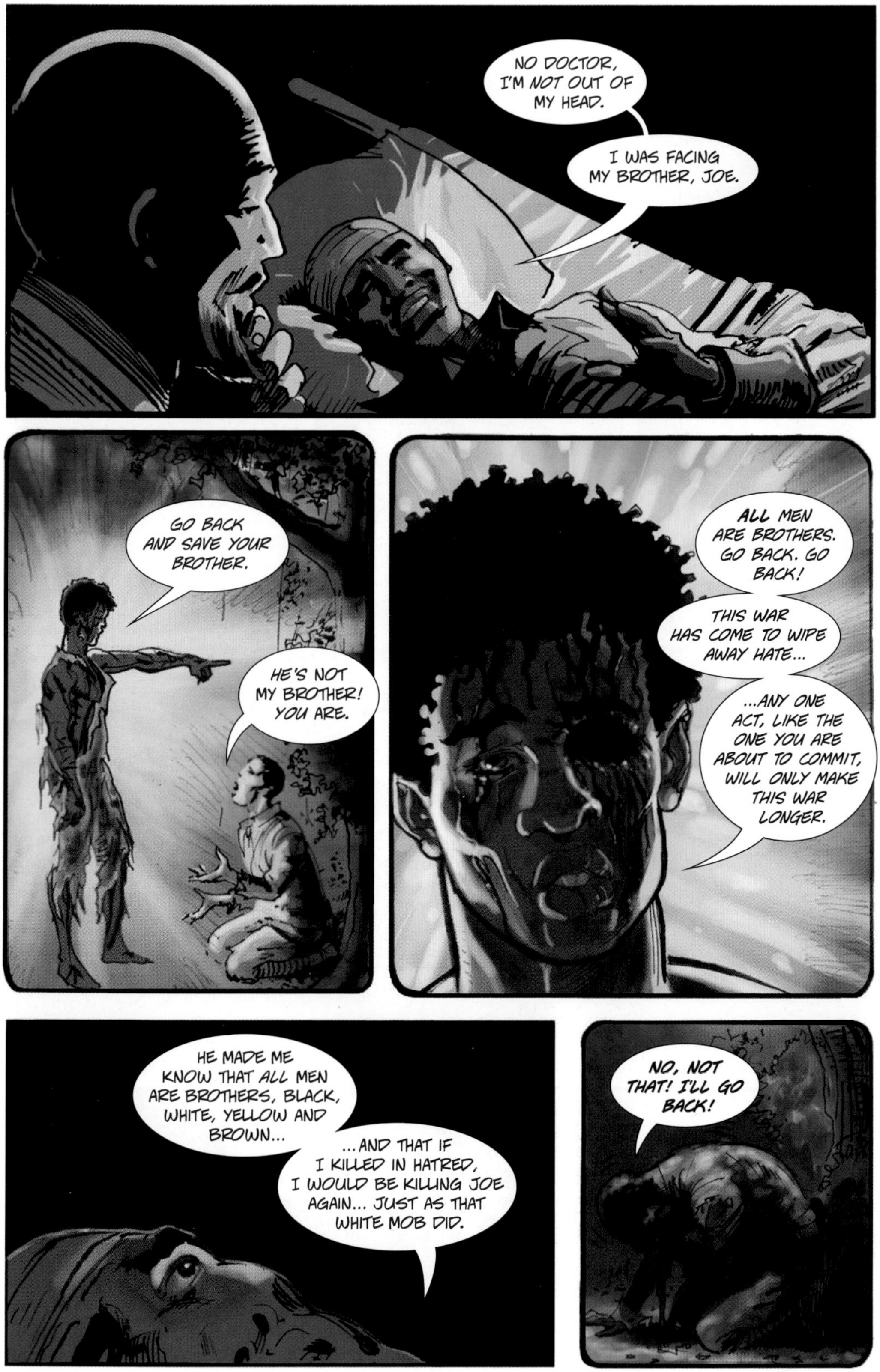
NO DOCTOR, I'M *NOT* OUT OF MY HEAD.
I WAS FACING MY BROTHER, JOE.
GO BACK AND SAVE YOUR BROTHER.
HE'S NOT MY BROTHER! YOU ARE.
ALL MEN ARE BROTHERS. GO BACK. GO BACK!
THIS WAR HAS COME TO WIPE AWAY HATE...
...ANY ONE ACT, LIKE THE ONE YOU ARE ABOUT TO COMMIT, WILL ONLY MAKE THIS WAR LONGER.
HE MADE ME KNOW THAT *ALL* MEN ARE BROTHERS, BLACK, WHITE, YELLOW AND BROWN...
...AND THAT IF I KILLED IN HATRED, I WOULD BE KILLING JOE AGAIN... JUST AS THAT WHITE MOB DID.
NO, NOT THAT! I'LL GO BACK!

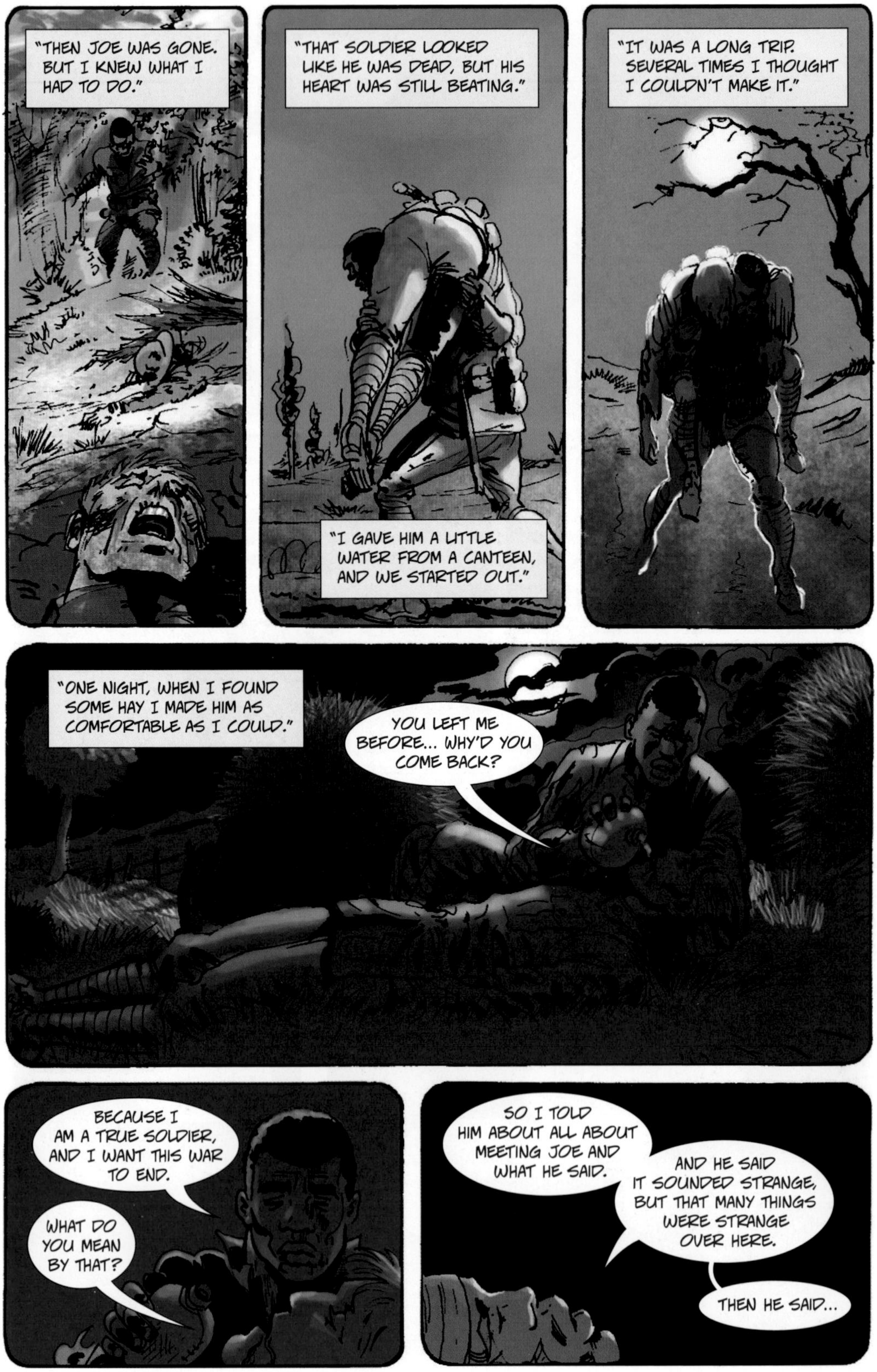
"THEN JOE WAS GONE. BUT I KNEW WHAT I HAD TO DO."
"THAT SOLDIER LOOKED LIKE HE WAS DEAD, BUT HIS HEART WAS STILL BEATING."
"I GAVE HIM A LITTLE WATER FROM A CANTEEN, AND WE STARTED OUT."
"IT WAS A LONG TRIP. SEVERAL TIMES I THOUGHT I COULDN'T MAKE IT."
"ONE NIGHT, WHEN I FOUND SOME HAY I MADE HIM AS COMFORTABLE AS I COULD."
YOU LEFT ME BEFORE... WHY'D YOU COME BACK?
BECAUSE I AM A TRUE SOLDIER, AND I WANT THIS WAR TO END.
WHAT DO YOU MEAN BY THAT?
SO I TOLD HIM ABOUT ALL ABOUT MEETING JOE AND WHAT HE SAID.
AND HE SAID IT SOUNDED STRANGE, BUT THAT MANY THINGS WERE STRANGE OVER HERE.
THEN HE SAID...

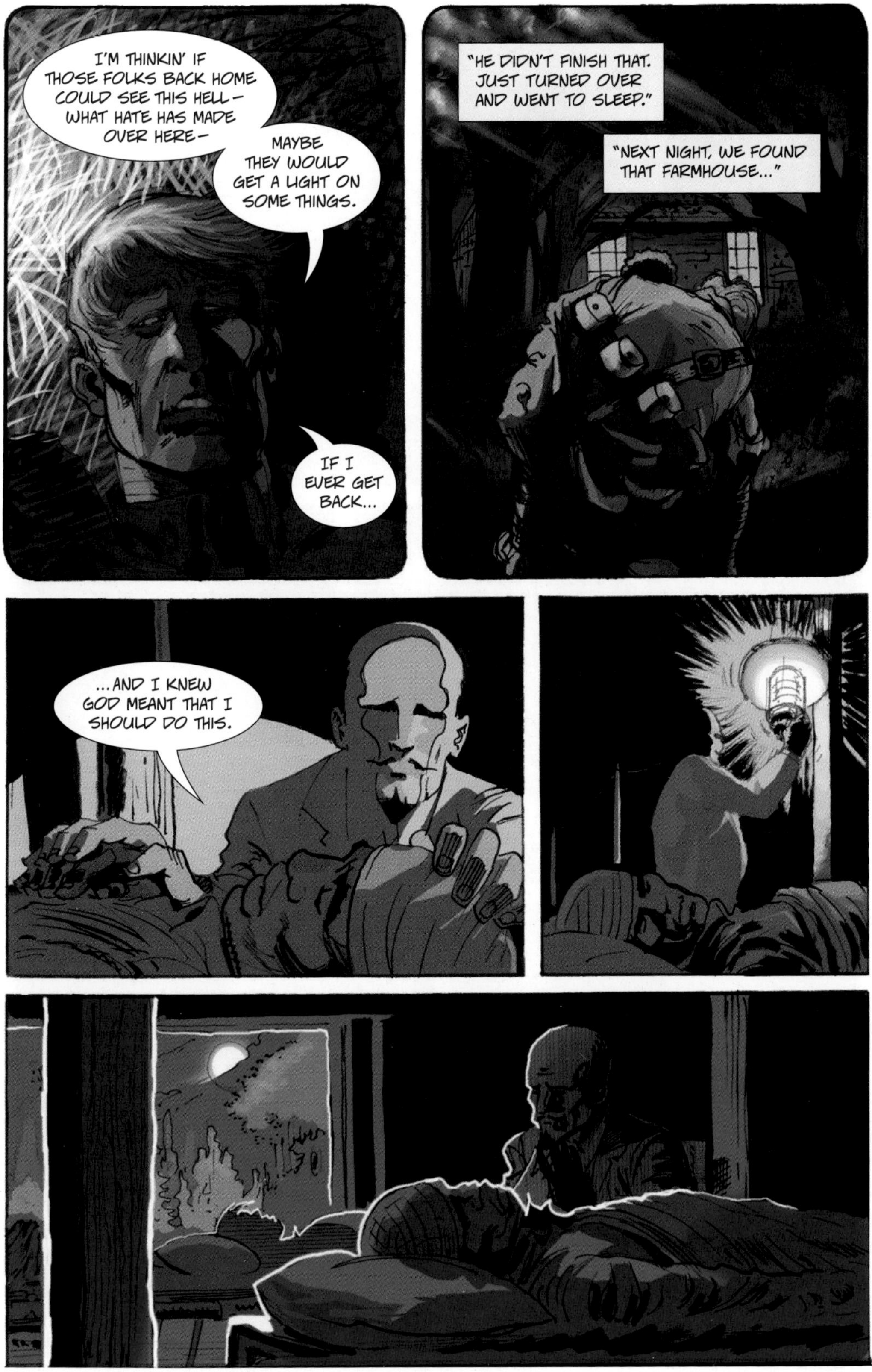
I'M THINKIN' IF THOSE FOLKS BACK HOME COULD SEE THIS HELL— WHAT HATE HAS MADE OVER HERE—
MAYBE THEY WOULD GET A LIGHT ON SOME THINGS.
IF I EVER GET BACK...
"HE DIDN'T FINISH THAT. JUST TURNED OVER AND WENT TO SLEEP."
"NEXT NIGHT, WE FOUND THAT FARMHOUSE..."
...AND I KNEW GOD MEANT THAT I SHOULD DO THIS.

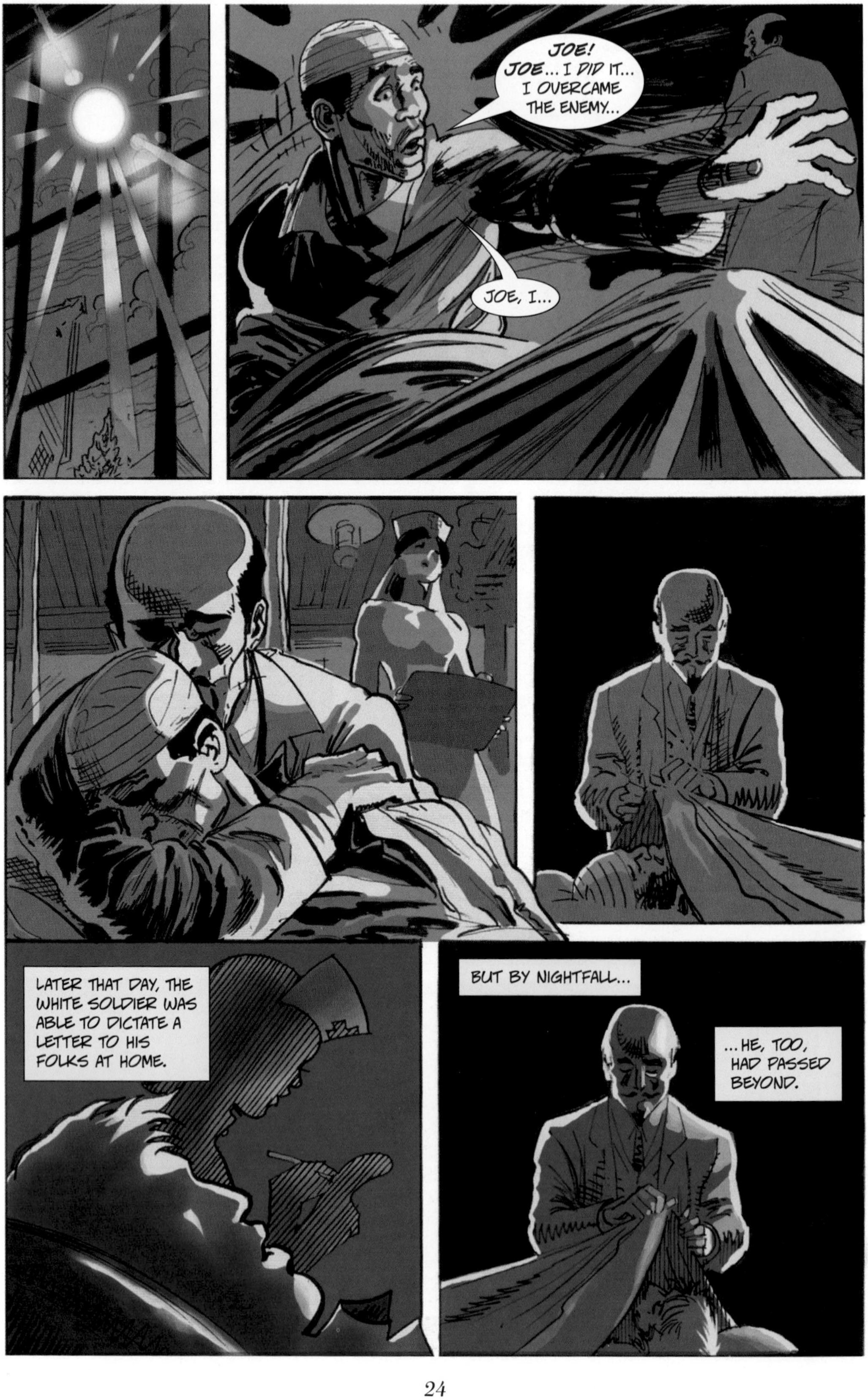
JOE!
JOE... I DID IT... I OVERCAME THE ENEMY...
JOE, I...
LATER THAT DAY, THE WHITE SOLDIER WAS ABLE TO DICTATE A LETTER TO HIS FOLKS AT HOME.
BUT BY NIGHTFALL...
...HE, TOO, HAD PASSED BEYOND.

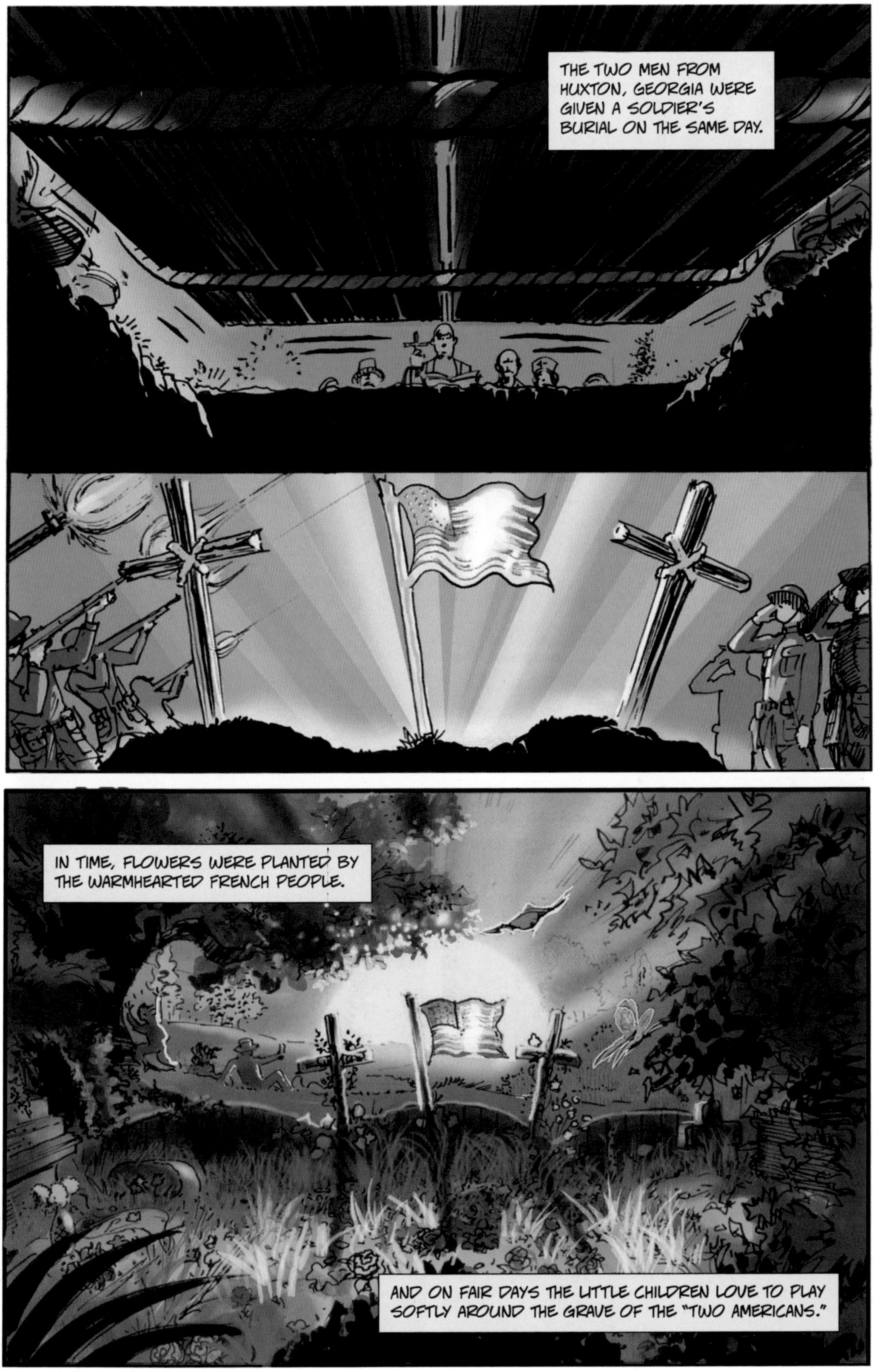
THE TWO MEN FROM HUXTON, GEORGIA WERE GIVEN A SOLDIER'S BURIAL ON THE SAME DAY.
IN TIME, FLOWERS WERE PLANTED BY THE WARMHEARTED FRENCH PEOPLE.
AND ON FAIR DAYS THE LITTLE CHILDREN LOVE TO PLAY SOFTLY AROUND THE GRAVE OF THE "TWO AMERICANS."

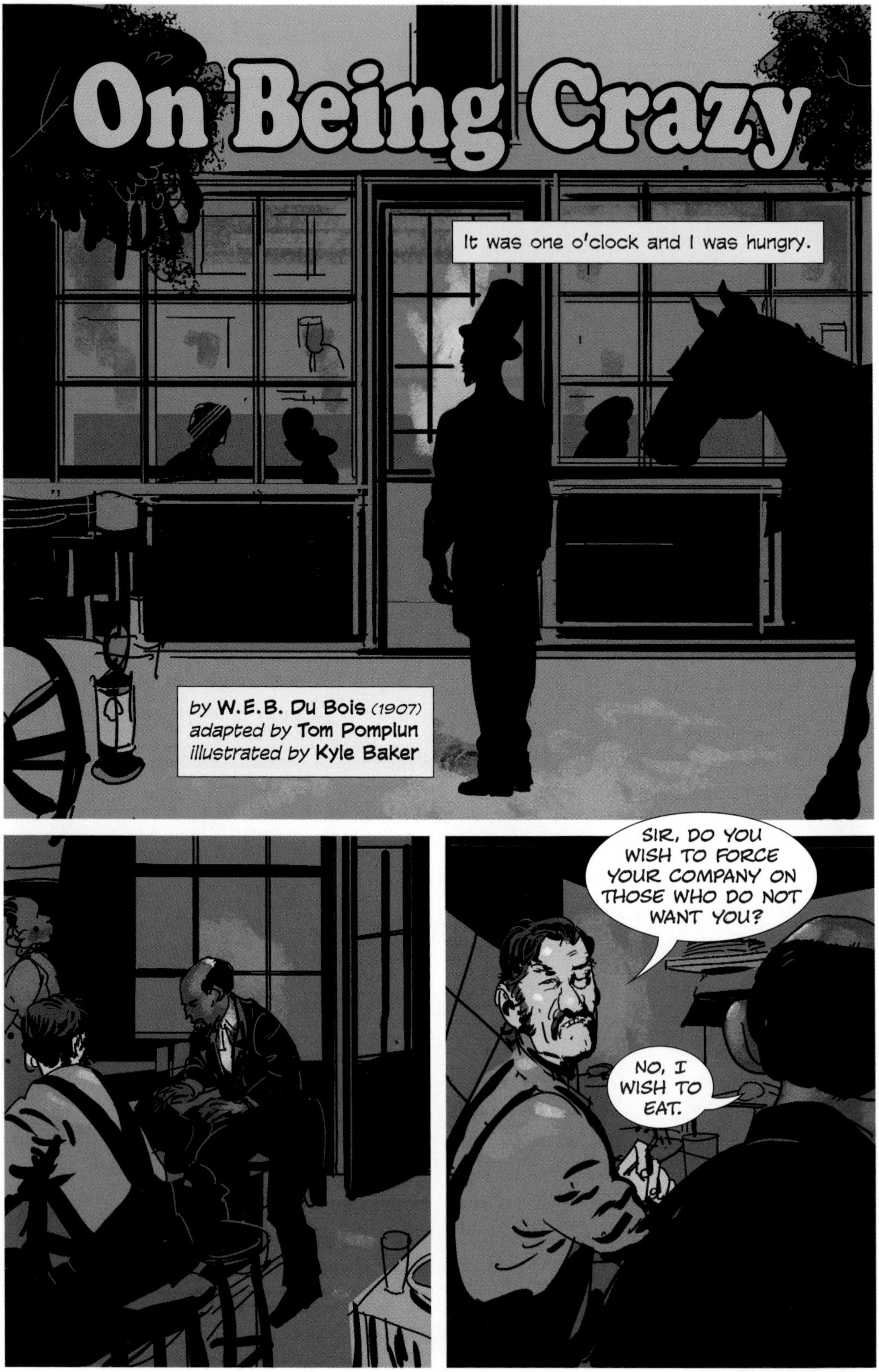
On Being Crazy
It was one o'clock and I was hungry.
by W.E.B. Du Bois (1907)
adapted by Tom Pomplun
illustrated by Kyle Baker
SIR, DO YOU WISH TO FORCE YOUR COMPANY ON THOSE WHO DO NOT WANT YOU?
NO, I WISH TO EAT.

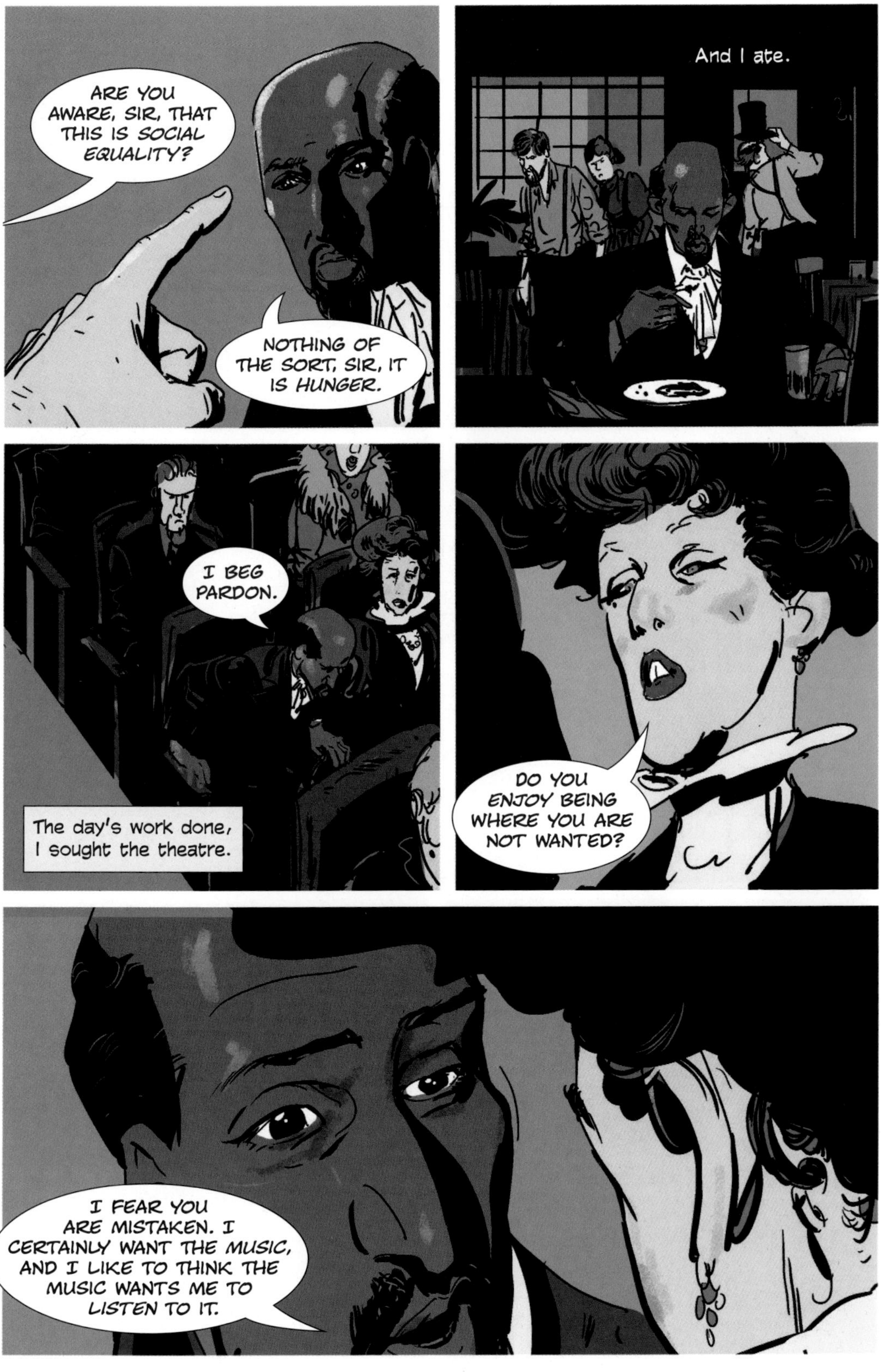
ARE YOU AWARE, SIR, THAT THIS IS SOCIAL EQUALITY?
NOTHING OF THE SORT, SIR, IT IS HUNGER.
And I ate.
The day's work done, I sought the theatre.
I BEG PARDON.
DO YOU ENJOY BEING WHERE YOU ARE NOT WANTED?
I FEAR YOU ARE MISTAKEN. I CERTAINLY WANT THE MUSIC, AND I LIKE TO THINK THE MUSIC WANTS ME TO LISTEN TO IT.

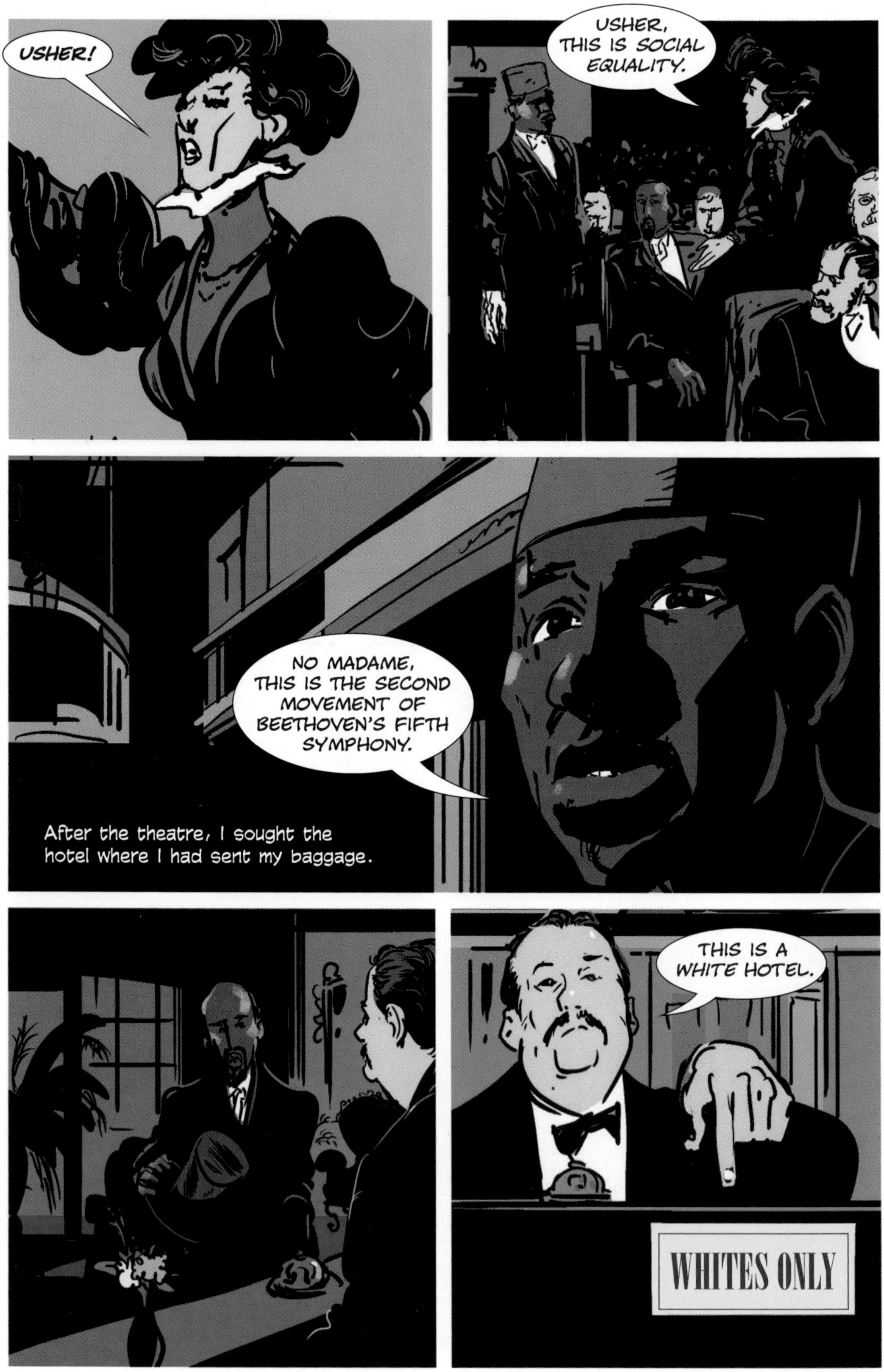
USHER!
USHER, THIS IS SOCIAL EQUALITY.
NO MADAME, THIS IS THE SECOND MOVEMENT OF BEETHOVEN'S FIFTH SYMPHONY.
After the theatre, I sought the hotel where I had sent my baggage.
THIS IS A WHITE HOTEL.
WHITES ONLY

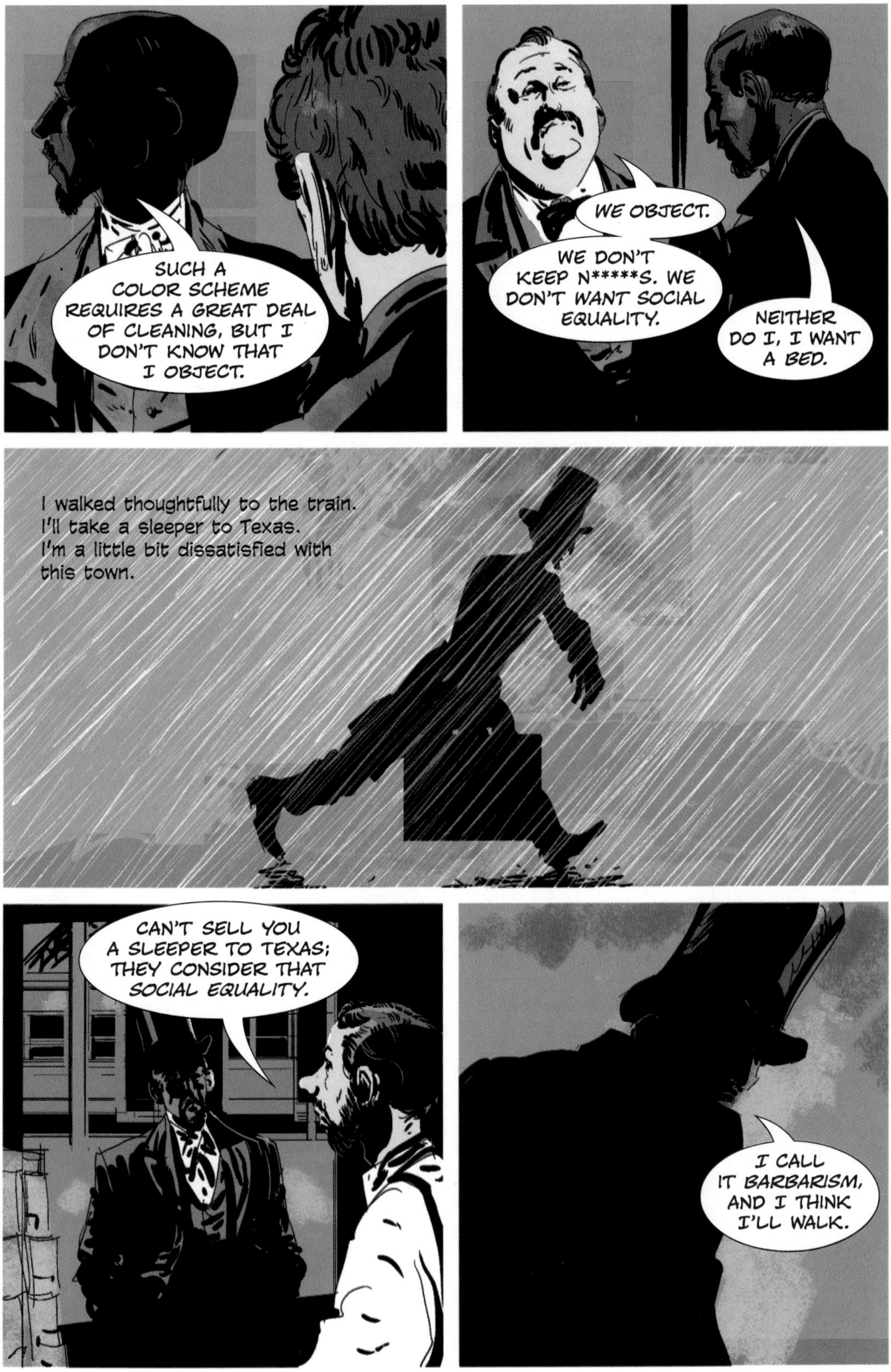
SUCH A COLOR SCHEME REQUIRES A GREAT DEAL OF CLEANING, BUT I DON'T KNOW THAT I OBJECT.
WE OBJECT.
WE DON'T KEEP N*****S. WE DON'T WANT SOCIAL EQUALITY.
NEITHER DO I, I WANT A BED.
I walked thoughtfully to the train.
I'll take a sleeper to Texas.
I'm a little bit dissatisfied with this town.
CAN'T SELL YOU A SLEEPER TO TEXAS; THEY CONSIDER THAT SOCIAL EQUALITY.
I CALL IT BARBARISM, AND I THINK I'LL WALK.

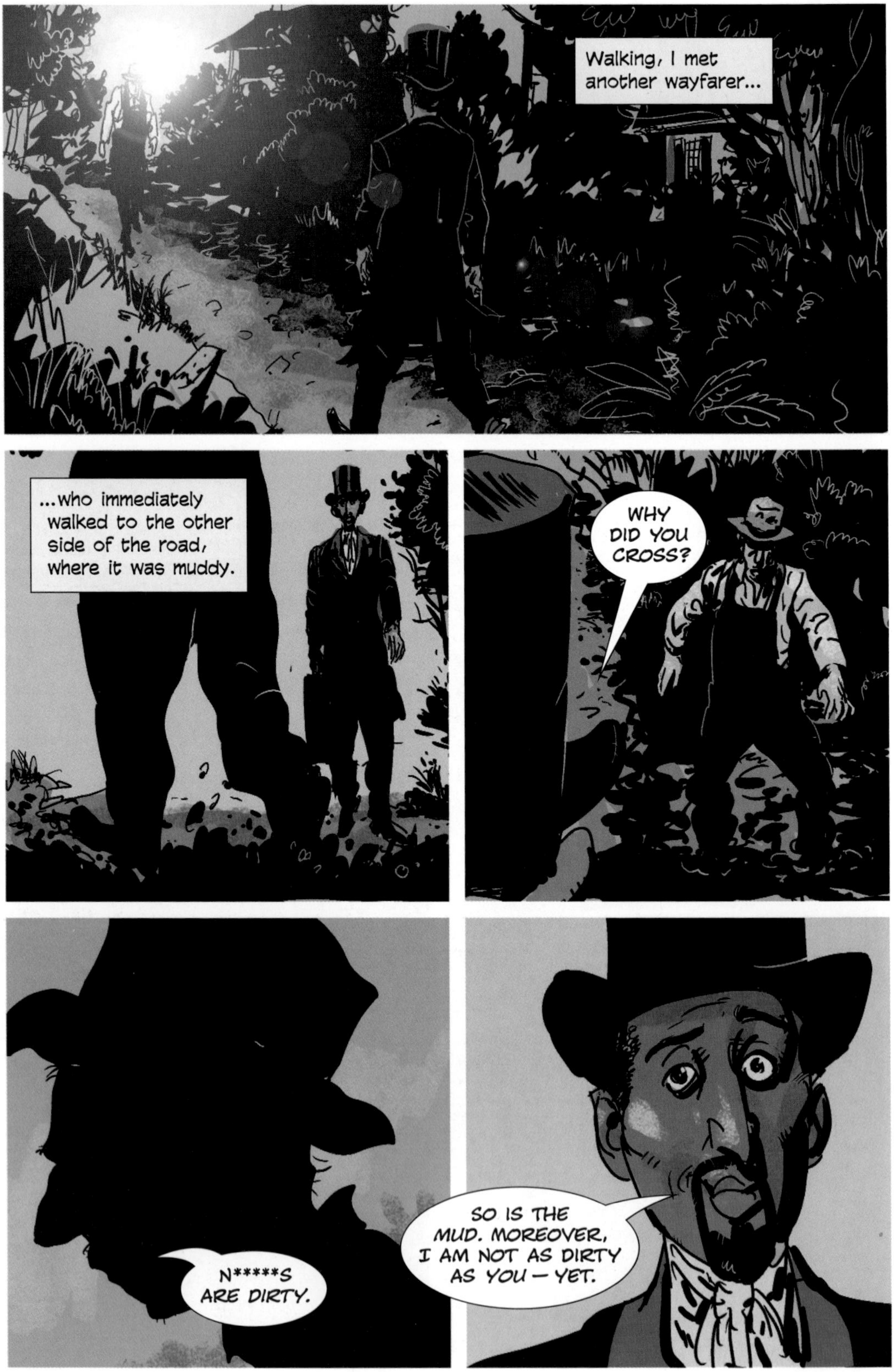
Walking, I met another wayfarer...
...who immediately walked to the other side of the road, where it was muddy.
WHY DID YOU CROSS?
N*****S ARE DIRTY.
SO IS THE MUD. MOREOVER, I AM NOT AS DIRTY AS YOU — YET.

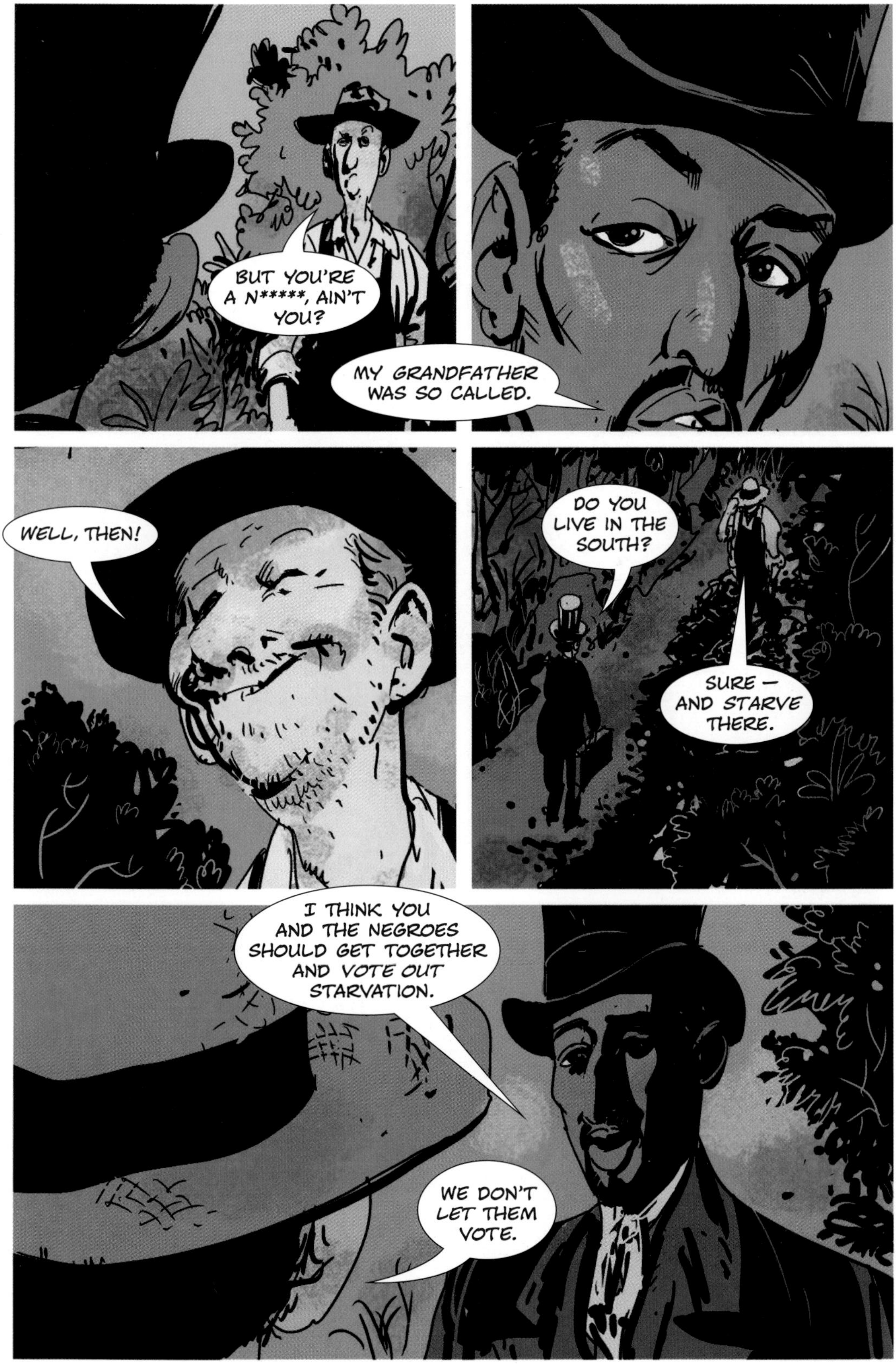
BUT YOU'RE A N*****, AIN'T YOU?
MY GRANDFATHER WAS SO CALLED.
WELL, THEN!
DO YOU LIVE IN THE SOUTH?
SURE — AND STARVE THERE.
I THINK YOU AND THE NEGROES SHOULD GET TOGETHER AND VOTE OUT STARVATION.
WE DON'T LET THEM VOTE.

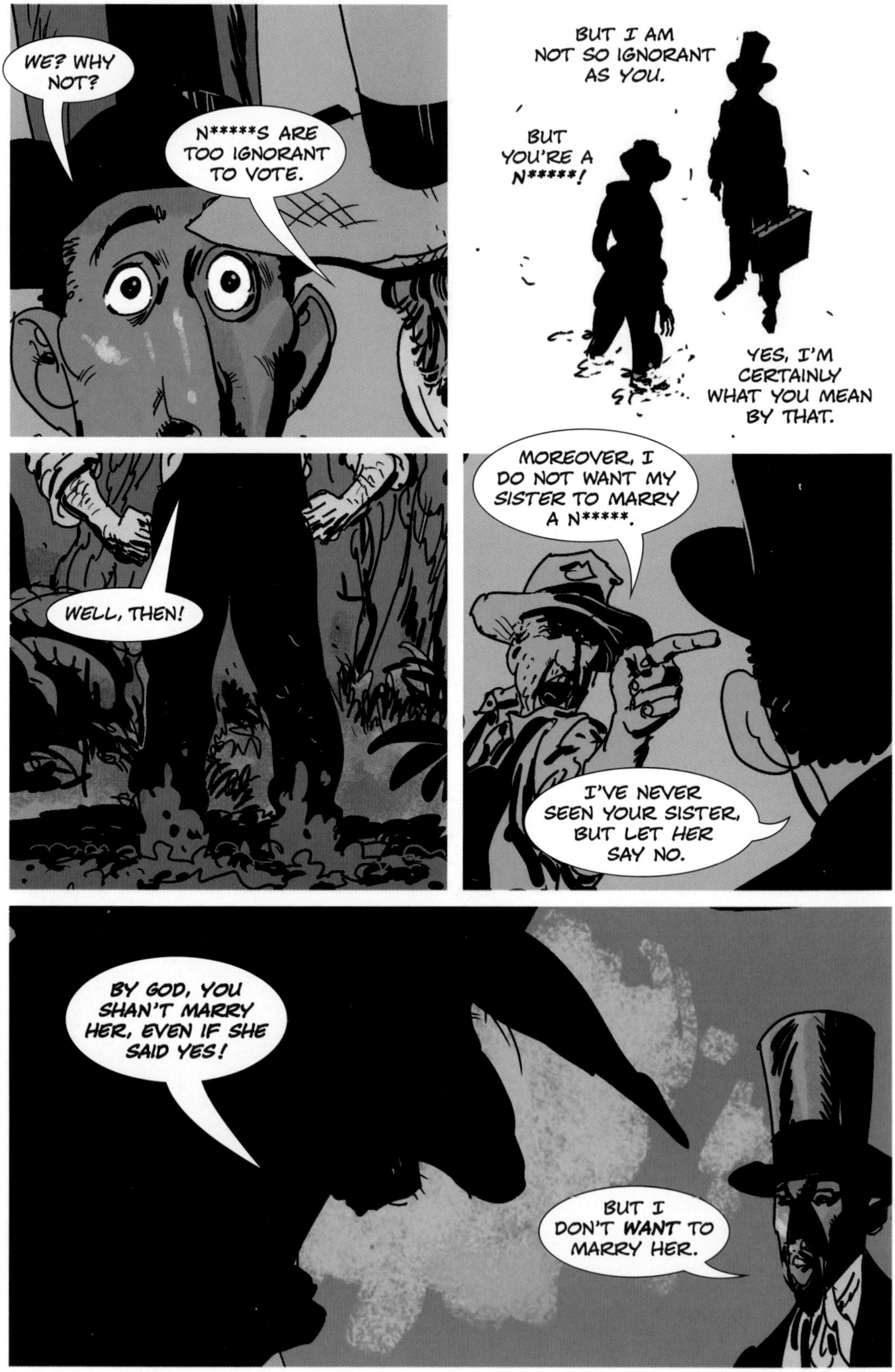
WE? WHY NOT?
N*****S ARE TOO IGNORANT TO VOTE.
BUT I AM NOT SO IGNORANT AS YOU.
BUT YOU'RE A N*****!
YES, I'M CERTAINLY WHAT YOU MEAN BY THAT.
WELL, THEN!
MOREOVER, I DO NOT WANT MY SISTER TO MARRY A N*****.
I'VE NEVER SEEN YOUR SISTER, BUT LET HER SAY NO.
BY GOD, YOU SHAN'T MARRY HER, EVEN IF SHE SAID YES!
BUT I DON'T WANT TO MARRY HER.

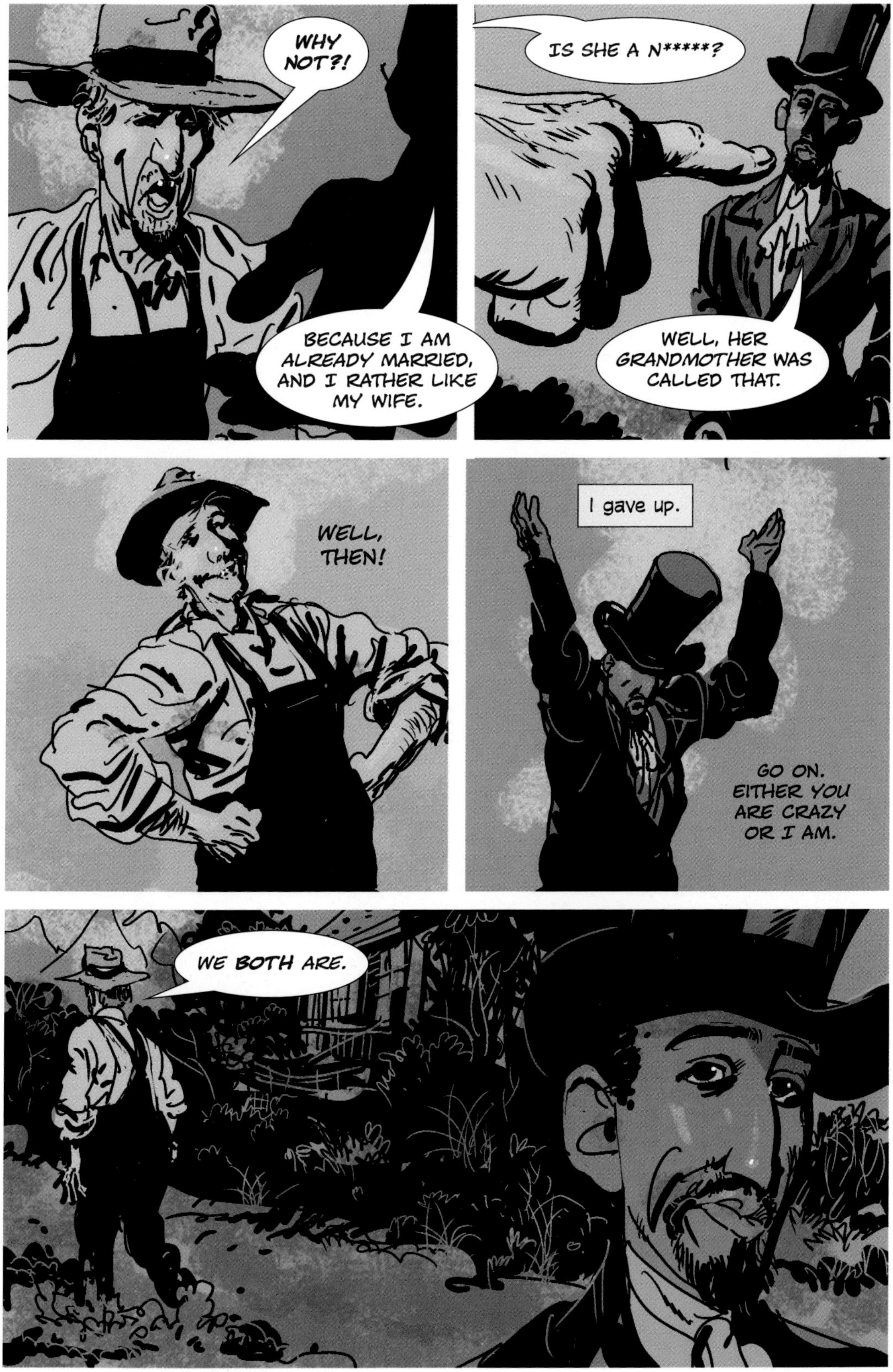
WHY NOT?!
BECAUSE I AM ALREADY MARRIED, AND I RATHER LIKE MY WIFE.
IS SHE A N*****?
WELL, HER GRANDMOTHER WAS CALLED THAT.
WELL, THEN!
I gave up.
GO ON. EITHER YOU ARE CRAZY OR I AM.
WE BOTH ARE.

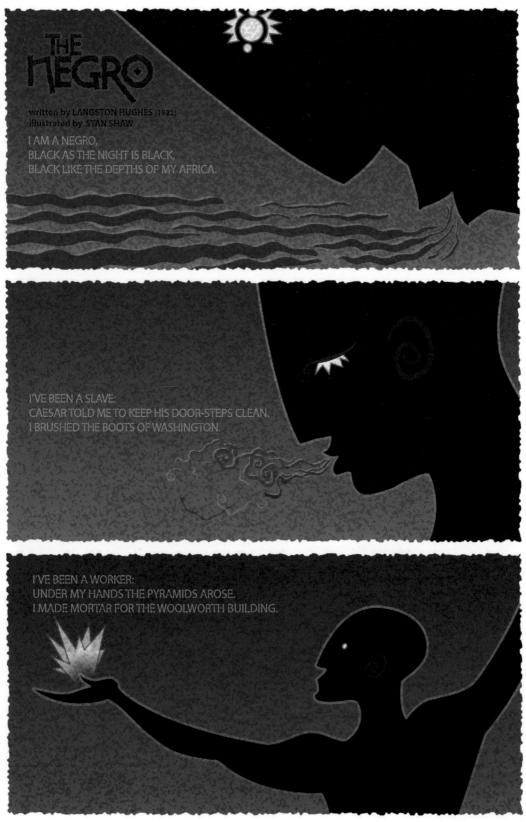

THE NEGRO

written by LANGSTON HUGHES (1922)
illustrated by STAN SHAW

I AM A NEGRO,
BLACK AS THE NIGHT IS BLACK,
BLACK LIKE THE DEPTHS OF MY AFRICA.

I'VE BEEN A SLAVE:
CAESAR TOLD ME TO KEEP HIS DOOR-STEPS CLEAN.
I BRUSHED THE BOOTS OF WASHINGTON.

I'VE BEEN A WORKER:
UNDER MY HANDS THE PYRAMIDS AROSE.
I MADE MORTAR FOR THE WOOLWORTH BUILDING.

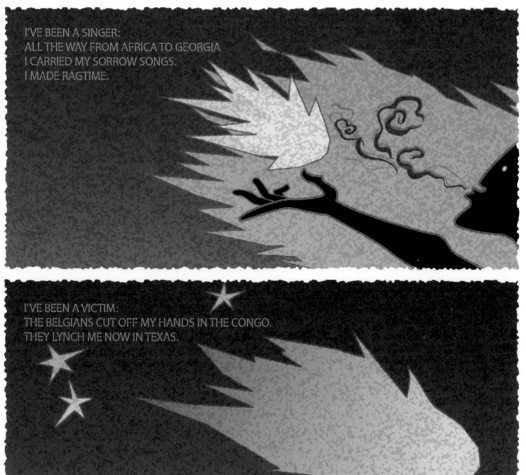

I'VE BEEN A SINGER:
ALL THE WAY FROM AFRICA TO GEORGIA
I CARRIED MY SORROW SONGS.
I MADE RAGTIME.

I'VE BEEN A VICTIM:
THE BELGIANS CUT OFF MY HANDS IN THE CONGO.
THEY LYNCH ME NOW IN TEXAS.

I AM NEGRO;
BLACK AS THE NIGHT IS BLACK,
BLACK LIKE THE DEPTHS OF MY AFRICA.

35

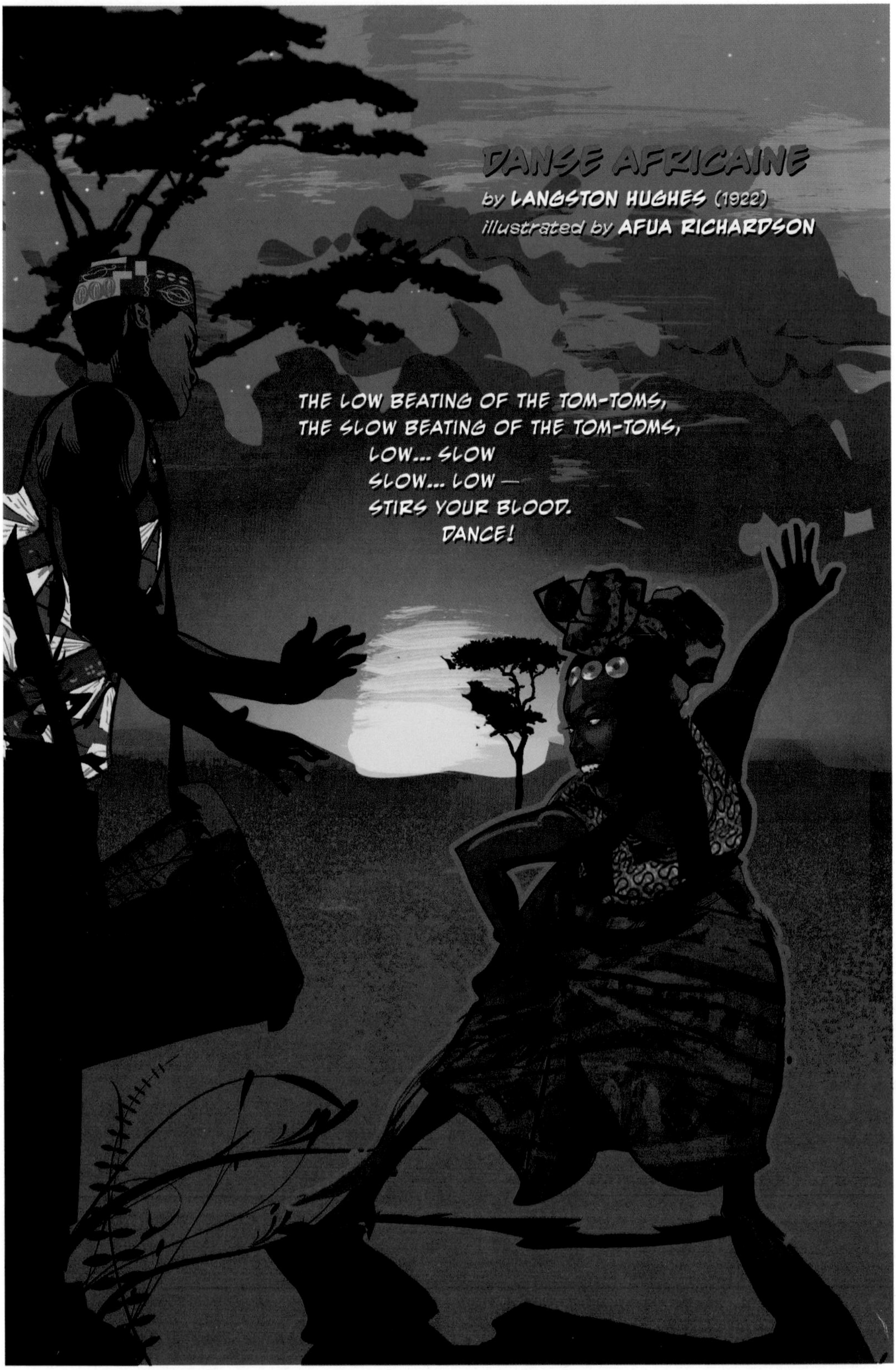
DANSE AFRICAINE
by LANGSTON HUGHES (1922)
illustrated by AFUA RICHARDSON
THE LOW BEATING OF THE TOM-TOMS,
THE SLOW BEATING OF THE TOM-TOMS,
LOW... SLOW
SLOW... LOW —
STIRS YOUR BLOOD.
DANCE!

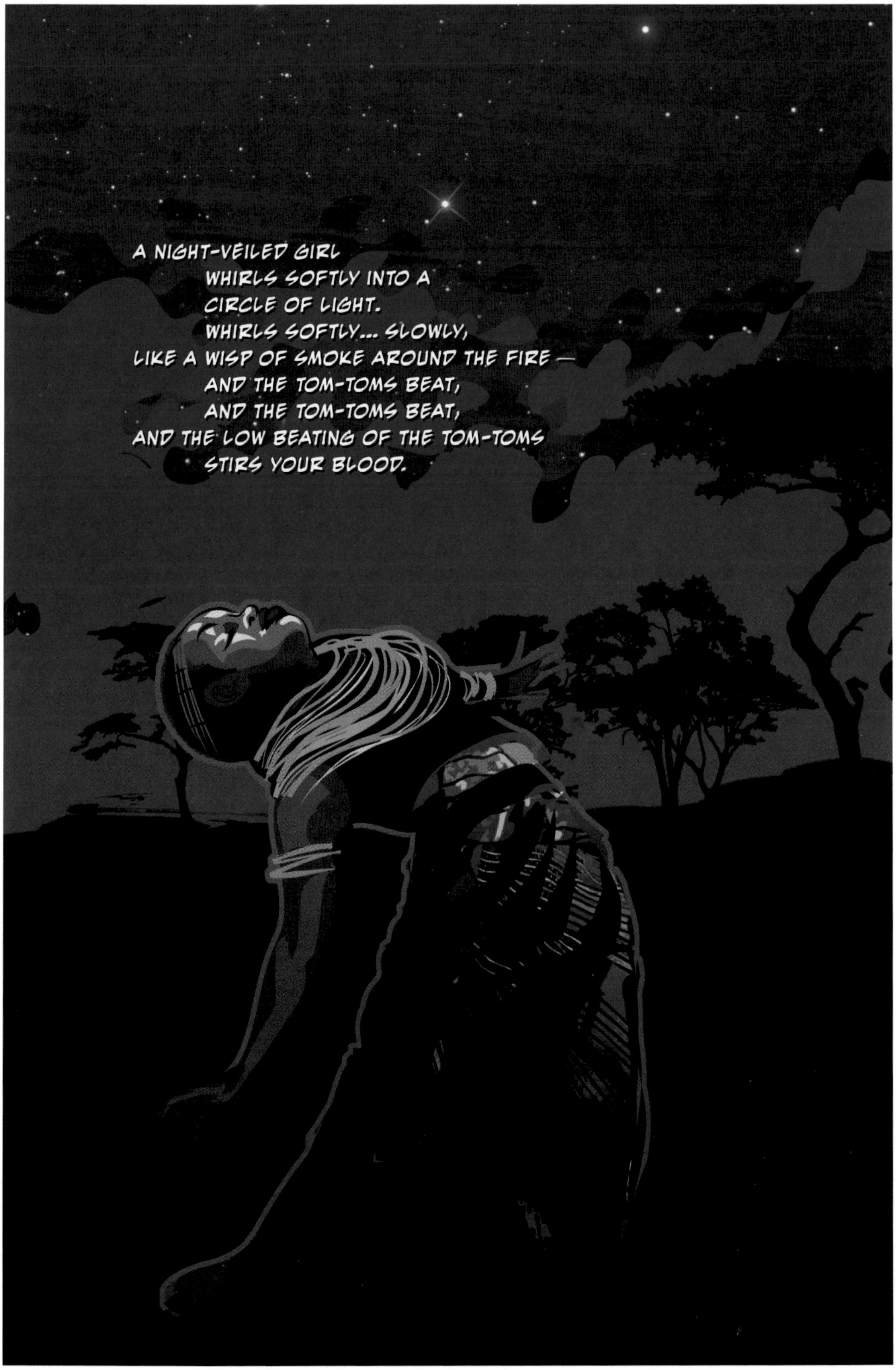
A NIGHT-VEILED GIRL
WHIRLS SOFTLY INTO A
CIRCLE OF LIGHT.
WHIRLS SOFTLY... SLOWLY,
LIKE A WISP OF SMOKE AROUND THE FIRE —
AND THE TOM-TOMS BEAT,
AND THE TOM-TOMS BEAT,
AND THE LOW BEATING OF THE TOM-TOMS
STIRS YOUR BLOOD.

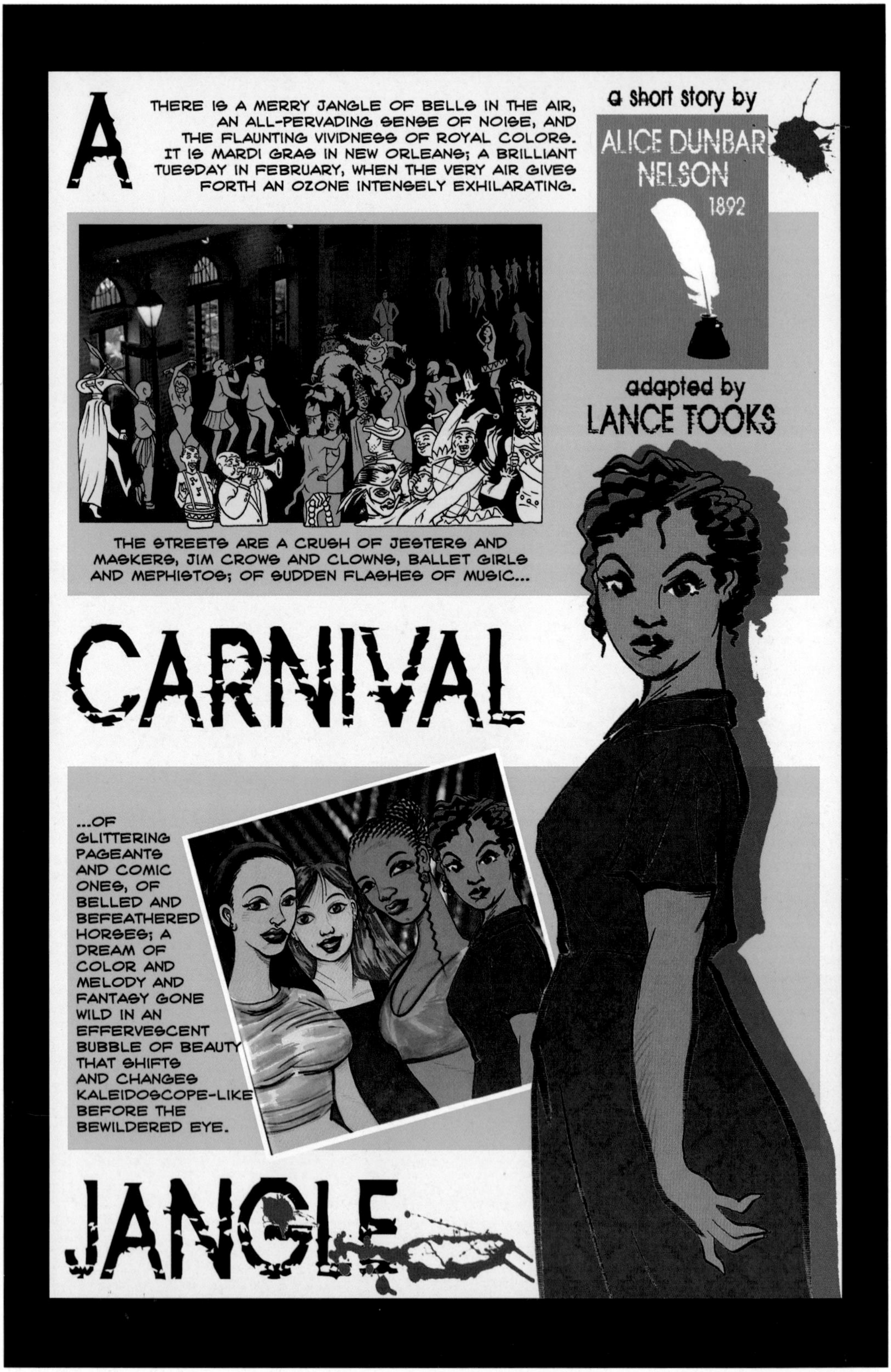
A THERE IS A MERRY JANGLE OF BELLS IN THE AIR, AN ALL-PERVADING SENSE OF NOISE, AND THE FLAUNTING VIVIDNESS OF ROYAL COLORS. IT IS MARDI GRAS IN NEW ORLEANS; A BRILLIANT TUESDAY IN FEBRUARY, WHEN THE VERY AIR GIVES FORTH AN OZONE INTENSELY EXHILARATING.
a short story by
ALICE DUNBAR NELSON
1892
adapted by
LANCE TOOKS
THE STREETS ARE A CRUSH OF JESTERS AND MASKERS, JIM CROWS AND CLOWNS, BALLET GIRLS AND MEPHISTOS; OF SUDDEN FLASHES OF MUSIC...
CARNIVAL
...OF GLITTERING PAGEANTS AND COMIC ONES, OF BELLED AND BEFEATHERED HORSES; A DREAM OF COLOR AND MELODY AND FANTASY GONE WILD IN AN EFFERVESCENT BUBBLE OF BEAUTY THAT SHIFTS AND CHANGES KALEIDOSCOPE-LIKE BEFORE THE BEWILDERED EYE.
JANGLE

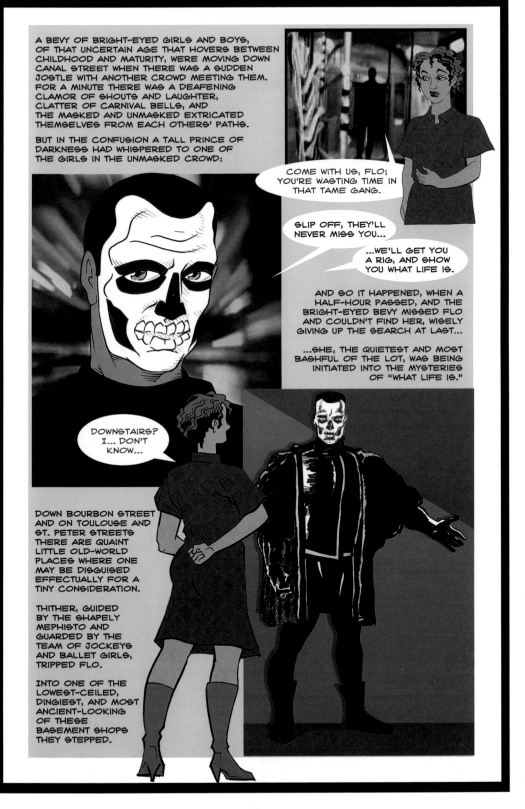

A BEVY OF BRIGHT-EYED GIRLS AND BOYS, OF THAT UNCERTAIN AGE THAT HOVERS BETWEEN CHILDHOOD AND MATURITY, WERE MOVING DOWN CANAL STREET WHEN THERE WAS A SUDDEN JOSTLE WITH ANOTHER CROWD MEETING THEM. FOR A MINUTE THERE WAS A DEAFENING CLAMOR OF SHOUTS AND LAUGHTER, CLATTER OF CARNIVAL BELLS, AND THE MASKED AND UNMASKED EXTRICATED THEMSELVES FROM EACH OTHERS' PATHS.

BUT IN THE CONFUSION A TALL PRINCE OF DARKNESS HAD WHISPERED TO ONE OF THE GIRLS IN THE UNMASKED CROWD:

COME WITH US, FLO; YOU'RE WASTING TIME IN THAT TAME GANG.

SLIP OFF, THEY'LL NEVER MISS YOU...

...WE'LL GET YOU A RIG, AND SHOW YOU WHAT LIFE IS.

AND SO IT HAPPENED, WHEN A HALF-HOUR PASSED, AND THE BRIGHT-EYED BEVY MISSED FLO AND COULDN'T FIND HER, WISELY GIVING UP THE SEARCH AT LAST...

...SHE, THE QUIETEST AND MOST BASHFUL OF THE LOT, WAS BEING INITIATED INTO THE MYSTERIES OF "WHAT LIFE IS."

DOWNSTAIRS? I... DON'T KNOW...

DOWN BOURBON STREET AND ON TOULOUSE AND ST. PETER STREETS THERE ARE QUAINT LITTLE OLD-WORLD PLACES WHERE ONE MAY BE DISGUISED EFFECTUALLY FOR A TINY CONSIDERATION.

THITHER, GUIDED BY THE SHAPELY MEPHISTO AND GUARDED BY THE TEAM OF JOCKEYS AND BALLET GIRLS, TRIPPED FLO.

INTO ONE OF THE LOWEST-CEILED, DINGIEST, AND MOST ANCIENT-LOOKING OF THESE BASEMENT SHOPS THEY STEPPED.

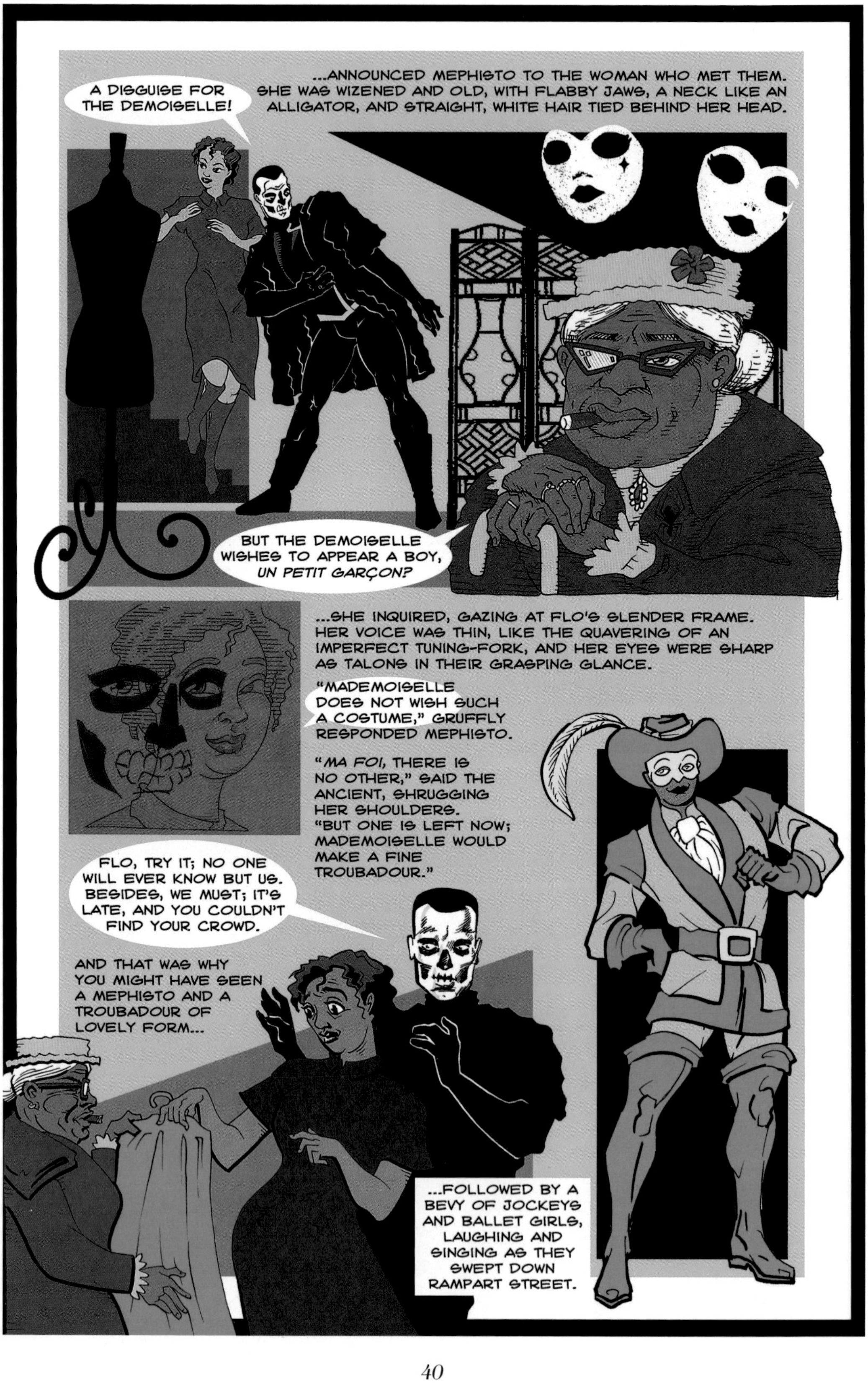
A DISGUISE FOR THE DEMOISELLE!
...ANNOUNCED MEPHISTO TO THE WOMAN WHO MET THEM. SHE WAS WIZENED AND OLD, WITH FLABBY JAWS, A NECK LIKE AN ALLIGATOR, AND STRAIGHT, WHITE HAIR TIED BEHIND HER HEAD.
BUT THE DEMOISELLE WISHES TO APPEAR A BOY, *UN PETIT GARÇON?*
...SHE INQUIRED, GAZING AT FLO'S SLENDER FRAME. HER VOICE WAS THIN, LIKE THE QUAVERING OF AN IMPERFECT TUNING-FORK, AND HER EYES WERE SHARP AS TALONS IN THEIR GRASPING GLANCE.
"MADEMOISELLE DOES NOT WISH SUCH A COSTUME," GRUFFLY RESPONDED MEPHISTO.
"*MA FOI,* THERE IS NO OTHER," SAID THE ANCIENT, SHRUGGING HER SHOULDERS. "BUT ONE IS LEFT NOW; MADEMOISELLE WOULD MAKE A FINE TROUBADOUR."
FLO, TRY IT; NO ONE WILL EVER KNOW BUT US. BESIDES, WE MUST; IT'S LATE, AND YOU COULDN'T FIND YOUR CROWD.
AND THAT WAS WHY YOU MIGHT HAVE SEEN A MEPHISTO AND A TROUBADOUR OF LOVELY FORM...
...FOLLOWED BY A BEVY OF JOCKEYS AND BALLET GIRLS, LAUGHING AND SINGING AS THEY SWEPT DOWN RAMPART STREET.

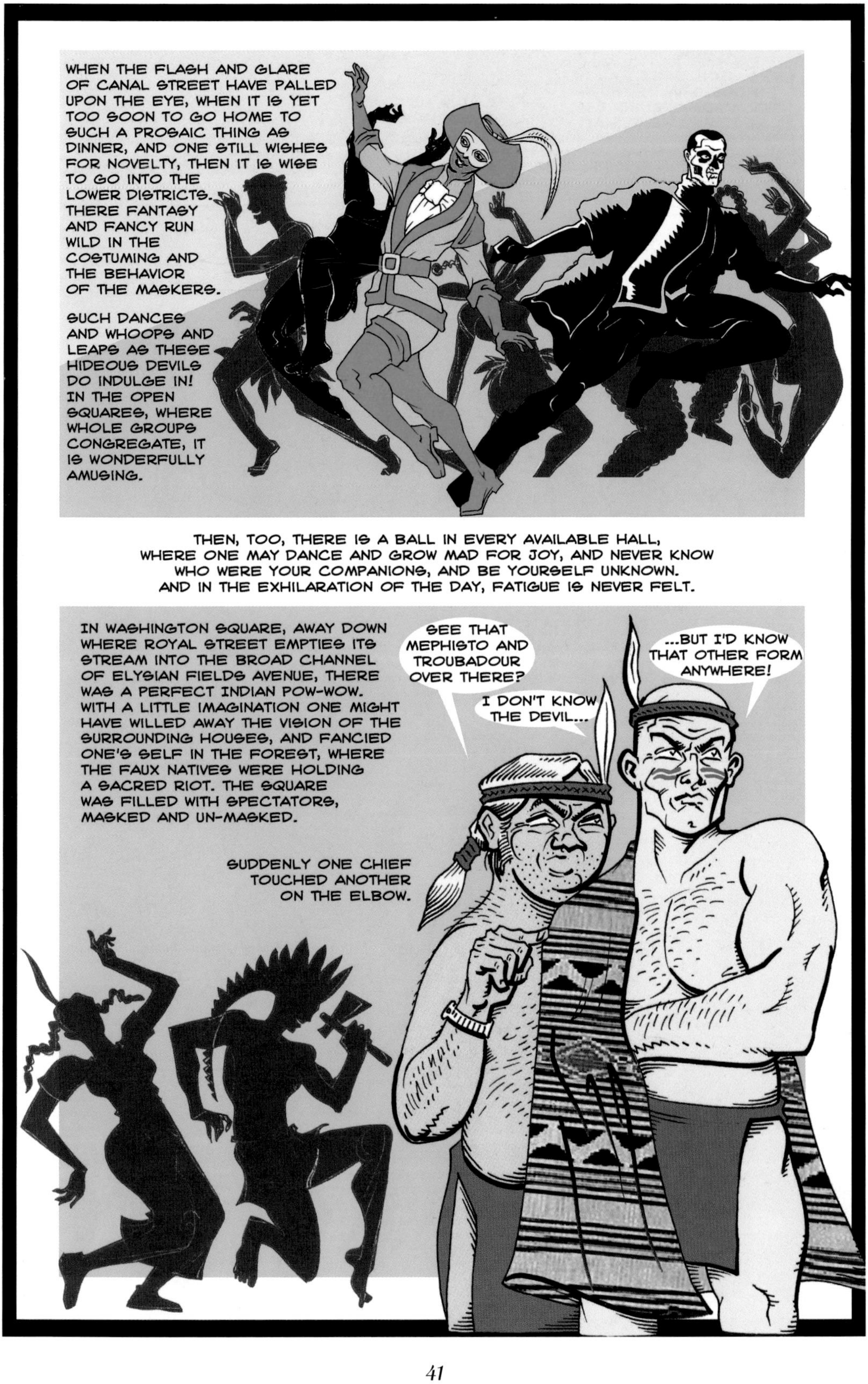
WHEN THE FLASH AND GLARE OF CANAL STREET HAVE PALLED UPON THE EYE, WHEN IT IS YET TOO SOON TO GO HOME TO SUCH A PROSAIC THING AS DINNER, AND ONE STILL WISHES FOR NOVELTY, THEN IT IS WISE TO GO INTO THE LOWER DISTRICTS. THERE FANTASY AND FANCY RUN WILD IN THE COSTUMING AND THE BEHAVIOR OF THE MASKERS.
SUCH DANCES AND WHOOPS AND LEAPS AS THESE HIDEOUS DEVILS DO INDULGE IN! IN THE OPEN SQUARES, WHERE WHOLE GROUPS CONGREGATE, IT IS WONDERFULLY AMUSING.
THEN, TOO, THERE IS A BALL IN EVERY AVAILABLE HALL, WHERE ONE MAY DANCE AND GROW MAD FOR JOY, AND NEVER KNOW WHO WERE YOUR COMPANIONS, AND BE YOURSELF UNKNOWN. AND IN THE EXHILARATION OF THE DAY, FATIGUE IS NEVER FELT.
IN WASHINGTON SQUARE, AWAY DOWN WHERE ROYAL STREET EMPTIES ITS STREAM INTO THE BROAD CHANNEL OF ELYSIAN FIELDS AVENUE, THERE WAS A PERFECT INDIAN POW-WOW. WITH A LITTLE IMAGINATION ONE MIGHT HAVE WILLED AWAY THE VISION OF THE SURROUNDING HOUSES, AND FANCIED ONE'S SELF IN THE FOREST, WHERE THE FAUX NATIVES WERE HOLDING A SACRED RIOT. THE SQUARE WAS FILLED WITH SPECTATORS, MASKED AND UN-MASKED.
SUDDENLY ONE CHIEF TOUCHED ANOTHER ON THE ELBOW.
SEE THAT MEPHISTO AND TROUBADOUR OVER THERE?
I DON'T KNOW THE DEVIL...
...BUT I'D KNOW THAT OTHER FORM ANYWHERE!

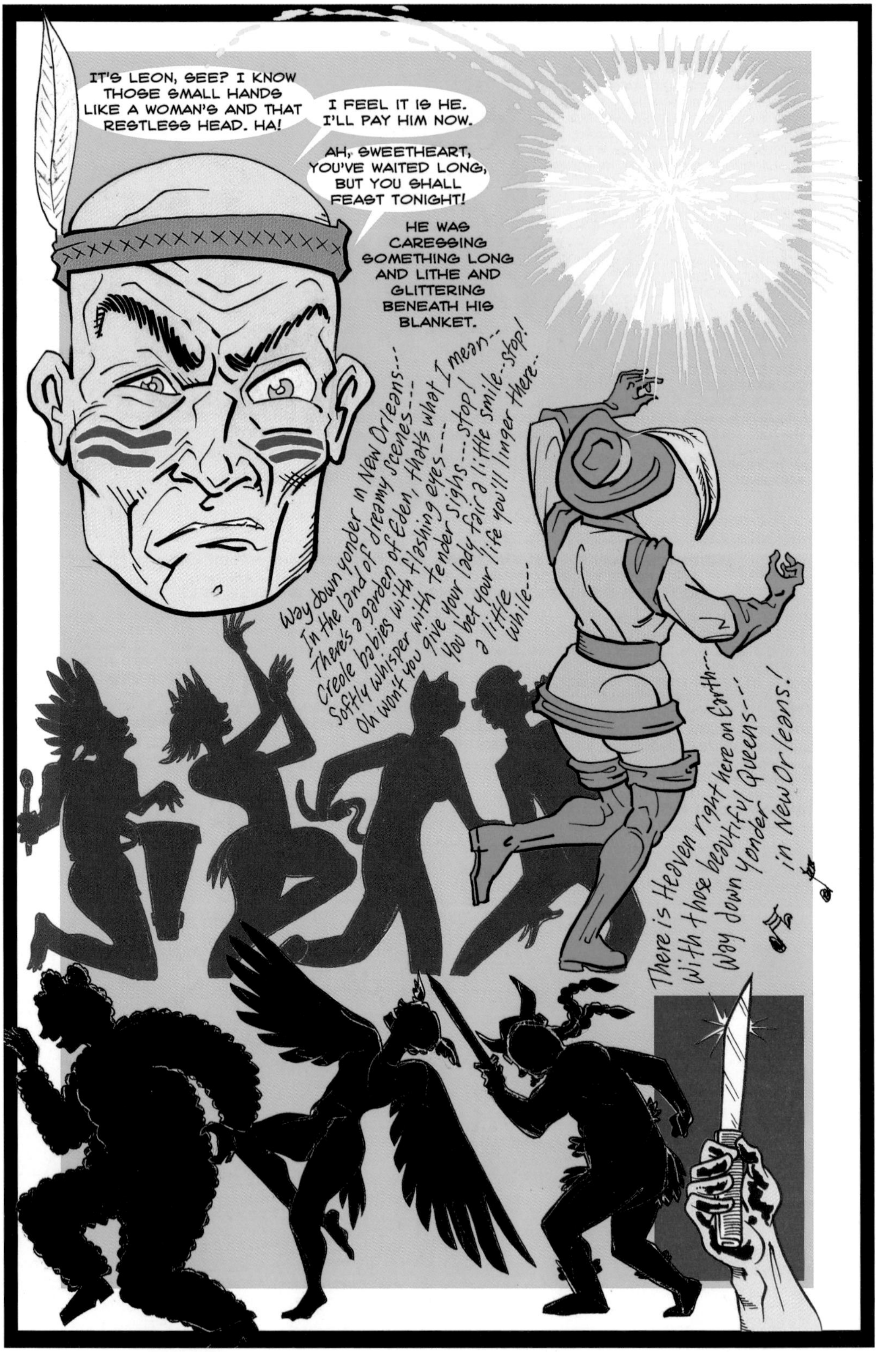
IT'S LEON, SEE? I KNOW THOSE SMALL HANDS LIKE A WOMAN'S AND THAT RESTLESS HEAD. HA!
I FEEL IT IS HE. I'LL PAY HIM NOW.
AH, SWEETHEART, YOU'VE WAITED LONG, BUT YOU SHALL FEAST TONIGHT!
HE WAS CARESSING SOMETHING LONG AND LITHE AND GLITTERING BENEATH HIS BLANKET.
Way down yonder in New Orleans...
In the land of dreamy scenes---
There's a garden of Eden, that's what I mean...
Creole babies with flashing eyes---
Softly whisper with tender sighs---stop!
Oh won't you give your lady fair a little smile--stop!
You bet your life you'll linger there--
a little while---
There is Heaven right here on Earth--
With those beautiful Queens---
Way down yonder
in New Orleans!

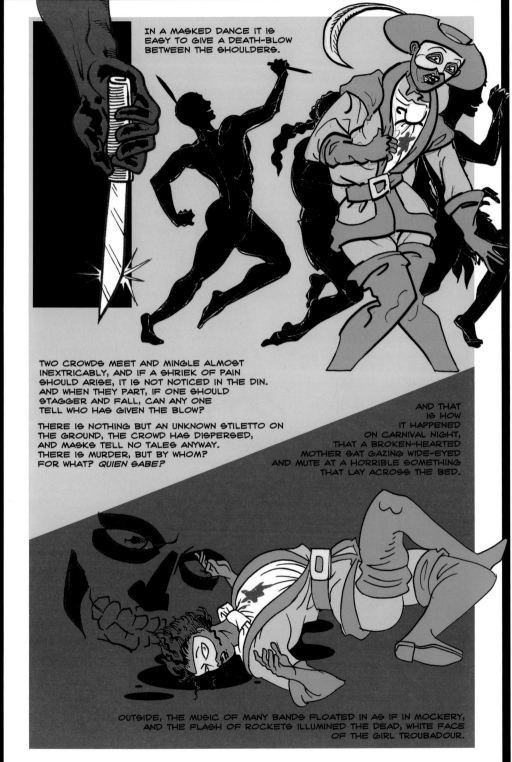

IN A MASKED DANCE IT IS EASY TO GIVE A DEATH-BLOW BETWEEN THE SHOULDERS.

TWO CROWDS MEET AND MINGLE ALMOST INEXTRICABLY, AND IF A SHRIEK OF PAIN SHOULD ARISE, IT IS NOT NOTICED IN THE DIN. AND WHEN THEY PART, IF ONE SHOULD STAGGER AND FALL, CAN ANY ONE TELL WHO HAS GIVEN THE BLOW?

THERE IS NOTHING BUT AN UNKNOWN STILETTO ON THE GROUND, THE CROWD HAS DISPERSED, AND MASKS TELL NO TALES ANYWAY. THERE IS MURDER, BUT BY WHOM? FOR WHAT? *QUIEN SABE?*

AND THAT IS HOW IT HAPPENED ON CARNIVAL NIGHT, THAT A BROKEN-HEARTED MOTHER SAT GAZING WIDE-EYED AND MUTE AT A HORRIBLE SOMETHING THAT LAY ACROSS THE BED.

OUTSIDE, THE MUSIC OF MANY BANDS FLOATED IN AS IF IN MOCKERY, AND THE FLASH OF ROCKETS ILLUMINED THE DEAD, WHITE FACE OF THE GIRL TROUBADOUR.

THE CASTAWAYS

by **Claude McKay** (1922)
illustrated by **Glenn Brewer**

The vivid grass with visible delight
Springing triumphant from the pregnant earth,
The butterflies, and sparrows in brief flight
Chirping and dancing for the season's birth,
The dandelions and rare daffodils
That touch the deep-stirred heart with hands of gold,
The thrushes sending forth their joyous trills,—
Not these, not these did I at first behold!
But seated on the benches daubed with green,
The castaways of life, a few asleep,
Some withered women desolate and mean,
And over all, life's shadows dark and deep.
Moaning I turned away, for misery
I have the strength to bear but not to see.

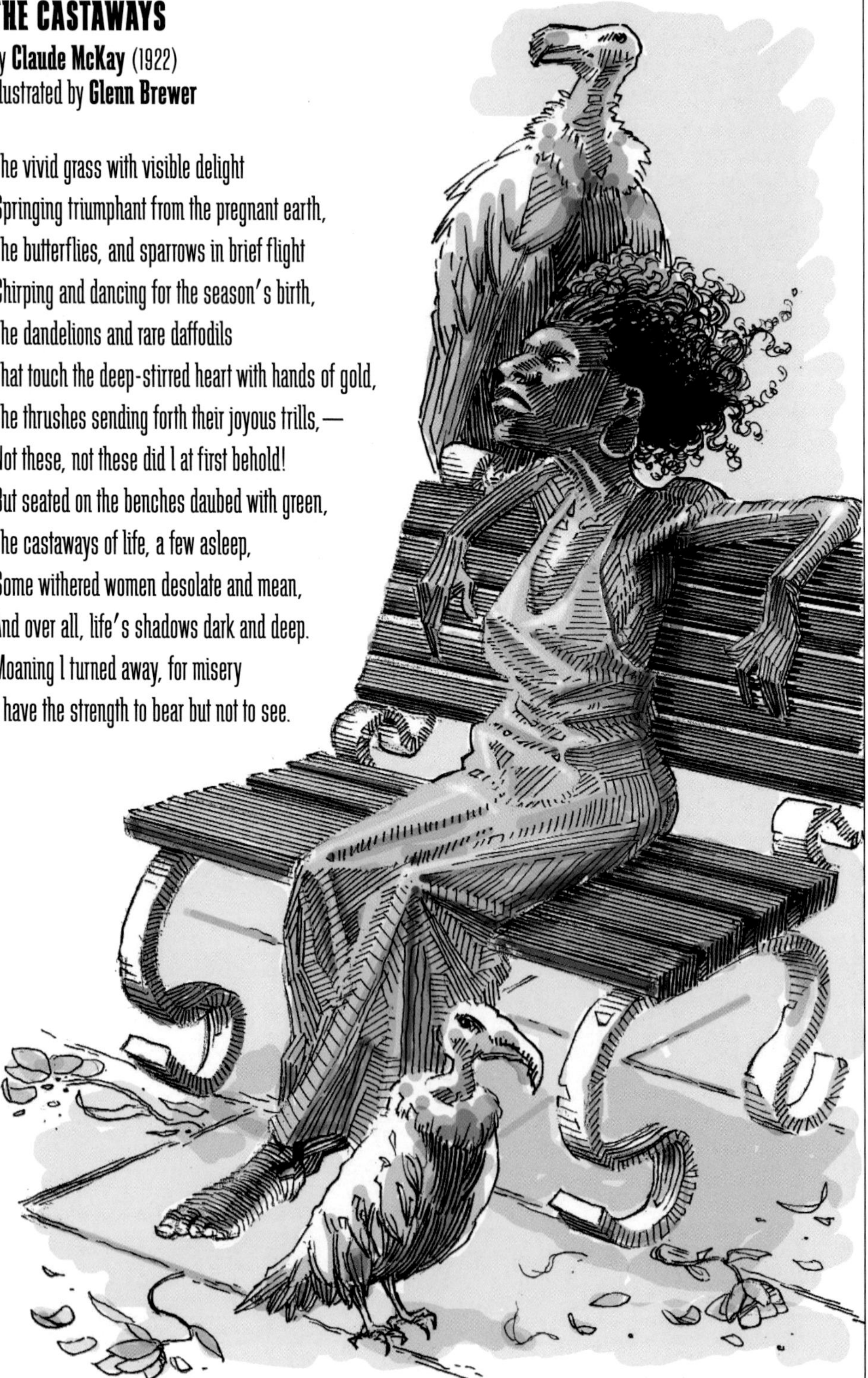

AMERICA

by **Claude McKay** (1922)
illustrated by **John Jennings**

Although she feeds me bread of bitterness,
And sinks into my throat her tiger's tooth,
Stealing my breath of life, I will confess
I love this cultured hell that tests my youth!
Her vigor flows like tides into my blood,
Giving me strength erect against her hate.
Her bigness sweeps my being like a flood.
Yet as a rebel fronts a king in state,
I stand within her walls with not a shred
Of terror, malice, not a word of jeer.
Darkly I gaze into the days ahead,
And see her might and granite wonders there,
Beneath the touch of Time's unerring hand,
Like priceless treasures sinking in the sand.

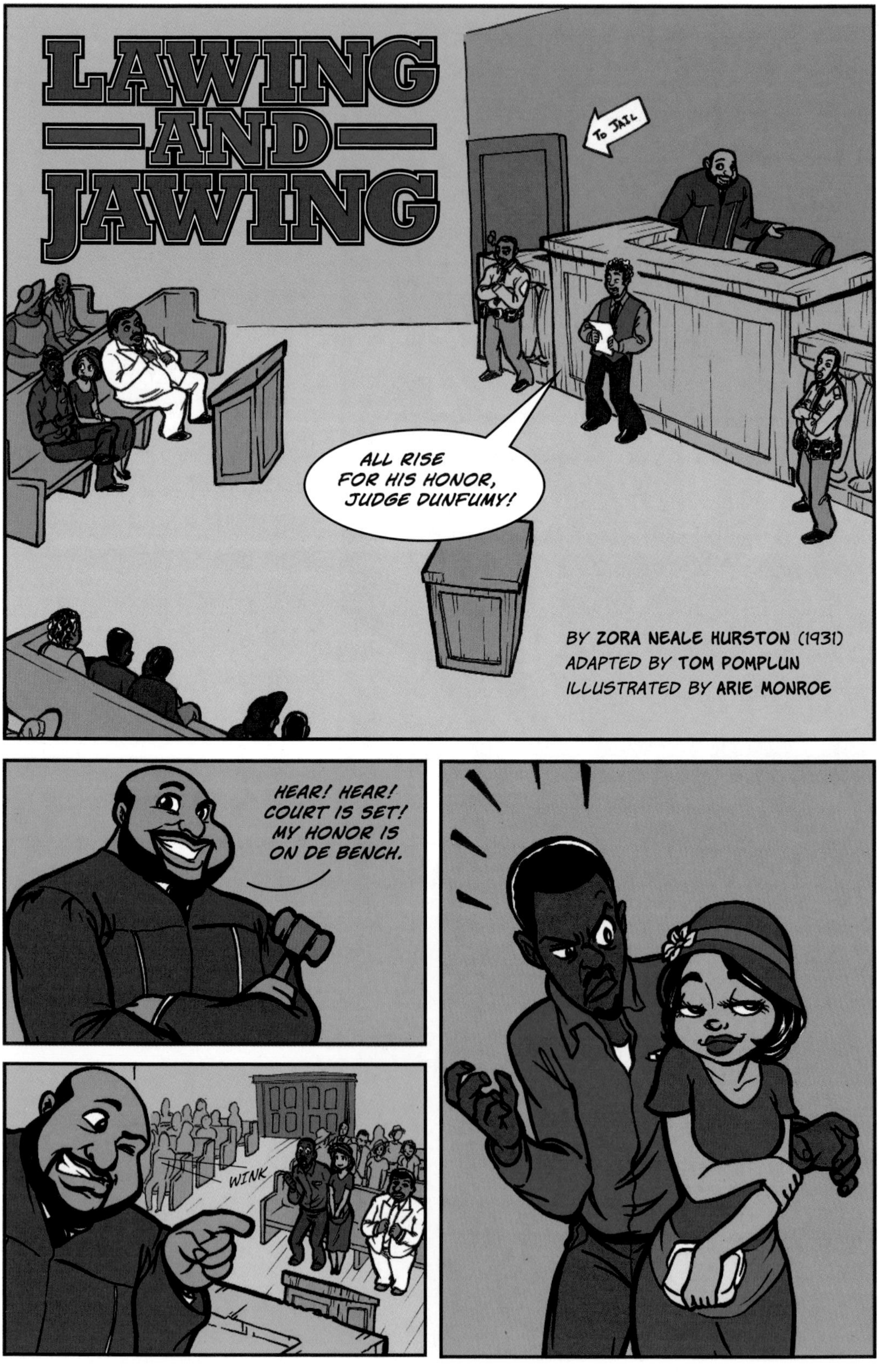
LAWING AND JAWING
TO JAIL
ALL RISE FOR HIS HONOR, JUDGE DUNFUMY!
BY ZORA NEALE HURSTON (1931)
ADAPTED BY TOM POMPLUN
ILLUSTRATED BY ARIE MONROE
HEAR! HEAR! COURT IS SET! MY HONOR IS ON DE BENCH.
WINK

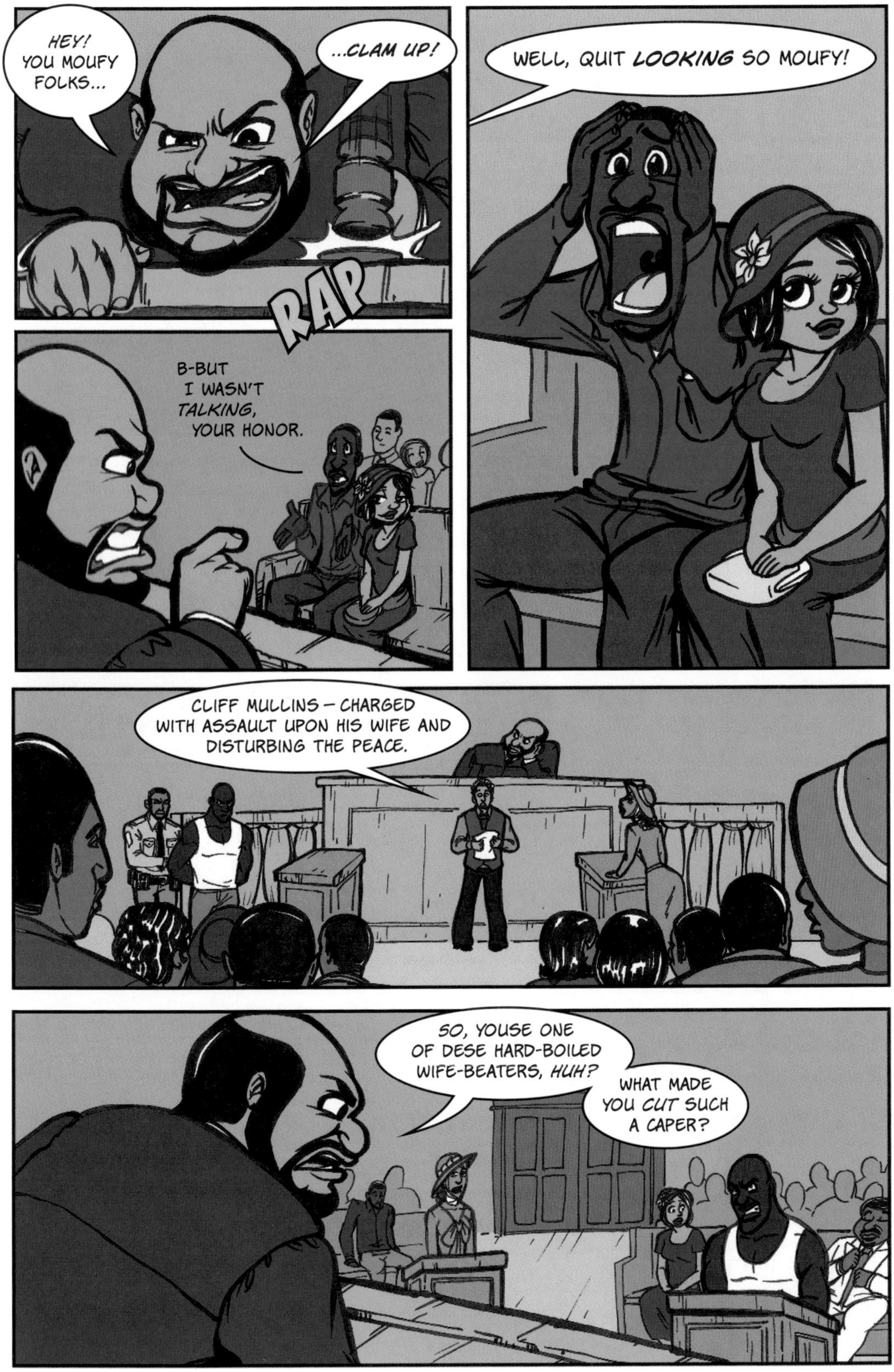
HEY! YOU MOUFY FOLKS...
...CLAM UP!
RAP
WELL, QUIT LOOKING SO MOUFY!
B-BUT I WASN'T TALKING, YOUR HONOR.
CLIFF MULLINS – CHARGED WITH ASSAULT UPON HIS WIFE AND DISTURBING THE PEACE.
SO, YOUSE ONE OF DESE HARD-BOILED WIFE-BEATERS, HUH?
WHAT MADE YOU CUT SUCH A CAPER?

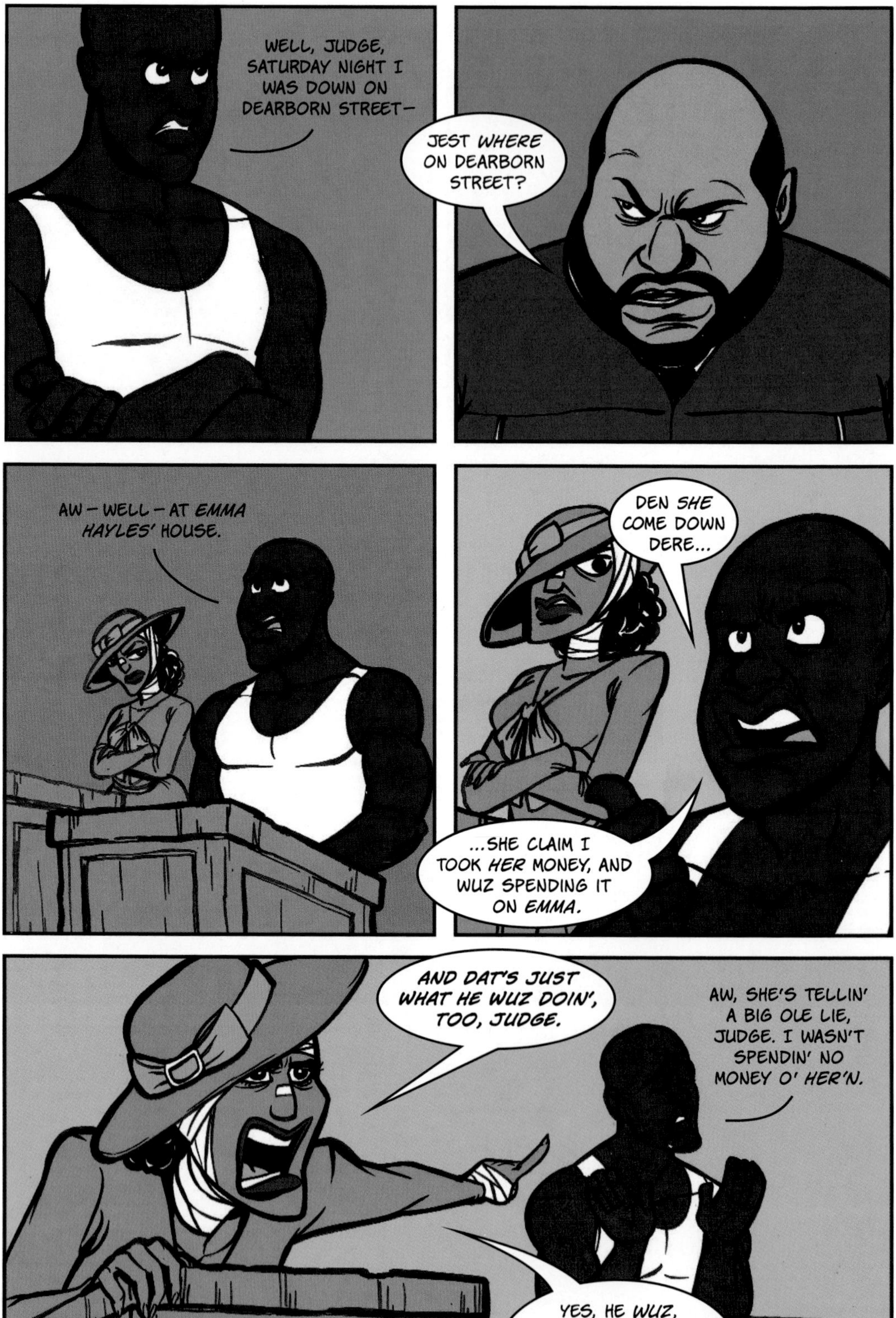
WELL, JUDGE, SATURDAY NIGHT I WAS DOWN ON DEARBORN STREET—
JEST *WHERE* ON DEARBORN STREET?
AW—WELL—AT *EMMA HAYLES'* HOUSE.
DEN *SHE* COME DOWN DERE...
...SHE CLAIM I TOOK *HER* MONEY, AND WUZ SPENDING IT ON *EMMA.*
AND DAT'S JUST WHAT HE WUZ DOIN', TOO, JUDGE.
AW, SHE'S TELLIN' A BIG OLE LIE, JUDGE. I WASN'T SPENDIN' NO MONEY O' *HER'N.*
YES, HE *WUZ*, JUDGE. HE AIN'T DONE A LICK O' WORK SINCE GOD BEEN TO MACON.

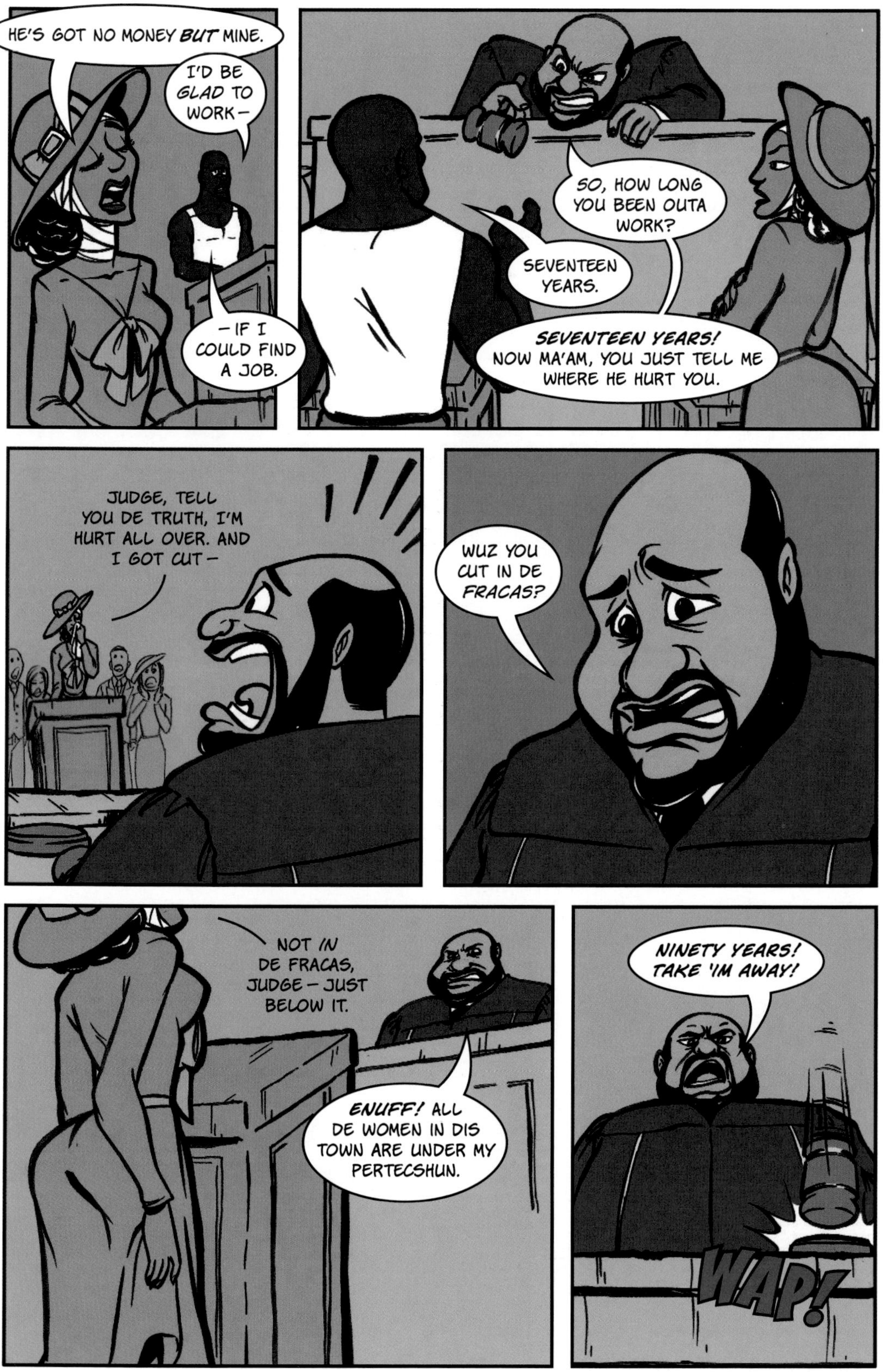
HE'S GOT NO MONEY **BUT** MINE.
I'D BE GLAD TO WORK–
–IF I COULD FIND A JOB.
SO, HOW LONG YOU BEEN OUTA WORK?
SEVENTEEN YEARS.
SEVENTEEN YEARS! NOW MA'AM, YOU JUST TELL ME WHERE HE HURT YOU.
JUDGE, TELL YOU DE TRUTH, I'M HURT ALL OVER. AND I GOT CUT–
WUZ YOU CUT IN DE *FRACAS?*
NOT *IN* DE FRACAS, JUDGE – JUST BELOW IT.
ENUFF! ALL DE WOMEN IN DIS TOWN ARE UNDER MY PERTECSHUN.
NINETY YEARS! TAKE 'IM AWAY!
WAP!

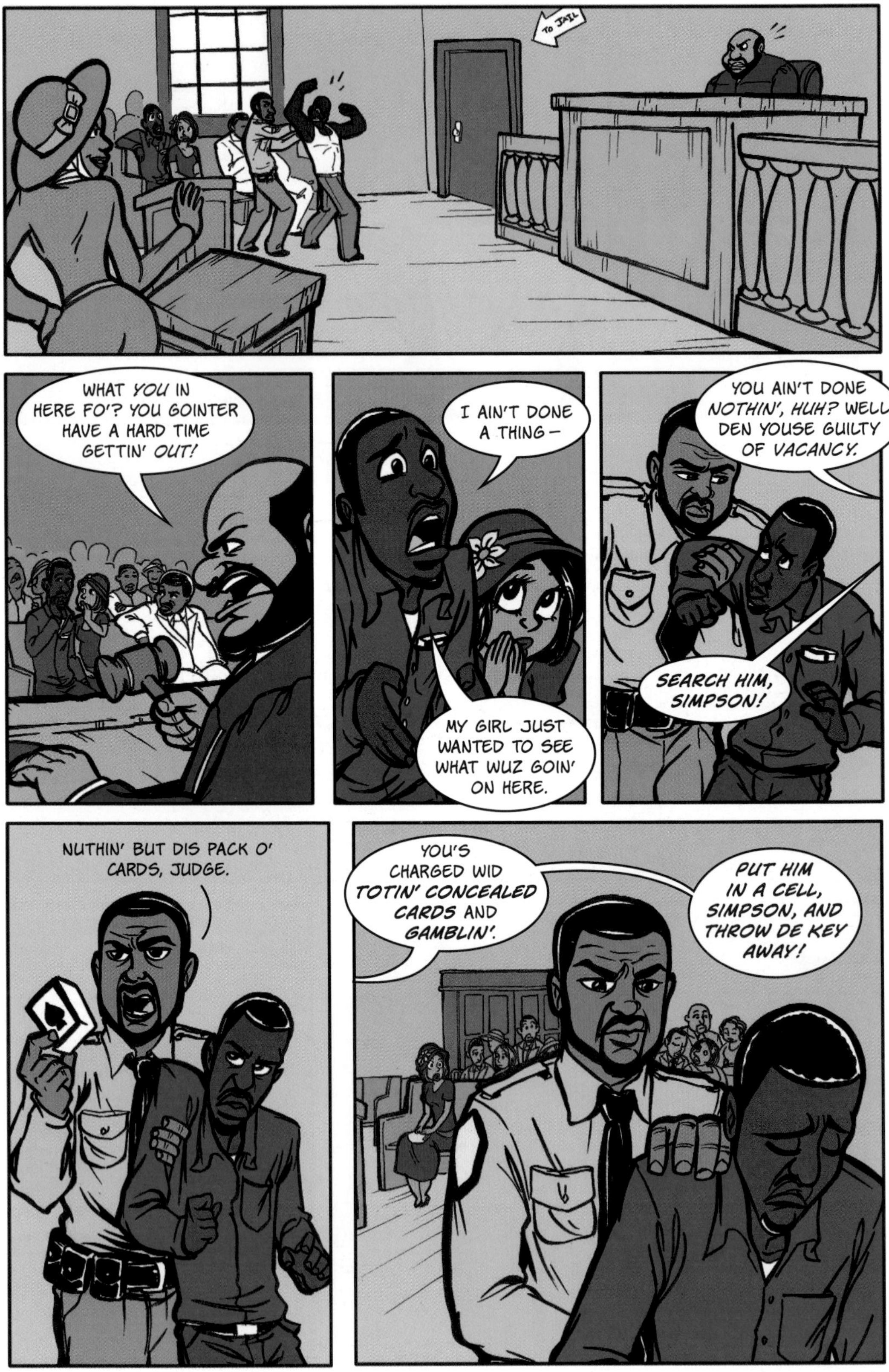
TO JAIL
WHAT YOU IN HERE FO'? YOU GOINTER HAVE A HARD TIME GETTIN' OUT!
I AIN'T DONE A THING—
MY GIRL JUST WANTED TO SEE WHAT WUZ GOIN' ON HERE.
YOU AIN'T DONE NOTHIN', HUH? WELL DEN YOUSE GUILTY OF VACANCY.
SEARCH HIM, SIMPSON!
NUTHIN' BUT DIS PACK O' CARDS, JUDGE.
YOU'S CHARGED WID TOTIN' CONCEALED CARDS AND GAMBLIN'.
PUT HIM IN A CELL, SIMPSON, AND THROW DE KEY AWAY!

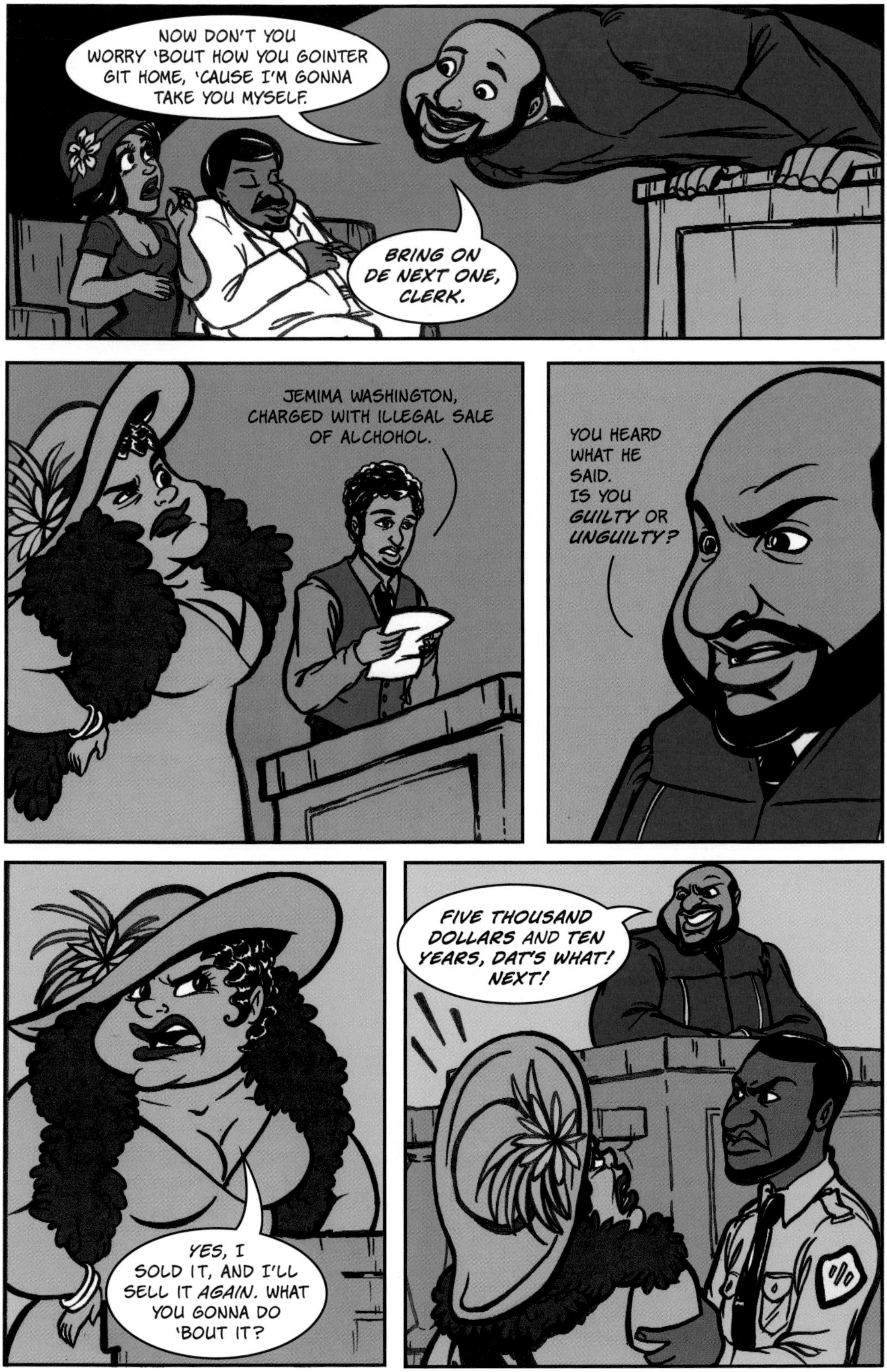
NOW DON'T YOU WORRY 'BOUT HOW YOU GOINTER GIT HOME, 'CAUSE I'M GONNA TAKE YOU MYSELF.
BRING ON DE NEXT ONE, CLERK.
JEMIMA WASHINGTON, CHARGED WITH ILLEGAL SALE OF ALCHOHOL.
YOU HEARD WHAT HE SAID. IS YOU GUILTY OR UNGUILTY?
YES, I SOLD IT, AND I'LL SELL IT AGAIN. WHAT YOU GONNA DO 'BOUT IT?
FIVE THOUSAND DOLLARS AND TEN YEARS, DAT'S WHAT! NEXT!

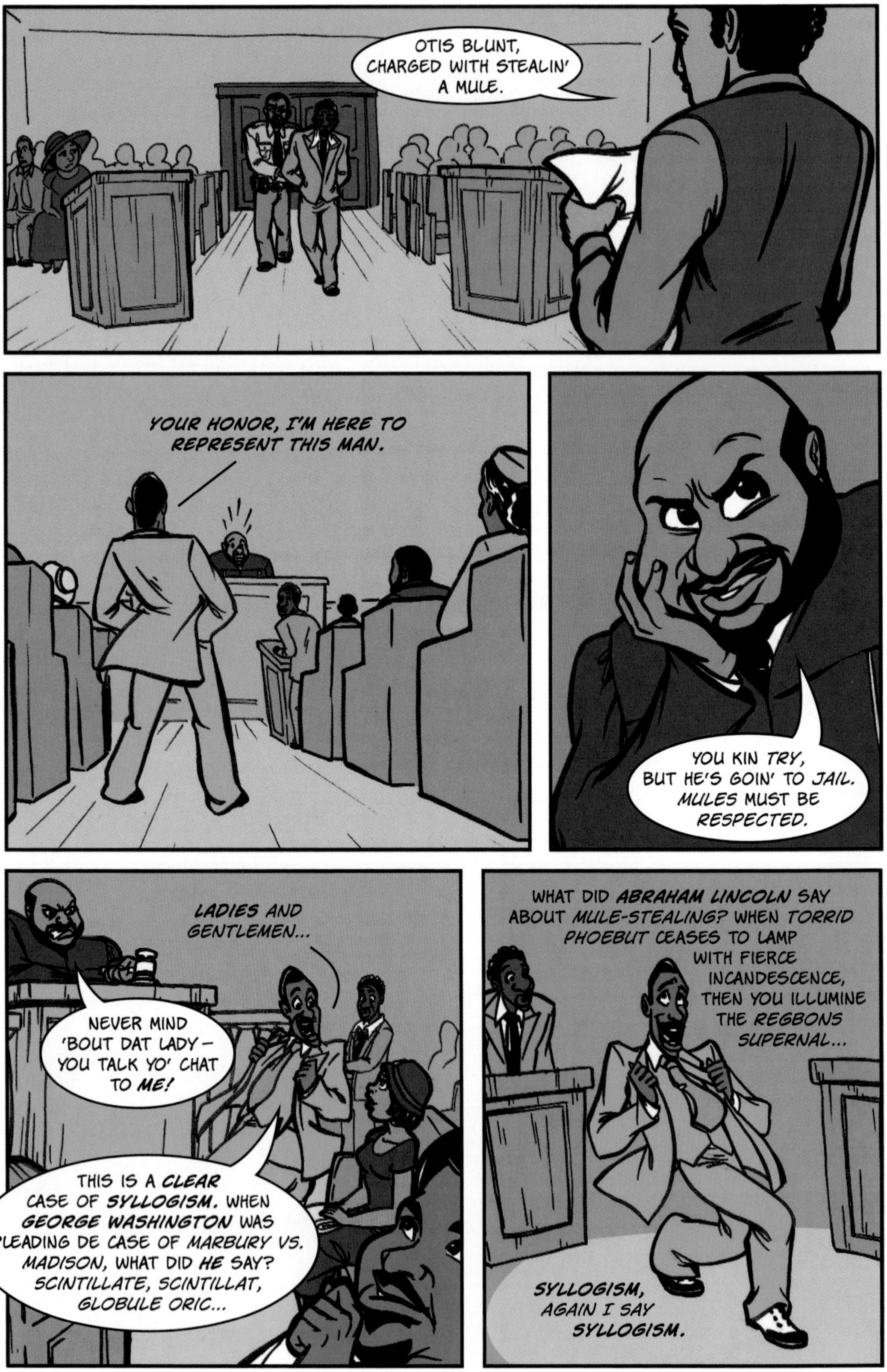
OTIS BLUNT, CHARGED WITH STEALIN' A MULE.
YOUR HONOR, I'M HERE TO REPRESENT THIS MAN.
YOU KIN TRY, BUT HE'S GOIN' TO JAIL. MULES MUST BE RESPECTED.
LADIES AND GENTLEMEN...
NEVER MIND 'BOUT DAT LADY – YOU TALK YO' CHAT TO ME!
THIS IS A CLEAR CASE OF SYLLOGISM. WHEN GEORGE WASHINGTON WAS PLEADING DE CASE OF MARBURY VS. MADISON, WHAT DID HE SAY? SCINTILLATE, SCINTILLAT, GLOBULE ORIC...
WHAT DID ABRAHAM LINCOLN SAY ABOUT MULE-STEALING? WHEN TORRID PHOEBUT CEASES TO LAMP WITH FIERCE INCANDESCENCE, THEN YOU ILLUMINE THE REGBONS SUPERNAL...
SYLLOGISM, AGAIN I SAY SYLLOGISM.

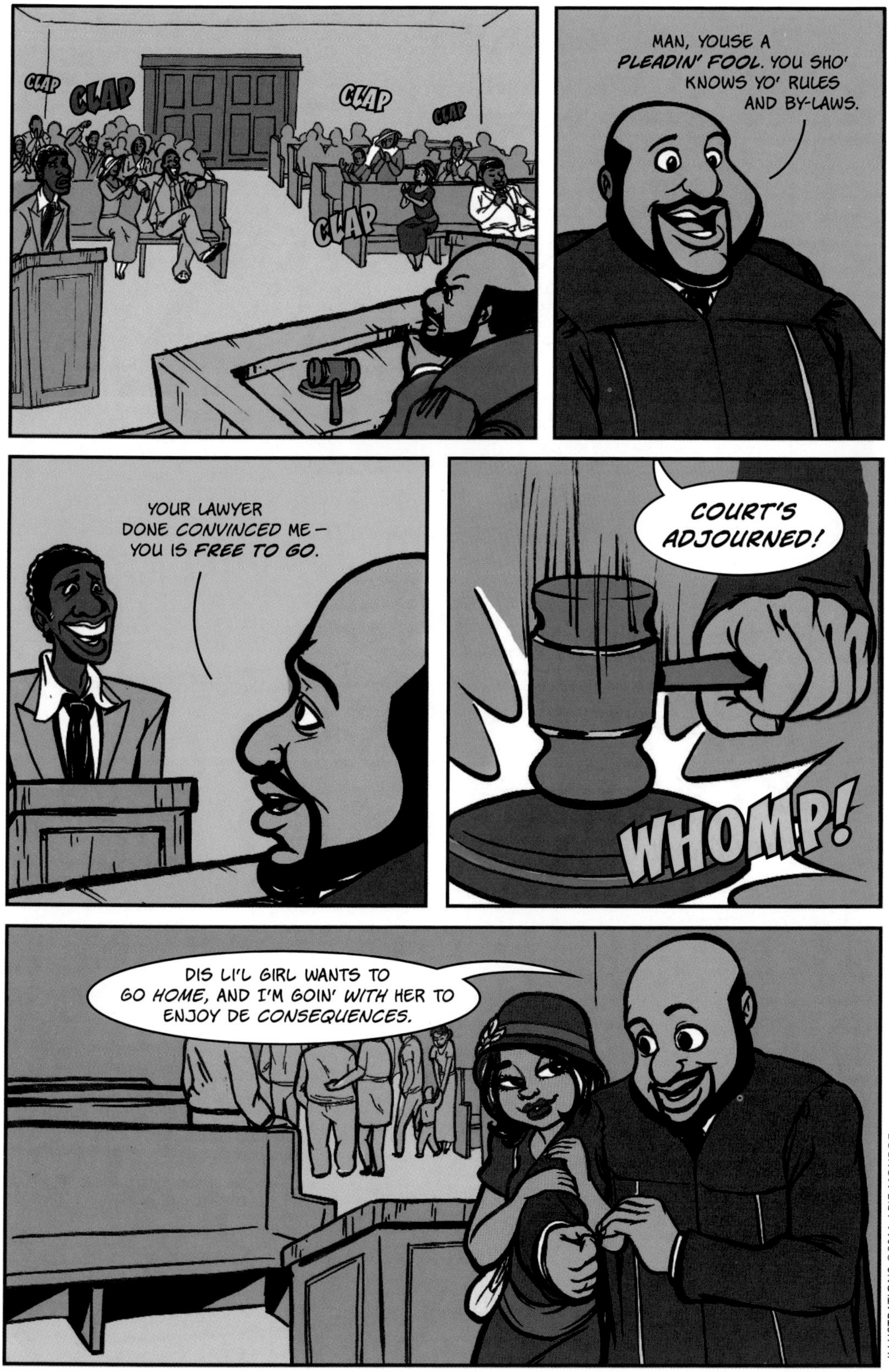
CLAP
CLAP
CLAP
CLAP
CLAP
MAN, YOUSE A PLEADIN' FOOL. YOU SHO' KNOWS YO' RULES AND BY-LAWS.
YOUR LAWYER DONE CONVINCED ME— YOU IS FREE TO GO.
COURT'S ADJOURNED!
WHOMP!
DIS LI'L GIRL WANTS TO GO HOME, AND I'M GOIN' WITH HER TO ENJOY DE CONSEQUENCES.

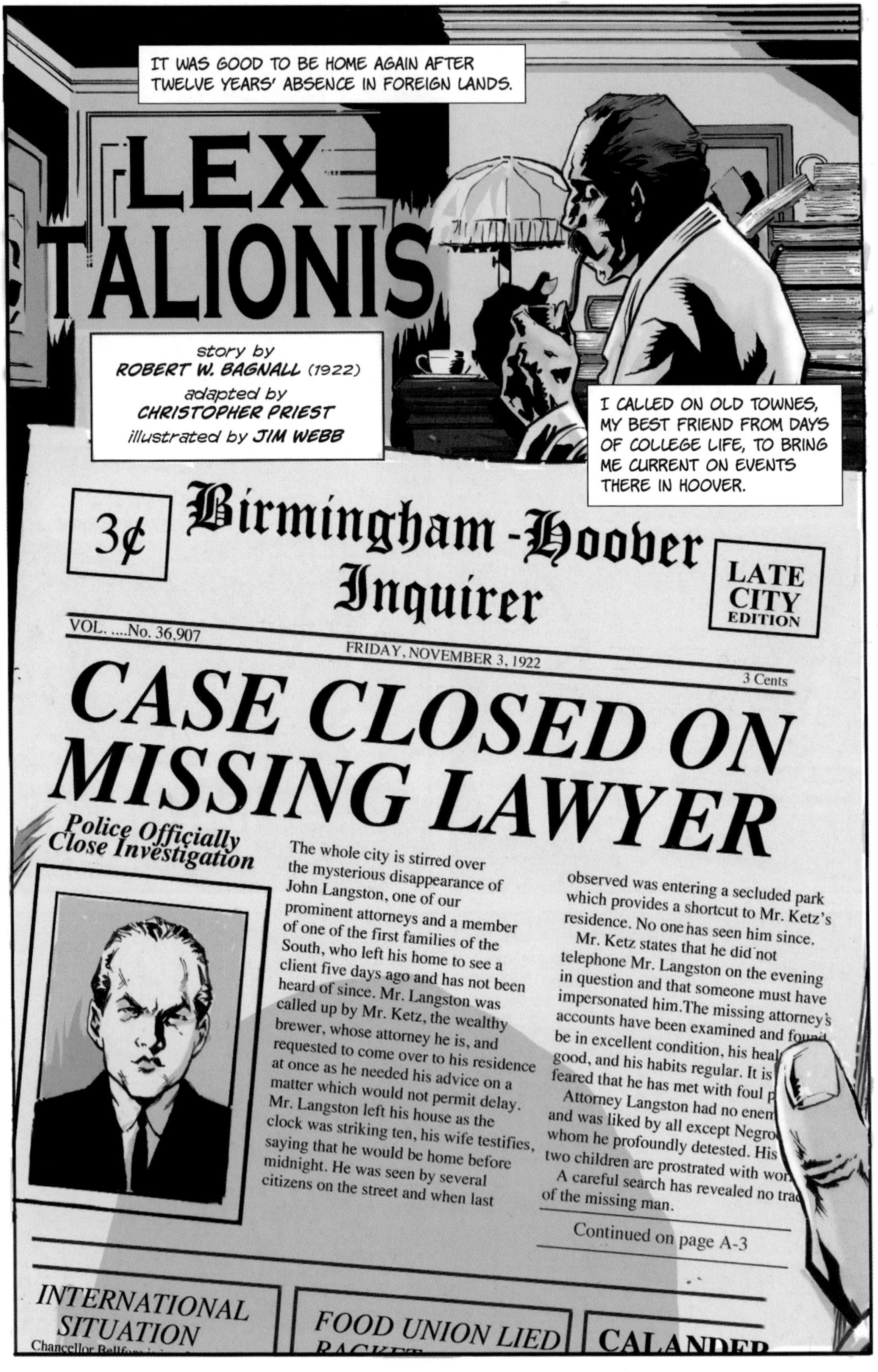
IT WAS GOOD TO BE HOME AGAIN AFTER TWELVE YEARS' ABSENCE IN FOREIGN LANDS.
LEX TALIONIS
story by ROBERT W. BAGNALL (1922) adapted by CHRISTOPHER PRIEST illustrated by JIM WEBB
I CALLED ON OLD TOWNES, MY BEST FRIEND FROM DAYS OF COLLEGE LIFE, TO BRING ME CURRENT ON EVENTS THERE IN HOOVER.
3¢
Birmingham-Hoover Inquirer
LATE CITY EDITION
VOL. ....No. 36,907
FRIDAY, NOVEMBER 3, 1922
3 Cents
CASE CLOSED ON MISSING LAWYER
Police Officially Close Investigation
The whole city is stirred over the mysterious disappearance of John Langston, one of our prominent attorneys and a member of one of the first families of the South, who left his home to see a client five days ago and has not been heard of since. Mr. Langston was called up by Mr. Ketz, the wealthy brewer, whose attorney he is, and requested to come over to his residence at once as he needed his advice on a matter which would not permit delay. Mr. Langston left his house as the clock was striking ten, his wife testifies, saying that he would be home before midnight. He was seen by several citizens on the street and when last observed was entering a secluded park which provides a shortcut to Mr. Ketz's residence. No one has seen him since.
Mr. Ketz states that he did not telephone Mr. Langston on the evening in question and that someone must have impersonated him. The missing attorney's accounts have been examined and fou good, and his habits regular. It is feared that he has met with foul p
be in excellent condition, his heal
Attorney Langston had no enem and was liked by all except Negro whom he profoundly detested. His two children are prostrated with wo
A careful search has revealed no tra of the missing man.
Continued on page A-3
INTERNATIONAL SITUATION
FOOD UNION LIED
CALANDER

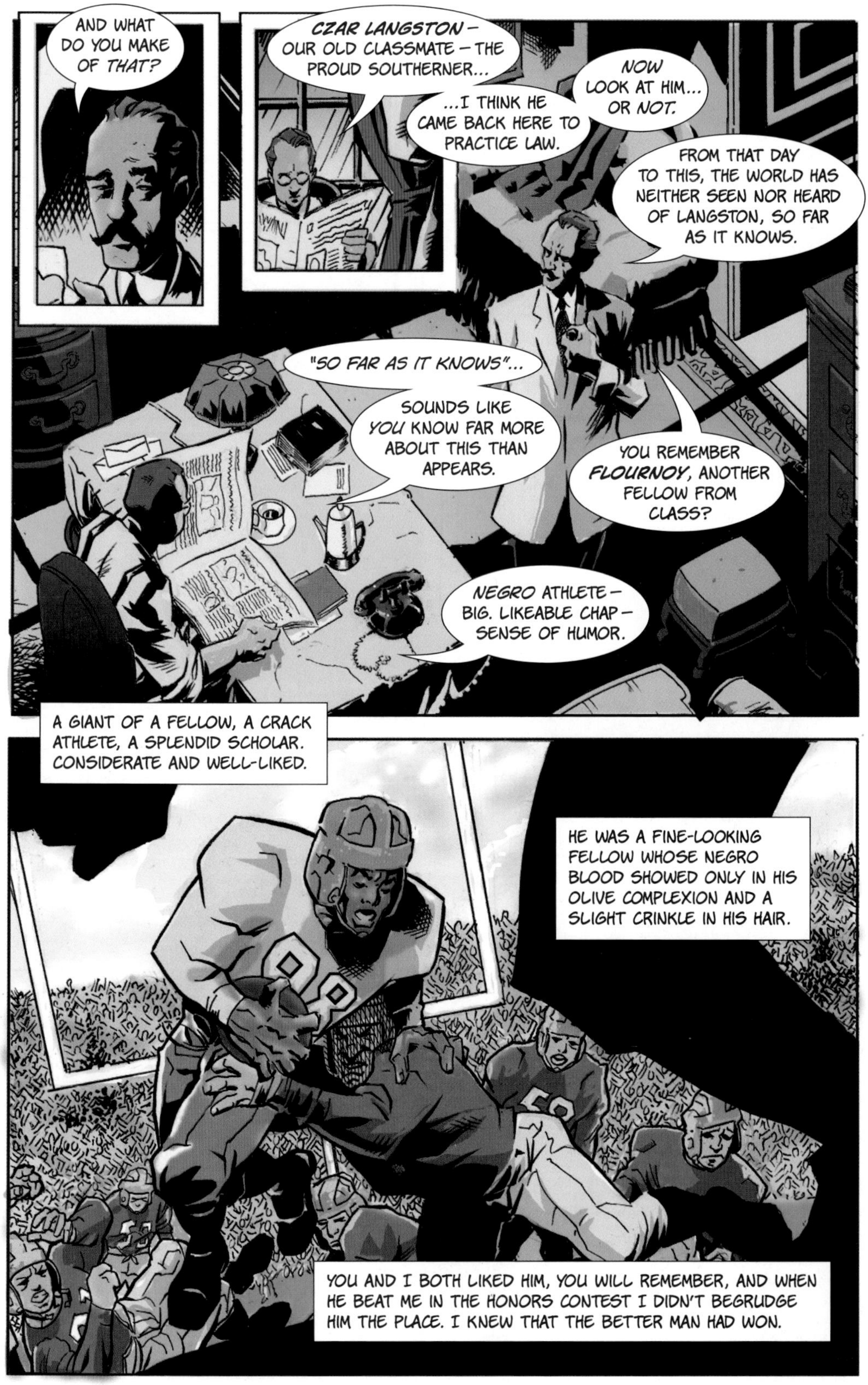
AND WHAT DO YOU MAKE OF *THAT*?
CZAR LANGSTON – OUR OLD CLASSMATE – THE PROUD SOUTHERNER...
...I THINK HE CAME BACK HERE TO PRACTICE LAW.
NOW LOOK AT HIM... OR *NOT*.
FROM THAT DAY TO THIS, THE WORLD HAS NEITHER SEEN NOR HEARD OF LANGSTON, SO FAR AS IT KNOWS.
"SO FAR AS IT KNOWS"...
SOUNDS LIKE *YOU* KNOW FAR MORE ABOUT THIS THAN APPEARS.
YOU REMEMBER ***FLOURNOY***, ANOTHER FELLOW FROM CLASS?
NEGRO ATHLETE – BIG. LIKEABLE CHAP – SENSE OF HUMOR.
A GIANT OF A FELLOW, A CRACK ATHLETE, A SPLENDID SCHOLAR. CONSIDERATE AND WELL-LIKED.
HE WAS A FINE-LOOKING FELLOW WHOSE NEGRO BLOOD SHOWED ONLY IN HIS OLIVE COMPLEXION AND A SLIGHT CRINKLE IN HIS HAIR.
YOU AND I BOTH LIKED HIM, YOU WILL REMEMBER, AND WHEN HE BEAT ME IN THE HONORS CONTEST I DIDN'T BEGRUDGE HIM THE PLACE. I KNEW THAT THE BETTER MAN HAD WON.

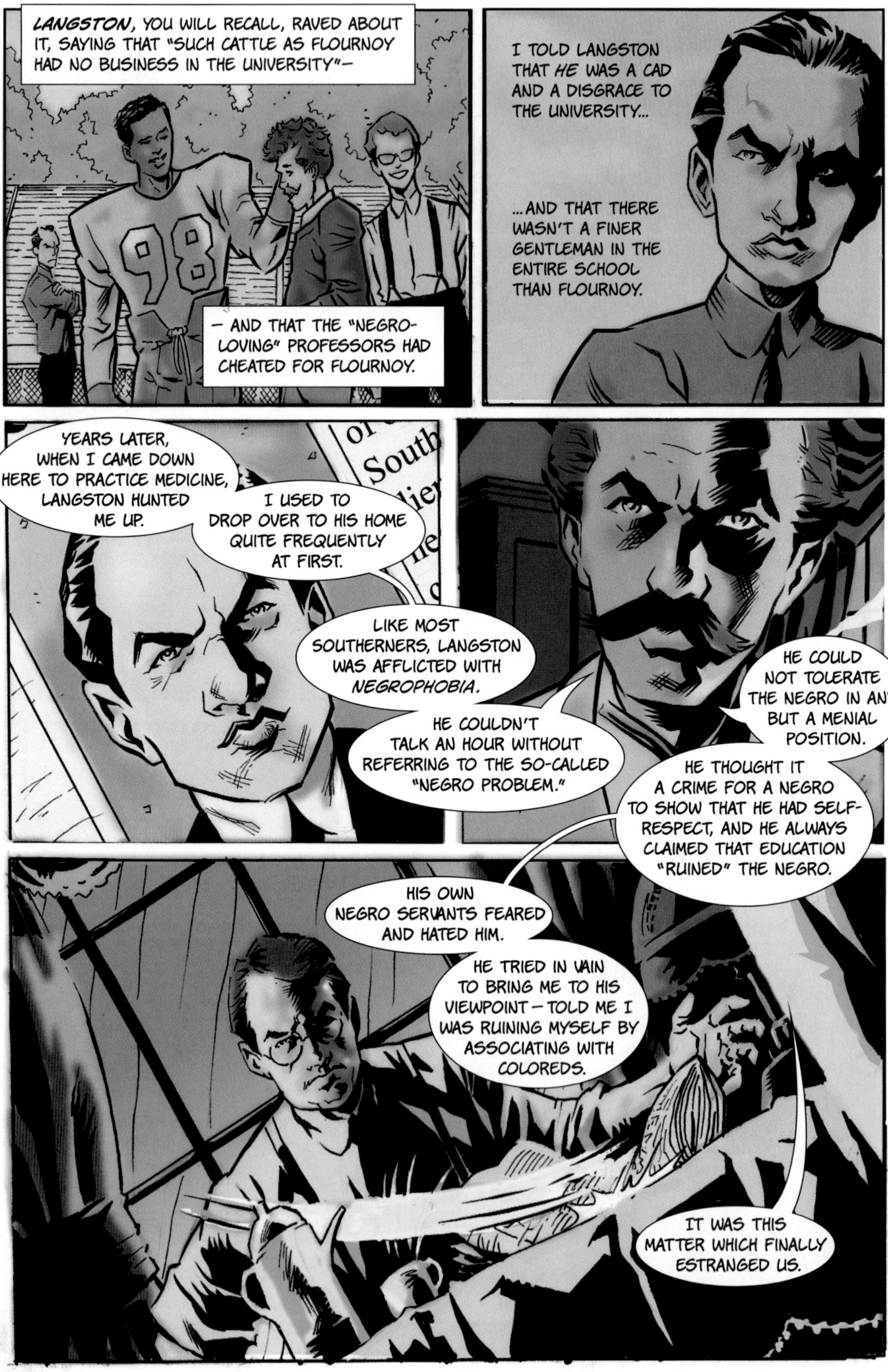
LANGSTON, YOU WILL RECALL, RAVED ABOUT IT, SAYING THAT "SUCH CATTLE AS FLOURNOY HAD NO BUSINESS IN THE UNIVERSITY"–
– AND THAT THE "NEGRO-LOVING" PROFESSORS HAD CHEATED FOR FLOURNOY.
I TOLD LANGSTON THAT HE WAS A CAD AND A DISGRACE TO THE UNIVERSITY...
...AND THAT THERE WASN'T A FINER GENTLEMAN IN THE ENTIRE SCHOOL THAN FLOURNOY.
YEARS LATER, WHEN I CAME DOWN HERE TO PRACTICE MEDICINE, LANGSTON HUNTED ME UP.
I USED TO DROP OVER TO HIS HOME QUITE FREQUENTLY AT FIRST.
LIKE MOST SOUTHERNERS, LANGSTON WAS AFFLICTED WITH NEGROPHOBIA.
HE COULDN'T TALK AN HOUR WITHOUT REFERRING TO THE SO-CALLED "NEGRO PROBLEM."
HE COULD NOT TOLERATE THE NEGRO IN ANY BUT A MENIAL POSITION.
HE THOUGHT IT A CRIME FOR A NEGRO TO SHOW THAT HE HAD SELF-RESPECT, AND HE ALWAYS CLAIMED THAT EDUCATION "RUINED" THE NEGRO.
HIS OWN NEGRO SERVANTS FEARED AND HATED HIM.
HE TRIED IN VAIN TO BRING ME TO HIS VIEWPOINT – TOLD ME I WAS RUINING MYSELF BY ASSOCIATING WITH COLOREDS.
IT WAS THIS MATTER WHICH FINALLY ESTRANGED US.

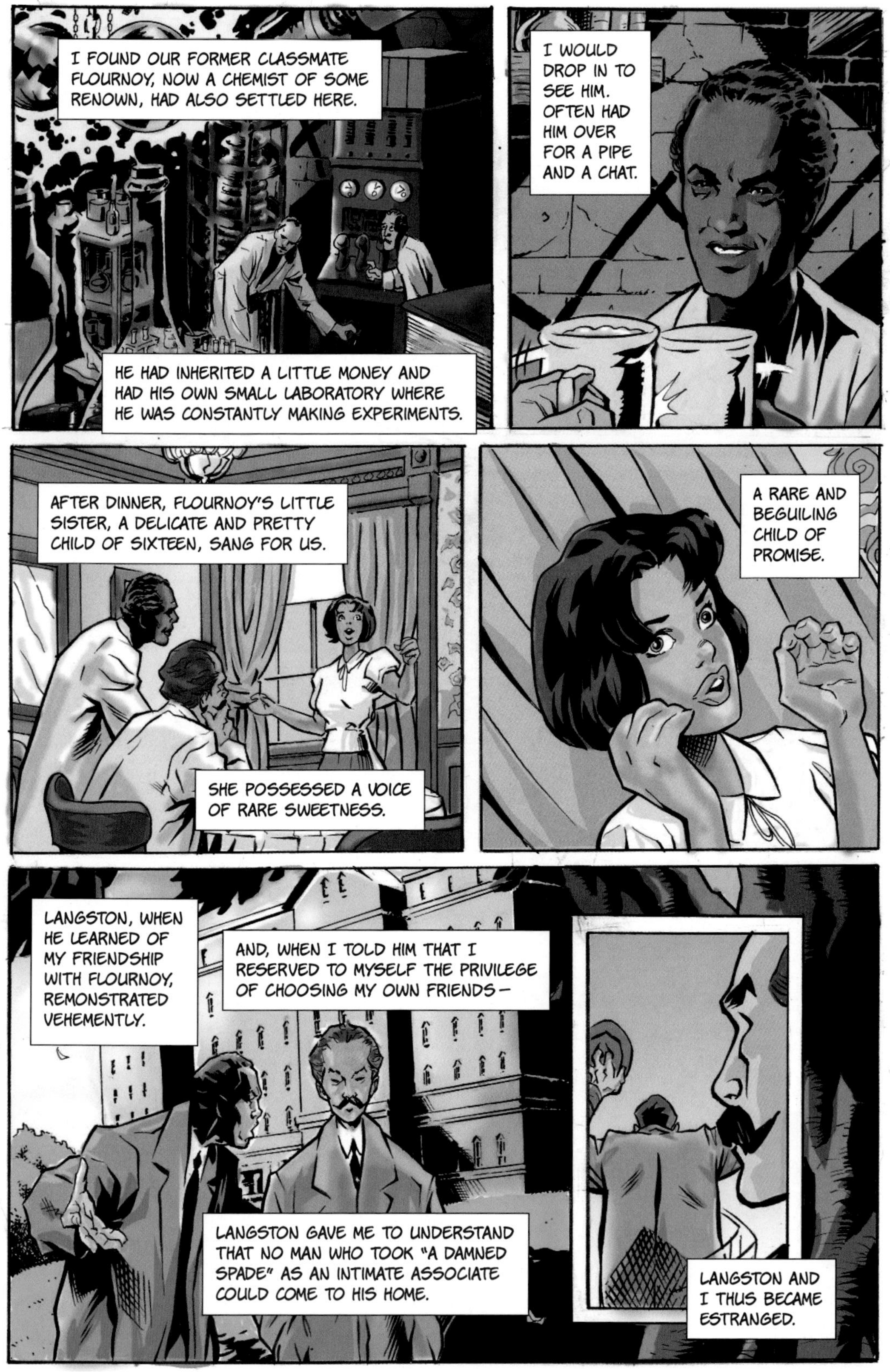
I FOUND OUR FORMER CLASSMATE FLOURNOY, NOW A CHEMIST OF SOME RENOWN, HAD ALSO SETTLED HERE.
HE HAD INHERITED A LITTLE MONEY AND HAD HIS OWN SMALL LABORATORY WHERE HE WAS CONSTANTLY MAKING EXPERIMENTS.
I WOULD DROP IN TO SEE HIM. OFTEN HAD HIM OVER FOR A PIPE AND A CHAT.
AFTER DINNER, FLOURNOY'S LITTLE SISTER, A DELICATE AND PRETTY CHILD OF SIXTEEN, SANG FOR US.
SHE POSSESSED A VOICE OF RARE SWEETNESS.
A RARE AND BEGUILING CHILD OF PROMISE.
LANGSTON, WHEN HE LEARNED OF MY FRIENDSHIP WITH FLOURNOY, REMONSTRATED VEHEMENTLY.
AND, WHEN I TOLD HIM THAT I RESERVED TO MYSELF THE PRIVILEGE OF CHOOSING MY OWN FRIENDS—
LANGSTON GAVE ME TO UNDERSTAND THAT NO MAN WHO TOOK "A DAMNED SPADE" AS AN INTIMATE ASSOCIATE COULD COME TO HIS HOME.
LANGSTON AND I THUS BECAME ESTRANGED.

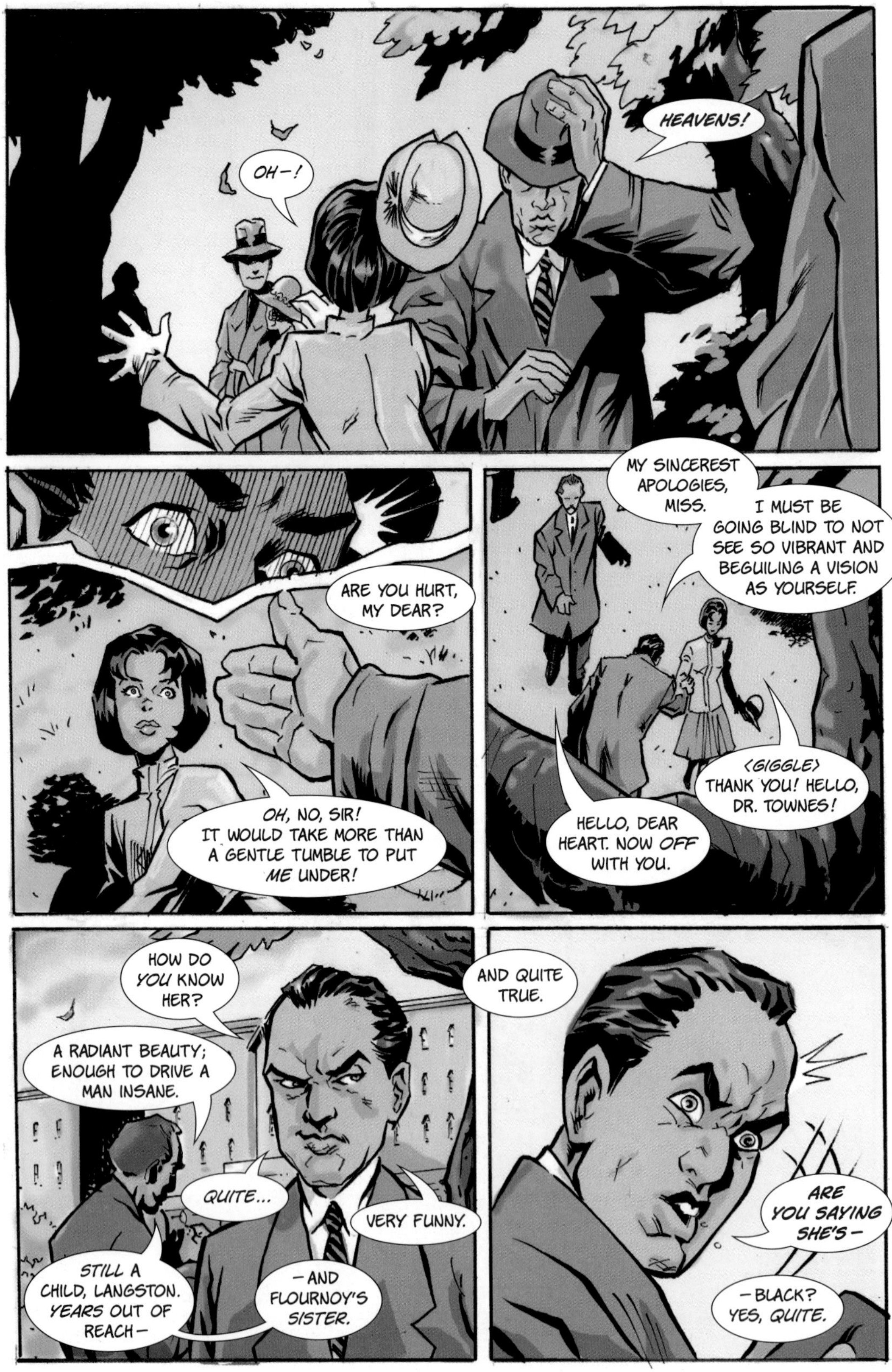
OH—!
HEAVENS!
ARE YOU HURT, MY DEAR?
OH, NO, SIR! IT WOULD TAKE MORE THAN A GENTLE TUMBLE TO PUT ME UNDER!
MY SINCEREST APOLOGIES, MISS.
I MUST BE GOING BLIND TO NOT SEE SO VIBRANT AND BEGUILING A VISION AS YOURSELF.
<GIGGLE> THANK YOU! HELLO, DR. TOWNES!
HELLO, DEAR HEART. NOW OFF WITH YOU.
HOW DO YOU KNOW HER?
A RADIANT BEAUTY; ENOUGH TO DRIVE A MAN INSANE.
QUITE...
STILL A CHILD, LANGSTON. YEARS OUT OF REACH—
—AND FLOURNOY'S SISTER.
VERY FUNNY.
AND QUITE TRUE.
ARE YOU SAYING SHE'S—
—BLACK? YES, QUITE.

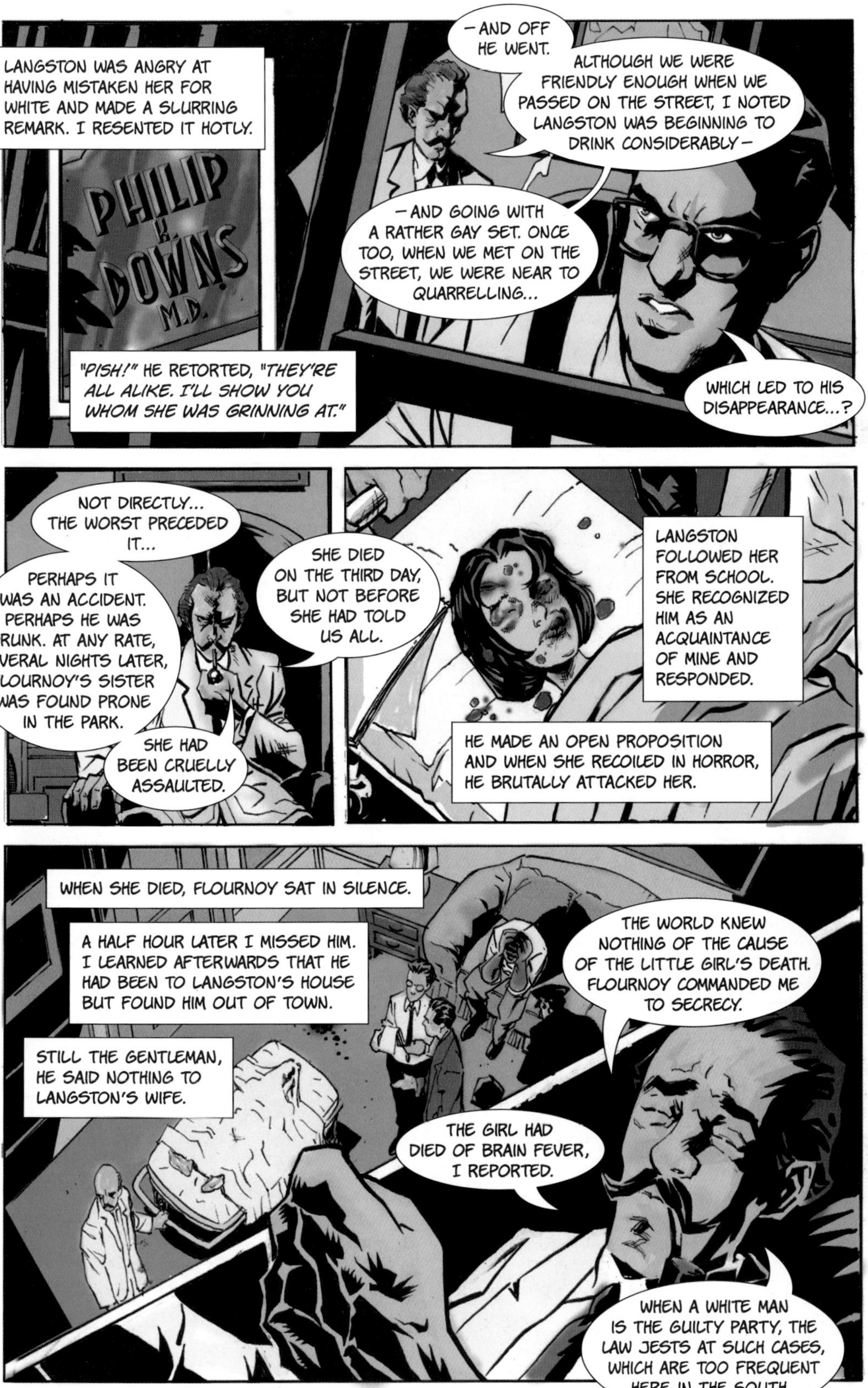
LANGSTON WAS ANGRY AT HAVING MISTAKEN HER FOR WHITE AND MADE A SLURRING REMARK. I RESENTED IT HOTLY.
PHILIP K. DOWNS M.D.
"PISH!" HE RETORTED, "THEY'RE ALL ALIKE. I'LL SHOW YOU WHOM SHE WAS GRINNING AT."
—AND OFF HE WENT.
ALTHOUGH WE WERE FRIENDLY ENOUGH WHEN WE PASSED ON THE STREET, I NOTED LANGSTON WAS BEGINNING TO DRINK CONSIDERABLY—
—AND GOING WITH A RATHER GAY SET. ONCE TOO, WHEN WE MET ON THE STREET, WE WERE NEAR TO QUARRELLING...
WHICH LED TO HIS DISAPPEARANCE...?
NOT DIRECTLY... THE WORST PRECEDED IT...
PERHAPS IT WAS AN ACCIDENT. PERHAPS HE WAS DRUNK. AT ANY RATE, SEVERAL NIGHTS LATER, FLOURNOY'S SISTER WAS FOUND PRONE IN THE PARK.
SHE HAD BEEN CRUELLY ASSAULTED.
SHE DIED ON THE THIRD DAY, BUT NOT BEFORE SHE HAD TOLD US ALL.
LANGSTON FOLLOWED HER FROM SCHOOL. SHE RECOGNIZED HIM AS AN ACQUAINTANCE OF MINE AND RESPONDED.
HE MADE AN OPEN PROPOSITION AND WHEN SHE RECOILED IN HORROR, HE BRUTALLY ATTACKED HER.
WHEN SHE DIED, FLOURNOY SAT IN SILENCE.
A HALF HOUR LATER I MISSED HIM. I LEARNED AFTERWARDS THAT HE HAD BEEN TO LANGSTON'S HOUSE BUT FOUND HIM OUT OF TOWN.
STILL THE GENTLEMAN, HE SAID NOTHING TO LANGSTON'S WIFE.
THE WORLD KNEW NOTHING OF THE CAUSE OF THE LITTLE GIRL'S DEATH. FLOURNOY COMMANDED ME TO SECRECY.
THE GIRL HAD DIED OF BRAIN FEVER, I REPORTED.
WHEN A WHITE MAN IS THE GUILTY PARTY, THE LAW JESTS AT SUCH CASES, WHICH ARE TOO FREQUENT HERE IN THE SOUTH...

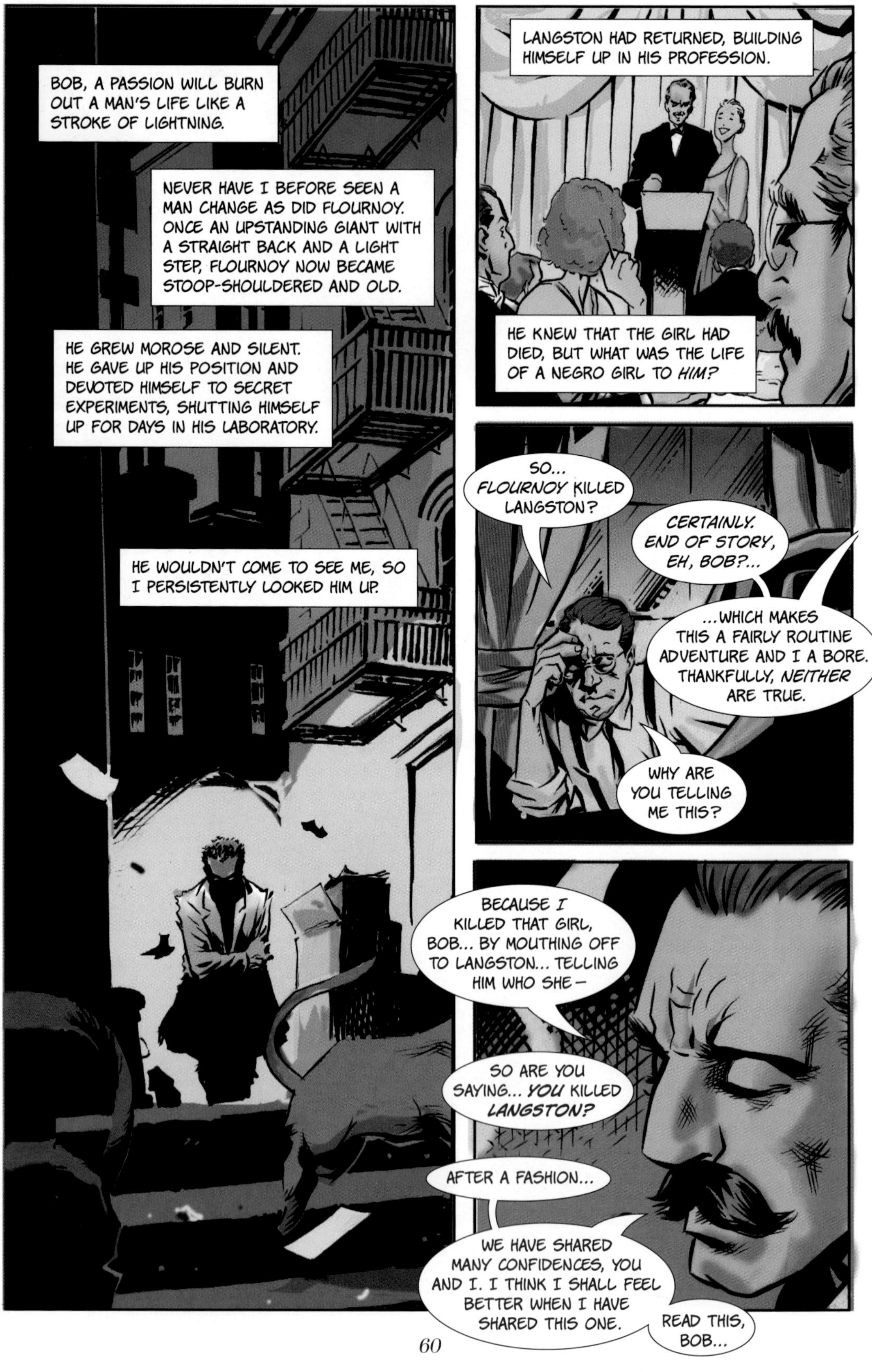
BOB, A PASSION WILL BURN OUT A MAN'S LIFE LIKE A STROKE OF LIGHTNING.
NEVER HAVE I BEFORE SEEN A MAN CHANGE AS DID FLOURNOY. ONCE AN UPSTANDING GIANT WITH A STRAIGHT BACK AND A LIGHT STEP, FLOURNOY NOW BECAME STOOP-SHOULDERED AND OLD.
HE GREW MOROSE AND SILENT. HE GAVE UP HIS POSITION AND DEVOTED HIMSELF TO SECRET EXPERIMENTS, SHUTTING HIMSELF UP FOR DAYS IN HIS LABORATORY.
HE WOULDN'T COME TO SEE ME, SO I PERSISTENTLY LOOKED HIM UP.
LANGSTON HAD RETURNED, BUILDING HIMSELF UP IN HIS PROFESSION.
HE KNEW THAT THE GIRL HAD DIED, BUT WHAT WAS THE LIFE OF A NEGRO GIRL TO *HIM?*
SO... *FLOURNOY* KILLED LANGSTON?
CERTAINLY. END OF STORY, EH, BOB?...
...WHICH MAKES THIS A FAIRLY ROUTINE ADVENTURE AND I A BORE. THANKFULLY, *NEITHER* ARE TRUE.
WHY ARE YOU TELLING ME THIS?
BECAUSE *I* KILLED THAT GIRL, BOB... BY MOUTHING OFF TO LANGSTON... TELLING HIM WHO SHE—
SO ARE YOU SAYING... ***YOU*** KILLED ***LANGSTON?***
AFTER A FASHION...
WE HAVE SHARED MANY CONFIDENCES, YOU AND I. I THINK I SHALL FEEL BETTER WHEN I HAVE SHARED THIS ONE.
READ THIS, BOB...

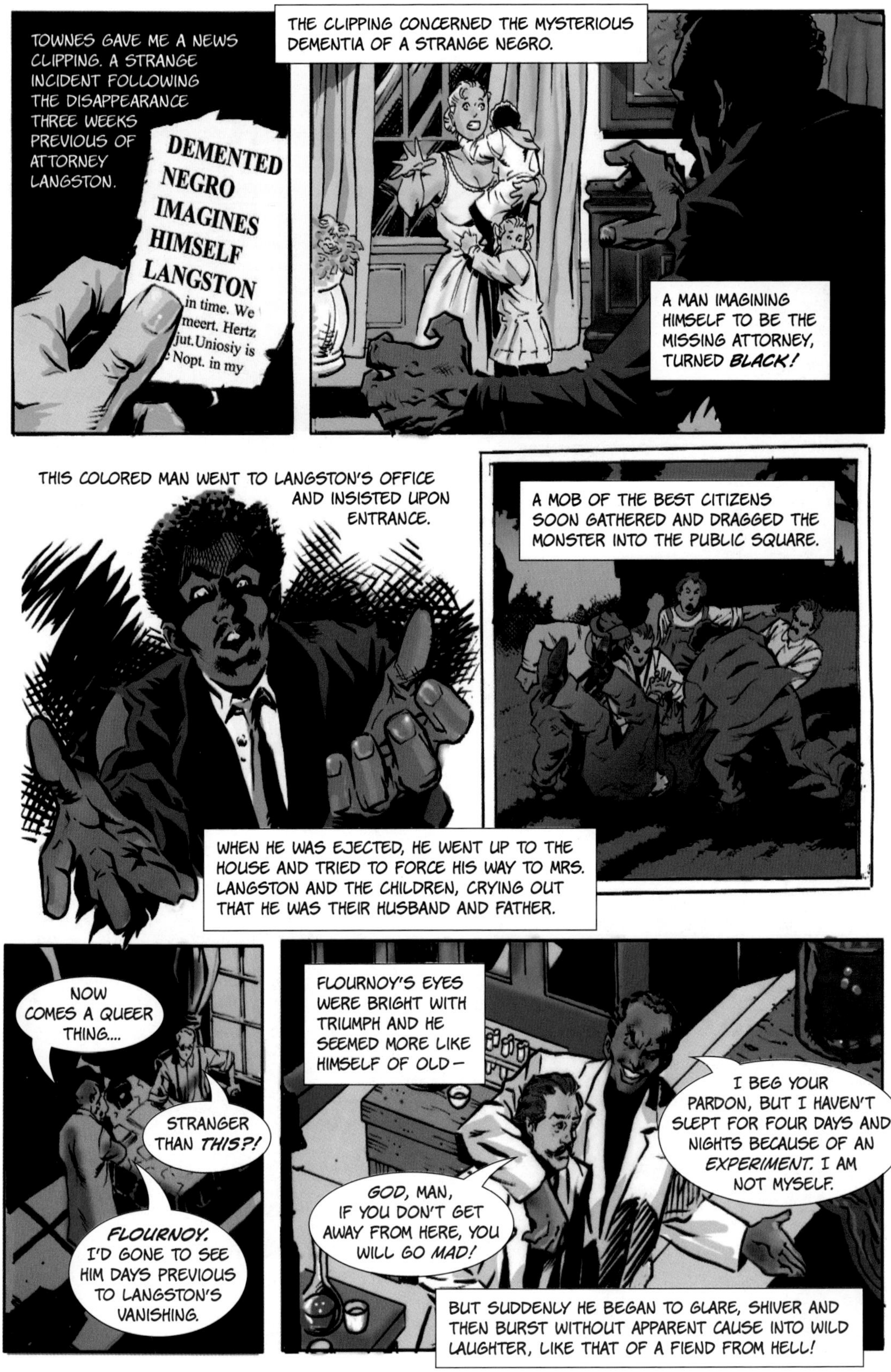
TOWNES GAVE ME A NEWS CLIPPING. A STRANGE INCIDENT FOLLOWING THE DISAPPEARANCE THREE WEEKS PREVIOUS OF ATTORNEY LANGSTON.
DEMENTED NEGRO IMAGINES HIMSELF LANGSTON
in time. We
meert. Hertz
jut.Uniosiy is
Nopt. in my
THE CLIPPING CONCERNED THE MYSTERIOUS DEMENTIA OF A STRANGE NEGRO.
A MAN IMAGINING HIMSELF TO BE THE MISSING ATTORNEY, TURNED *BLACK!*
THIS COLORED MAN WENT TO LANGSTON'S OFFICE AND INSISTED UPON ENTRANCE.
A MOB OF THE BEST CITIZENS SOON GATHERED AND DRAGGED THE MONSTER INTO THE PUBLIC SQUARE.
WHEN HE WAS EJECTED, HE WENT UP TO THE HOUSE AND TRIED TO FORCE HIS WAY TO MRS. LANGSTON AND THE CHILDREN, CRYING OUT THAT HE WAS THEIR HUSBAND AND FATHER.
NOW COMES A QUEER THING....
STRANGER THAN *THIS?!*
FLOURNOY. I'D GONE TO SEE HIM DAYS PREVIOUS TO LANGSTON'S VANISHING.
FLOURNOY'S EYES WERE BRIGHT WITH TRIUMPH AND HE SEEMED MORE LIKE HIMSELF OF OLD—
I BEG YOUR PARDON, BUT I HAVEN'T SLEPT FOR FOUR DAYS AND NIGHTS BECAUSE OF AN *EXPERIMENT.* I AM NOT MYSELF.
GOD, MAN, IF YOU DON'T GET AWAY FROM HERE, YOU WILL GO *MAD!*
BUT SUDDENLY HE BEGAN TO GLARE, SHIVER AND THEN BURST WITHOUT APPARENT CAUSE INTO WILD LAUGHTER, LIKE THAT OF A FIEND FROM HELL!

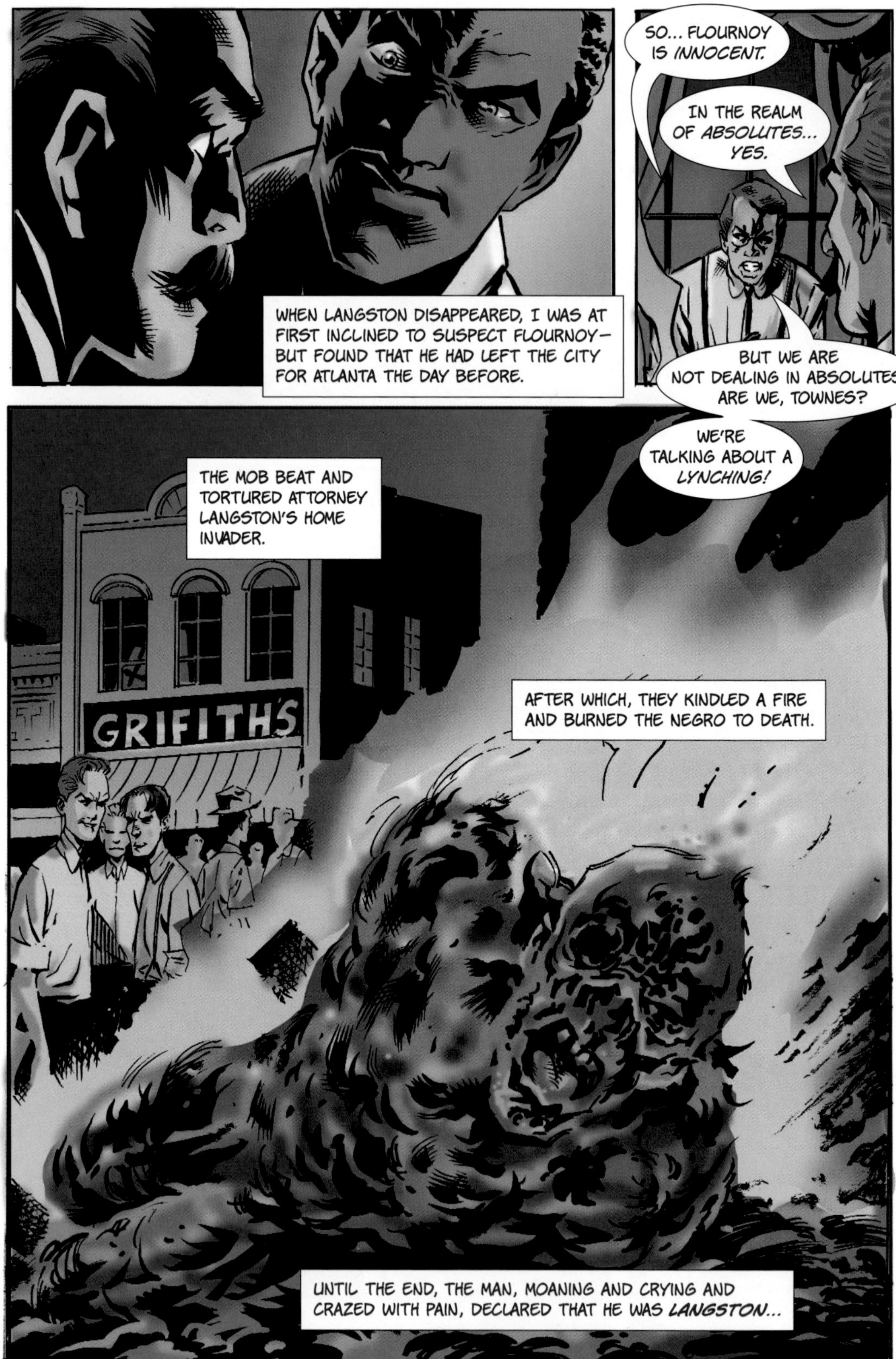
WHEN LANGSTON DISAPPEARED, I WAS AT FIRST INCLINED TO SUSPECT FLOURNOY—BUT FOUND THAT HE HAD LEFT THE CITY FOR ATLANTA THE DAY BEFORE.
SO... FLOURNOY IS *INNOCENT.*
IN THE REALM OF *ABSOLUTES...* *YES.*
BUT WE ARE NOT DEALING IN ABSOLUTES, ARE WE, TOWNES?
WE'RE TALKING ABOUT A *LYNCHING!*
THE MOB BEAT AND TORTURED ATTORNEY LANGSTON'S HOME INVADER.
GRIFITH'S
AFTER WHICH, THEY KINDLED A FIRE AND BURNED THE NEGRO TO DEATH.
UNTIL THE END, THE MAN, MOANING AND CRYING AND CRAZED WITH PAIN, DECLARED THAT HE WAS *LANGSTON...*

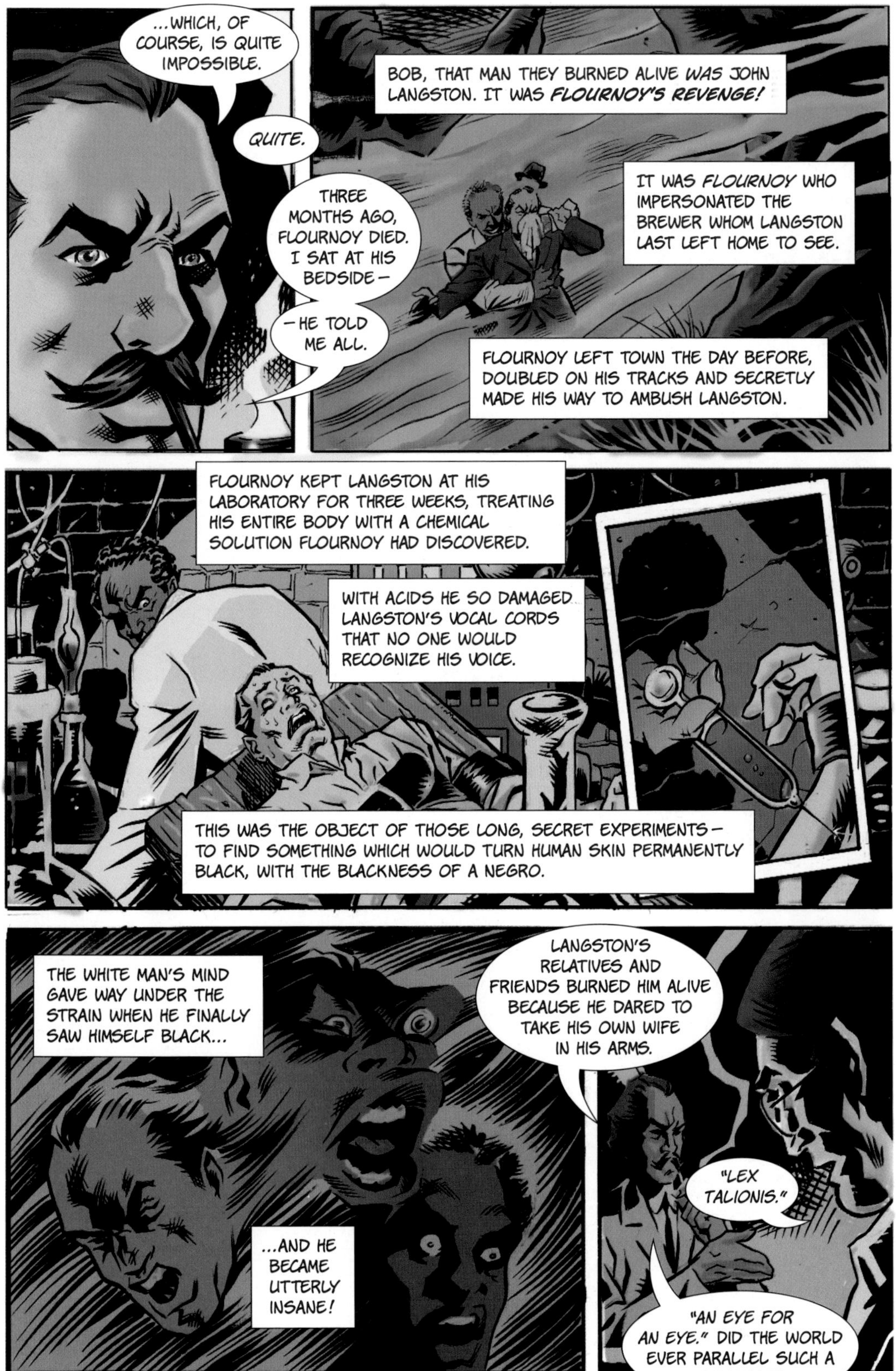
...WHICH, OF COURSE, IS QUITE IMPOSSIBLE.
QUITE.
THREE MONTHS AGO, FLOURNOY DIED. I SAT AT HIS BEDSIDE—
—HE TOLD ME ALL.
BOB, THAT MAN THEY BURNED ALIVE *WAS* JOHN LANGSTON. IT WAS *FLOURNOY'S REVENGE!*
IT WAS *FLOURNOY* WHO IMPERSONATED THE BREWER WHOM LANGSTON LAST LEFT HOME TO SEE.
FLOURNOY LEFT TOWN THE DAY BEFORE, DOUBLED ON HIS TRACKS AND SECRETLY MADE HIS WAY TO AMBUSH LANGSTON.
FLOURNOY KEPT LANGSTON AT HIS LABORATORY FOR THREE WEEKS, TREATING HIS ENTIRE BODY WITH A CHEMICAL SOLUTION FLOURNOY HAD DISCOVERED.
WITH ACIDS HE SO DAMAGED LANGSTON'S VOCAL CORDS THAT NO ONE WOULD RECOGNIZE HIS VOICE.
THIS WAS THE OBJECT OF THOSE LONG, SECRET EXPERIMENTS—TO FIND SOMETHING WHICH WOULD TURN HUMAN SKIN PERMANENTLY BLACK, WITH THE BLACKNESS OF A NEGRO.
THE WHITE MAN'S MIND GAVE WAY UNDER THE STRAIN WHEN HE FINALLY SAW HIMSELF BLACK...
...AND HE BECAME UTTERLY INSANE!
LANGSTON'S RELATIVES AND FRIENDS BURNED HIM ALIVE BECAUSE HE DARED TO TAKE HIS OWN WIFE IN HIS ARMS.
"LEX TALIONIS."
"AN EYE FOR AN EYE." DID THE WORLD EVER PARALLEL SUCH A REVENGE?

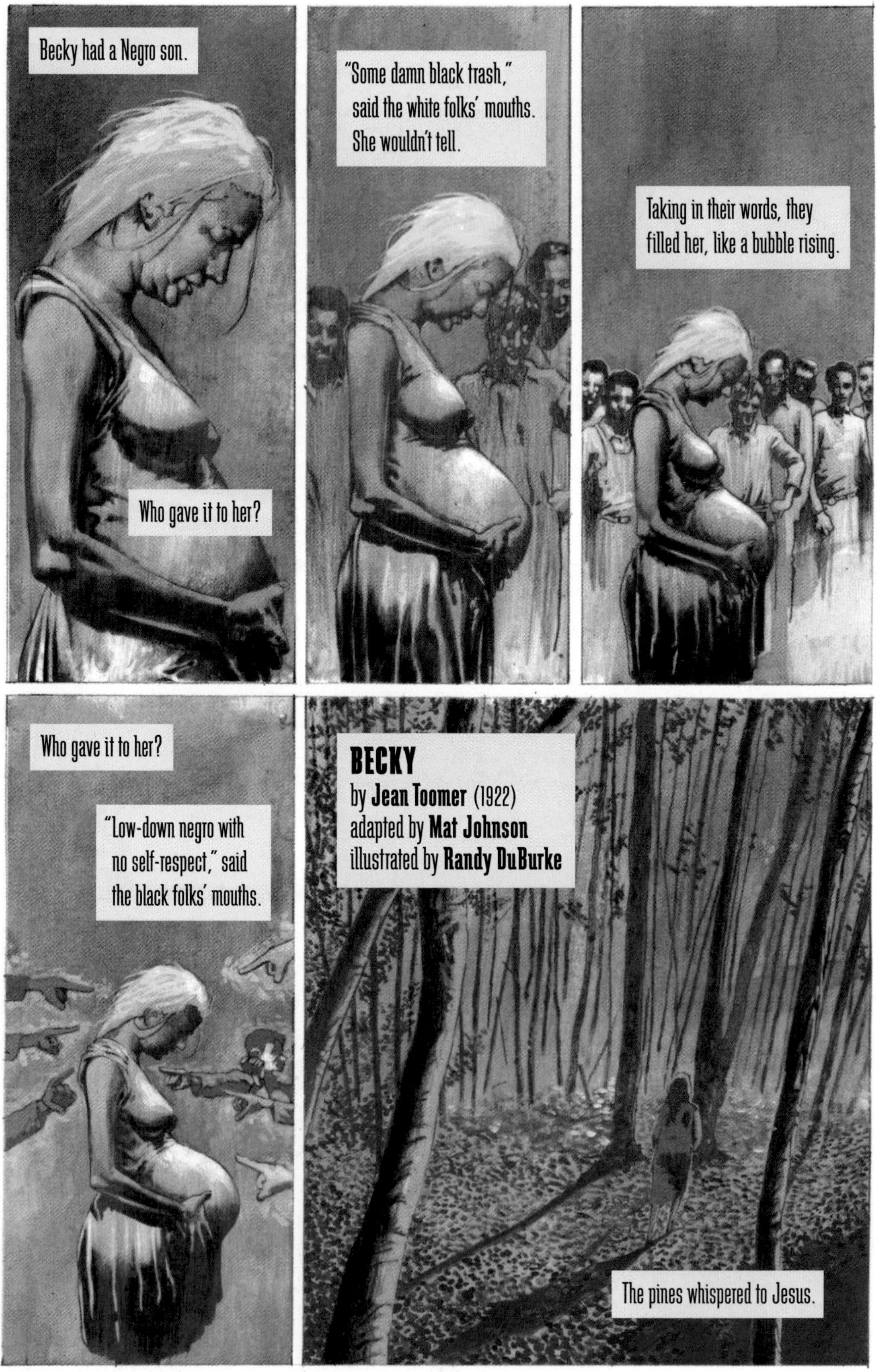
Becky had a Negro son.
Who gave it to her?
"Some damn black trash," said the white folks' mouths. She wouldn't tell.
Taking in their words, they filled her, like a bubble rising.
Who gave it to her?
"Low-down negro with no self-respect," said the black folks' mouths.
BECKY
by Jean Toomer (1922)
adapted by Mat Johnson
illustrated by Randy DuBurke
The pines whispered to Jesus.

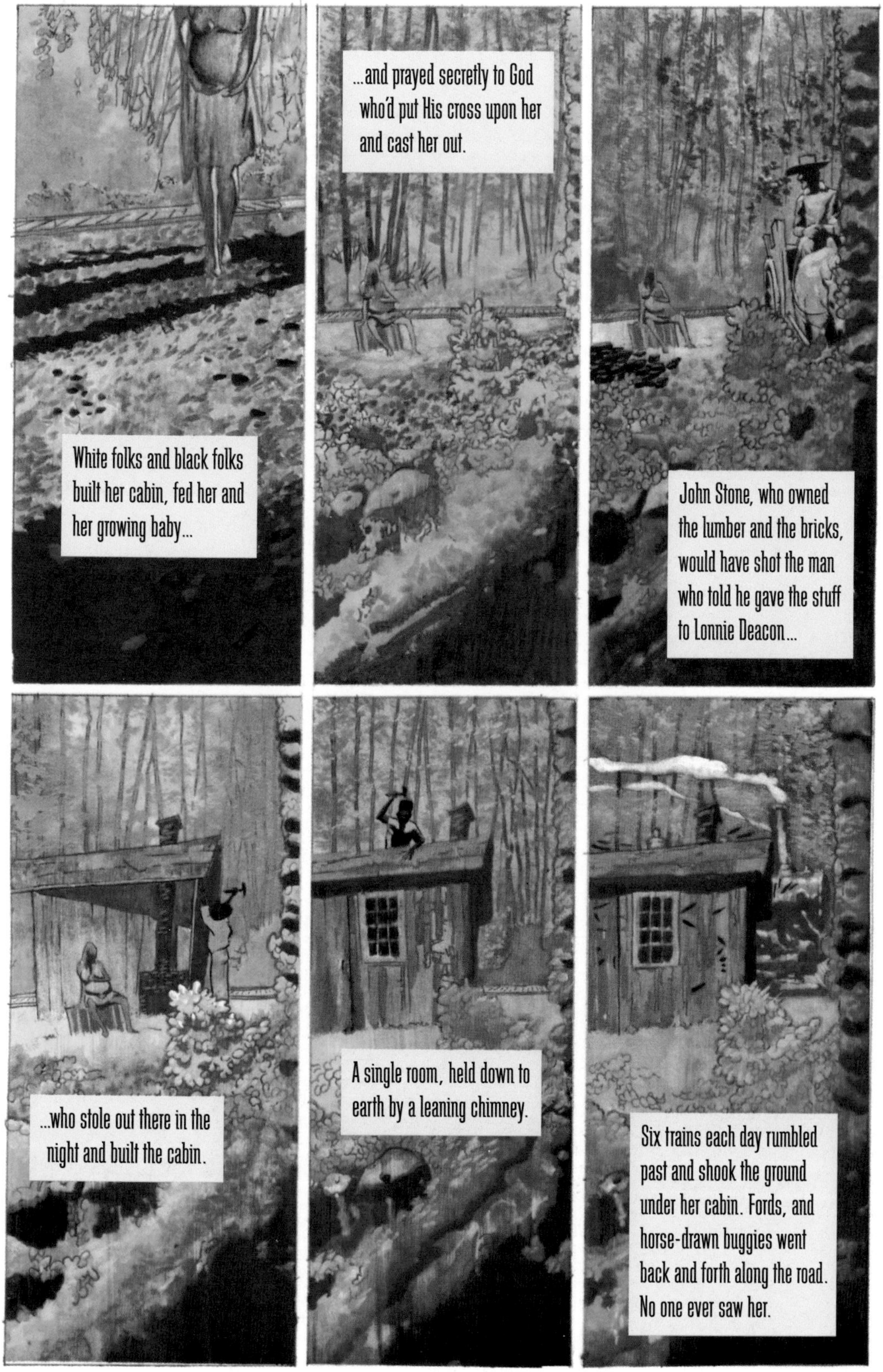
White folks and black folks built her cabin, fed her and her growing baby...
...and prayed secretly to God who'd put His cross upon her and cast her out.
John Stone, who owned the lumber and the bricks, would have shot the man who told he gave the stuff to Lonnie Deacon...
...who stole out there in the night and built the cabin.
A single room, held down to earth by a leaning chimney.
Six trains each day rumbled past and shook the ground under her cabin. Fords, and horse-drawn buggies went back and forth along the road. No one ever saw her.

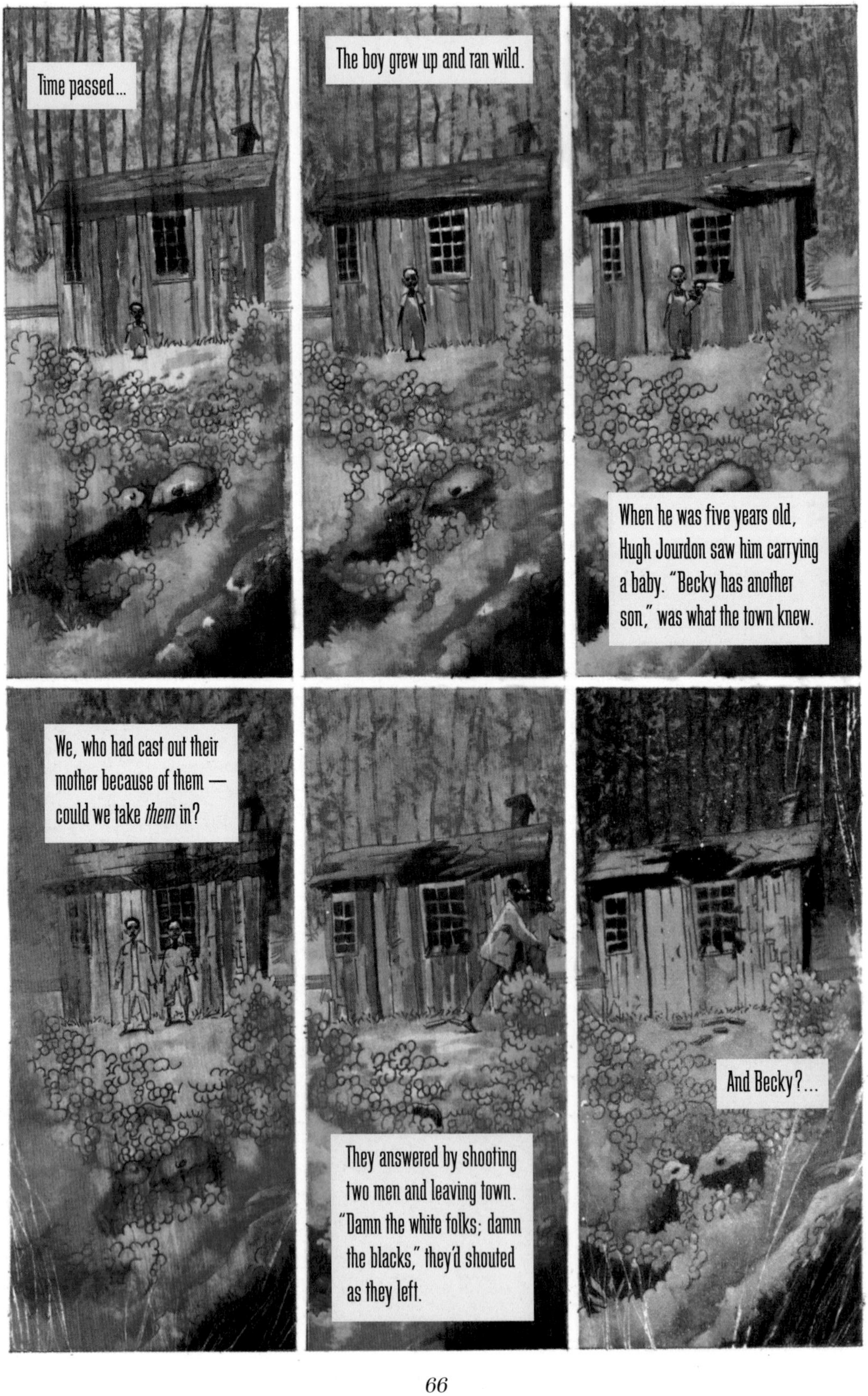
Time passed...
The boy grew up and ran wild.
When he was five years old, Hugh Jourdon saw him carrying a baby. "Becky has another son," was what the town knew.
We, who had cast out their mother because of them — could we take *them* in?
They answered by shooting two men and leaving town. "Damn the white folks; damn the blacks," they'd shouted as they left.
And Becky?...

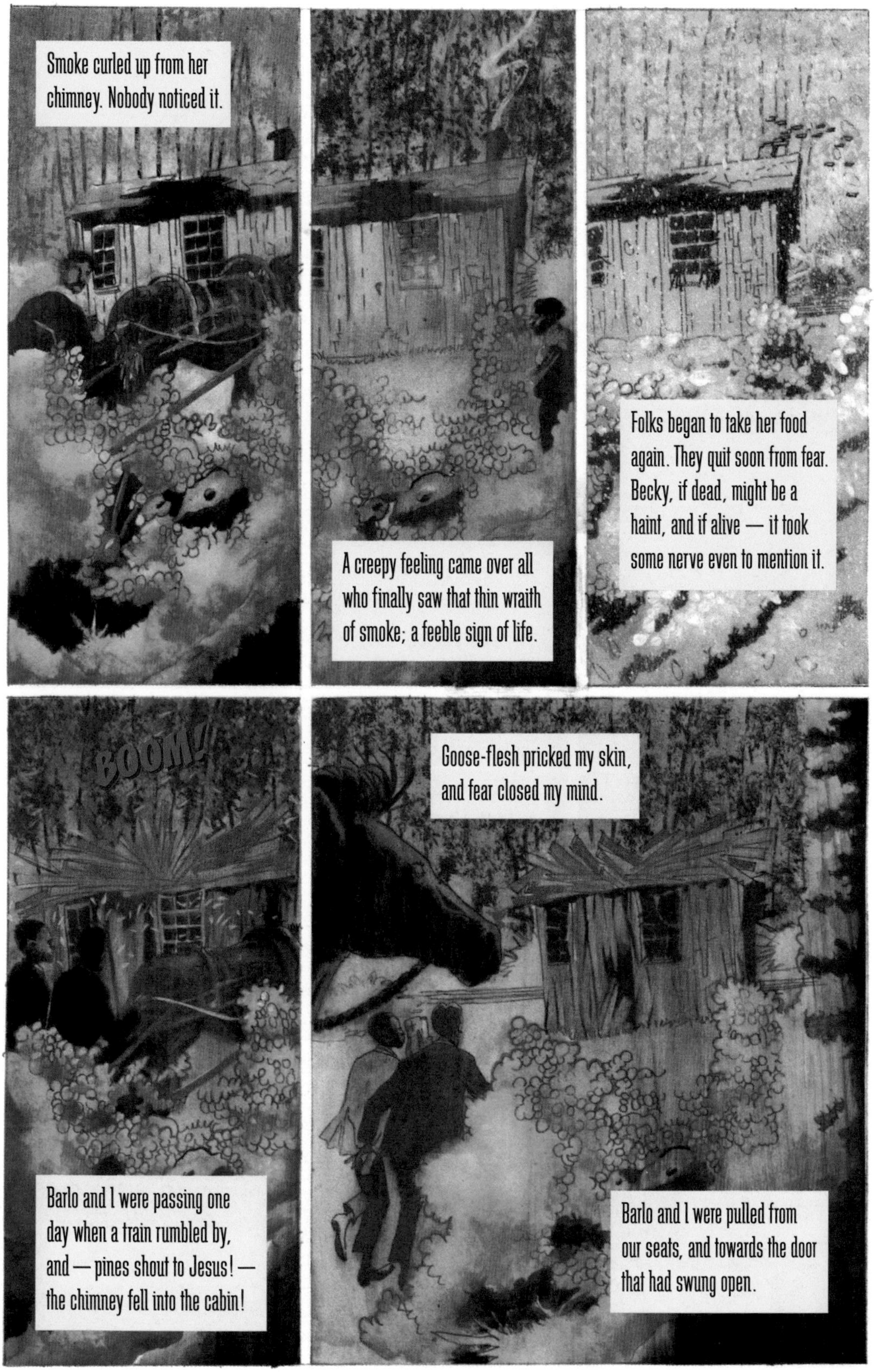
BOOM!
Smoke curled up from her chimney. Nobody noticed it.
A creepy feeling came over all who finally saw that thin wraith of smoke; a feeble sign of life.
Folks began to take her food again. They quit soon from fear. Becky, if dead, might be a haint, and if alive — it took some nerve even to mention it.
Barlo and I were passing one day when a train rumbled by, and — pines shout to Jesus! — the chimney fell into the cabin!
Goose-flesh pricked my skin, and fear closed my mind.
Barlo and I were pulled from our seats, and towards the door that had swung open.

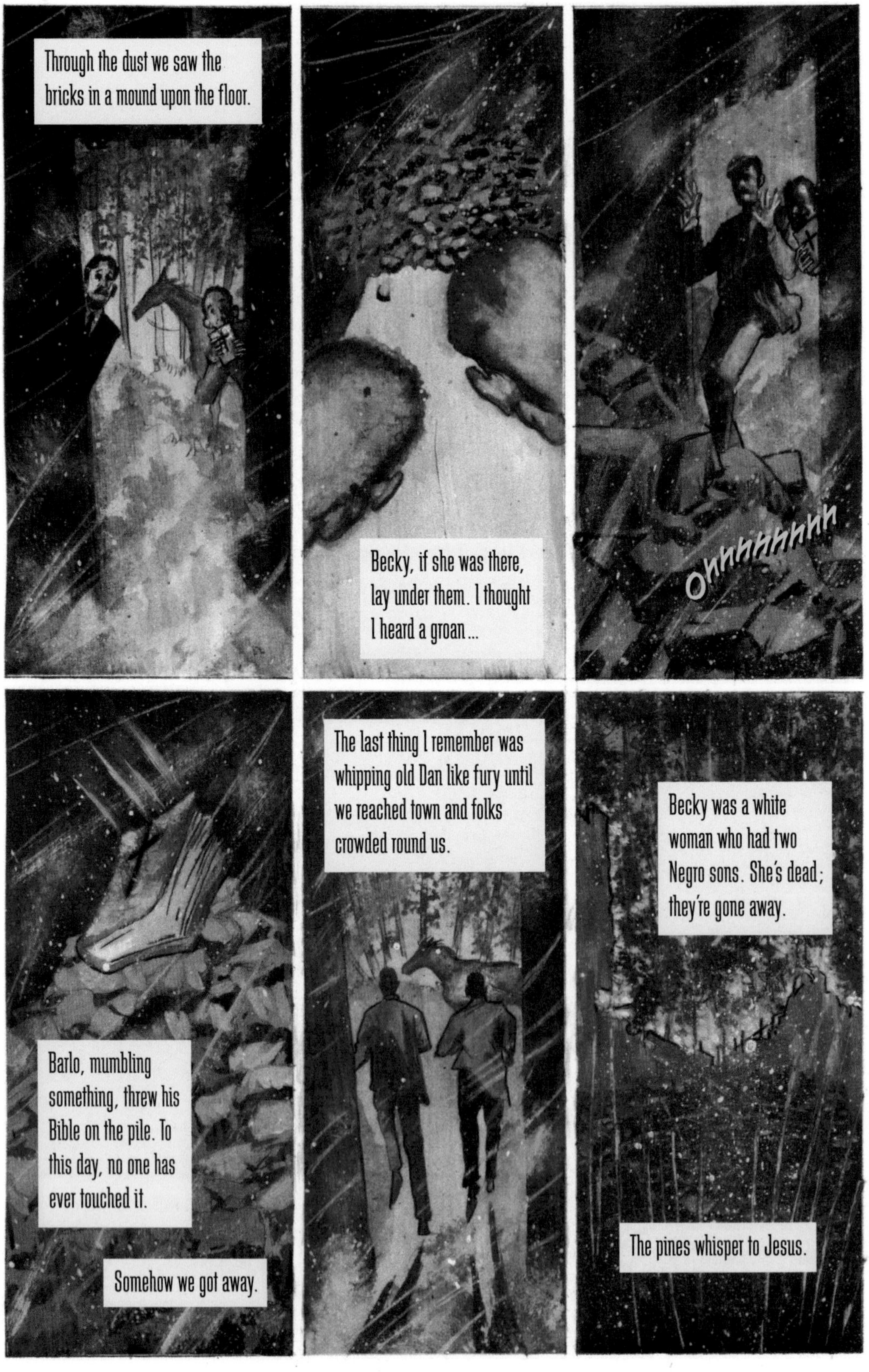
Through the dust we saw the bricks in a mound upon the floor.
Becky, if she was there, lay under them. I thought I heard a groan...
Ohhhhhhhh
Barlo, mumbling something, threw his Bible on the pile. To this day, no one has ever touched it.
Somehow we got away.
The last thing I remember was whipping old Dan like fury until we reached town and folks crowded round us.
Becky was a white woman who had two Negro sons. She's dead; they're gone away.
The pines whisper to Jesus.

IN THE MATTER OF TWO MEN

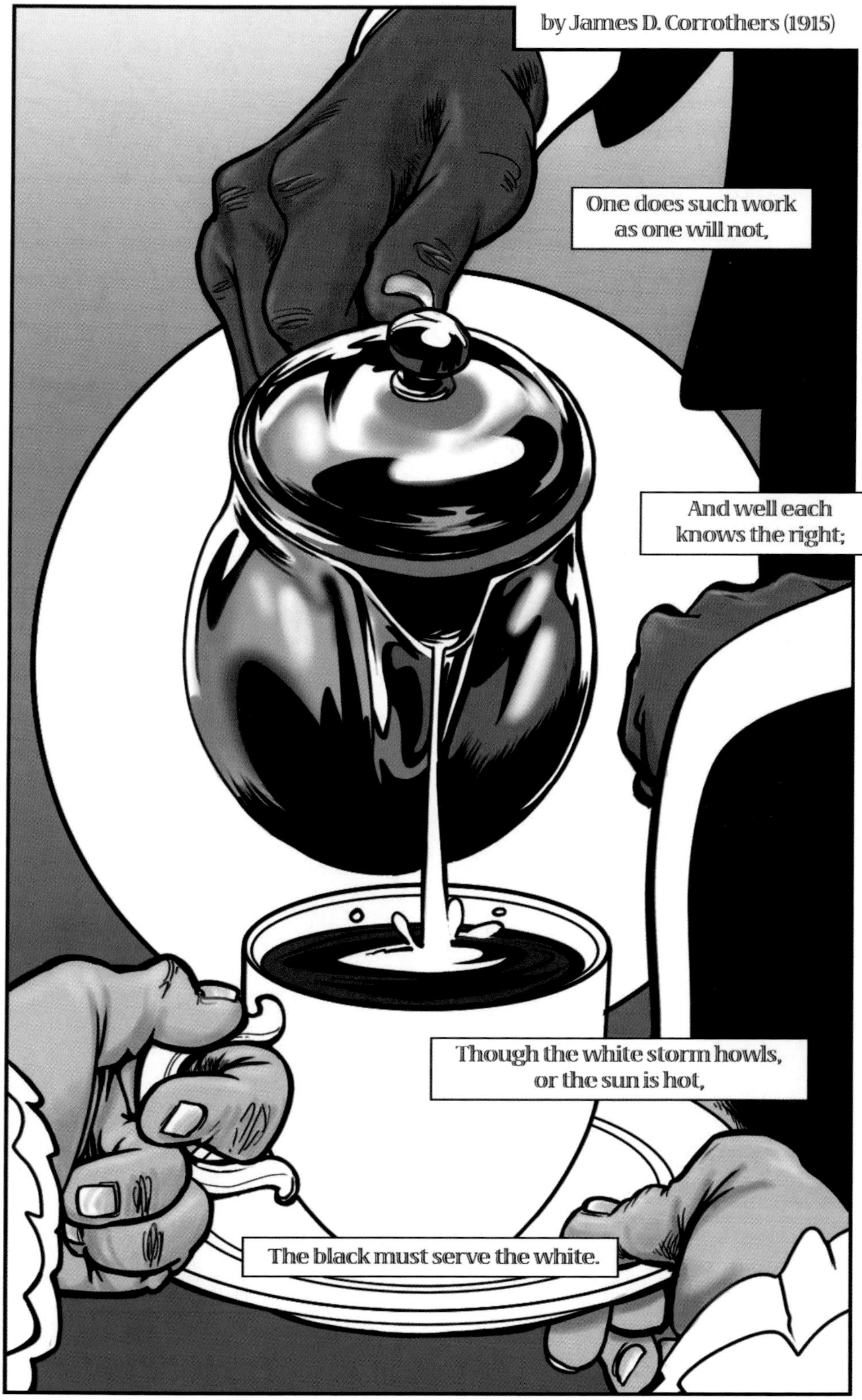
by James D. Corrothers (1915)
One does such work as one will not,
And well each knows the right;
Though the white storm howls, or the sun is hot,
The black must serve the white.

illustrated by Kenjji

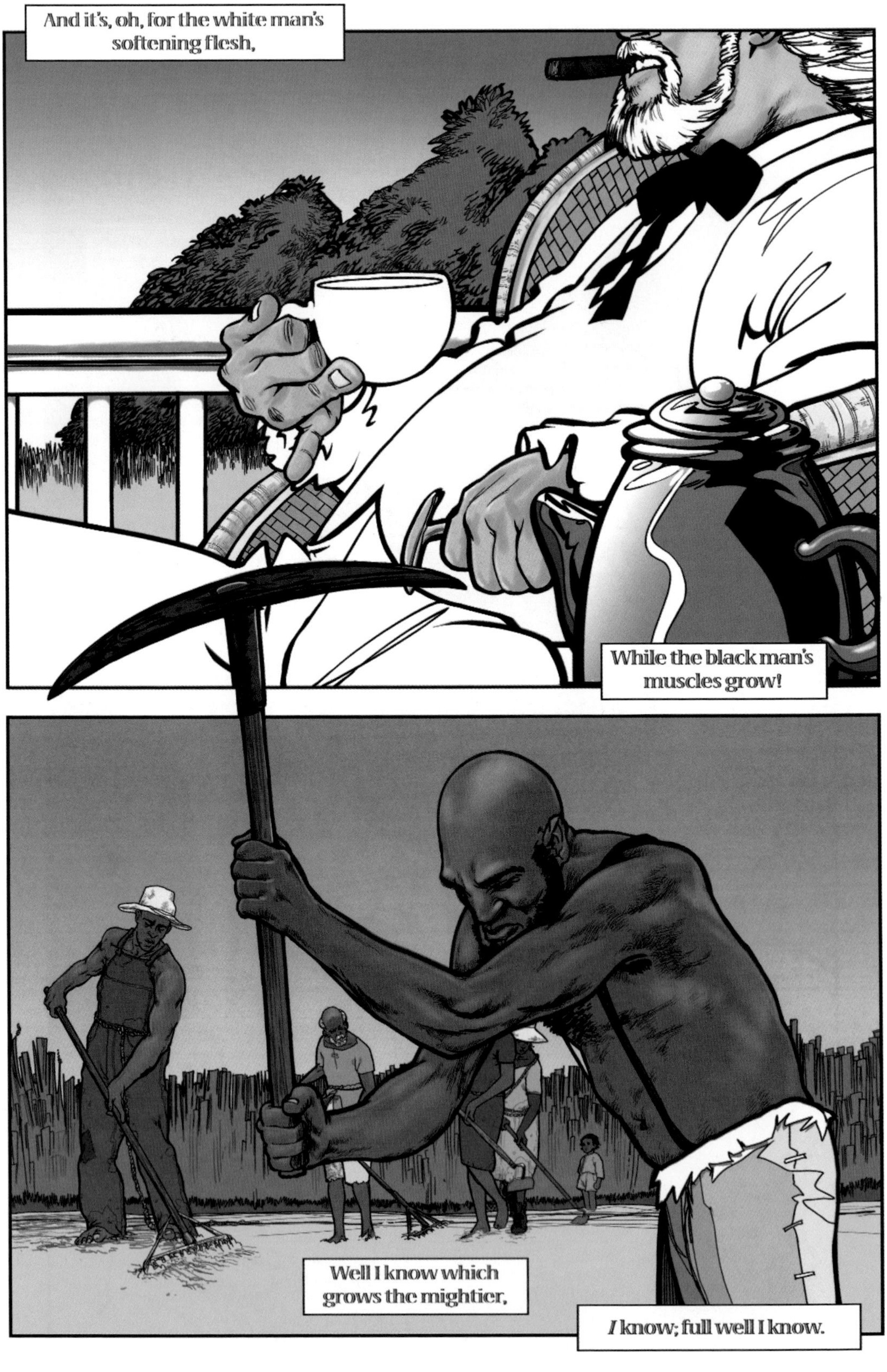
And it's, oh, for the white man's softening flesh,
While the black man's muscles grow!
Well I know which grows the mightier,
I know; full well I know.

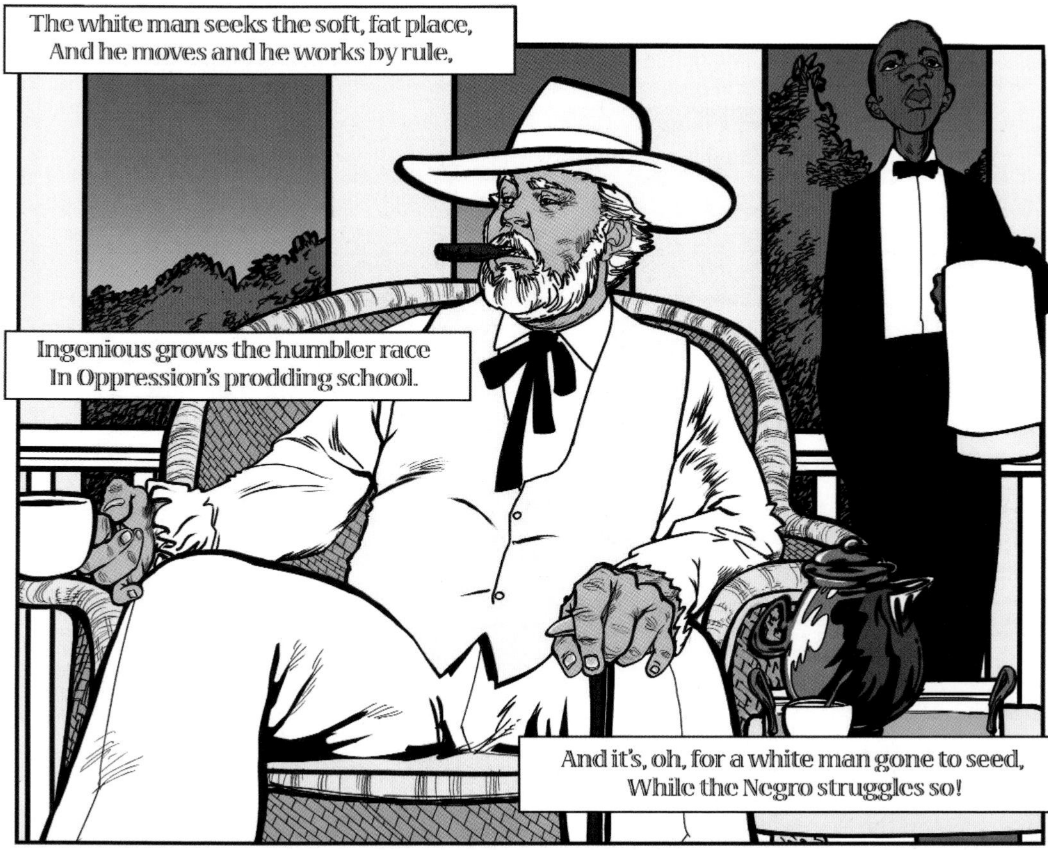
The white man seeks the soft, fat place,
And he moves and he works by rule,
Ingenious grows the humbler race
In Oppression's prodding school.
And it's, oh, for a white man gone to seed,
While the Negro struggles so!

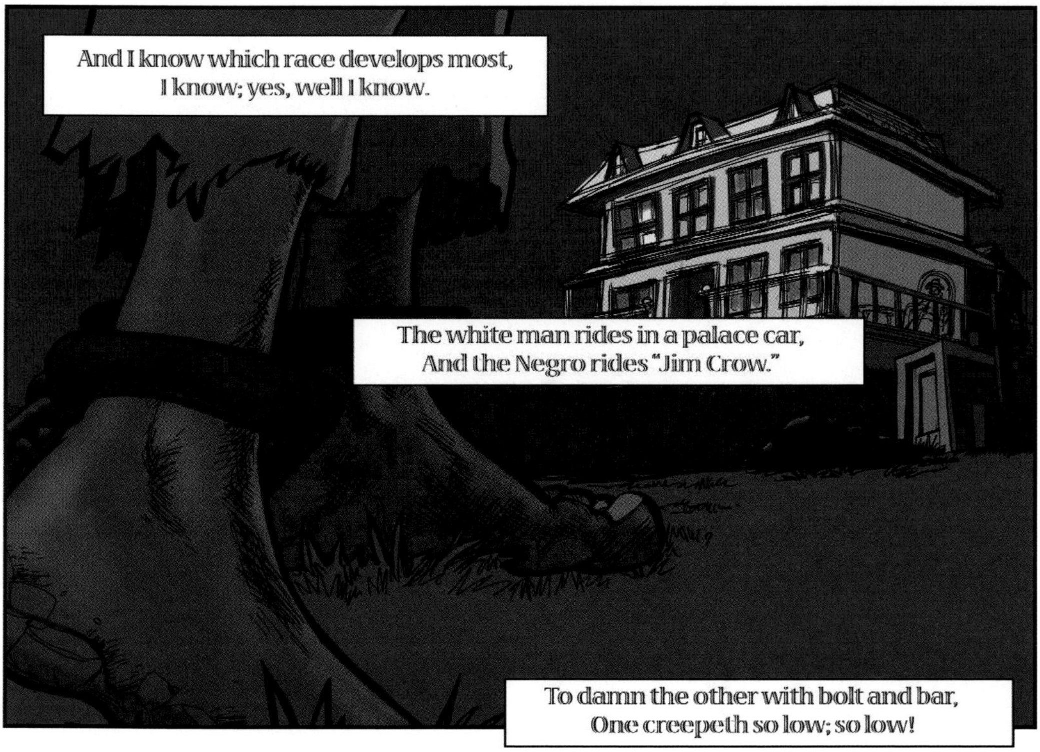
And I know which race develops most,
I know; yes, well I know.
The white man rides in a palace car,
And the Negro rides "Jim Crow."
To damn the other with bolt and bar,
One creepeth so low; so low!

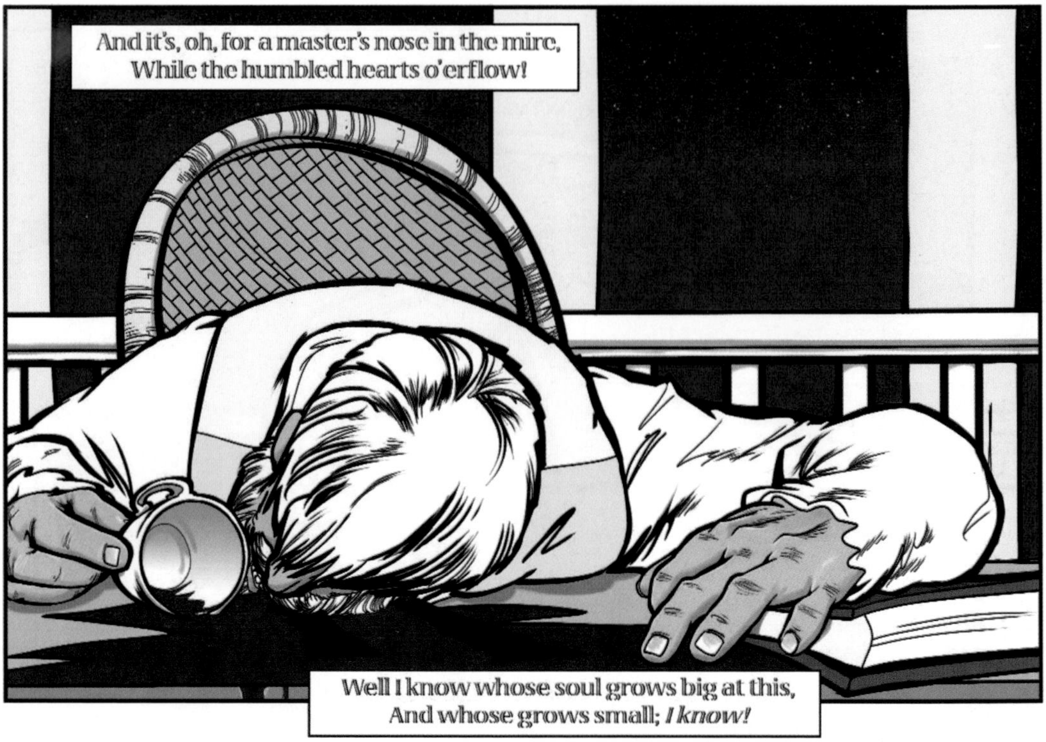
And it's, oh, for a master's nose in the mire,
While the humbled hearts o'erflow!
Well I know whose soul grows big at this,
And whose grows small; *I know!*

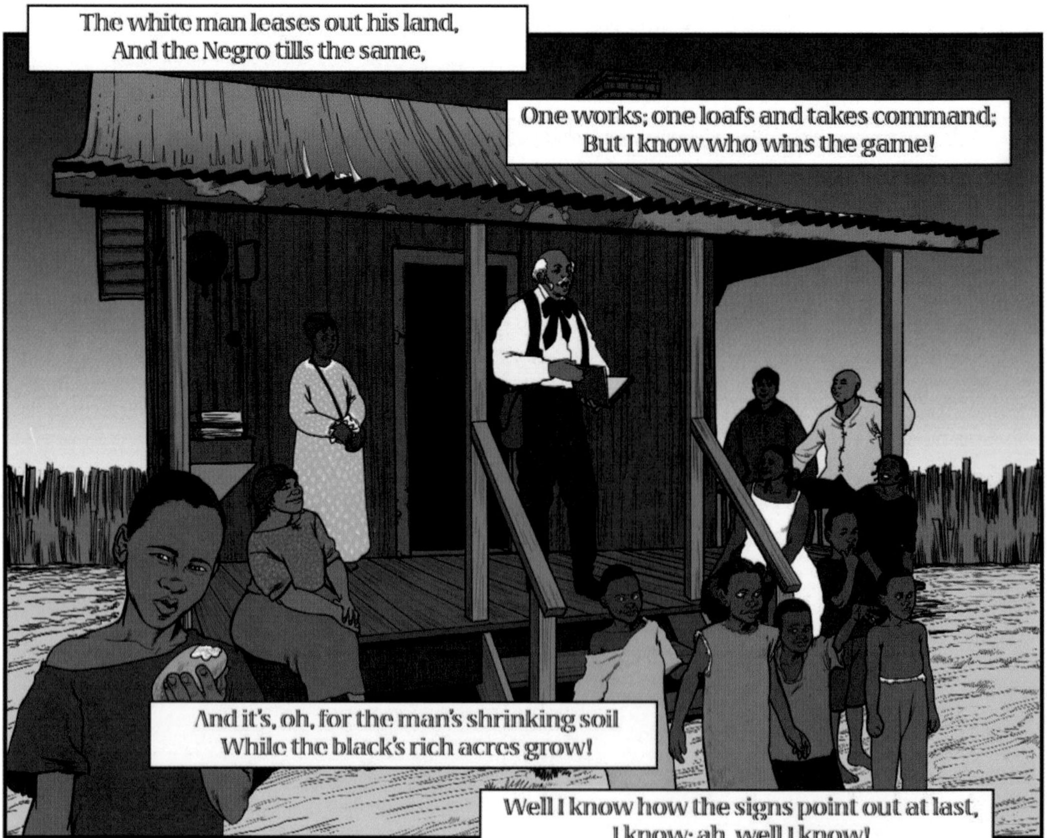
The white man leases out his land,
And the Negro tills the same,
One works; one loafs and takes command;
But I know who wins the game!
And it's, oh, for the man's shrinking soil
While the black's rich acres grow!
Well I know how the signs point out at last,
I know; ah, well I know!

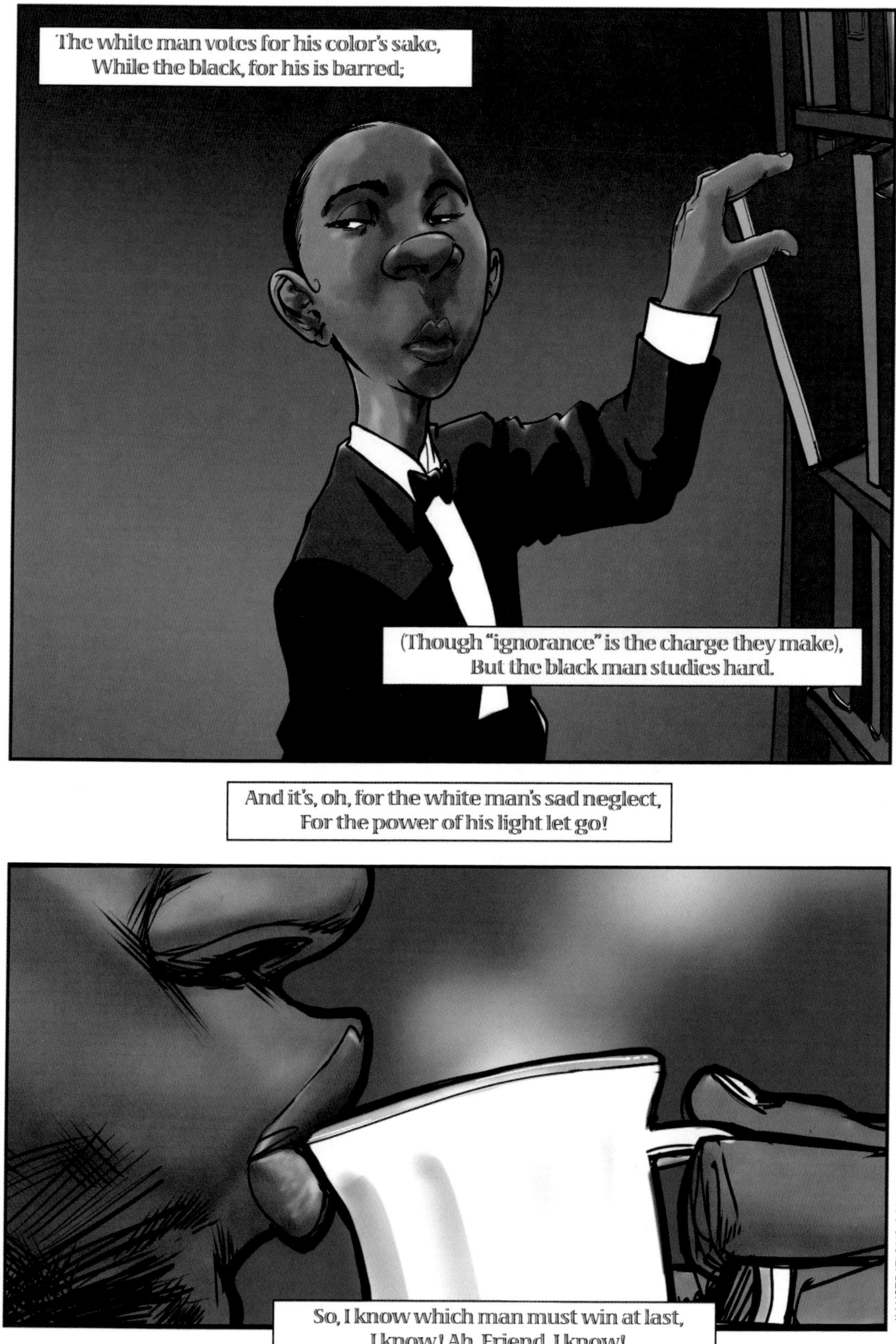
The white man votes for his color's sake,
While the black, for his is barred;
(Though "ignorance" is the charge they make),
But the black man studies hard.
And it's, oh, for the white man's sad neglect,
For the power of his light let go!
So, I know which man must win at last,
I know! Ah, Friend, I know!

SYMPATHY

by **Paul Laurence Dunbar** (1899)
illustrated by **Lance Tooks**

I know what the caged bird feels, alas!
    When the sun is bright on the upland slopes;
When the wind stirs soft through the springing grass,
And the river flows like a stream of glass;
    When the first bird sings and the first bud opes,
And the faint perfume from its chalice steals —
I know what the caged bird feels!

I know why the caged bird beats his wing
    Till its blood is red on the cruel bars;
For he must fly back to his perch and cling
When he fain would be on the bough a-swing;
    And a pain still throbs in the old, old scars
And they pulse again with a keener sting —
I know why he beats his wing!

I know why the caged bird sings, ah me,
    When his wing is bruised and his bosom sore —
When he beats his bars and he would be free;
It is not a carol of joy or glee,
    But a prayer that he sends from his heart's deep core,
But a plea, that upward to Heaven he flings —
I know why the caged bird sings!

WE WEAR THE MASK

by **Paul Laurence Dunbar** (1896)
illustrated by **Larry Poncho Brown**

We wear the mask that grins and lies,
It hides our cheeks and shades our eyes —
This debt we pay to human guile;
With torn and bleeding hearts we smile,
And mouth with myriad subtleties.

Why should the world be over-wise,
In counting all our tears and sighs?
Nay, let them only see us, while
　　We wear the mask.

We smile, but, O great Christ, our cries
To thee from tortured souls arise.
We sing, but oh the clay is vile
Beneath our feet, and long the mile;
But let the world dream otherwise,
　　We wear the mask!

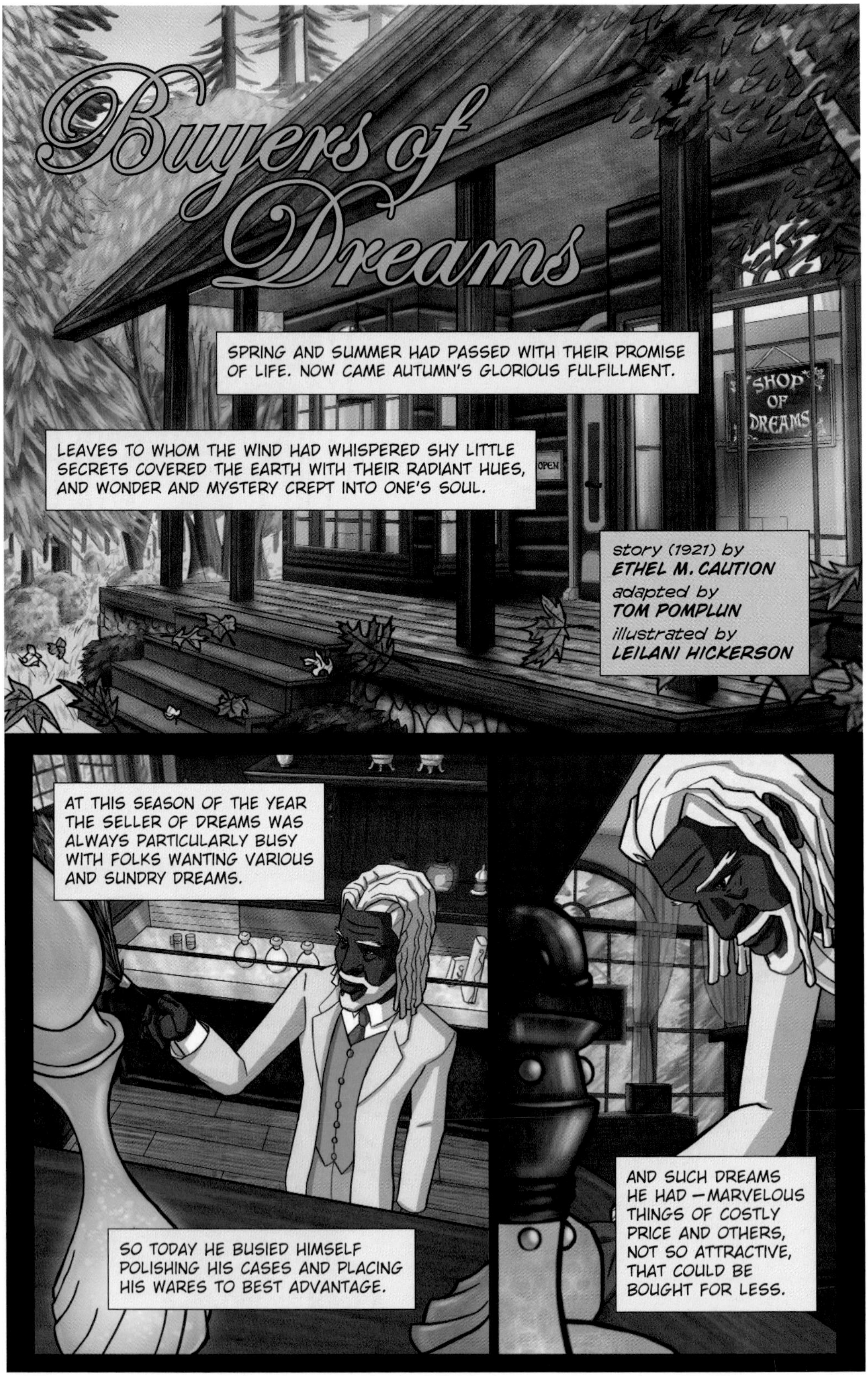
Buyers of Dreams
SPRING AND SUMMER HAD PASSED WITH THEIR PROMISE OF LIFE. NOW CAME AUTUMN'S GLORIOUS FULFILLMENT.
SHOP OF DREAMS
LEAVES TO WHOM THE WIND HAD WHISPERED SHY LITTLE SECRETS COVERED THE EARTH WITH THEIR RADIANT HUES, AND WONDER AND MYSTERY CREPT INTO ONE'S SOUL.
OPEN
story (1921) by ETHEL M. CAUTION
adapted by TOM POMPLUN
illustrated by LEILANI HICKERSON
AT THIS SEASON OF THE YEAR THE SELLER OF DREAMS WAS ALWAYS PARTICULARLY BUSY WITH FOLKS WANTING VARIOUS AND SUNDRY DREAMS.
SO TODAY HE BUSIED HIMSELF POLISHING HIS CASES AND PLACING HIS WARES TO BEST ADVANTAGE.
AND SUCH DREAMS HE HAD—MARVELOUS THINGS OF COSTLY PRICE AND OTHERS, NOT SO ATTRACTIVE, THAT COULD BE BOUGHT FOR LESS.

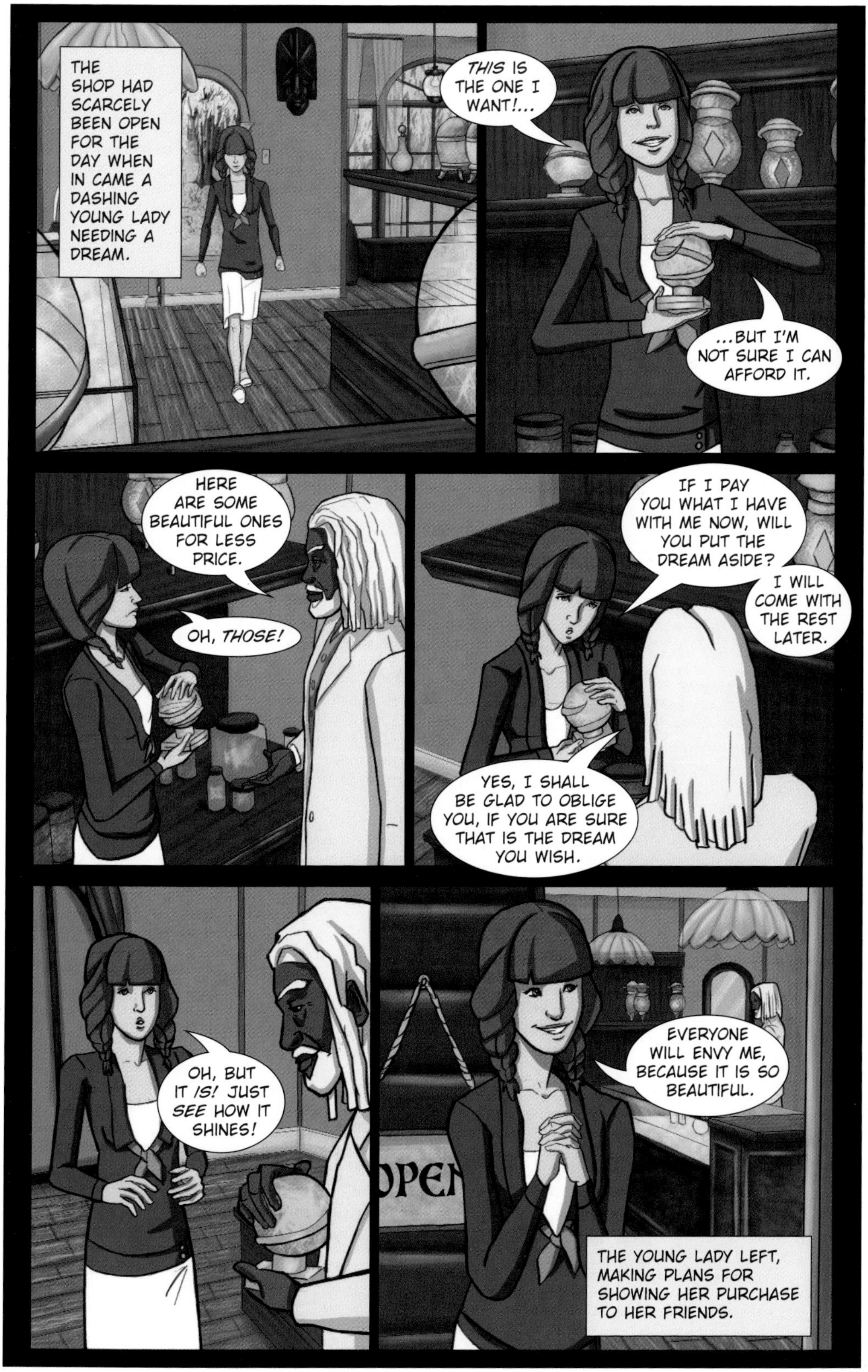
THE SHOP HAD SCARCELY BEEN OPEN FOR THE DAY WHEN IN CAME A DASHING YOUNG LADY NEEDING A DREAM.
THIS IS THE ONE I WANT!...
...BUT I'M NOT SURE I CAN AFFORD IT.
HERE ARE SOME BEAUTIFUL ONES FOR LESS PRICE.
OH, *THOSE!*
IF I PAY YOU WHAT I HAVE WITH ME NOW, WILL YOU PUT THE DREAM ASIDE?
I WILL COME WITH THE REST LATER.
YES, I SHALL BE GLAD TO OBLIGE YOU, IF YOU ARE SURE THAT IS THE DREAM YOU WISH.
OH, BUT IT *IS!* JUST *SEE* HOW IT SHINES!
EVERYONE WILL ENVY ME, BECAUSE IT IS SO BEAUTIFUL.
OPEN
THE YOUNG LADY LEFT, MAKING PLANS FOR SHOWING HER PURCHASE TO HER FRIENDS.

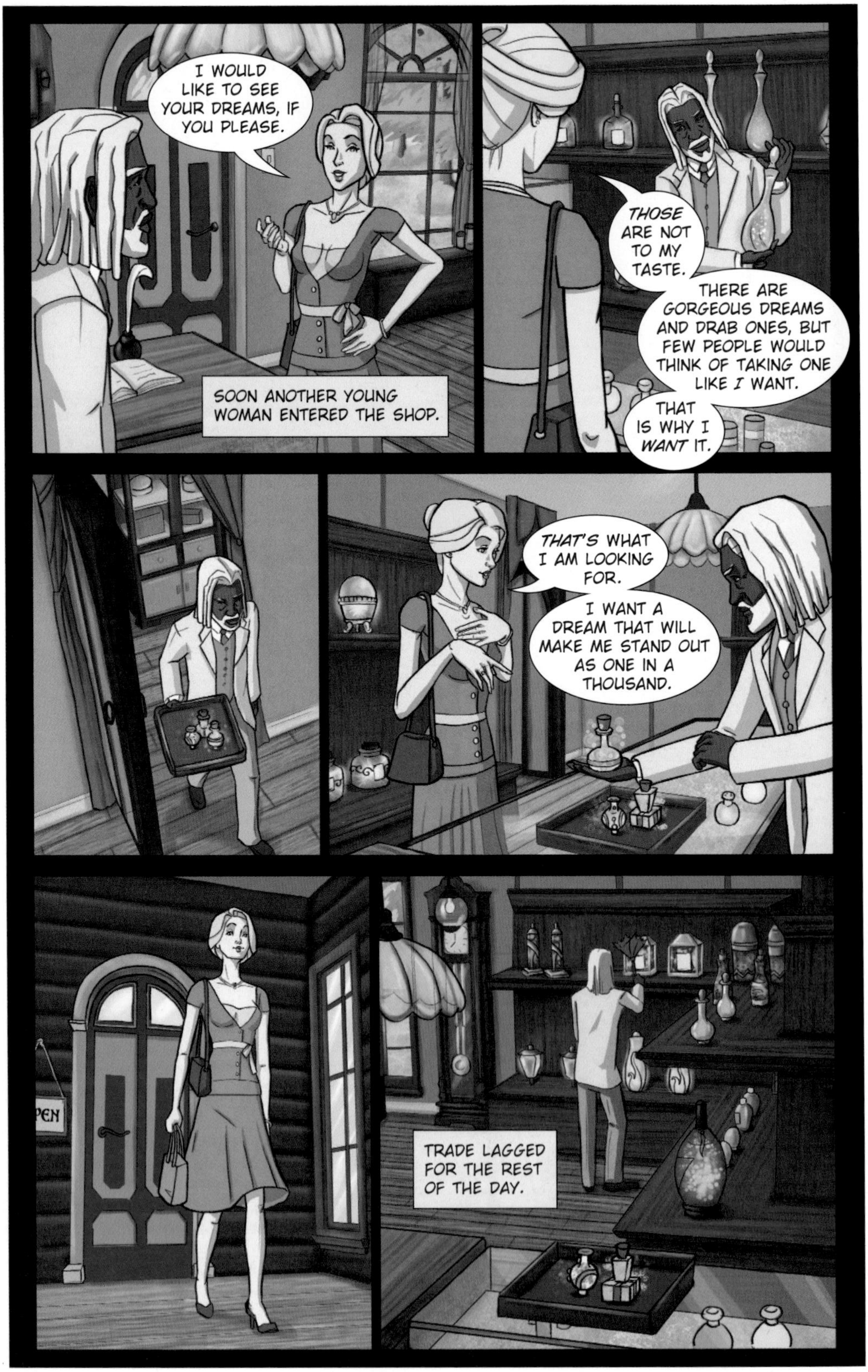
I WOULD LIKE TO SEE YOUR DREAMS, IF YOU PLEASE.
SOON ANOTHER YOUNG WOMAN ENTERED THE SHOP.
THOSE ARE NOT TO MY TASTE.
THERE ARE GORGEOUS DREAMS AND DRAB ONES, BUT FEW PEOPLE WOULD THINK OF TAKING ONE LIKE I WANT.
THAT IS WHY I WANT IT.
THAT'S WHAT I AM LOOKING FOR.
I WANT A DREAM THAT WILL MAKE ME STAND OUT AS ONE IN A THOUSAND.
PEN
TRADE LAGGED FOR THE REST OF THE DAY.

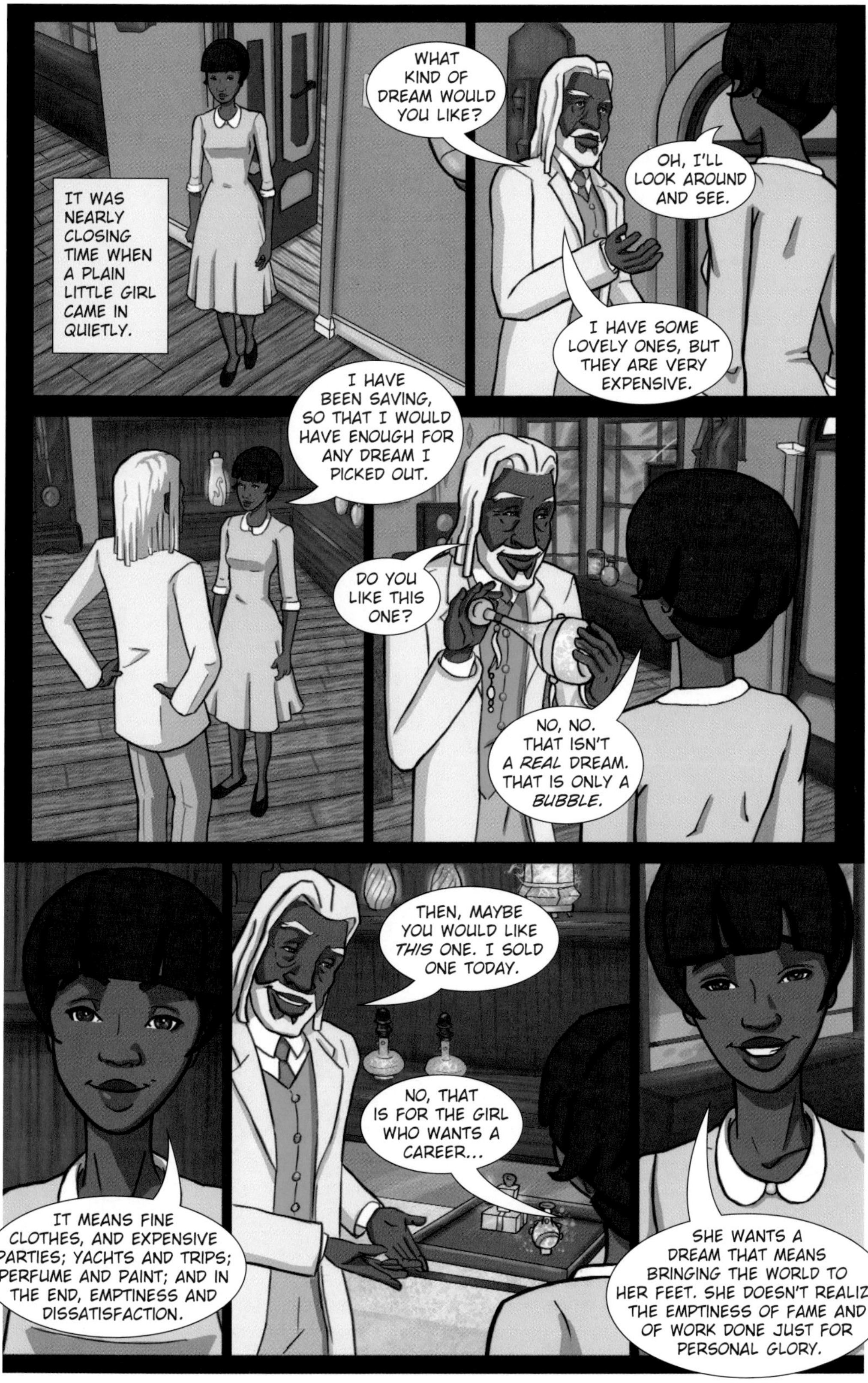
IT WAS NEARLY CLOSING TIME WHEN A PLAIN LITTLE GIRL CAME IN QUIETLY.
WHAT KIND OF DREAM WOULD YOU LIKE?
OH, I'LL LOOK AROUND AND SEE.
I HAVE SOME LOVELY ONES, BUT THEY ARE VERY EXPENSIVE.
I HAVE BEEN SAVING, SO THAT I WOULD HAVE ENOUGH FOR ANY DREAM I PICKED OUT.
DO YOU LIKE THIS ONE?
NO, NO. THAT ISN'T A *REAL* DREAM. THAT IS ONLY A *BUBBLE*.
THEN, MAYBE YOU WOULD LIKE *THIS* ONE. I SOLD ONE TODAY.
NO, THAT IS FOR THE GIRL WHO WANTS A CAREER...
IT MEANS FINE CLOTHES, AND EXPENSIVE PARTIES; YACHTS AND TRIPS; PERFUME AND PAINT; AND IN THE END, EMPTINESS AND DISSATISFACTION.
SHE WANTS A DREAM THAT MEANS BRINGING THE WORLD TO HER FEET. SHE DOESN'T REALIZE THE EMPTINESS OF FAME AND OF WORK DONE JUST FOR PERSONAL GLORY.

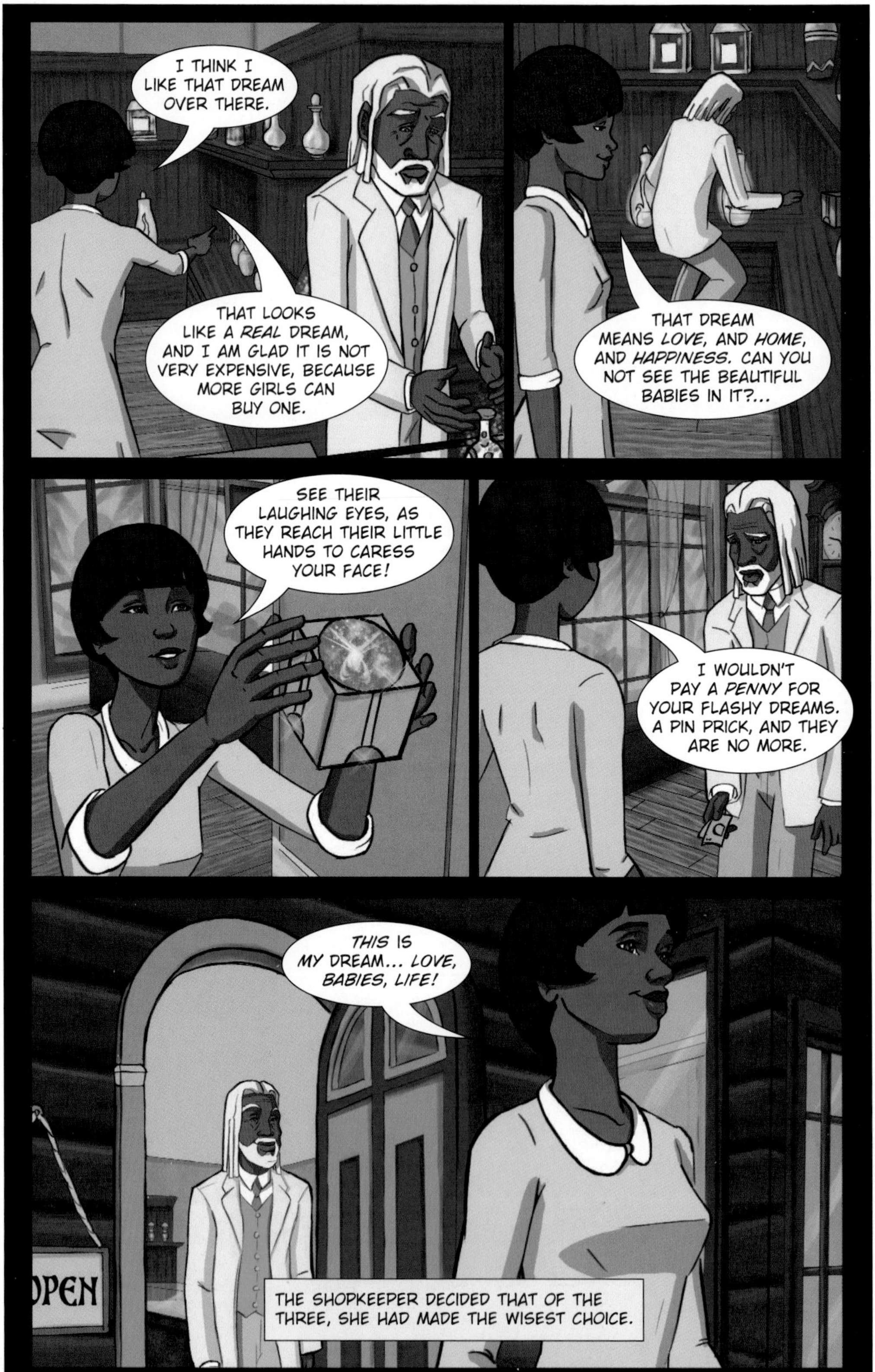
I THINK I LIKE THAT DREAM OVER THERE.
THAT LOOKS LIKE A *REAL* DREAM, AND I AM GLAD IT IS NOT VERY EXPENSIVE, BECAUSE MORE GIRLS CAN BUY ONE.
THAT DREAM MEANS *LOVE*, AND *HOME*, AND *HAPPINESS*. CAN YOU NOT SEE THE BEAUTIFUL BABIES IN IT?...
SEE THEIR LAUGHING EYES, AS THEY REACH THEIR LITTLE HANDS TO CARESS YOUR FACE!
I WOULDN'T PAY A *PENNY* FOR YOUR FLASHY DREAMS. A PIN PRICK, AND THEY ARE NO MORE.
THIS IS MY DREAM... *LOVE, BABIES, LIFE!*
OPEN
THE SHOPKEEPER DECIDED THAT OF THE THREE, SHE HAD MADE THE WISEST CHOICE.

THE BRONZE LEGACY
(To a Brown Boy)

(1922)

by **Effie Lee Newsome** / *illustrated by* **Keith Mallett**

'Tis a noble gift to be brown, all brown
Like the strongest things that make up this earth,
Like the mountains grave and grand,
Even like the very land,
Even like the trunks of trees –
Even oaks, to be like these!
God builds His strength in bronze.

To be brown like thrush and lark!
Like the subtle wren so dark!
Nay, the king of beasts wears brown;
Eagles are of this same hue,
I thank God, then, I am brown,
Brown has mighty things to do.

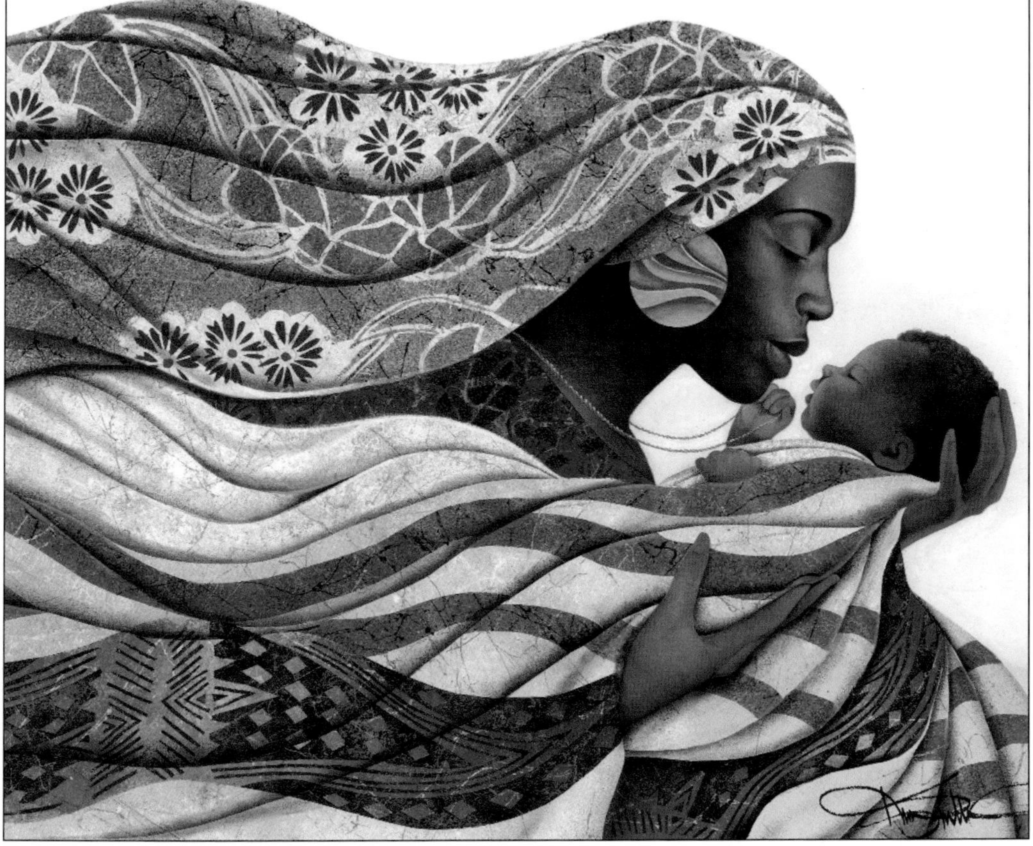

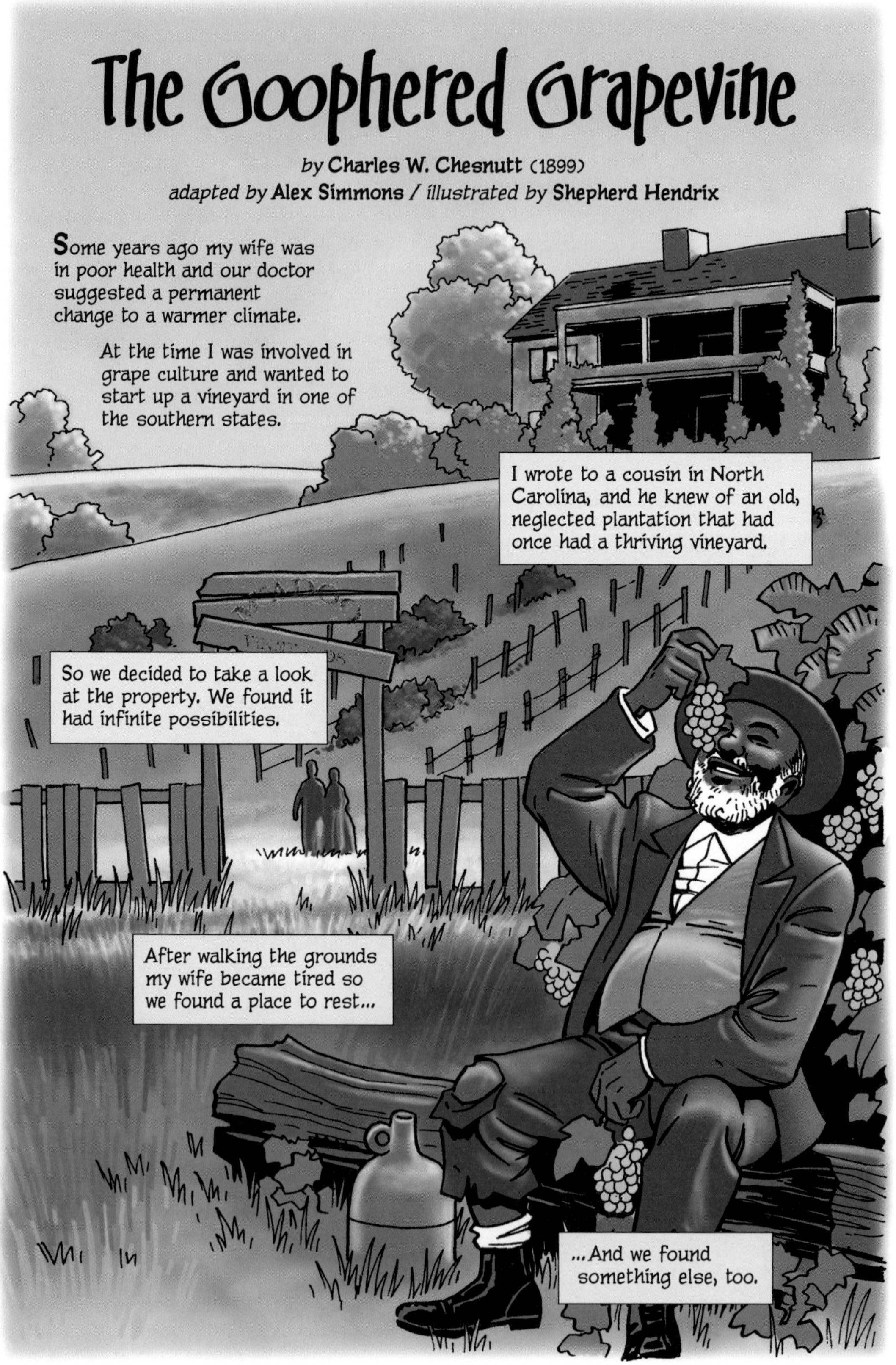
The Goophered Grapevine
by Charles W. Chesnutt (1899)
adapted by Alex Simmons / illustrated by Shepherd Hendrix
Some years ago my wife was in poor health and our doctor suggested a permanent change to a warmer climate.
At the time I was involved in grape culture and wanted to start up a vineyard in one of the southern states.
I wrote to a cousin in North Carolina, and he knew of an old, neglected plantation that had once had a thriving vineyard.
So we decided to take a look at the property. We found it had infinite possibilities.
After walking the grounds my wife became tired so we found a place to rest...
...And we found something else, too.

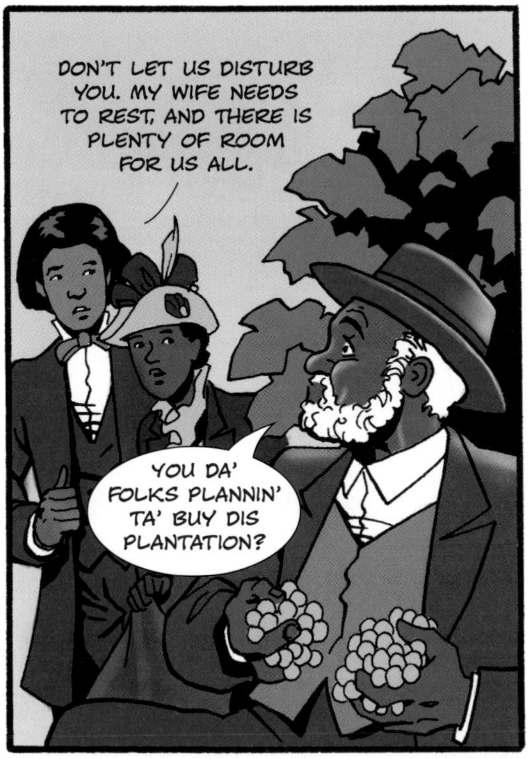
DON'T LET US DISTURB YOU. MY WIFE NEEDS TO REST, AND THERE IS PLENTY OF ROOM FOR US ALL.
YOU DA' FOLKS PLANNIN' TA' BUY DIS PLANTATION?

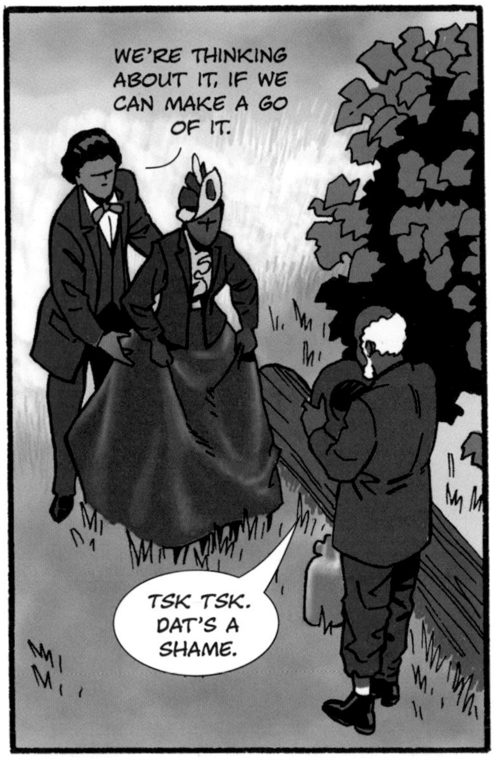
WE'RE THINKING ABOUT IT, IF WE CAN MAKE A GO OF IT.
TSK TSK. DAT'S A SHAME.

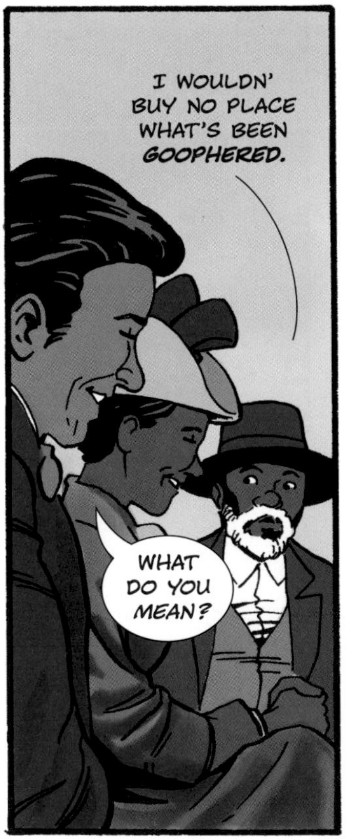
I WOULDN' BUY NO PLACE WHAT'S BEEN GOOPHERED.
WHAT DO YOU MEAN?

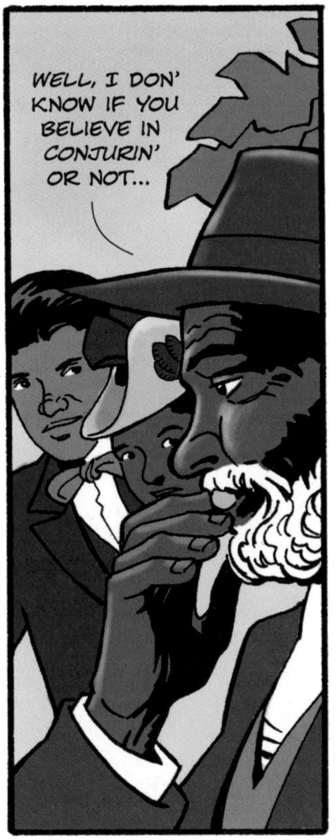
WELL, I DON' KNOW IF YOU BELIEVE IN CONJURIN' OR NOT...

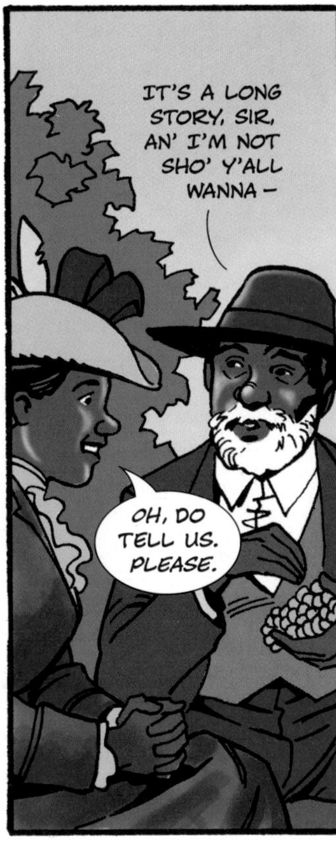
IT'S A LONG STORY, SIR, AN' I'M NOT SHO' Y'ALL WANNA –
OH, DO TELL US. PLEASE.

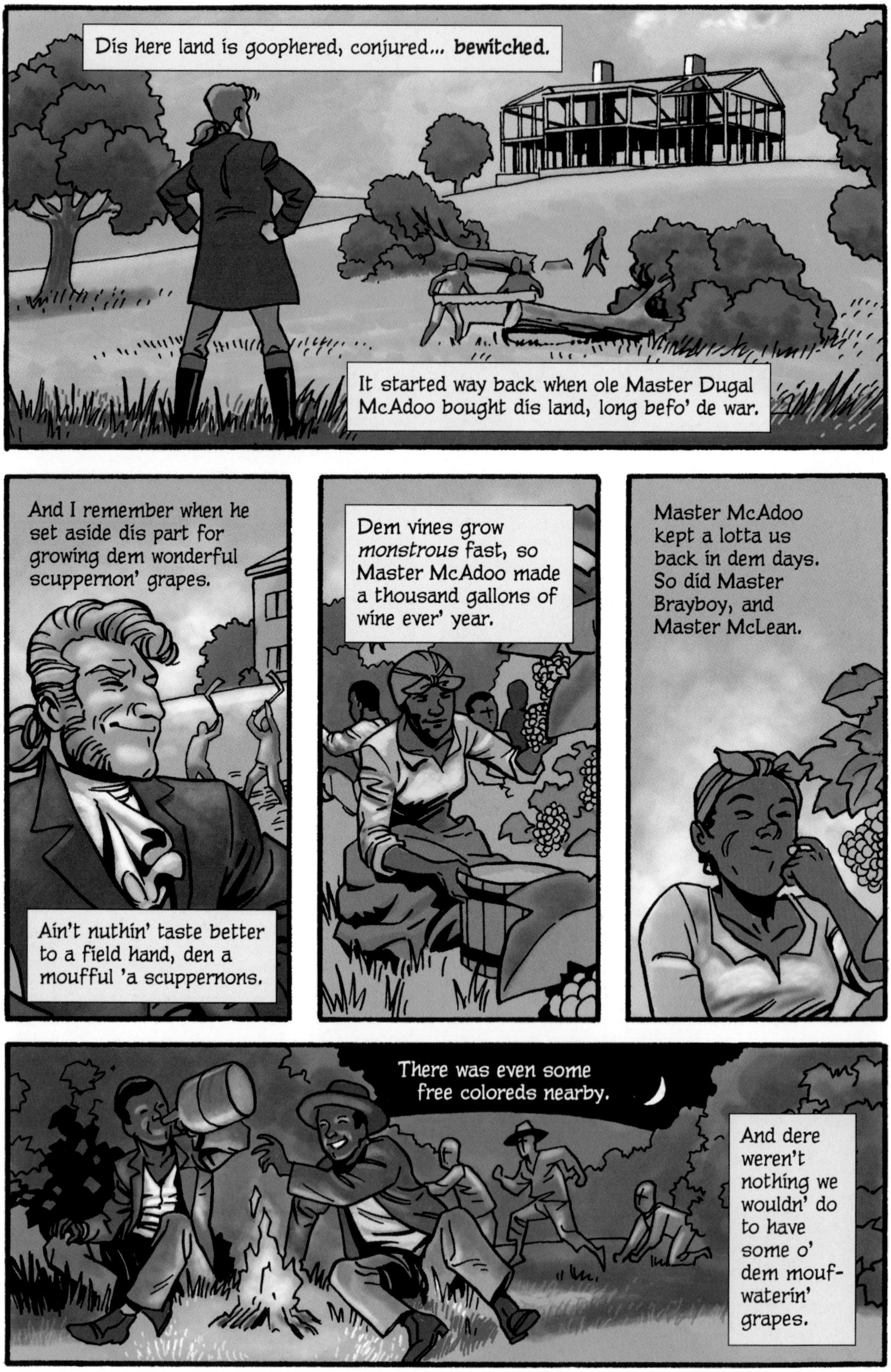
Dis here land is goophered, conjured... **bewitched.**
It started way back when ole Master Dugal McAdoo bought dis land, long befo' de war.
And I remember when he set aside dis part for growing dem wonderful scuppernon' grapes.
Ain't nuthin' taste better to a field hand, den a moufful 'a scuppernons.
Dem vines grow *monstrous* fast, so Master McAdoo made a thousand gallons of wine ever' year.
Master McAdoo kept a lotta us back in dem days. So did Master Brayboy, and Master McLean.
There was even some free coloreds nearby.
And dere weren't nothing we wouldn' do to have some o' dem mouf-waterin' grapes.

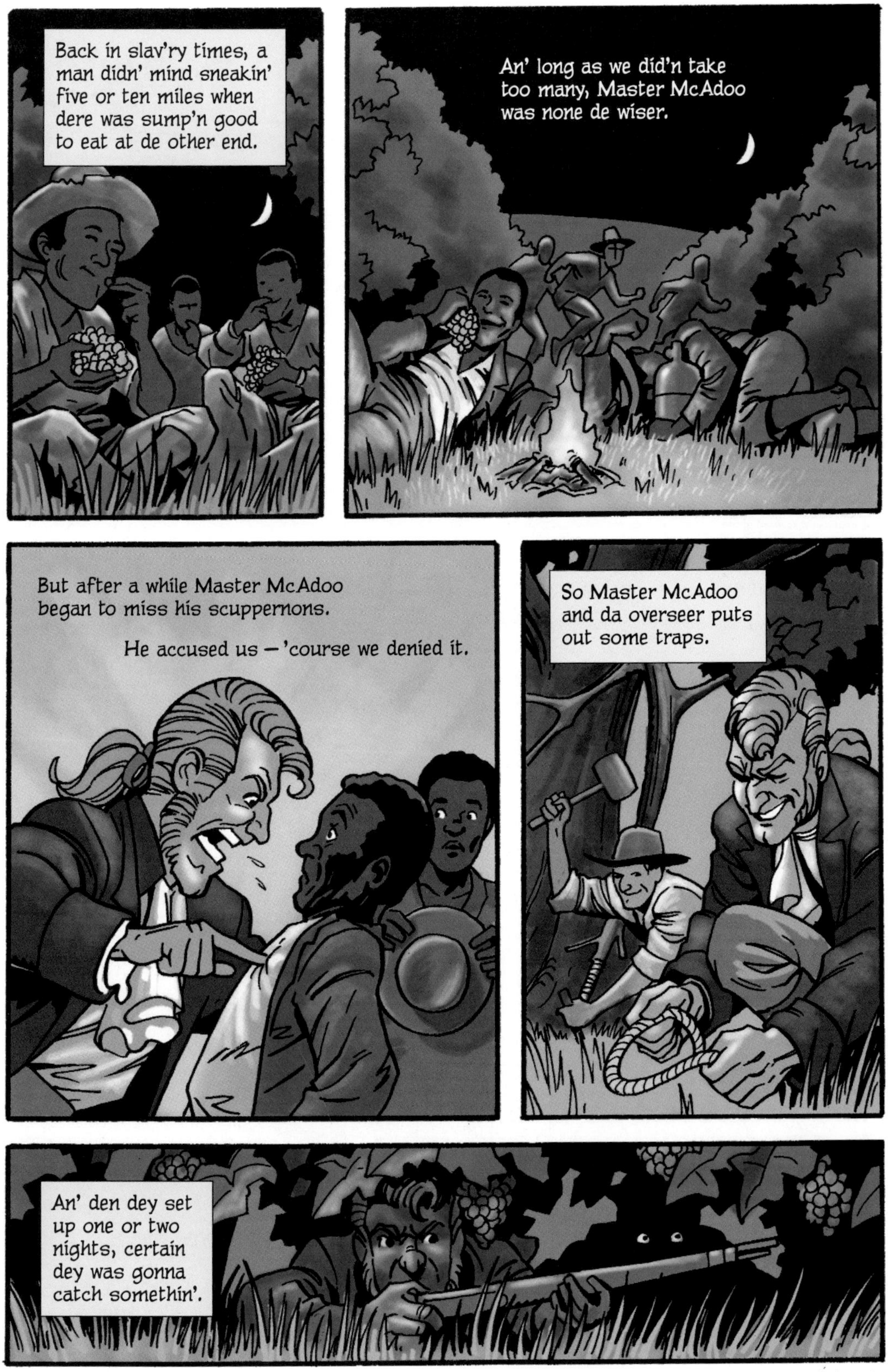
Back in slav'ry times, a man didn' mind sneakin' five or ten miles when dere was sump'n good to eat at de other end.
An' long as we did'n take too many, Master McAdoo was none de wiser.
But after a while Master McAdoo began to miss his scuppernons.
He accused us — 'course we denied it.
So Master McAdoo and da overseer puts out some traps.
An' den dey set up one or two nights, certain dey was gonna catch somethin'.

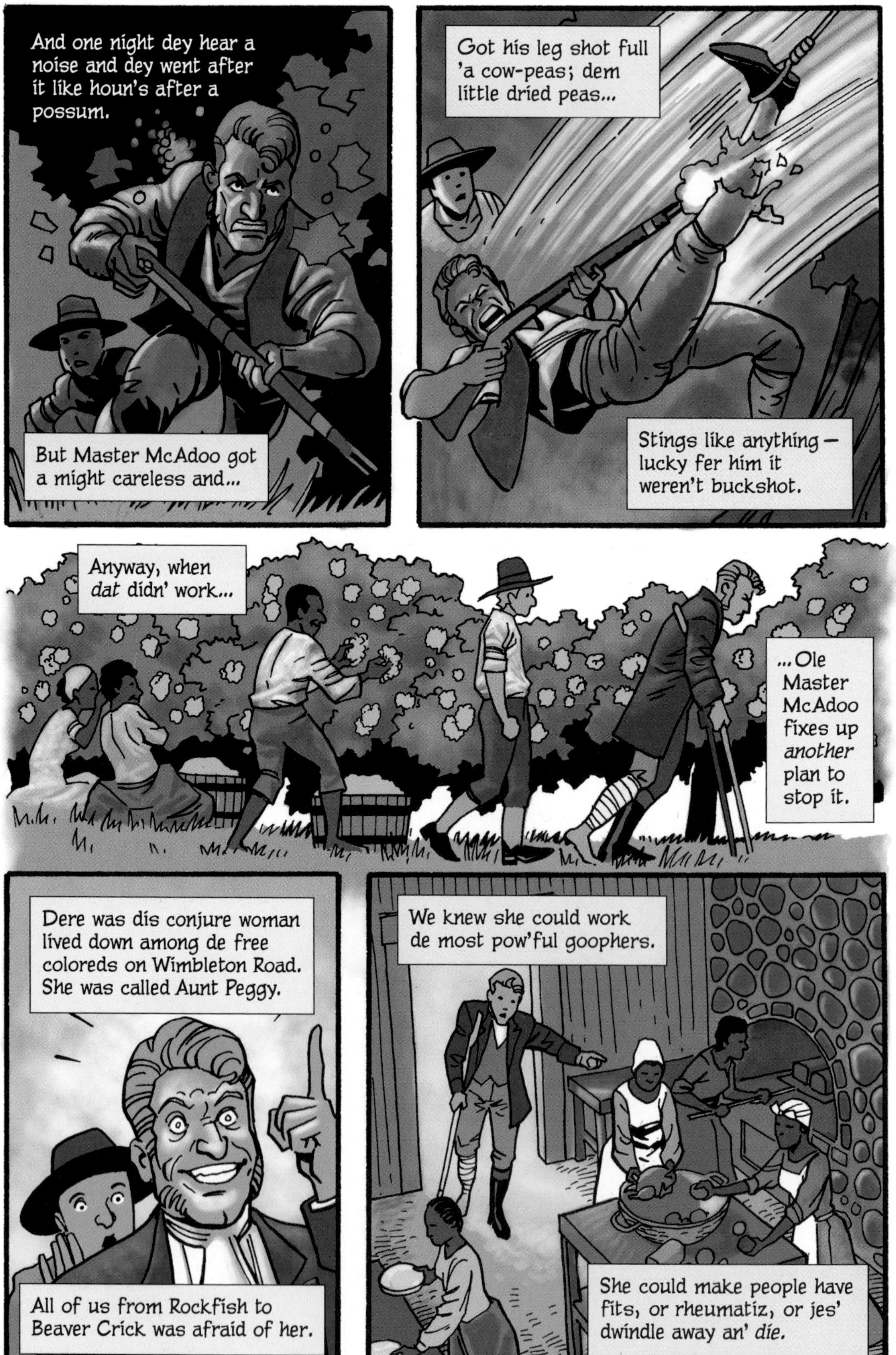
And one night dey hear a noise and dey went after it like houn's after a possum.
But Master McAdoo got a might careless and...
Got his leg shot full 'a cow-peas; dem little dried peas...
Stings like anything — lucky fer him it weren't buckshot.
Anyway, when *dat* didn' work...
...Ole Master McAdoo fixes up *another* plan to stop it.
Dere was dis conjure woman lived down among de free coloreds on Wimbleton Road. She was called Aunt Peggy.
All of us from Rockfish to Beaver Crick was afraid of her.
We knew she could work de most pow'ful goophers.
She could make people have fits, or rheumatiz, or jes' dwindle away an' *die*.

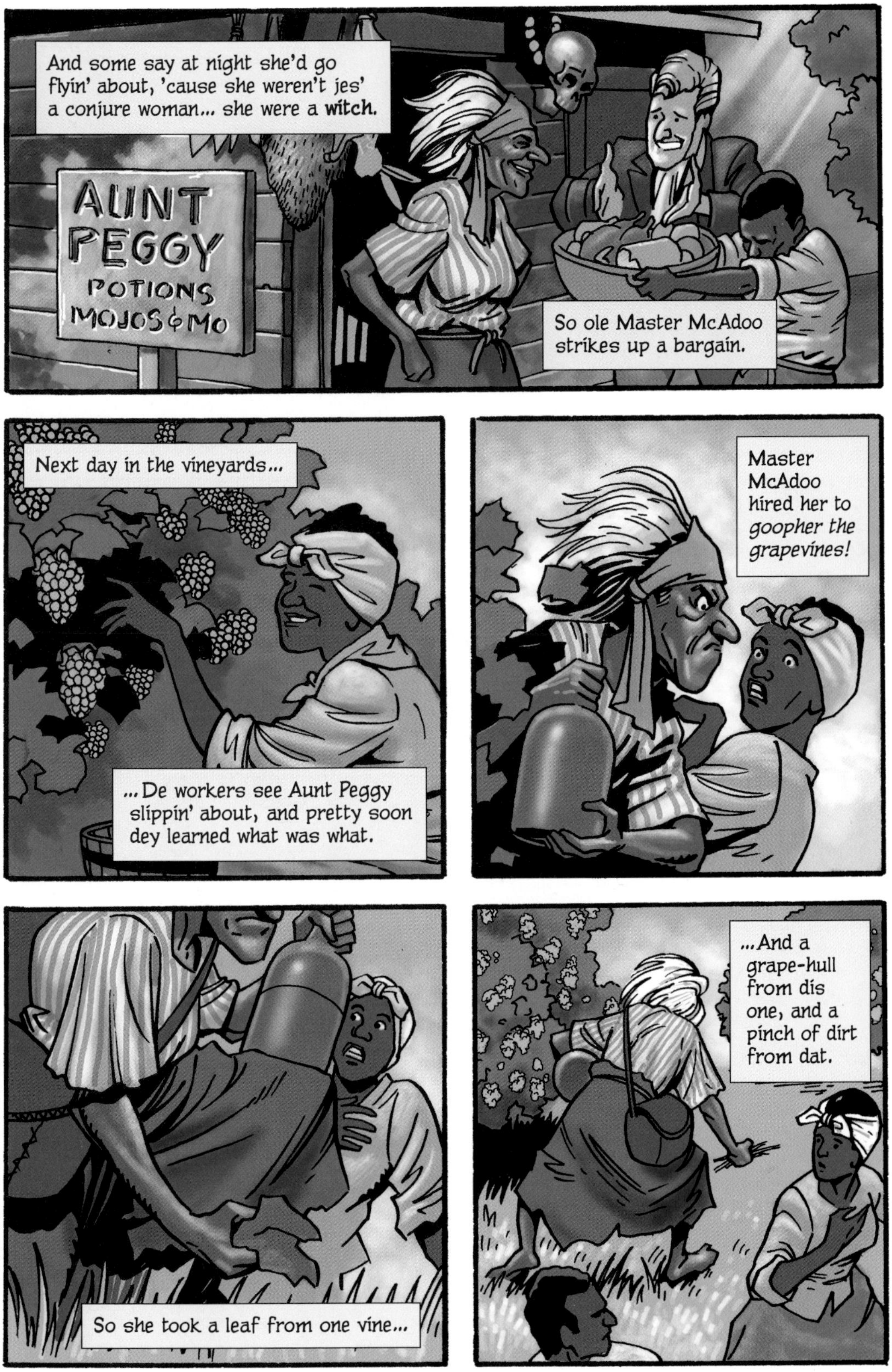
And some say at night she'd go flyin' about, 'cause she weren't jes' a conjure woman... she were a **witch**.
AUNT PEGGY
POTIONS
MOJOS & MO
So ole Master McAdoo strikes up a bargain.
Next day in the vineyards...
...De workers see Aunt Peggy slippin' about, and pretty soon dey learned what was what.
Master McAdoo hired her to *goopher the grapevines!*
So she took a leaf from one vine...
...And a grape-hull from dis one, and a pinch of dirt from dat.

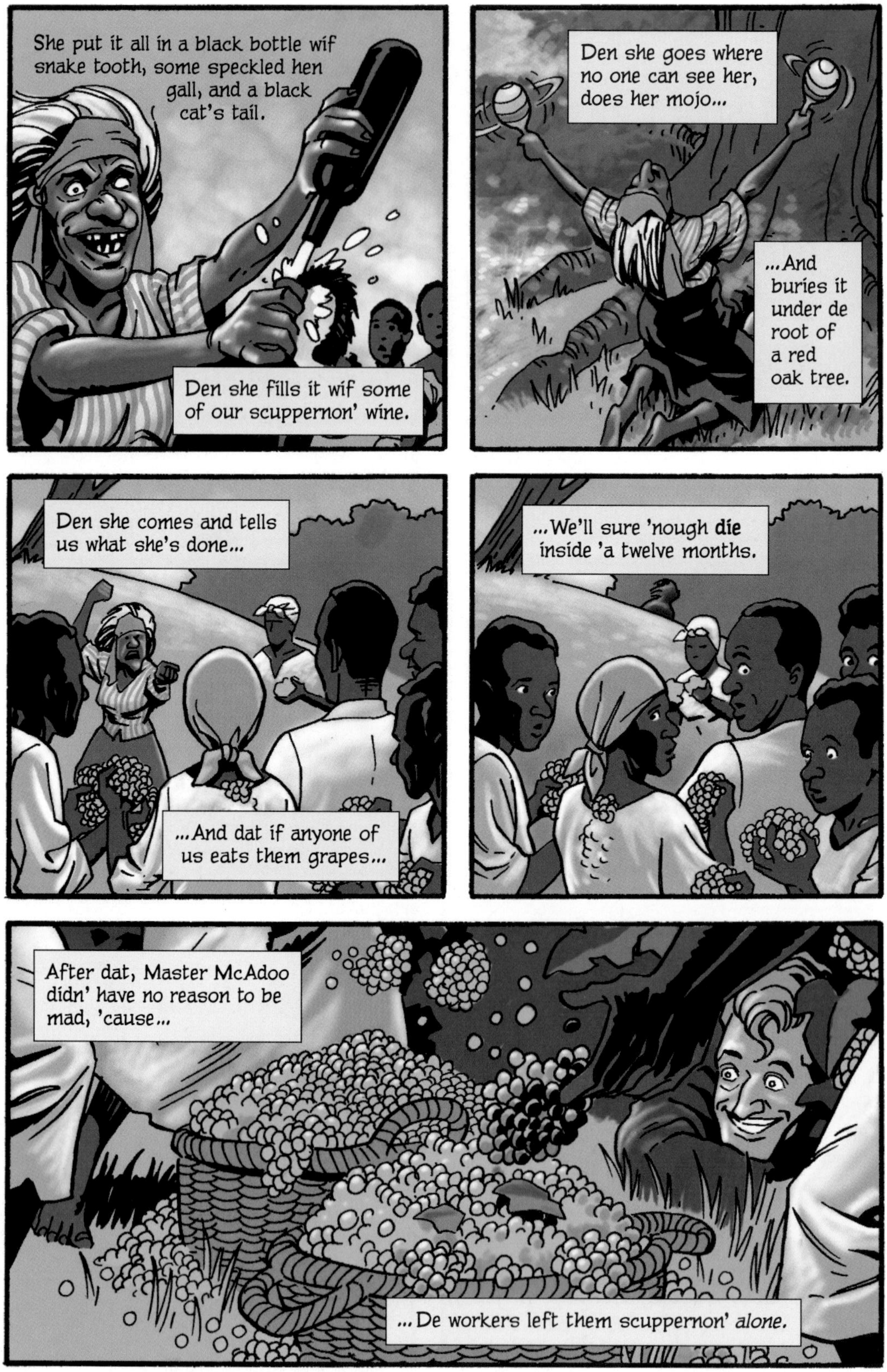
She put it all in a black bottle wif snake tooth, some speckled hen gall, and a black cat's tail.
Den she fills it wif some of our scuppernon' wine.
Den she goes where no one can see her, does her mojo...
...And buries it under de root of a red oak tree.
Den she comes and tells us what she's done...
...And dat if anyone of us eats them grapes...
...We'll sure 'nough **die** inside 'a twelve months.
After dat, Master McAdoo didn' have no reason to be mad, 'cause...
...De workers left them scuppernon' *alone.*

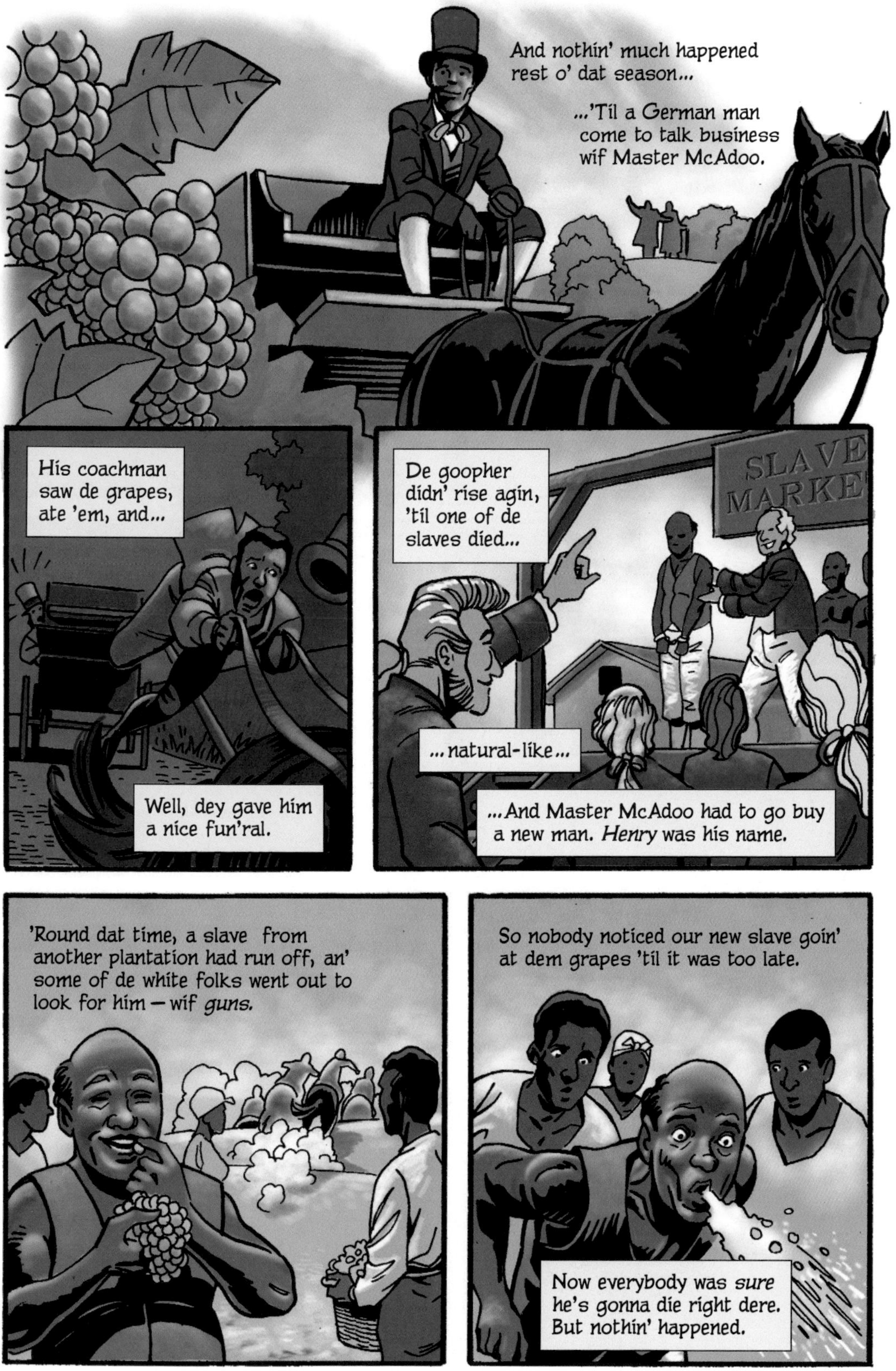
And nothin' much happened rest o' dat season...
...'Til a German man come to talk business wif Master McAdoo.
His coachman saw de grapes, ate 'em, and...
Well, dey gave him a nice fun'ral.
De goopher didn' rise agin, 'til one of de slaves died...
...natural-like...
...And Master McAdoo had to go buy a new man. *Henry* was his name.
'Round dat time, a slave from another plantation had run off, an' some of de white folks went out to look for him — wif *guns.*
So nobody noticed our new slave goin' at dem grapes 'til it was too late.
Now everybody was *sure* he's gonna die right dere. But nothin' happened.

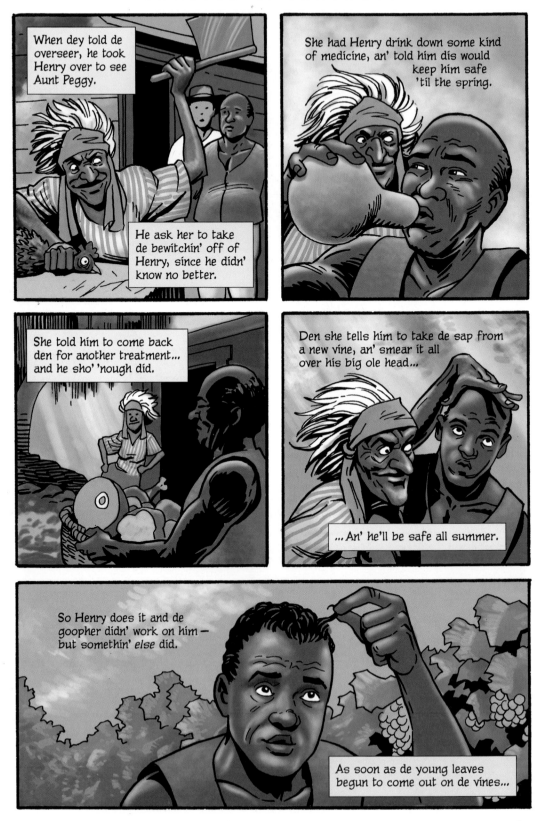

When dey told de overseer, he took Henry over to see Aunt Peggy.

He ask her to take de bewitchin' off of Henry, since he didn' know no better.

She had Henry drink down some kind of medicine, an' told him dis would keep him safe 'til the spring.

She told him to come back den for another treatment... and he sho' 'nough did.

Den she tells him to take de sap from a new vine, an' smear it all over his big ole head...

...An' he'll be safe all summer.

So Henry does it and de goopher didn' work on him — but somethin' else did.

As soon as de young leaves begun to come out on de vines...

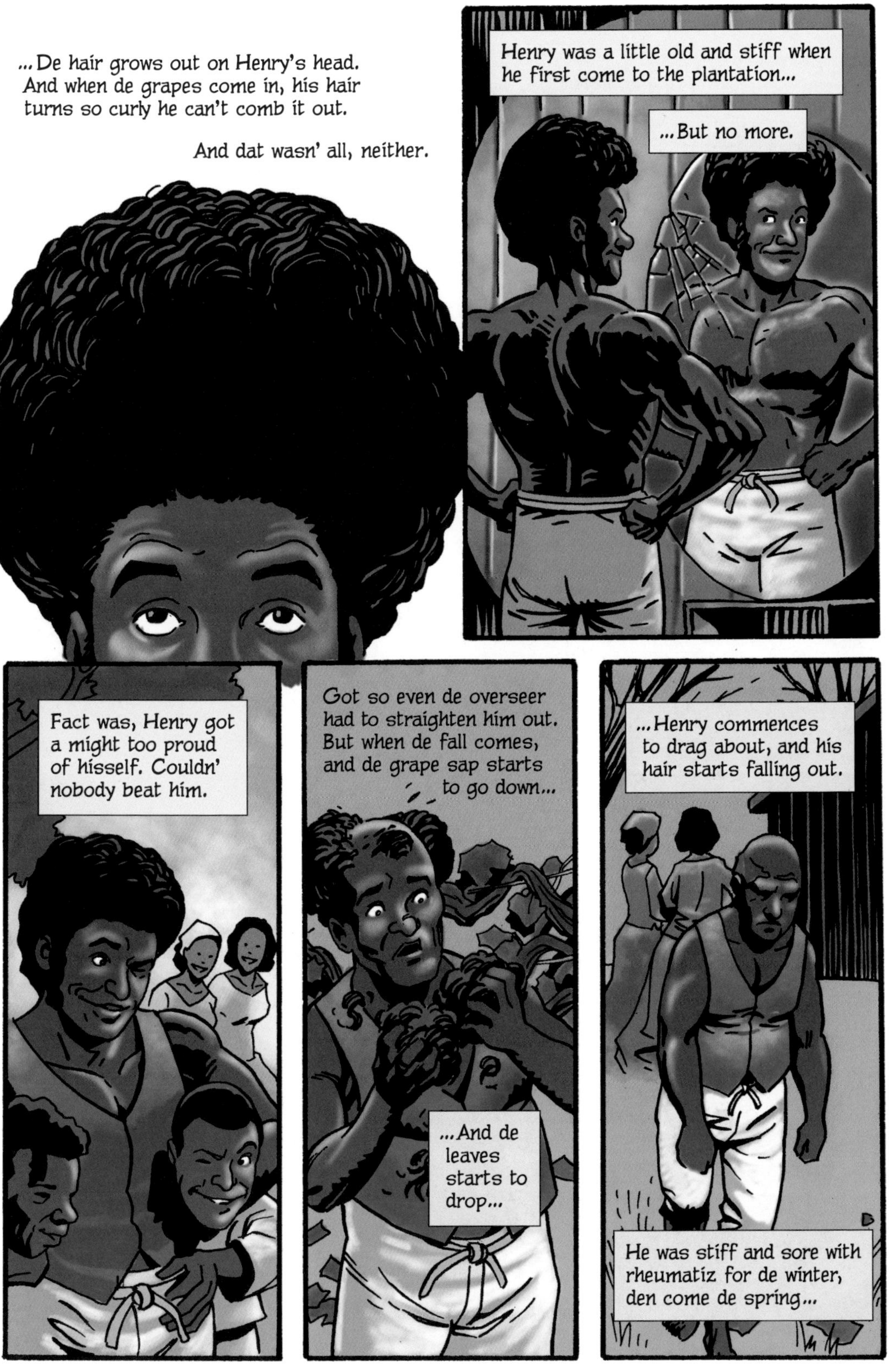
...De hair grows out on Henry's head. And when de grapes come in, his hair turns so curly he can't comb it out.
And dat wasn' all, neither.
Henry was a little old and stiff when he first come to the plantation...
...But no more.
Fact was, Henry got a might too proud of hisself. Couldn' nobody beat him.
Got so even de overseer had to straighten him out. But when de fall comes, and de grape sap starts to go down...
...And de leaves starts to drop...
...Henry commences to drag about, and his hair starts falling out.
He was stiff and sore with rheumatiz for de winter, den come de spring...

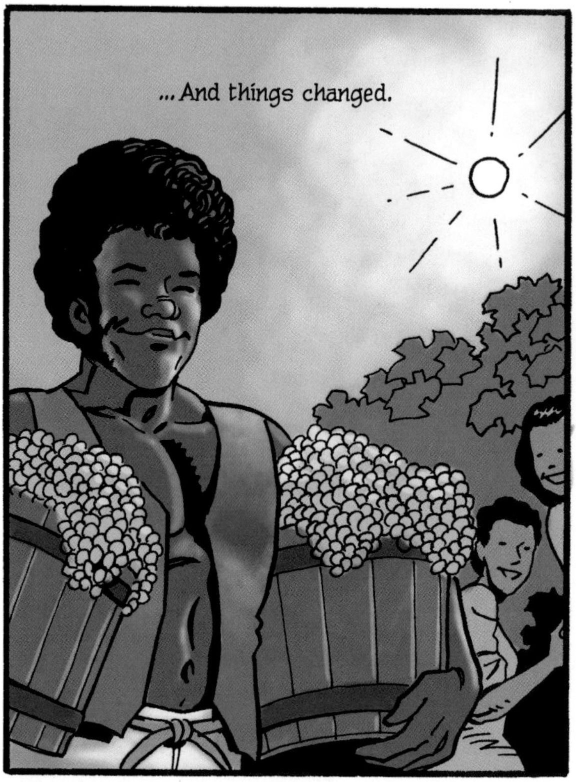
...And things changed.

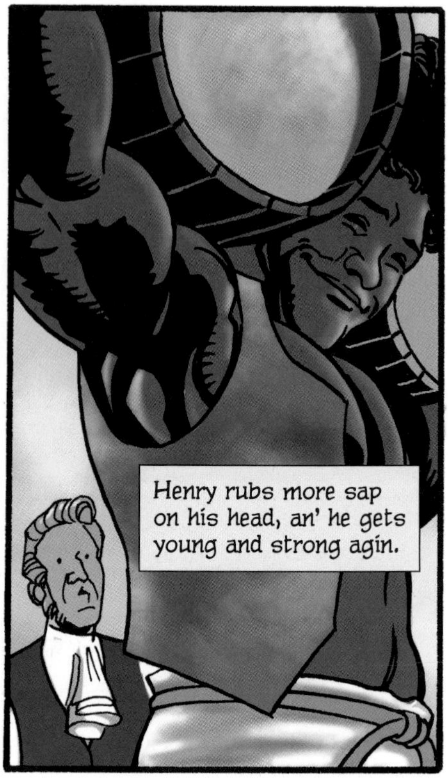
Henry rubs more sap on his head, an' he gets young and strong agin.

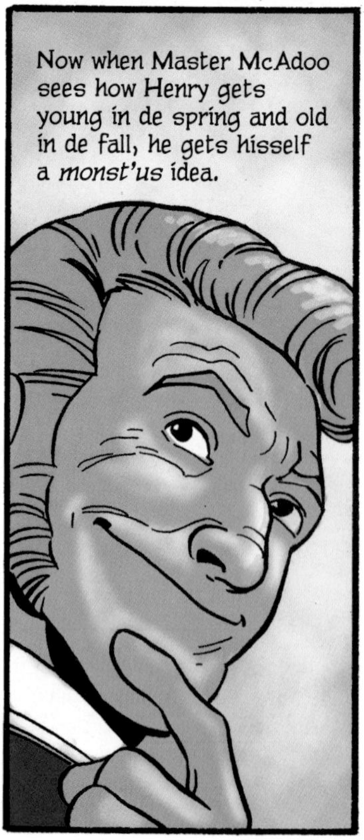
Now when Master McAdoo sees how Henry gets young in de spring and old in de fall, he gets hisself a *monst'us* idea.

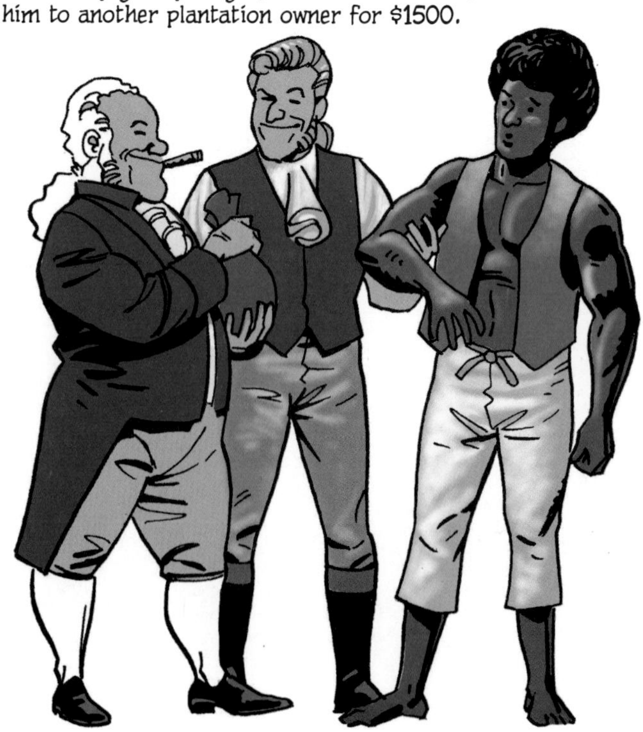
So come next spring, when de sap starts to rise, and Henry gets younger, Master McAdoo sells him to another plantation owner for $1500.

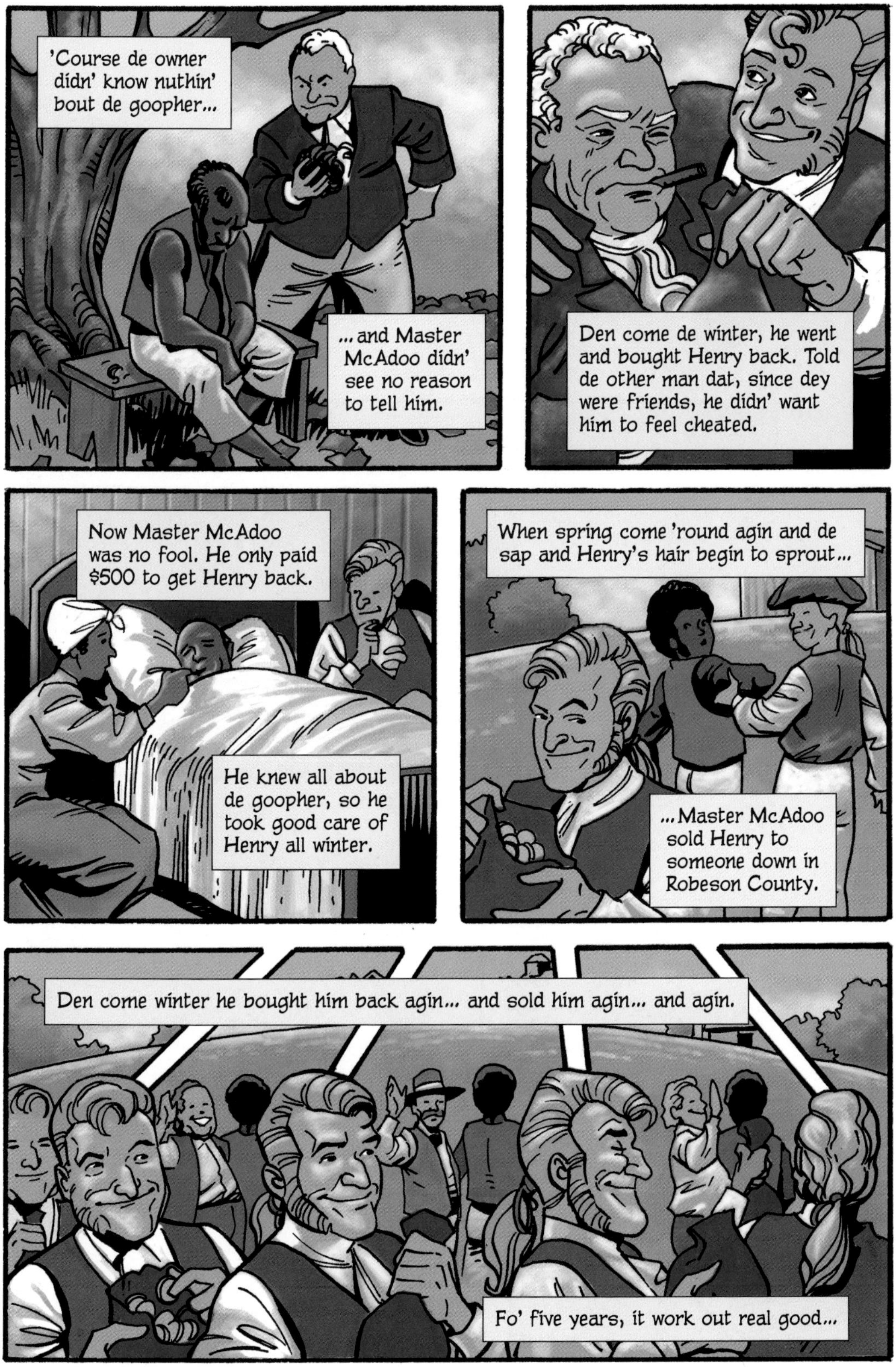
'Course de owner didn' know nuthin' bout de goopher...
...and Master McAdoo didn' see no reason to tell him.
Den come de winter, he went and bought Henry back. Told de other man dat, since dey were friends, he didn' want him to feel cheated.
Now Master McAdoo was no fool. He only paid $500 to get Henry back.
He knew all about de goopher, so he took good care of Henry all winter.
When spring come 'round agin and de sap and Henry's hair begin to sprout...
...Master McAdoo sold Henry to someone down in Robeson County.
Den come winter he bought him back agin... and sold him agin... and agin.
Fo' five years, it work out real good...

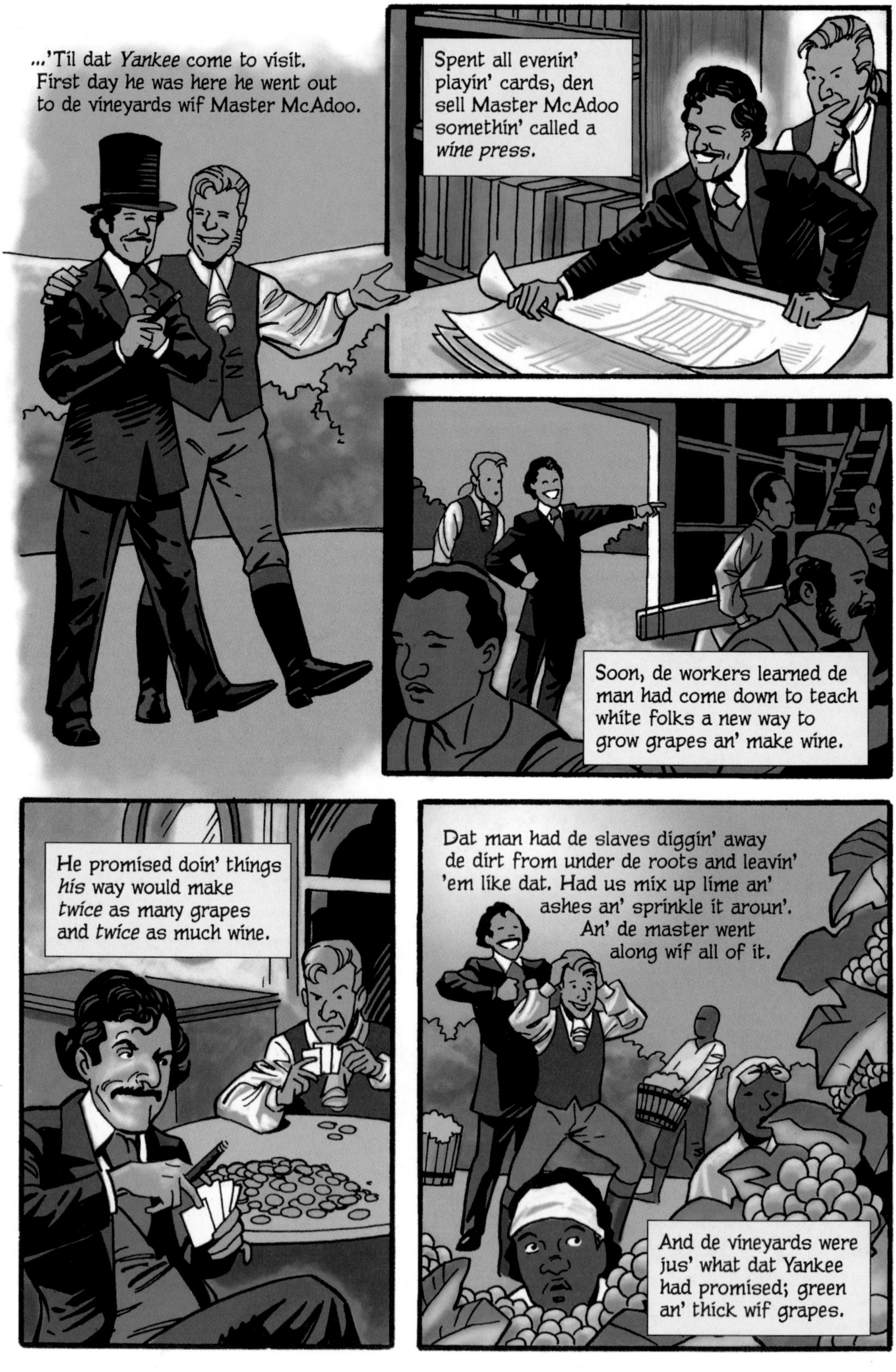
...'Til dat *Yankee* come to visit. First day he was here he went out to de vineyards wif Master McAdoo.
Spent all evenin' playin' cards, den sell Master McAdoo somethin' called a *wine press*.
Soon, de workers learned de man had come down to teach white folks a new way to grow grapes an' make wine.
He promised doin' things *his* way would make *twice* as many grapes and *twice* as much wine.
Dat man had de slaves diggin' away de dirt from under de roots and leavin' 'em like dat. Had us mix up lime an' ashes an' sprinkle it aroun'. An' de master went along wif all of it.
And de vineyards were jus' what dat Yankee had promised; green an' thick wif grapes.

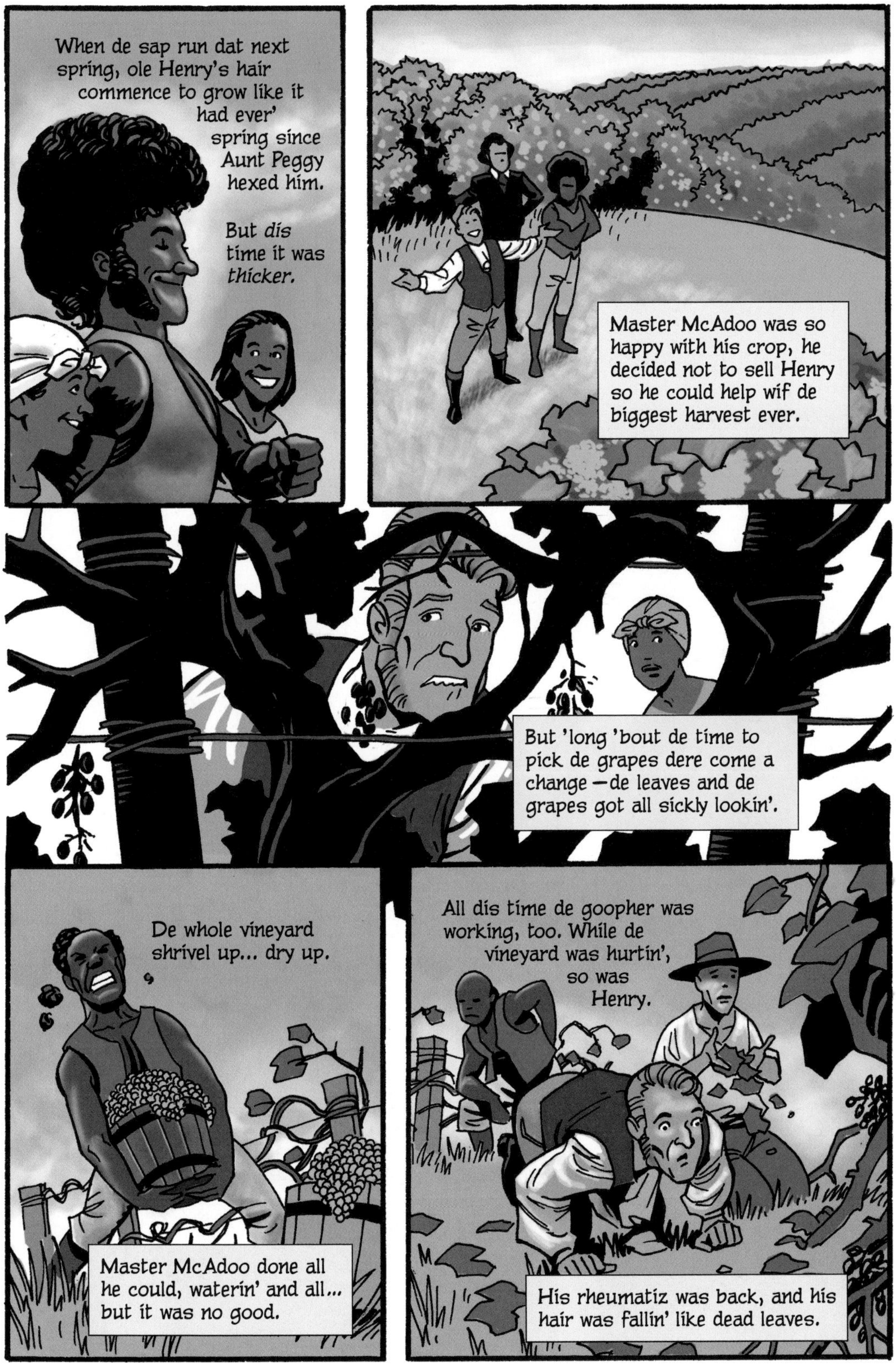
When de sap run dat next spring, ole Henry's hair commence to grow like it had ever' spring since Aunt Peggy hexed him.
But *dis* time it was *thicker.*
Master McAdoo was so happy with his crop, he decided not to sell Henry so he could help wif de biggest harvest ever.
But 'long 'bout de time to pick de grapes dere come a change—de leaves and de grapes got all sickly lookin'.
De whole vineyard shrivel up... dry up.
Master McAdoo done all he could, waterin' and all... but it was no good.
All dis time de goopher was working, too. While de vineyard was hurtin', so was Henry.
His rheumatiz was back, and his hair was fallin' like dead leaves.

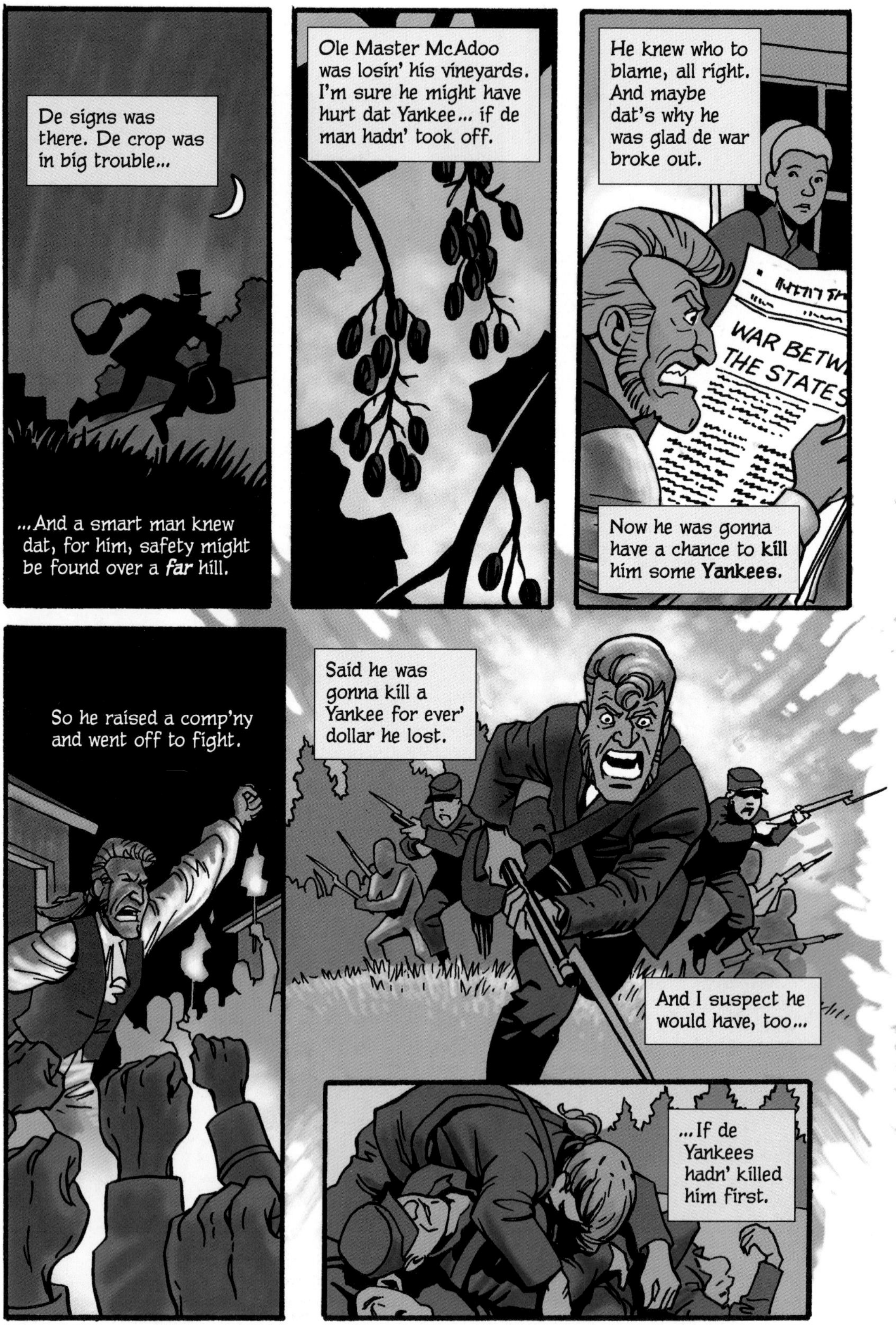
De signs was there. De crop was in big trouble...
...And a smart man knew dat, for him, safety might be found over a *far* hill.
Ole Master McAdoo was losin' his vineyards. I'm sure he might have hurt dat Yankee... if de man hadn' took off.
He knew who to blame, all right. And maybe dat's why he was glad de war broke out.
WAR BETW THE STATES
Now he was gonna have a chance to **kill** him some **Yankees**.
So he raised a comp'ny and went off to fight.
Said he was gonna kill a Yankee for ever' dollar he lost.
And I suspect he would have, too...
...If de Yankees hadn' killed him first.

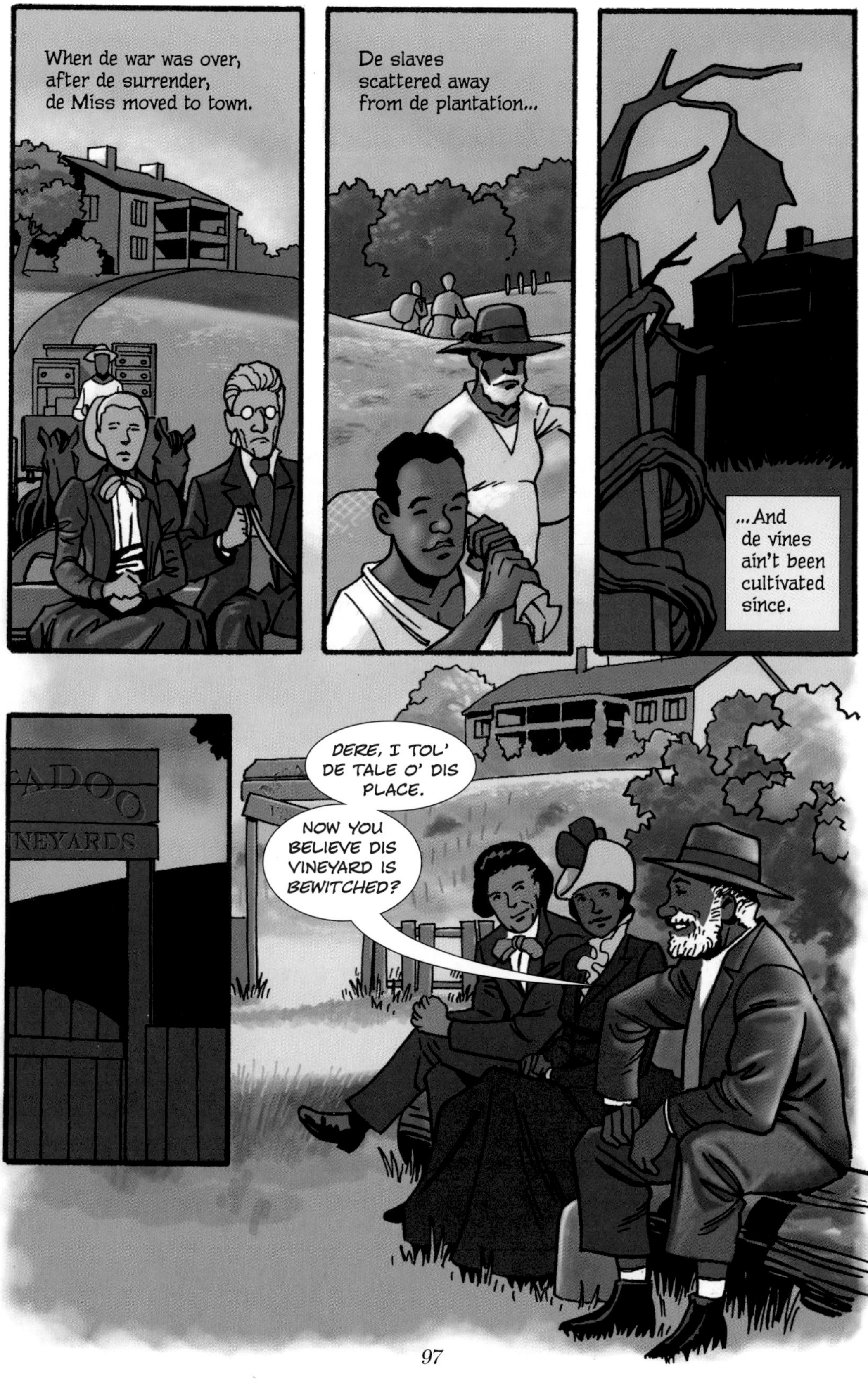
When de war was over, after de surrender, de Miss moved to town.
De slaves scattered away from de plantation...
...And de vines ain't been cultivated since.
DERE, I TOL' DE TALE O' DIS PLACE.
NOW YOU BELIEVE DIS VINEYARD IS BEWITCHED?

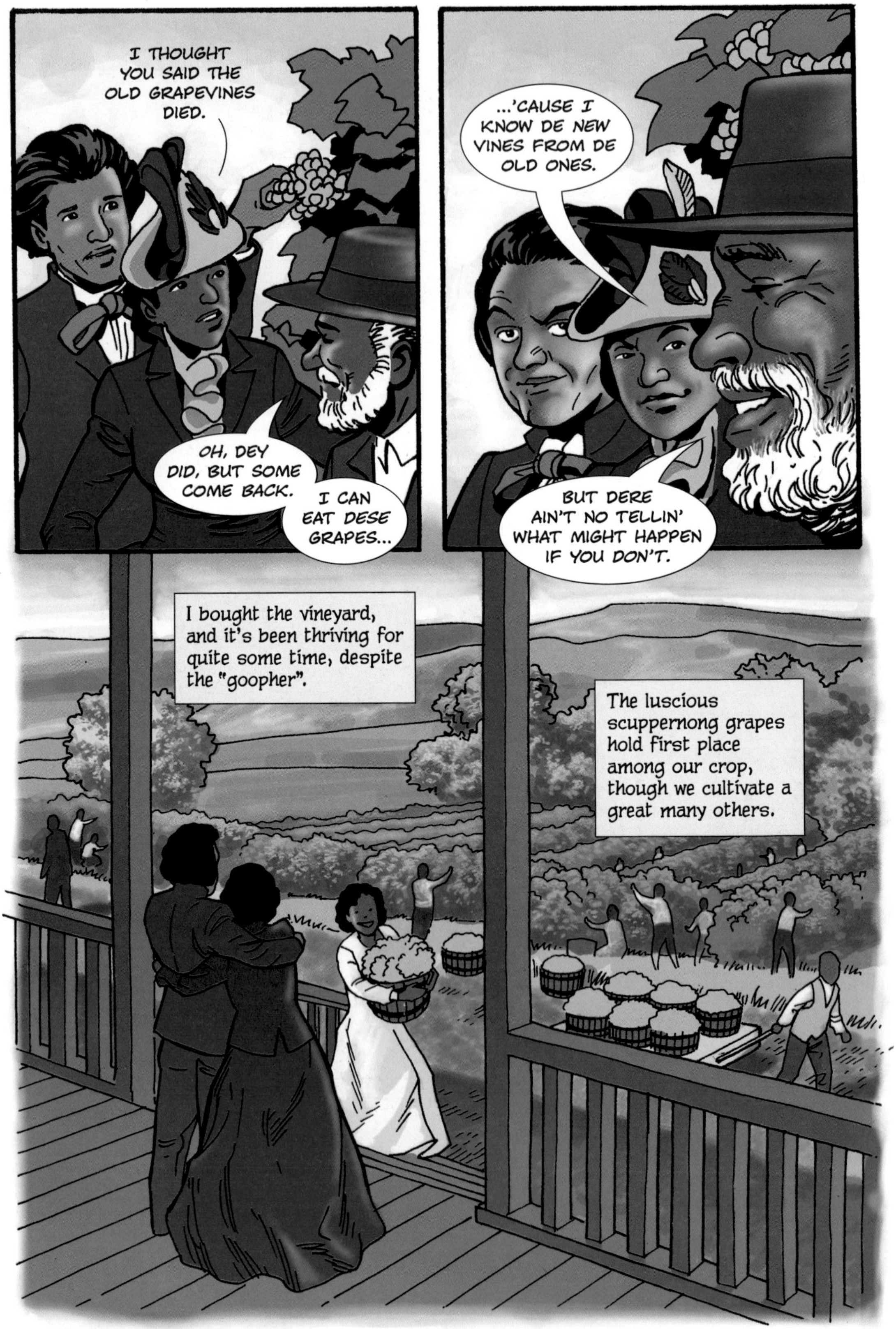
I THOUGHT YOU SAID THE OLD GRAPEVINES DIED.
OH, DEY DID, BUT SOME COME BACK.
I CAN EAT DESE GRAPES...
...'CAUSE I KNOW DE NEW VINES FROM DE OLD ONES.
BUT DERE AIN'T NO TELLIN' WHAT MIGHT HAPPEN IF YOU DON'T.
I bought the vineyard, and it's been thriving for quite some time, despite the "goopher".
The luscious scuppernong grapes hold first place among our crop, though we cultivate a great many others.

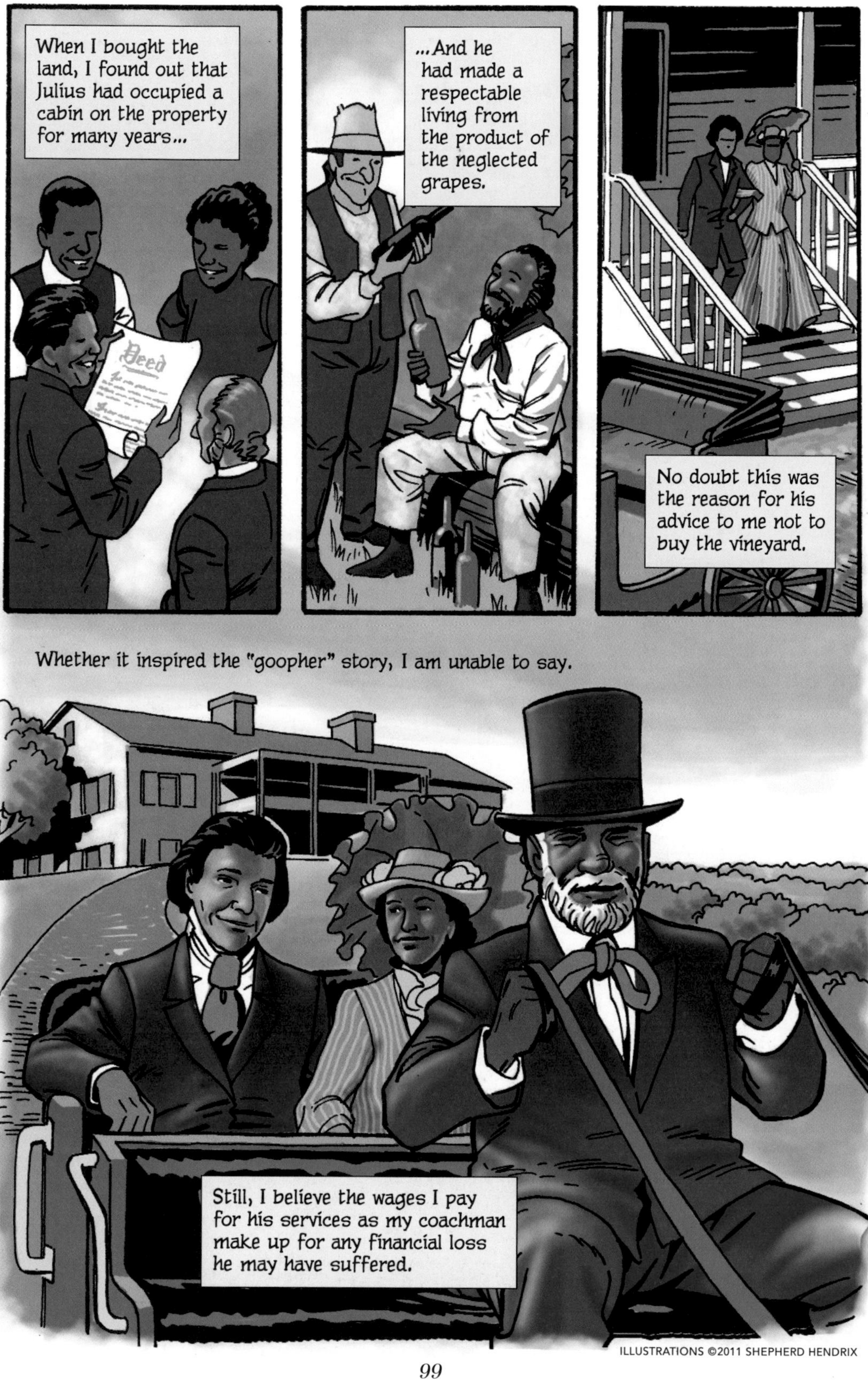
When I bought the land, I found out that Julius had occupied a cabin on the property for many years...
...And he had made a respectable living from the product of the neglected grapes.
No doubt this was the reason for his advice to me not to buy the vineyard.
Whether it inspired the "goopher" story, I am unable to say.
Still, I believe the wages I pay for his services as my coachman make up for any financial loss he may have suffered.

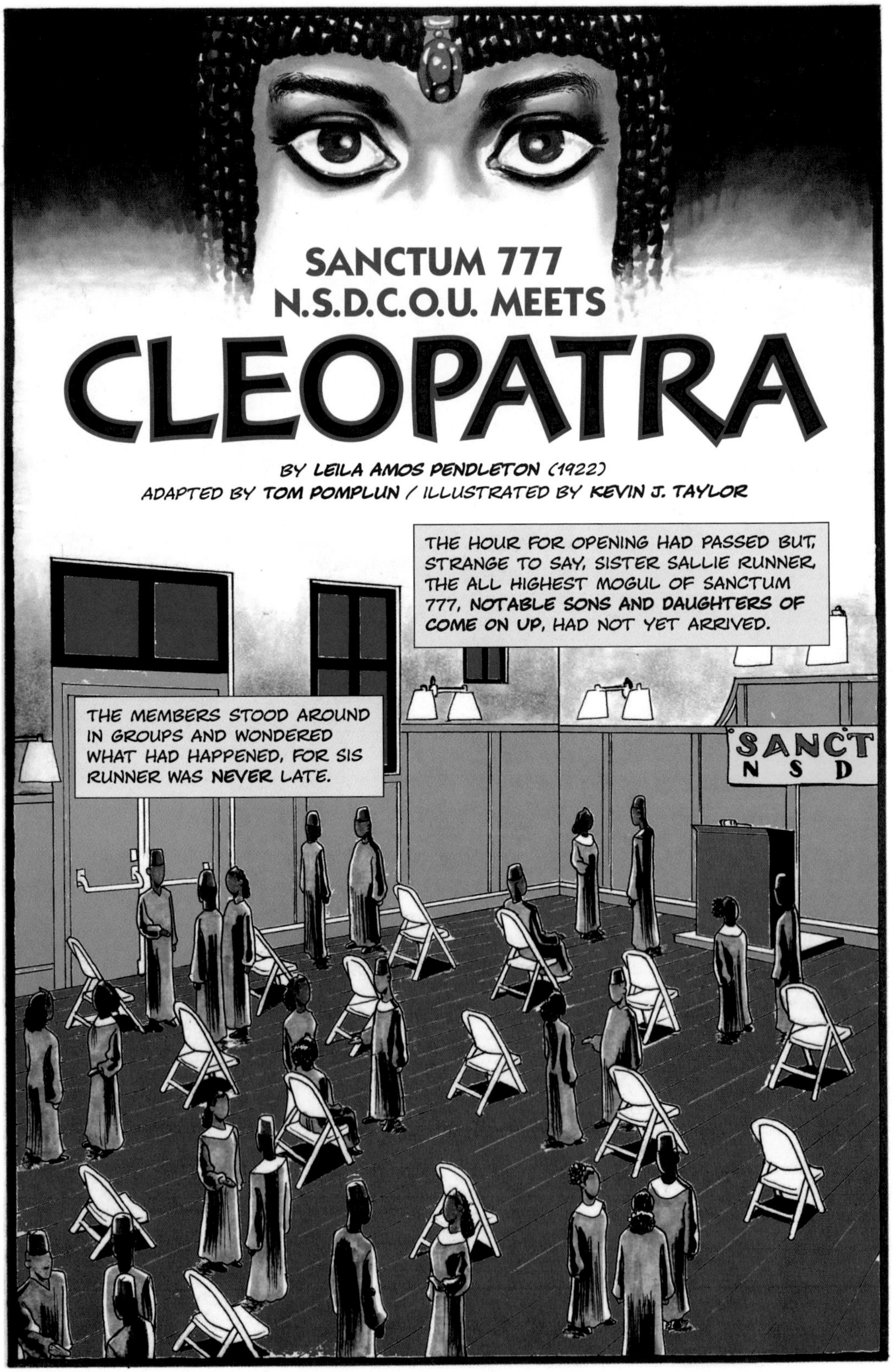
SANCTUM 777
N.S.D.C.O.U. MEETS
CLEOPATRA
BY LEILA AMOS PENDLETON (1922)
ADAPTED BY TOM POMPLUN / ILLUSTRATED BY KEVIN J. TAYLOR
THE HOUR FOR OPENING HAD PASSED BUT, STRANGE TO SAY, SISTER SALLIE RUNNER, THE ALL HIGHEST MOGUL OF SANCTUM 777, NOTABLE SONS AND DAUGHTERS OF COME ON UP, HAD NOT YET ARRIVED.
THE MEMBERS STOOD AROUND IN GROUPS AND WONDERED WHAT HAD HAPPENED, FOR SIS RUNNER WAS NEVER LATE.
SANCT
N S D

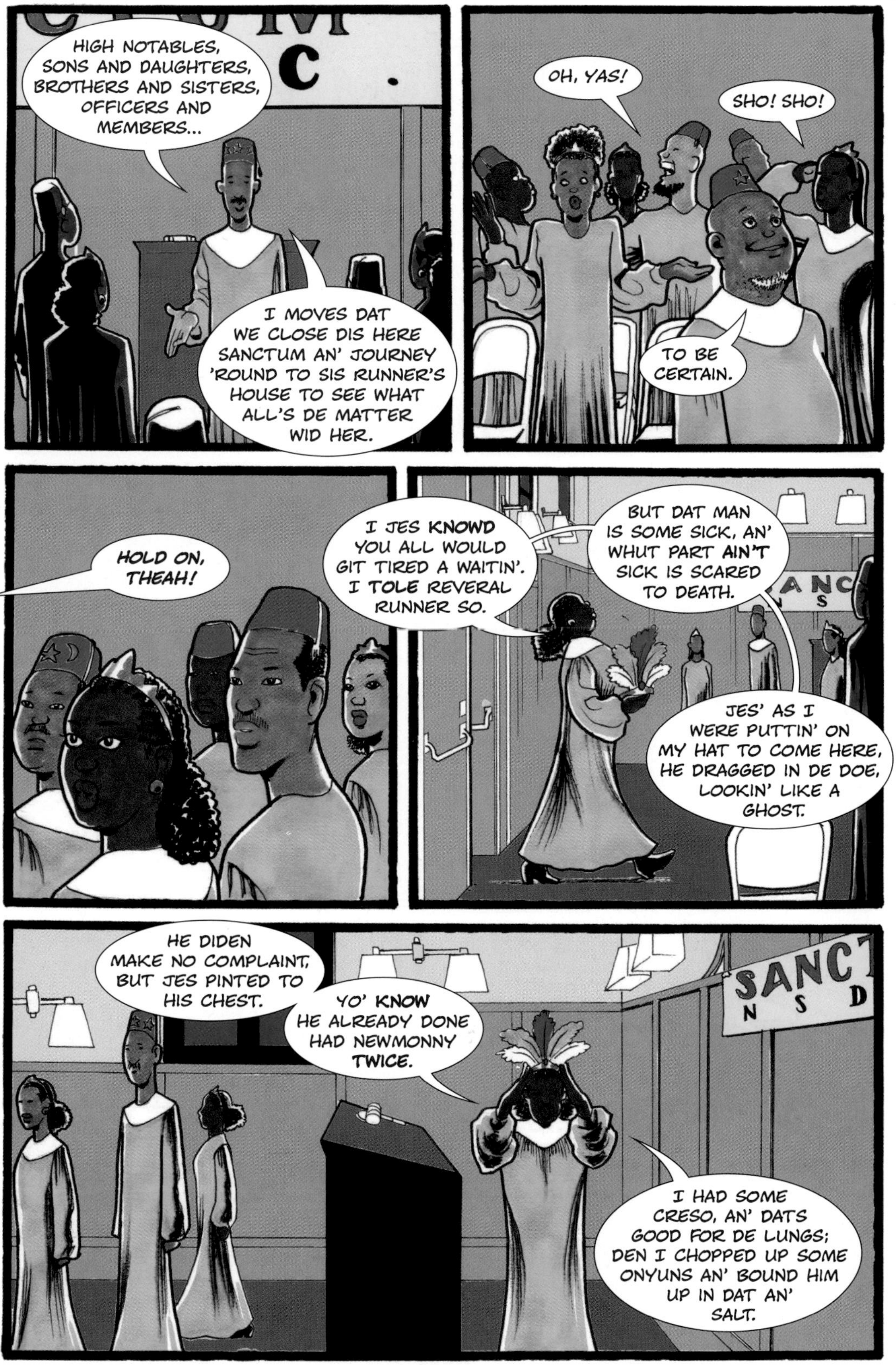
HIGH NOTABLES, SONS AND DAUGHTERS, BROTHERS AND SISTERS, OFFICERS AND MEMBERS...
I MOVES DAT WE CLOSE DIS HERE SANCTUM AN' JOURNEY 'ROUND TO SIS RUNNER'S HOUSE TO SEE WHAT ALL'S DE MATTER WID HER.
OH, YAS!
SHO! SHO!
TO BE CERTAIN.
HOLD ON, THEAH!
I JES **KNOWD** YOU ALL WOULD GIT TIRED A WAITIN'. I **TOLE** REVERAL RUNNER SO.
BUT DAT MAN IS SOME SICK, AN' WHUT PART **AIN'T** SICK IS SCARED TO DEATH.
JES' AS I WERE PUTTIN' ON MY HAT TO COME HERE, HE DRAGGED IN DE DOE, LOOKIN' LIKE A GHOST.
HE DIDEN MAKE NO COMPLAINT, BUT JES PINTED TO HIS CHEST.
YO' **KNOW** HE ALREADY DONE HAD NEWMONNY **TWICE**.
I HAD SOME CRESO, AN' DATS GOOD FOR DE LUNGS; DEN I CHOPPED UP SOME ONYUNS AN' BOUND HIM UP IN DAT AN' SALT.

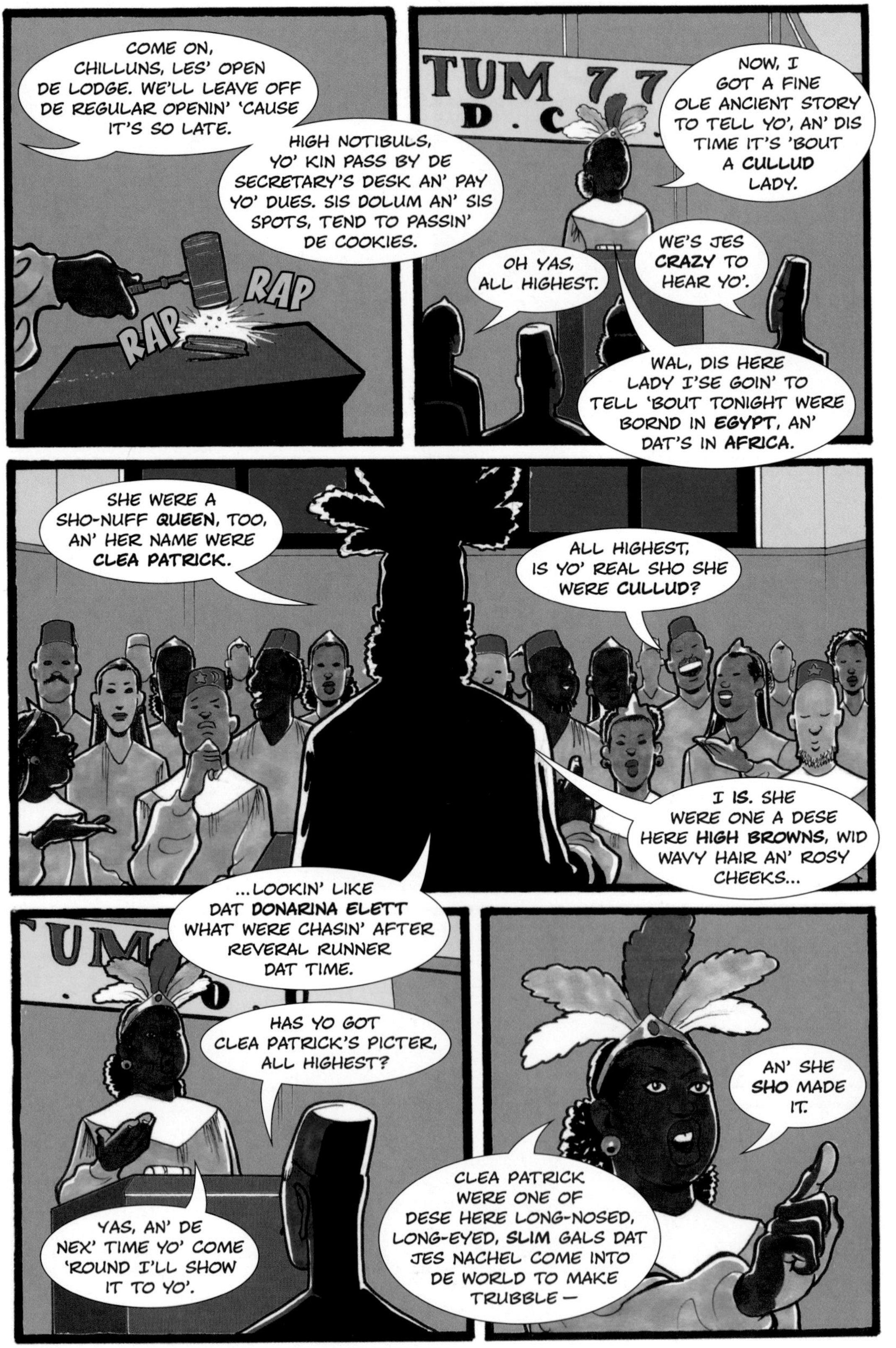
COME ON, CHILLUNS, LES' OPEN DE LODGE. WE'LL LEAVE OFF DE REGULAR OPENIN' 'CAUSE IT'S SO LATE.
HIGH NOTIBULS, YO' KIN PASS BY DE SECRETARY'S DESK AN' PAY YO' DUES. SIS DOLUM AN' SIS SPOTS, TEND TO PASSIN' DE COOKIES.
RAP
RAP
TUM 7 7
D. C.
NOW, I GOT A FINE OLE ANCIENT STORY TO TELL YO', AN' DIS TIME IT'S 'BOUT A CULLUD LADY.
OH YAS, ALL HIGHEST.
WE'S JES CRAZY TO HEAR YO'.
WAL, DIS HERE LADY I'SE GOIN' TO TELL 'BOUT TONIGHT WERE BORND IN EGYPT, AN' DAT'S IN AFRICA.
SHE WERE A SHO-NUFF QUEEN, TOO, AN' HER NAME WERE CLEA PATRICK.
ALL HIGHEST, IS YO' REAL SHO SHE WERE CULLUD?
I IS. SHE WERE ONE A DESE HERE HIGH BROWNS, WID WAVY HAIR AN' ROSY CHEEKS...
...LOOKIN' LIKE DAT DONARINA ELETT WHAT WERE CHASIN' AFTER REVERAL RUNNER DAT TIME.
HAS YO GOT CLEA PATRICK'S PICTER, ALL HIGHEST?
YAS, AN' DE NEX' TIME YO' COME 'ROUND I'LL SHOW IT TO YO'.
CLEA PATRICK WERE ONE OF DESE HERE LONG-NOSED, LONG-EYED, SLIM GALS DAT JES NACHEL COME INTO DE WORLD TO MAKE TRUBBLE —
AN' SHE SHO MADE IT.

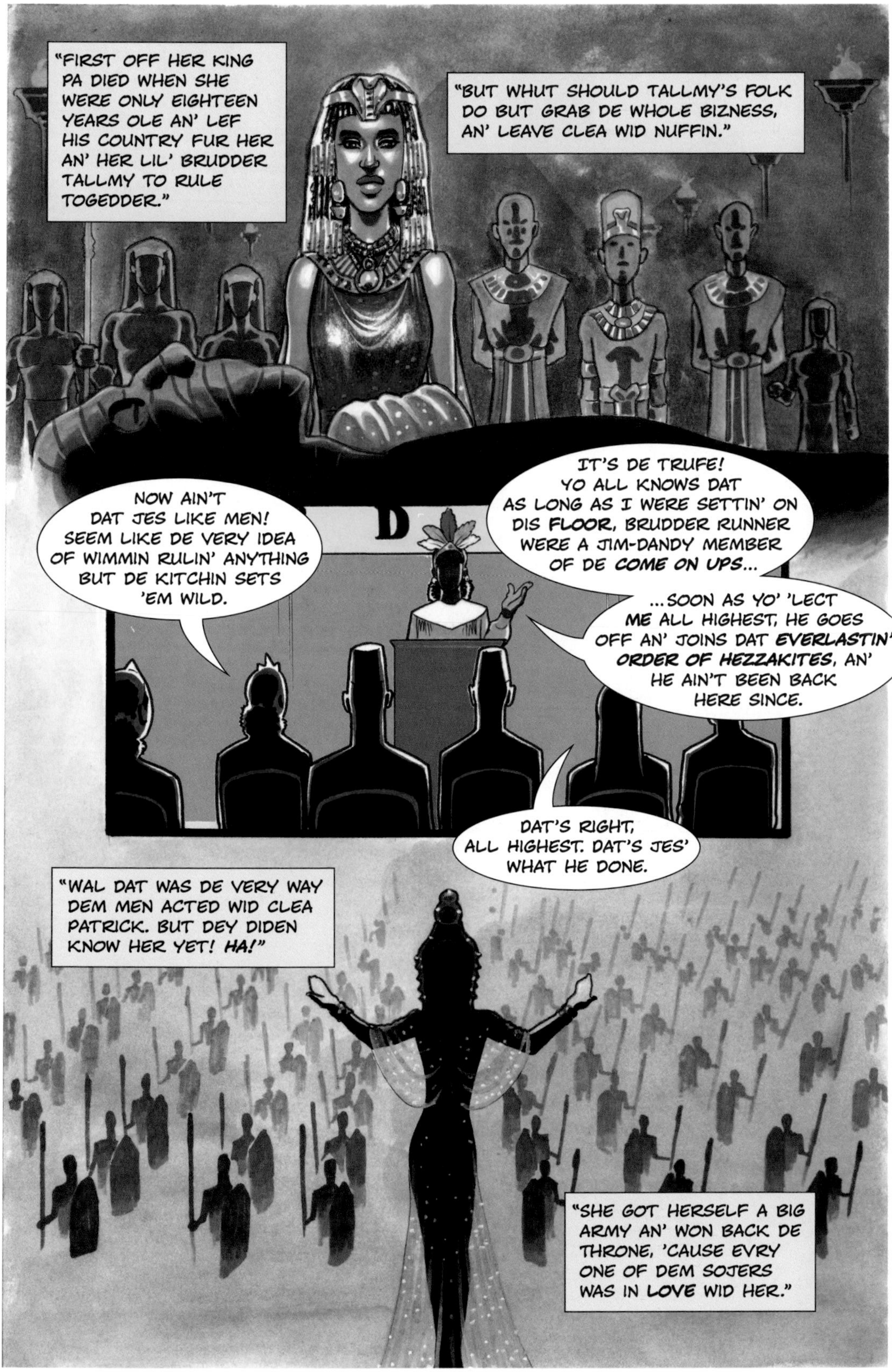
"FIRST OFF HER KING PA DIED WHEN SHE WERE ONLY EIGHTEEN YEARS OLE AN' LEF HIS COUNTRY FUR HER AN' HER LIL' BRUDDER TALLMY TO RULE TOGEDDER."
"BUT WHUT SHOULD TALLMY'S FOLK DO BUT GRAB DE WHOLE BIZNESS, AN' LEAVE CLEA WID NUFFIN."
NOW AIN'T DAT JES LIKE MEN! SEEM LIKE DE VERY IDEA OF WIMMIN RULIN' ANYTHING BUT DE KITCHIN SETS 'EM WILD.
IT'S DE TRUFE! YO ALL KNOWS DAT AS LONG AS I WERE SETTIN' ON DIS **FLOOR**, BRUDDER RUNNER WERE A JIM-DANDY MEMBER OF DE ***COME ON UPS***...
...SOON AS YO' 'LECT **ME** ALL HIGHEST, HE GOES OFF AN' JOINS DAT ***EVERLASTIN' ORDER OF HEZZAKITES***, AN' HE AIN'T BEEN BACK HERE SINCE.
DAT'S RIGHT, ALL HIGHEST. DAT'S JES' WHAT HE DONE.
"WAL DAT WAS DE VERY WAY DEM MEN ACTED WID CLEA PATRICK. BUT DEY DIDEN KNOW HER YET! ***HA!***"
"SHE GOT HERSELF A BIG ARMY AN' WON BACK DE THRONE, 'CAUSE EVRY ONE OF DEM SOJERS WAS IN **LOVE** WID HER."

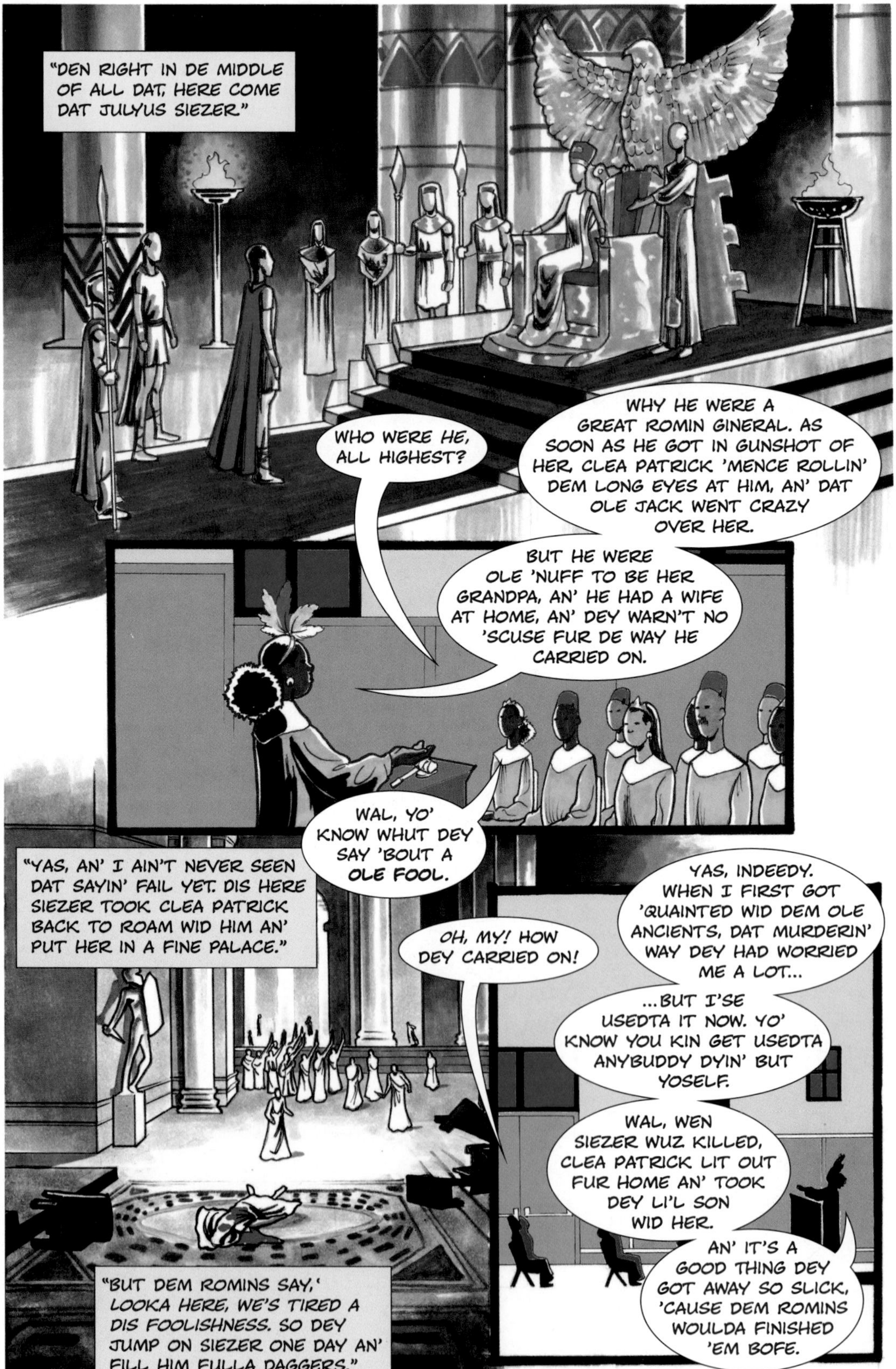
"DEN RIGHT IN DE MIDDLE OF ALL DAT, HERE COME DAT JULYUS SIEZER."
WHO WERE HE, ALL HIGHEST?
WHY HE WERE A GREAT ROMIN GINERAL. AS SOON AS HE GOT IN GUNSHOT OF HER, CLEA PATRICK 'MENCE ROLLIN' DEM LONG EYES AT HIM, AN' DAT OLE JACK WENT CRAZY OVER HER.
BUT HE WERE OLE 'NUFF TO BE HER GRANDPA, AN' HE HAD A WIFE AT HOME, AN' DEY WARN'T NO 'SCUSE FUR DE WAY HE CARRIED ON.
WAL, YO' KNOW WHUT DEY SAY 'BOUT A **OLE FOOL.**
"YAS, AN' I AIN'T NEVER SEEN DAT SAYIN' FAIL YET. DIS HERE SIEZER TOOK CLEA PATRICK BACK TO ROAM WID HIM AN' PUT HER IN A FINE PALACE."
"BUT DEM ROMINS SAY,' LOOKA HERE, WE'S TIRED A DIS FOOLISHNESS. SO DEY JUMP ON SIEZER ONE DAY AN' FILL HIM FULLA DAGGERS."
OH, MY! HOW DEY CARRIED ON!
YAS, INDEEDY. WHEN I FIRST GOT 'QUAINTED WID DEM OLE ANCIENTS, DAT MURDERIN' WAY DEY HAD WORRIED ME A LOT...
...BUT I'SE USEDTA IT NOW. YO' KNOW YOU KIN GET USEDTA ANYBUDDY DYIN' BUT YOSELF.
WAL, WEN SIEZER WUZ KILLED, CLEA PATRICK LIT OUT FUR HOME AN' TOOK DEY LI'L SON WID HER.
AN' IT'S A GOOD THING DEY GOT AWAY SO SLICK, 'CAUSE DEM ROMINS WOULDA FINISHED 'EM BOFE.

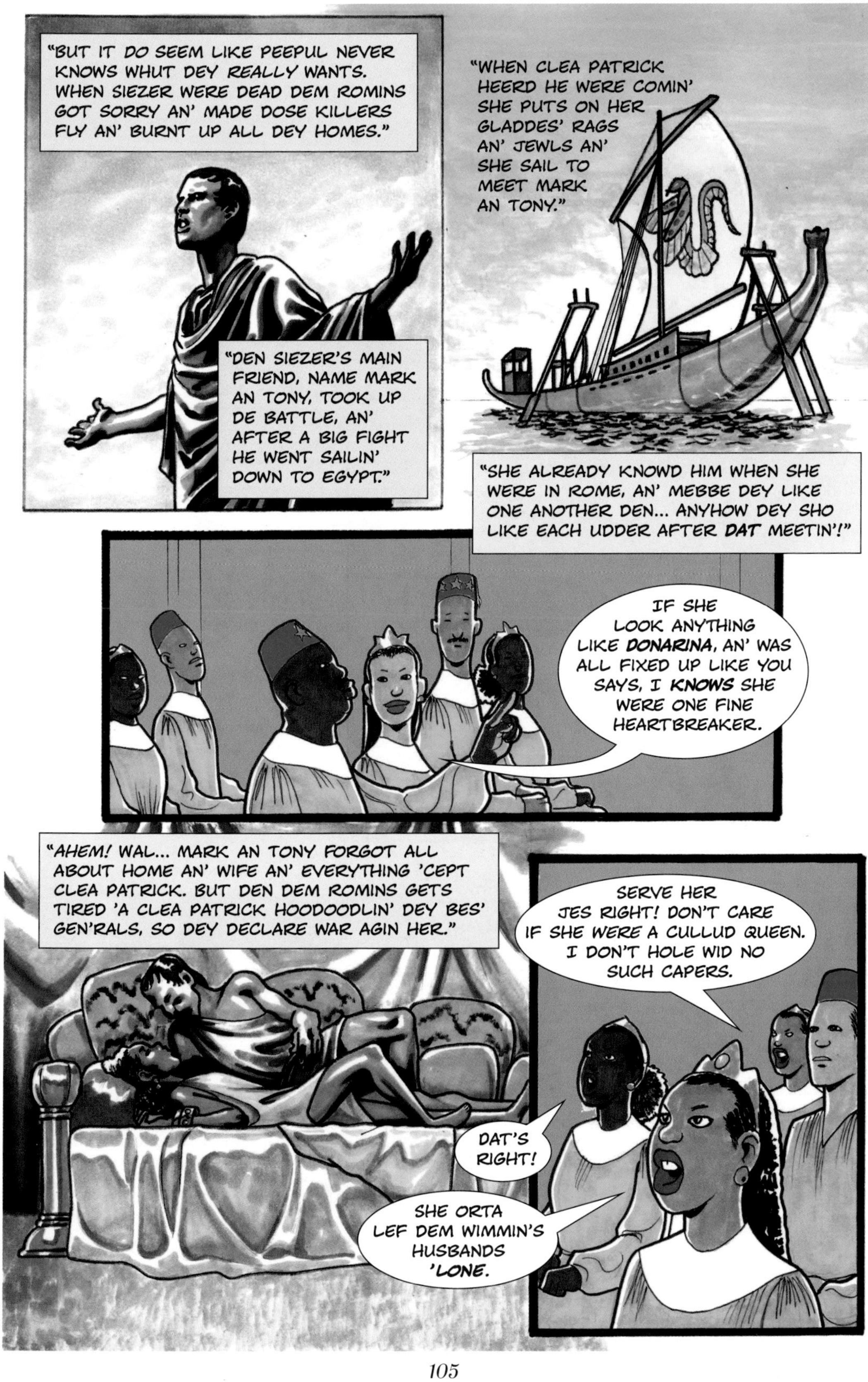
"BUT IT DO SEEM LIKE PEEPUL NEVER KNOWS WHUT DEY REALLY WANTS. WHEN SIEZER WERE DEAD DEM ROMINS GOT SORRY AN' MADE DOSE KILLERS FLY AN' BURNT UP ALL DEY HOMES."
"DEN SIEZER'S MAIN FRIEND, NAME MARK AN TONY, TOOK UP DE BATTLE, AN' AFTER A BIG FIGHT HE WENT SAILIN' DOWN TO EGYPT."
"WHEN CLEA PATRICK HEERD HE WERE COMIN' SHE PUTS ON HER GLADDES' RAGS AN' JEWLS AN' SHE SAIL TO MEET MARK AN TONY."
"SHE ALREADY KNOWD HIM WHEN SHE WERE IN ROME, AN' MEBBE DEY LIKE ONE ANOTHER DEN... ANYHOW DEY SHO LIKE EACH UDDER AFTER DAT MEETIN'!"
IF SHE LOOK ANYTHING LIKE DONARINA, AN' WAS ALL FIXED UP LIKE YOU SAYS, I KNOWS SHE WERE ONE FINE HEARTBREAKER.
"AHEM! WAL... MARK AN TONY FORGOT ALL ABOUT HOME AN' WIFE AN' EVERYTHING 'CEPT CLEA PATRICK. BUT DEN DEM ROMINS GETS TIRED 'A CLEA PATRICK HOODOODLIN' DEY BES' GEN'RALS, SO DEY DECLARE WAR AGIN HER."
SERVE HER JES RIGHT! DON'T CARE IF SHE WERE A CULLUD QUEEN. I DON'T HOLE WID NO SUCH CAPERS.
DAT'S RIGHT!
SHE ORTA LEF DEM WIMMIN'S HUSBANDS 'LONE.

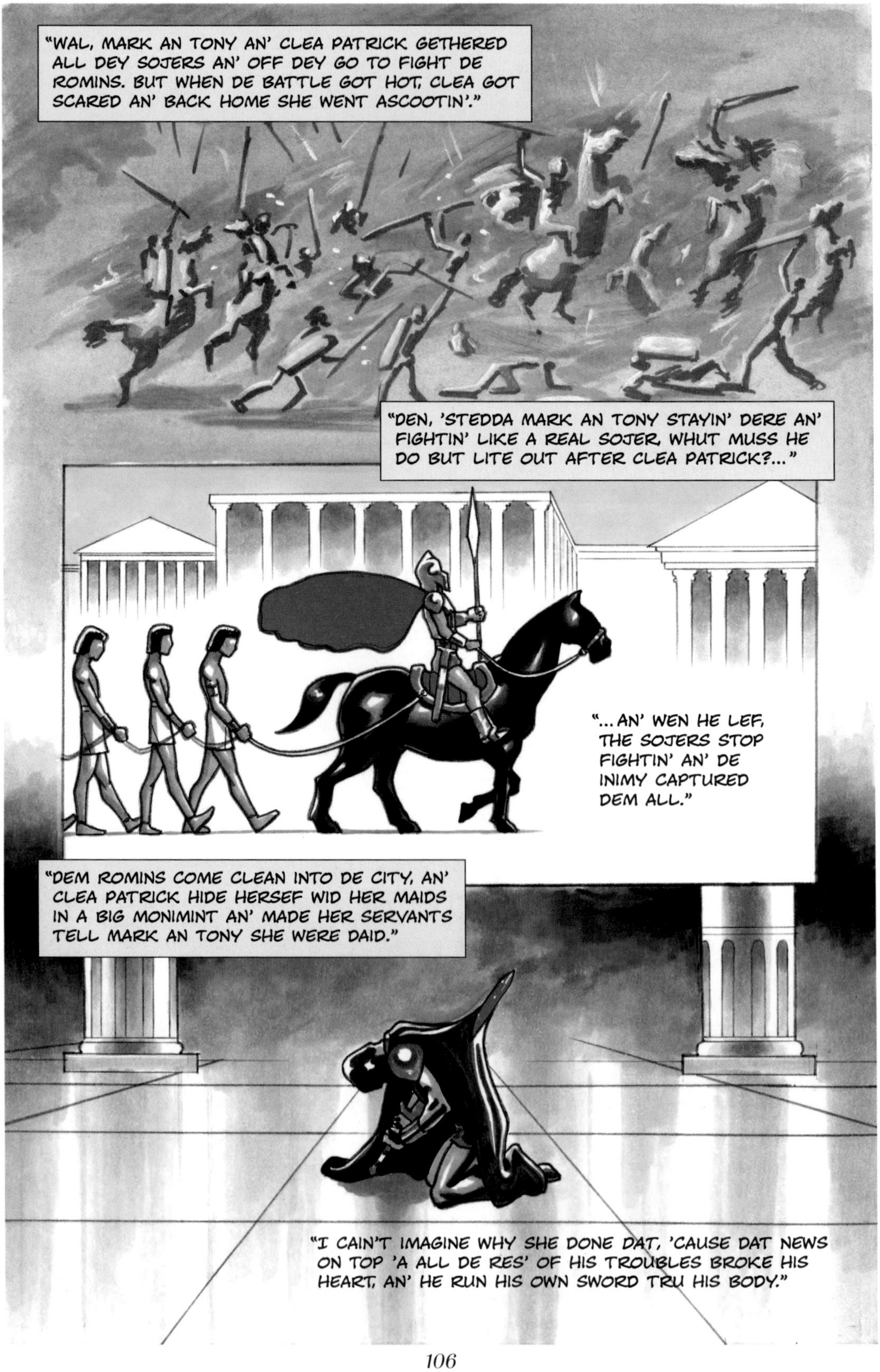
"WAL, MARK AN TONY AN' CLEA PATRICK GETHERED ALL DEY SOJERS AN' OFF DEY GO TO FIGHT DE ROMINS. BUT WHEN DE BATTLE GOT HOT, CLEA GOT SCARED AN' BACK HOME SHE WENT ASCOOTIN'."
"DEN, 'STEDDA MARK AN TONY STAYIN' DERE AN' FIGHTIN' LIKE A REAL SOJER, WHUT MUSS HE DO BUT LITE OUT AFTER CLEA PATRICK?..."
"...AN' WEN HE LEF, THE SOJERS STOP FIGHTIN' AN' DE INIMY CAPTURED DEM ALL."
"DEM ROMINS COME CLEAN INTO DE CITY, AN' CLEA PATRICK HIDE HERSEF WID HER MAIDS IN A BIG MONIMINT AN' MADE HER SERVANTS TELL MARK AN TONY SHE WERE DAID."
"I CAIN'T IMAGINE WHY SHE DONE DAT, 'CAUSE DAT NEWS ON TOP 'A ALL DE RES' OF HIS TROUBLES BROKE HIS HEART, AN' HE RUN HIS OWN SWORD TRU HIS BODY."

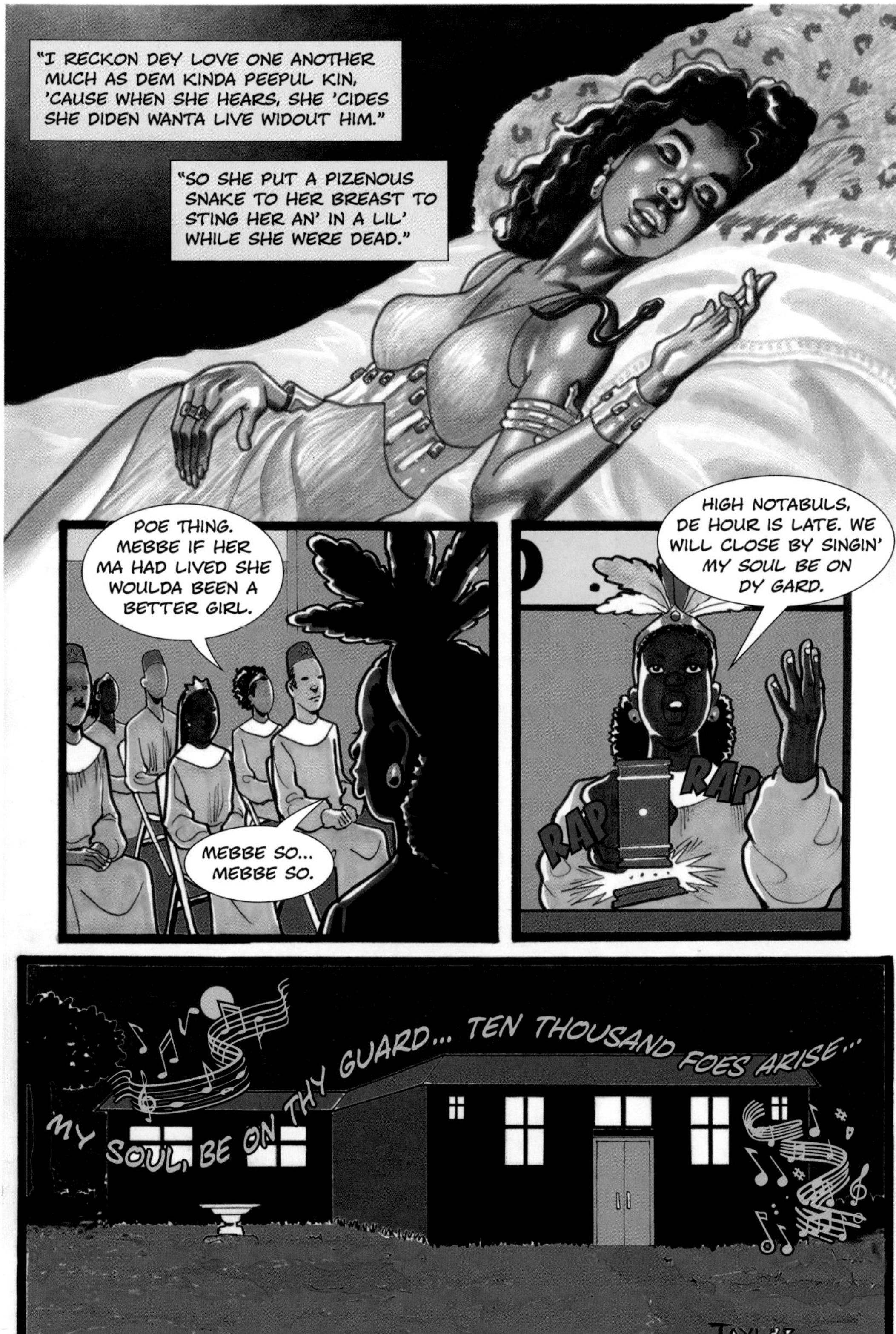
"I RECKON DEY LOVE ONE ANOTHER MUCH AS DEM KINDA PEEPUL KIN, 'CAUSE WHEN SHE HEARS, SHE 'CIDES SHE DIDEN WANTA LIVE WIDOUT HIM."
"SO SHE PUT A PIZENOUS SNAKE TO HER BREAST TO STING HER AN' IN A LIL' WHILE SHE WERE DEAD."
POE THING. MEBBE IF HER MA HAD LIVED SHE WOULDA BEEN A BETTER GIRL.
MEBBE SO... MEBBE SO.
HIGH NOTABULS, DE HOUR IS LATE. WE WILL CLOSE BY SINGIN' MY SOUL BE ON DY GARD.
RAP
RAP
MY SOUL, BE ON THY GUARD... TEN THOUSAND FOES ARISE...
TAYLOR ©2011

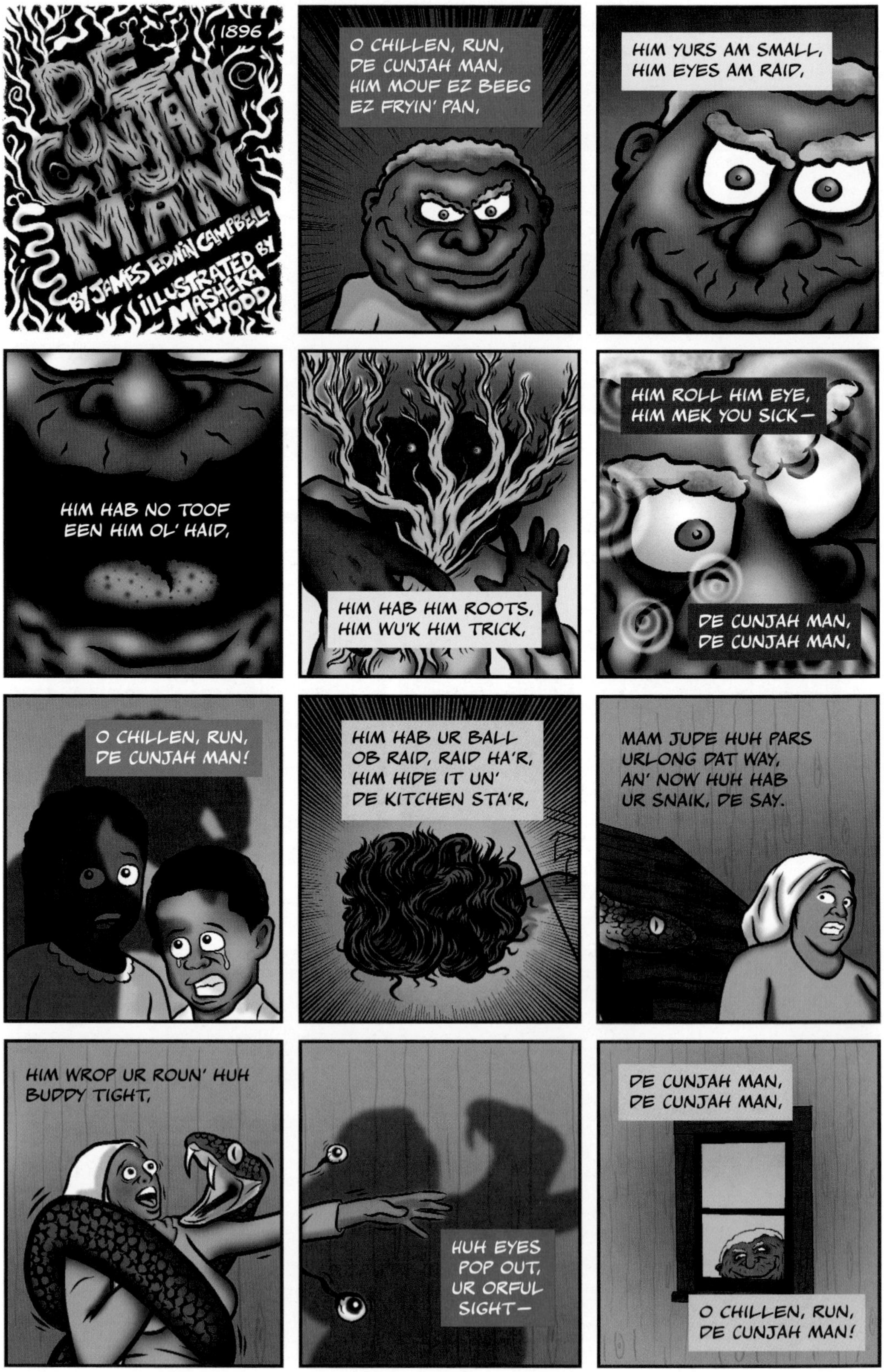
1896
DE CUNJAH MAN
BY JAMES EDWIN CAMPBELL
ILLUSTRATED BY MASHEKA WOOD
O CHILLEN, RUN, DE CUNJAH MAN, HIM MOUF EZ BEEG EZ FRYIN' PAN,
HIM YURS AM SMALL, HIM EYES AM RAID,
HIM HAB NO TOOF EEN HIM OL' HAID,
HIM HAB HIM ROOTS, HIM WU'K HIM TRICK,
HIM ROLL HIM EYE, HIM MEK YOU SICK—
DE CUNJAH MAN, DE CUNJAH MAN,
O CHILLEN, RUN, DE CUNJAH MAN!
HIM HAB UR BALL OB RAID, RAID HA'R, HIM HIDE IT UN' DE KITCHEN STA'R,
MAM JUDE HUH PARS URLONG DAT WAY, AN' NOW HUH HAB UR SNAIK, DE SAY.
HIM WROP UR ROUN' HUH BUDDY TIGHT,
HUH EYES POP OUT, UR ORFUL SIGHT—
DE CUNJAH MAN, DE CUNJAH MAN,
O CHILLEN, RUN, DE CUNJAH MAN!

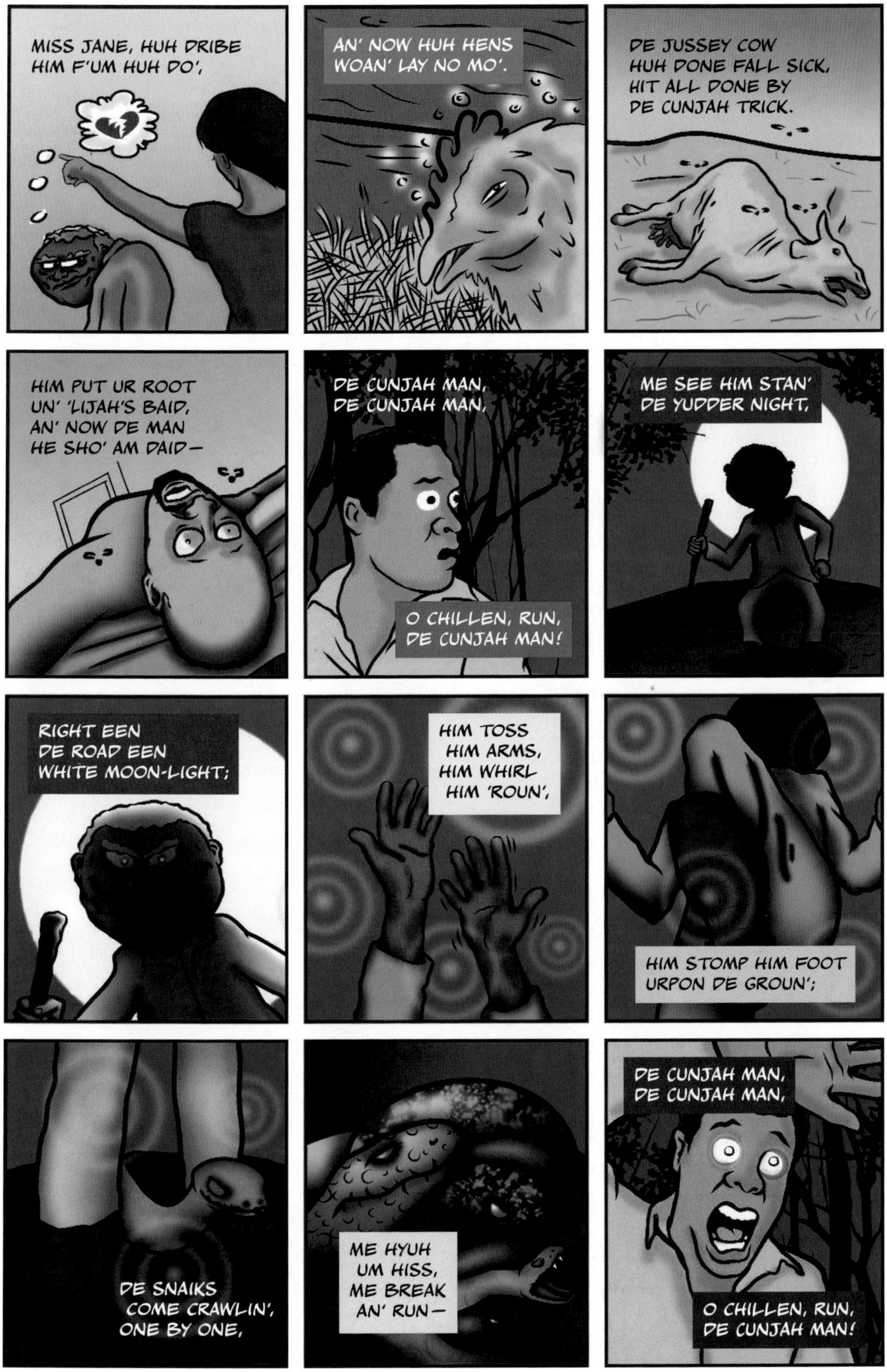
MISS JANE, HUH DRIBE HIM F'UM HUH DO',
AN' NOW HUH HENS WOAN' LAY NO MO'.
DE JUSSEY COW HUH DONE FALL SICK, HIT ALL DONE BY DE CUNJAH TRICK.
HIM PUT UR ROOT UN' 'LIJAH'S BAID, AN' NOW DE MAN HE SHO' AM DAID—
DE CUNJAH MAN, DE CUNJAH MAN,
O CHILLEN, RUN, DE CUNJAH MAN!
ME SEE HIM STAN' DE YUDDER NIGHT,
RIGHT EEN DE ROAD EEN WHITE MOON-LIGHT;
HIM TOSS HIM ARMS, HIM WHIRL HIM 'ROUN',
HIM STOMP HIM FOOT URPON DE GROUN';
DE SNAIKS COME CRAWLIN', ONE BY ONE,
ME HYUH UM HISS, ME BREAK AN' RUN—
DE CUNJAH MAN, DE CUNJAH MAN,
O CHILLEN, RUN, DE CUNJAH MAN!

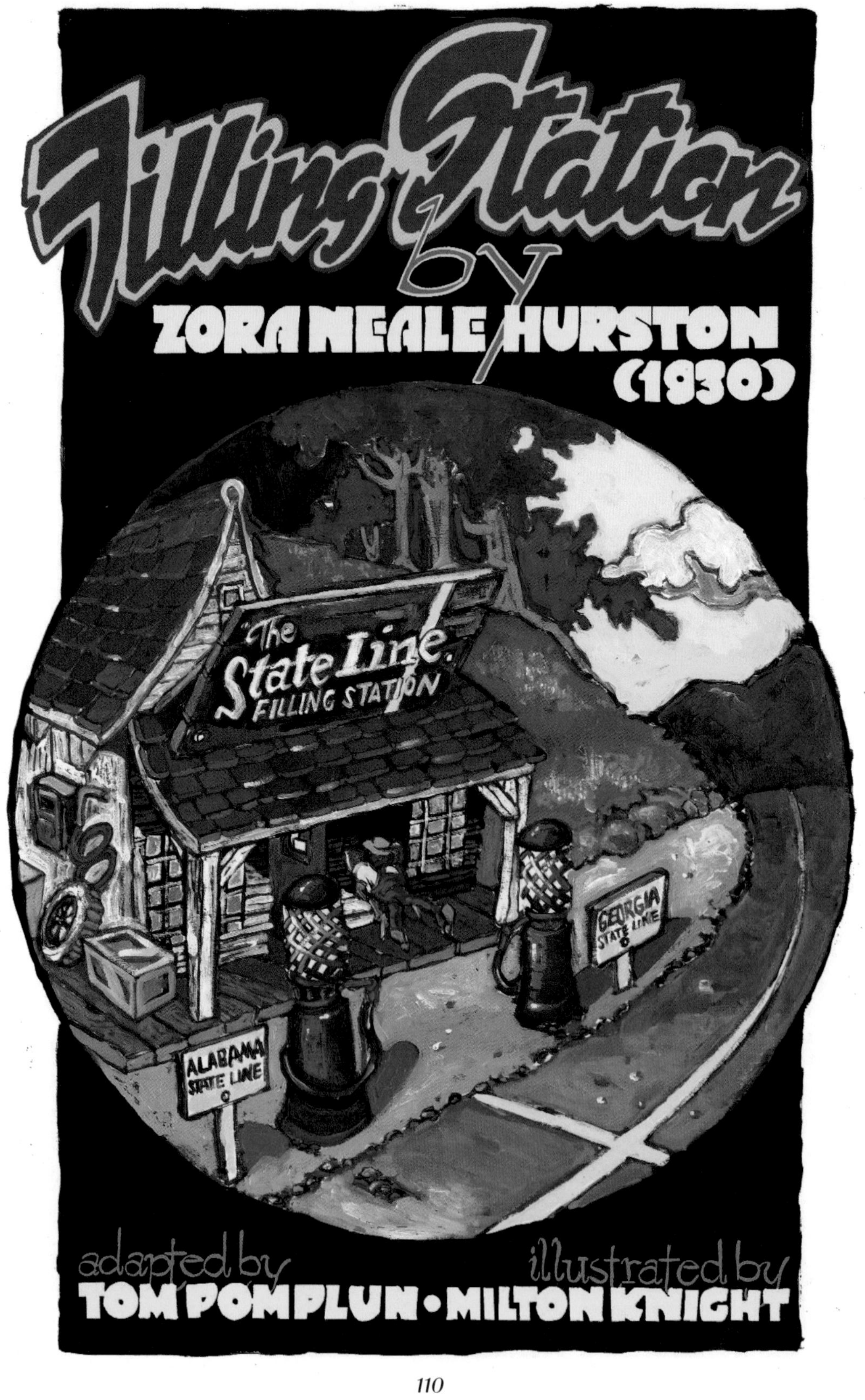
Filling Station
by
ZORA NEALE HURSTON
(1930)
"The State Line" FILLING STATION
GEORGIA STATE LINE
ALABAMA STATE LINE
adapted by
TOM POMPLUN
illustrated by
MILTON KNIGHT

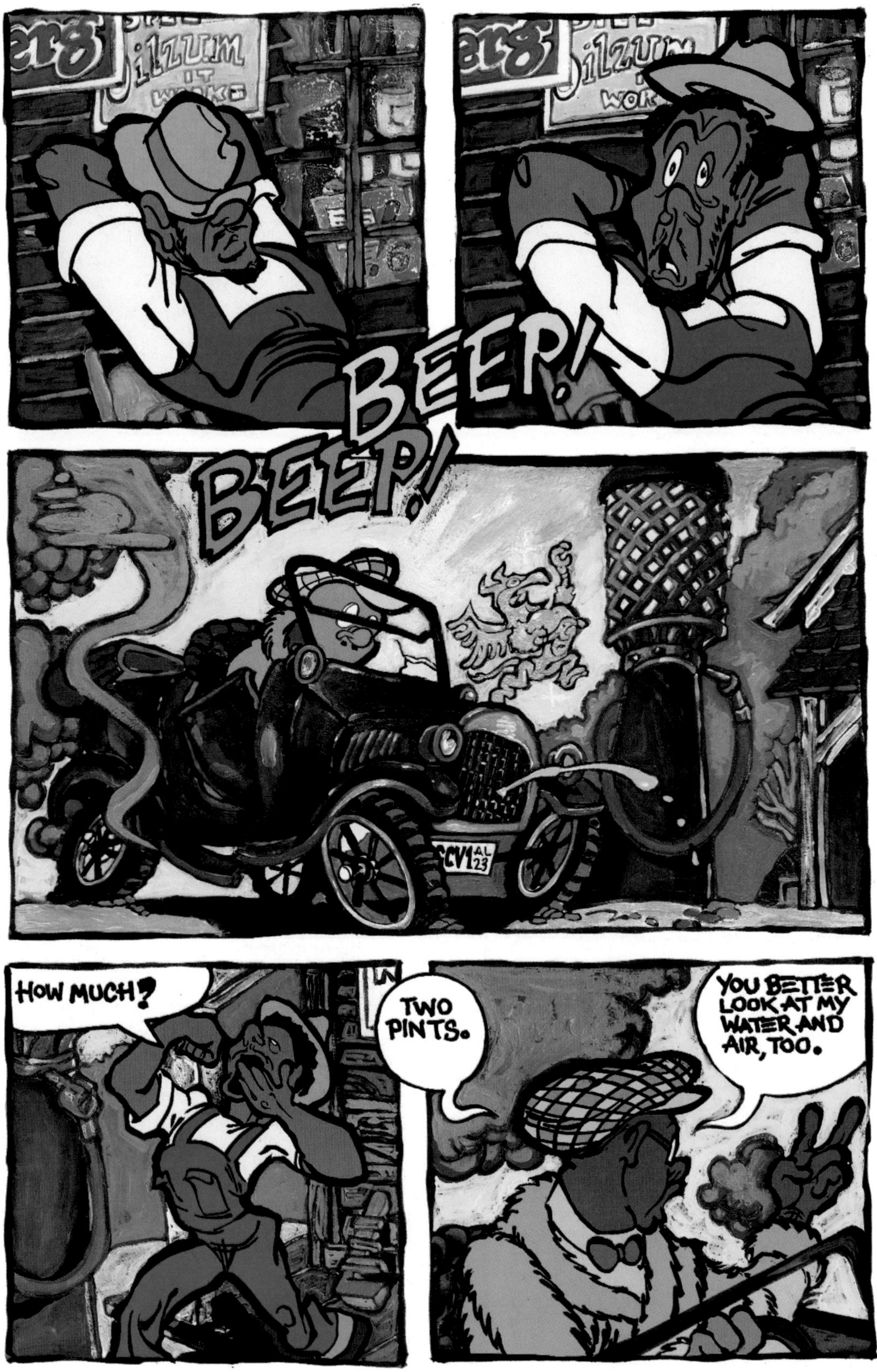
BEEP!
BEEP!
HOW MUCH?
TWO PINTS.
YOU BETTER LOOK AT MY WATER AND AIR, TOO.

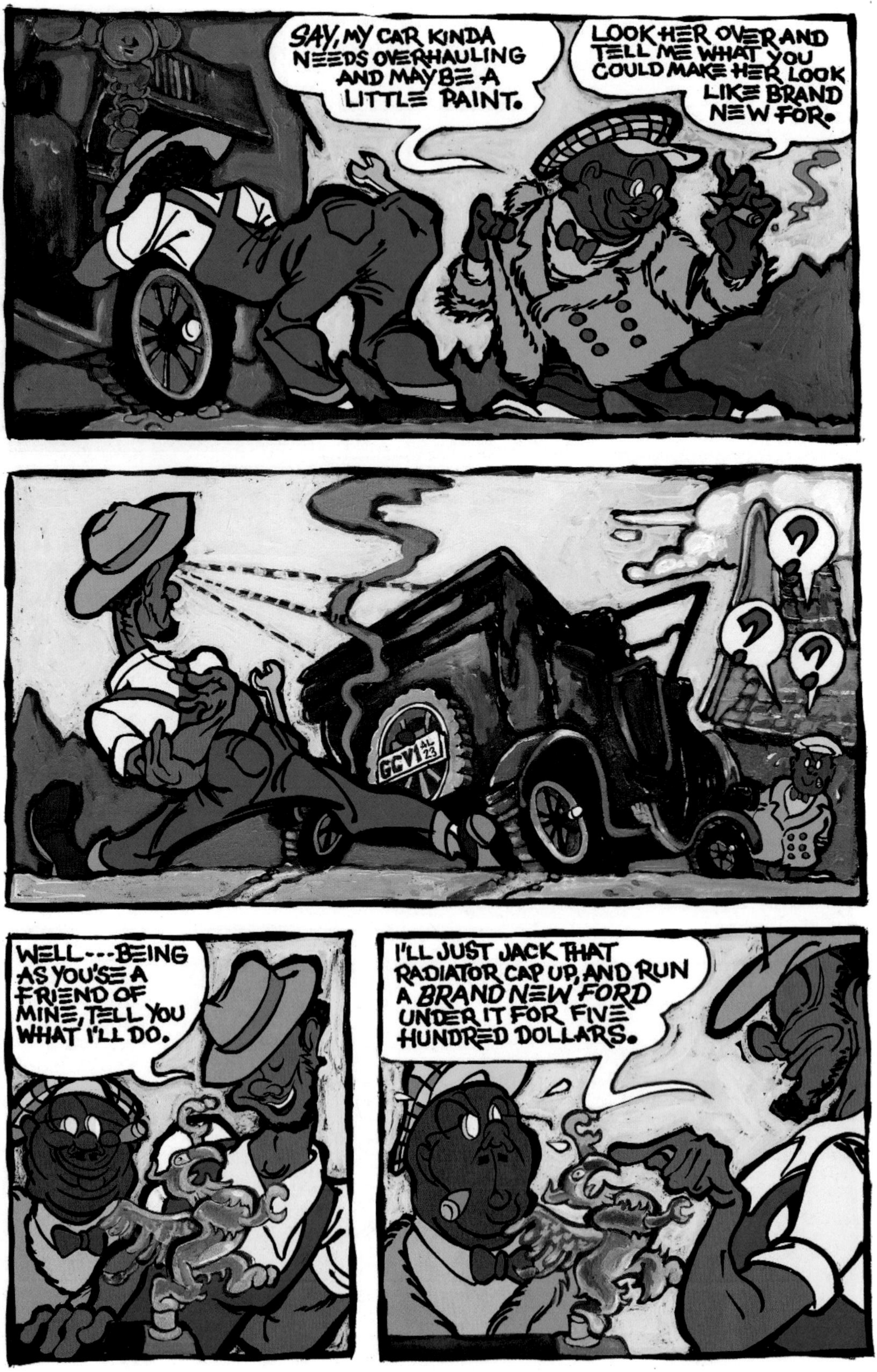
SAY, MY CAR KINDA NEEDS OVERHAULING AND MAYBE A LITTLE PAINT.
LOOK HER OVER AND TELL ME WHAT YOU COULD MAKE HER LOOK LIKE BRAND NEW FOR.
?
?
?
GCV1 AL 23
WELL---BEING AS YOU'SE A FRIEND OF MINE, TELL YOU WHAT I'LL DO.
I'LL JUST JACK THAT RADIATOR CAP UP, AND RUN A *BRAND NEW FORD* UNDER IT FOR FIVE HUNDRED DOLLARS.

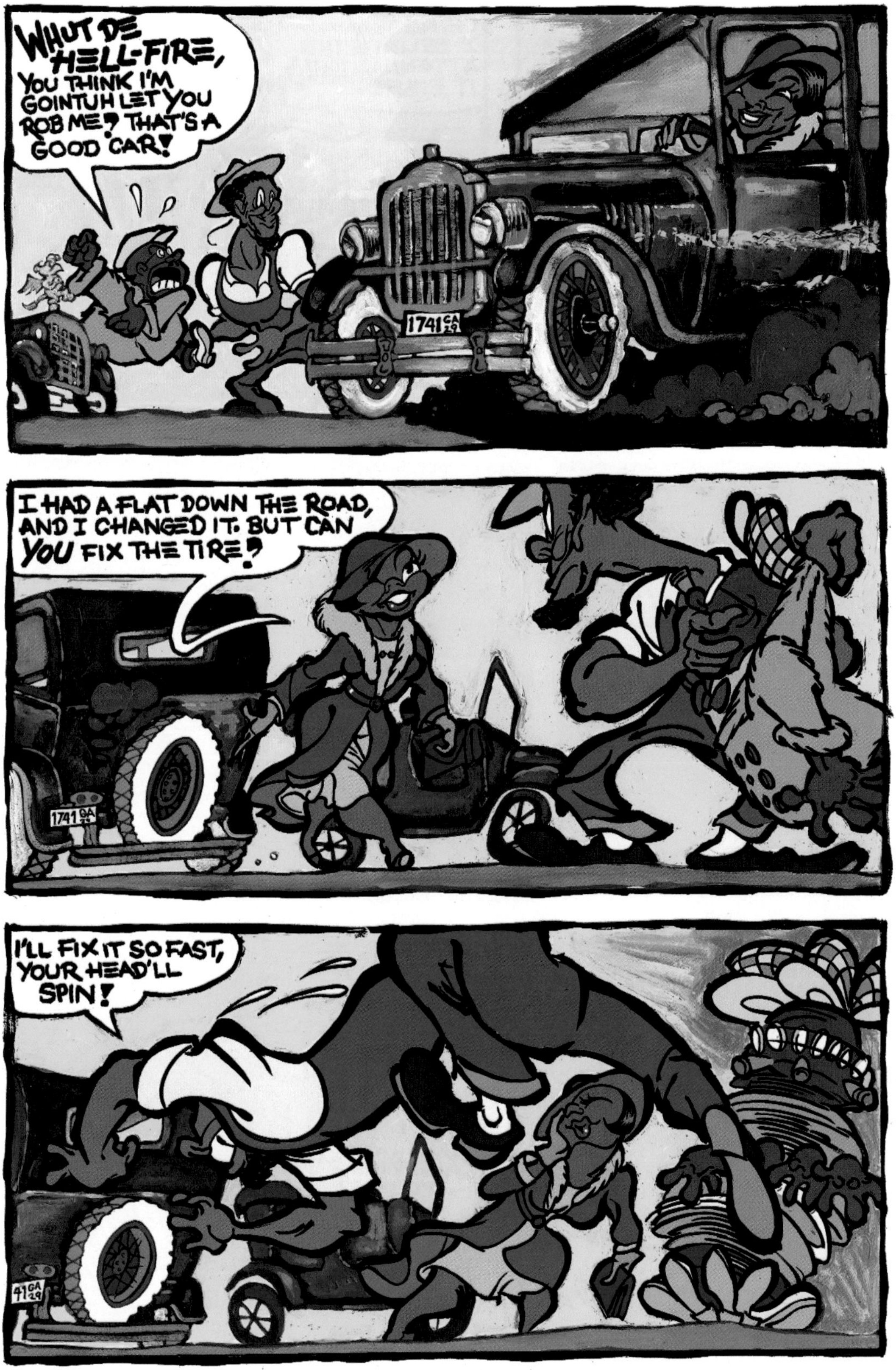
WHUT DE HELL-FIRE, YOU THINK I'M GOINTUH LET YOU ROB ME? THAT'S A GOOD CAR!
I HAD A FLAT DOWN THE ROAD, AND I CHANGED IT. BUT CAN YOU FIX THE TIRE?
I'LL FIX IT SO FAST, YOUR HEAD'LL SPIN!

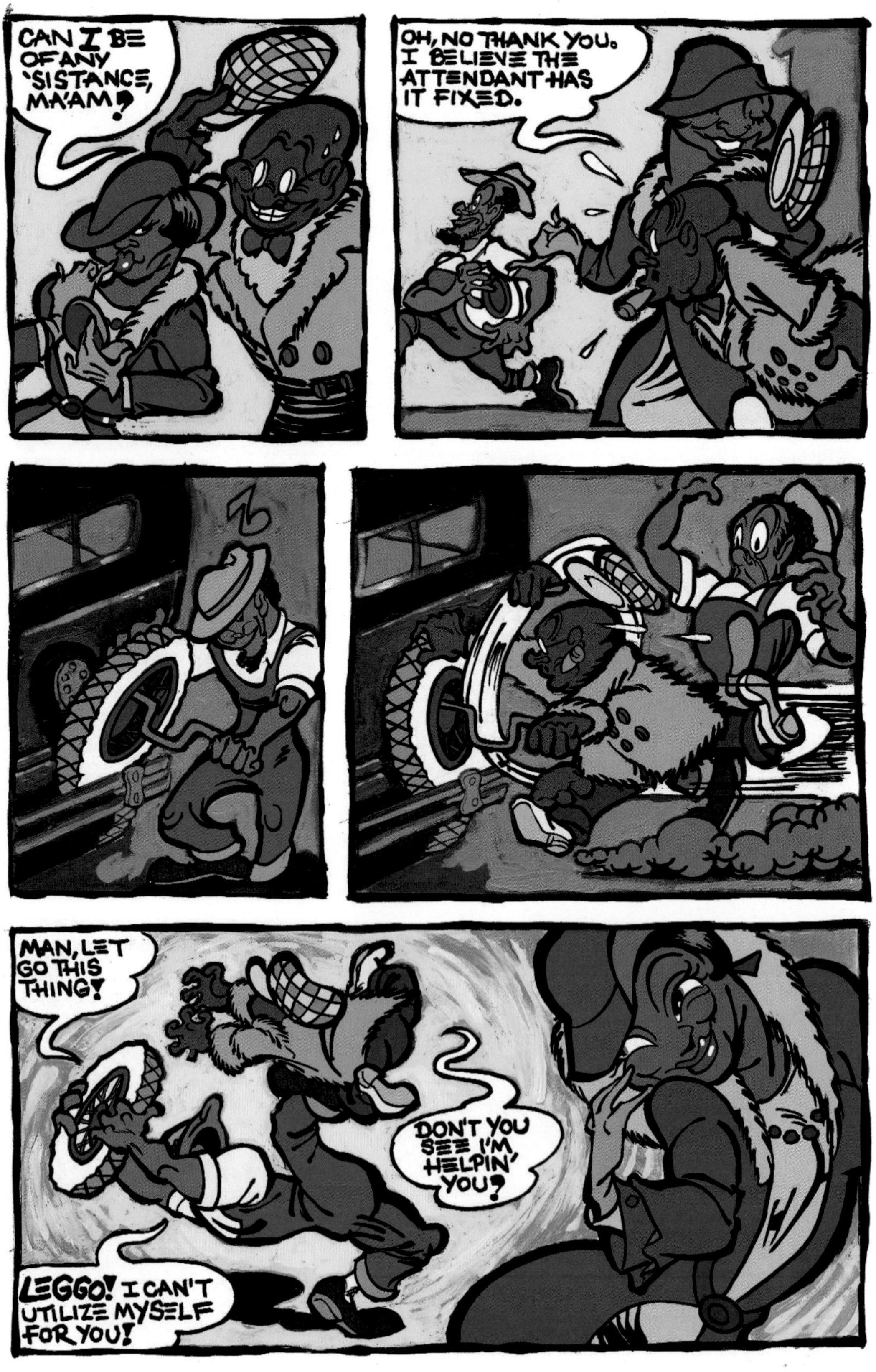
CAN I BE OF ANY 'SISTANCE, MA'AM?
OH, NO THANK YOU. I BELIEVE THE ATTENDANT HAS IT FIXED.
MAN, LET GO THIS THING!
DON'T YOU SEE I'M HELPIN' YOU?
LEGGO! I CAN'T UTILIZE MYSELF FOR YOU!

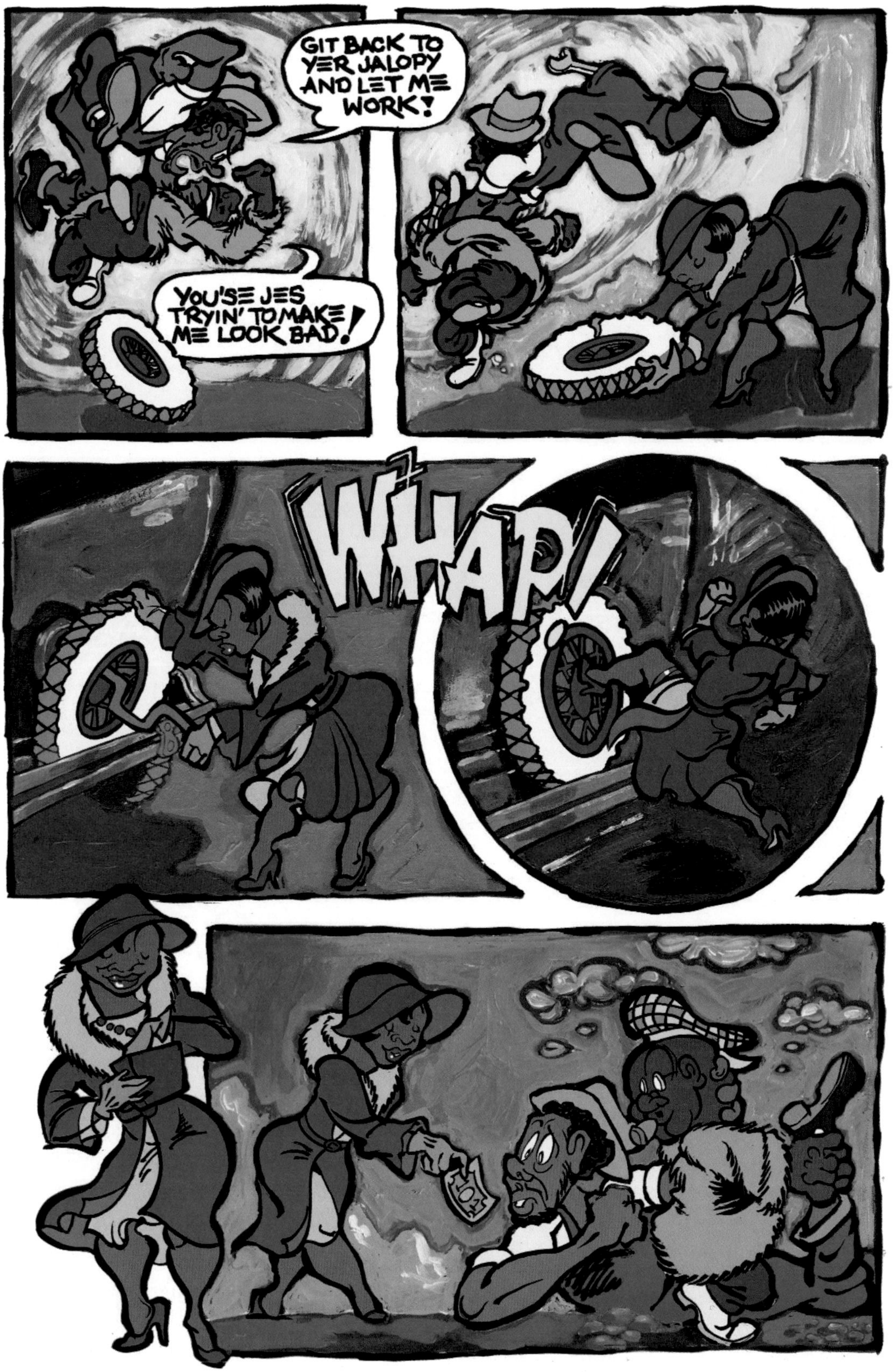
GIT BACK TO YER JALOPY AND LET ME WORK!
YOU'SE JES TRYIN' TO MAKE ME LOOK BAD!
WHAP!

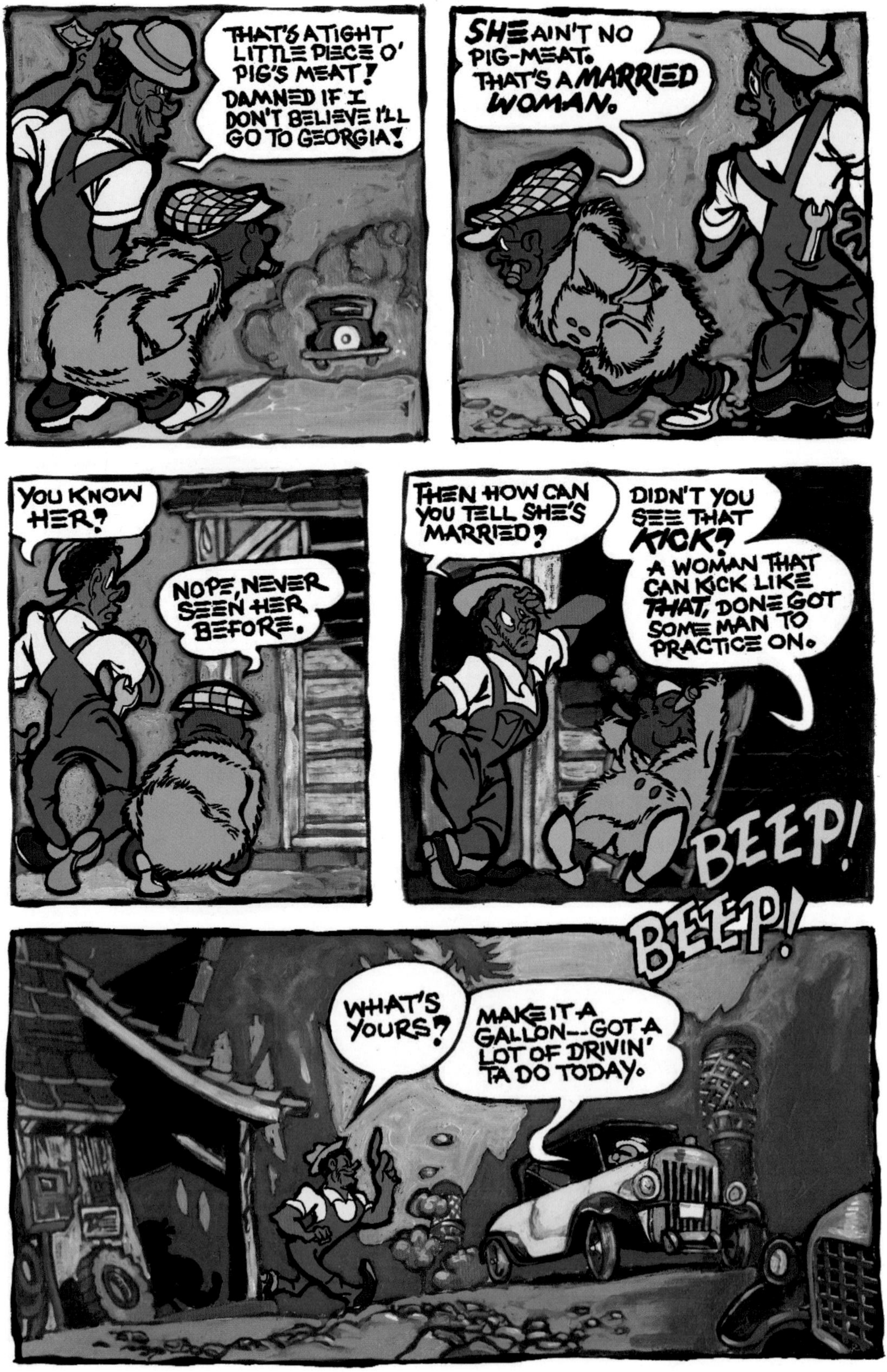
THAT'S A TIGHT LITTLE PIECE O' PIG'S MEAT! DAMNED IF I DON'T BELIEVE I'LL GO TO GEORGIA!
SHE AIN'T NO PIG-MEAT. THAT'S A MARRIED WOMAN.
YOU KNOW HER?
NOPE, NEVER SEEN HER BEFORE.
THEN HOW CAN YOU TELL SHE'S MARRIED?
DIDN'T YOU SEE THAT KICK? A WOMAN THAT CAN KICK LIKE THAT, DONE GOT SOME MAN TO PRACTICE ON.
BEEP!
BEEP!
WHAT'S YOURS?
MAKE IT A GALLON--GOT A LOT OF DRIVIN' TA DO TODAY.

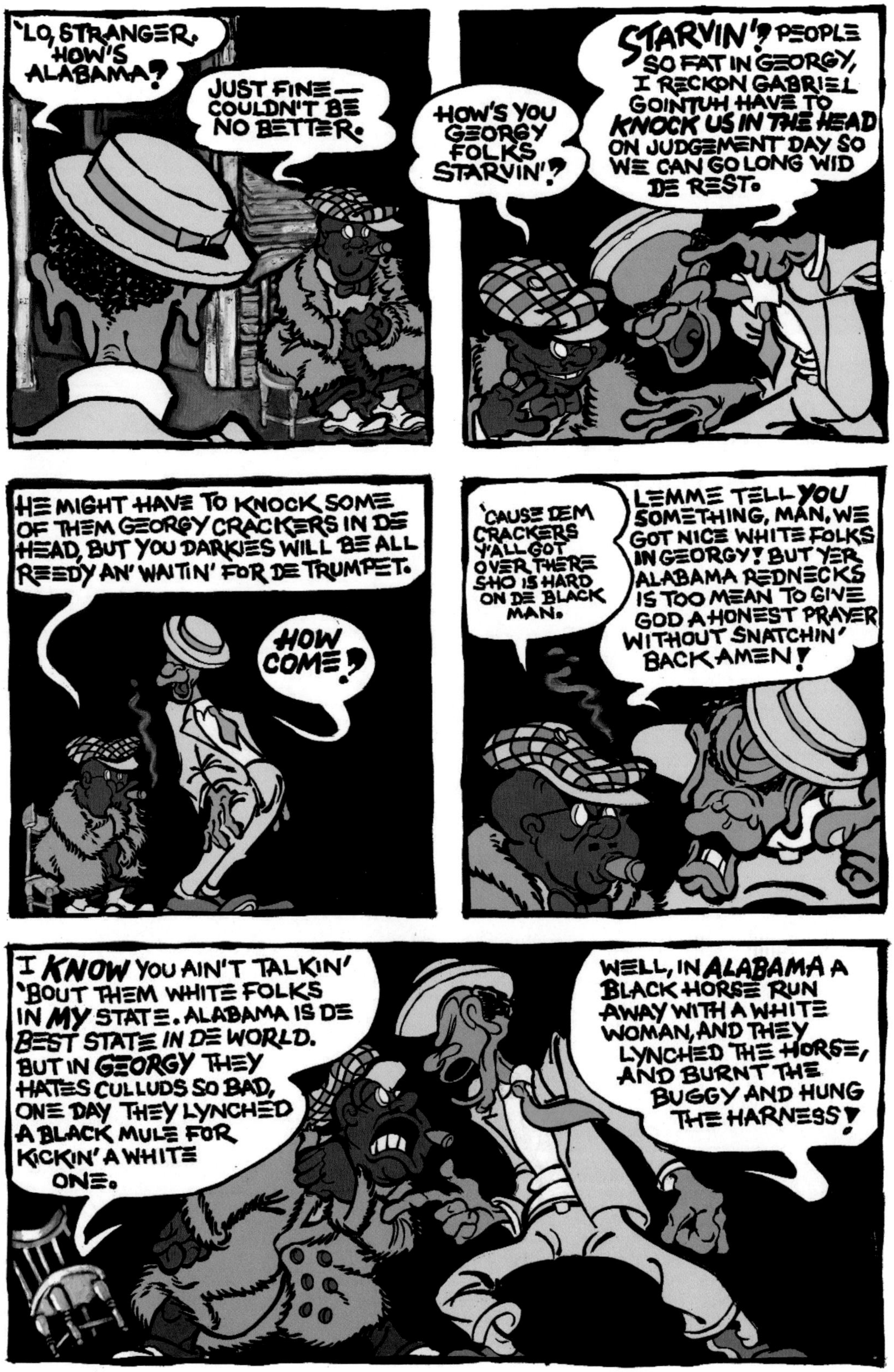
'LO, STRANGER. HOW'S ALABAMA?
JUST FINE— COULDN'T BE NO BETTER.
HOW'S YOU GEORGY FOLKS STARVIN'?
STARVIN'? PEOPLE SO FAT IN GEORGY, I RECKON GABRIEL GOINTUH HAVE TO KNOCK US IN THE HEAD ON JUDGEMENT DAY SO WE CAN GO LONG WID DE REST.
HE MIGHT HAVE TO KNOCK SOME OF THEM GEORGY CRACKERS IN DE HEAD, BUT YOU DARKIES WILL BE ALL REEDY AN' WAITIN' FOR DE TRUMPET.
HOW COME?
'CAUSE DEM CRACKERS Y'ALL GOT OVER THERE SHO IS HARD ON DE BLACK MAN.
LEMME TELL YOU SOMETHING, MAN. WE GOT NICE WHITE FOLKS IN GEORGY! BUT YER ALABAMA REDNECKS IS TOO MEAN TO GIVE GOD A HONEST PRAYER WITHOUT SNATCHIN' BACK AMEN!
I KNOW YOU AIN'T TALKIN' 'BOUT THEM WHITE FOLKS IN MY STATE. ALABAMA IS DE BEST STATE IN DE WORLD. BUT IN GEORGY THEY HATES CULLUDS SO BAD, ONE DAY THEY LYNCHED A BLACK MULE FOR KICKIN' A WHITE ONE.
WELL, IN ALABAMA A BLACK HORSE RUN AWAY WITH A WHITE WOMAN, AND THEY LYNCHED THE HORSE, AND BURNT THE BUGGY AND HUNG THE HARNESS!

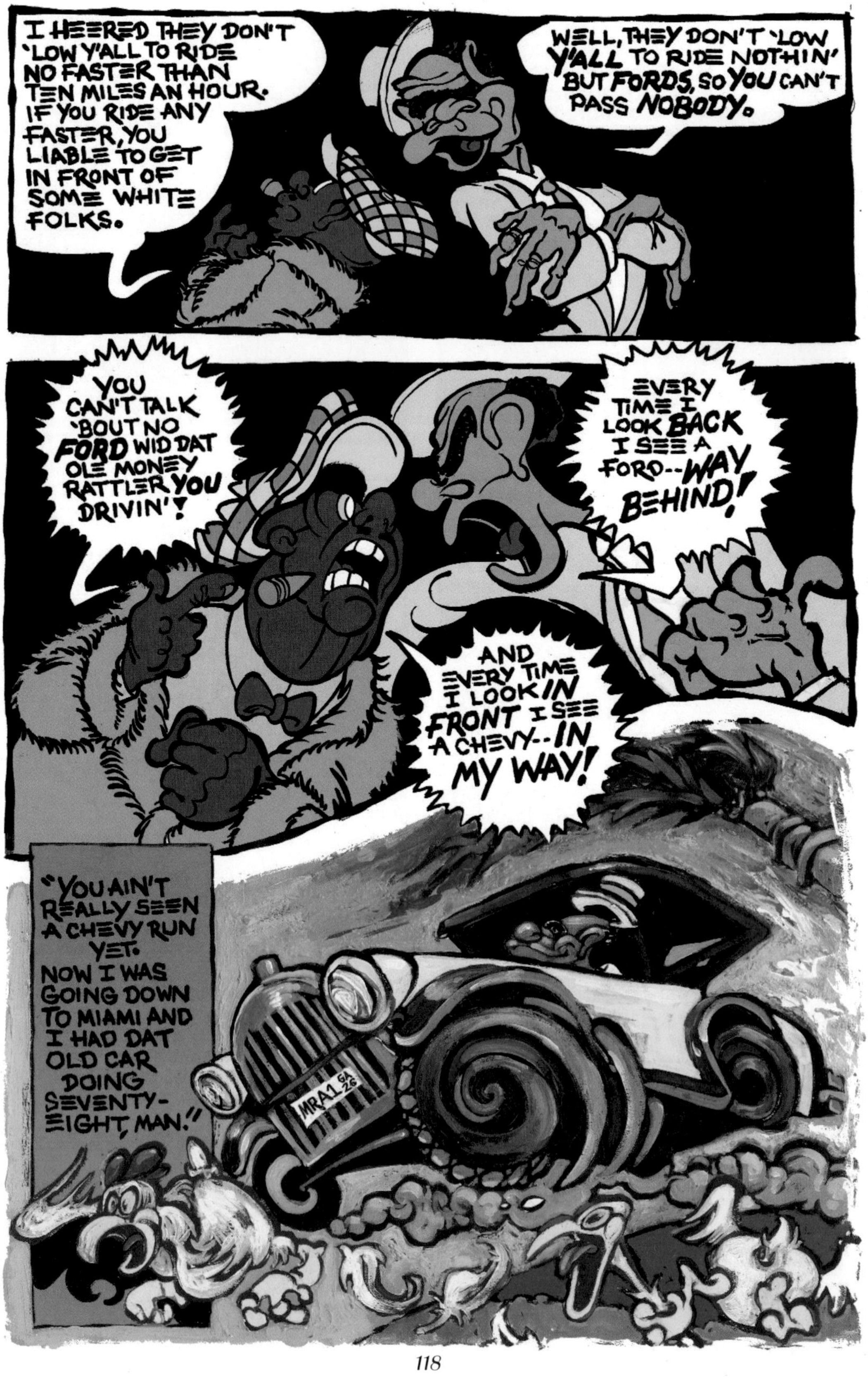
I HEERED THEY DON'T 'LOW Y'ALL TO RIDE NO FASTER THAN TEN MILES AN HOUR. IF YOU RIDE ANY FASTER, YOU LIABLE TO GET IN FRONT OF SOME WHITE FOLKS.
WELL, THEY DON'T 'LOW Y'ALL TO RIDE NOTHIN' BUT FORDS, SO YOU CAN'T PASS NOBODY.
YOU CAN'T TALK 'BOUT NO FORD WID DAT OLE MONEY RATTLER YOU DRIVIN'!
EVERY TIME I LOOK BACK I SEE A FORD--WAY BEHIND!
AND EVERY TIME I LOOK IN FRONT I SEE A CHEVY--IN MY WAY!
"YOU AIN'T REALLY SEEN A CHEVY RUN YET. NOW I WAS GOING DOWN TO MIAMI AND I HAD DAT OLD CAR DOING SEVENTY-EIGHT, MAN!"
MRA1 GA 26

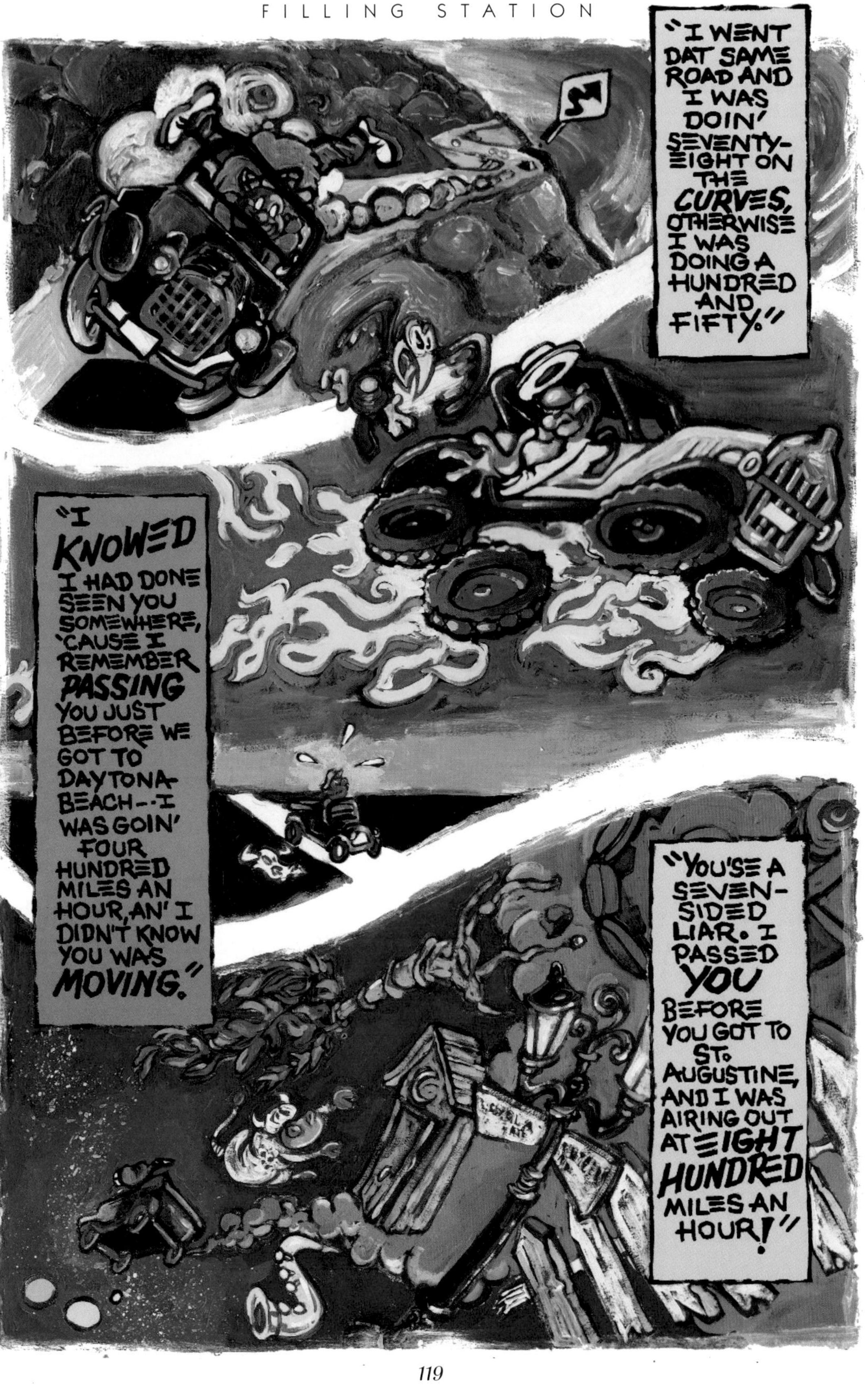
"I WENT DAT SAME ROAD AND I WAS DOIN' SEVENTY-EIGHT ON THE CURVES, OTHERWISE I WAS DOING A HUNDRED AND FIFTY."
"I KNOWED I HAD DONE SEEN YOU SOMEWHERE, 'CAUSE I REMEMBER PASSING YOU JUST BEFORE WE GOT TO DAYTONA BEACH--I WAS GOIN' FOUR HUNDRED MILES AN HOUR, AN' I DIDN'T KNOW YOU WAS MOVING."
"YOU'SE A SEVEN-SIDED LIAR. I PASSED YOU BEFORE YOU GOT TO ST. AUGUSTINE, AND I WAS AIRING OUT AT EIGHT HUNDRED MILES AN HOUR!"

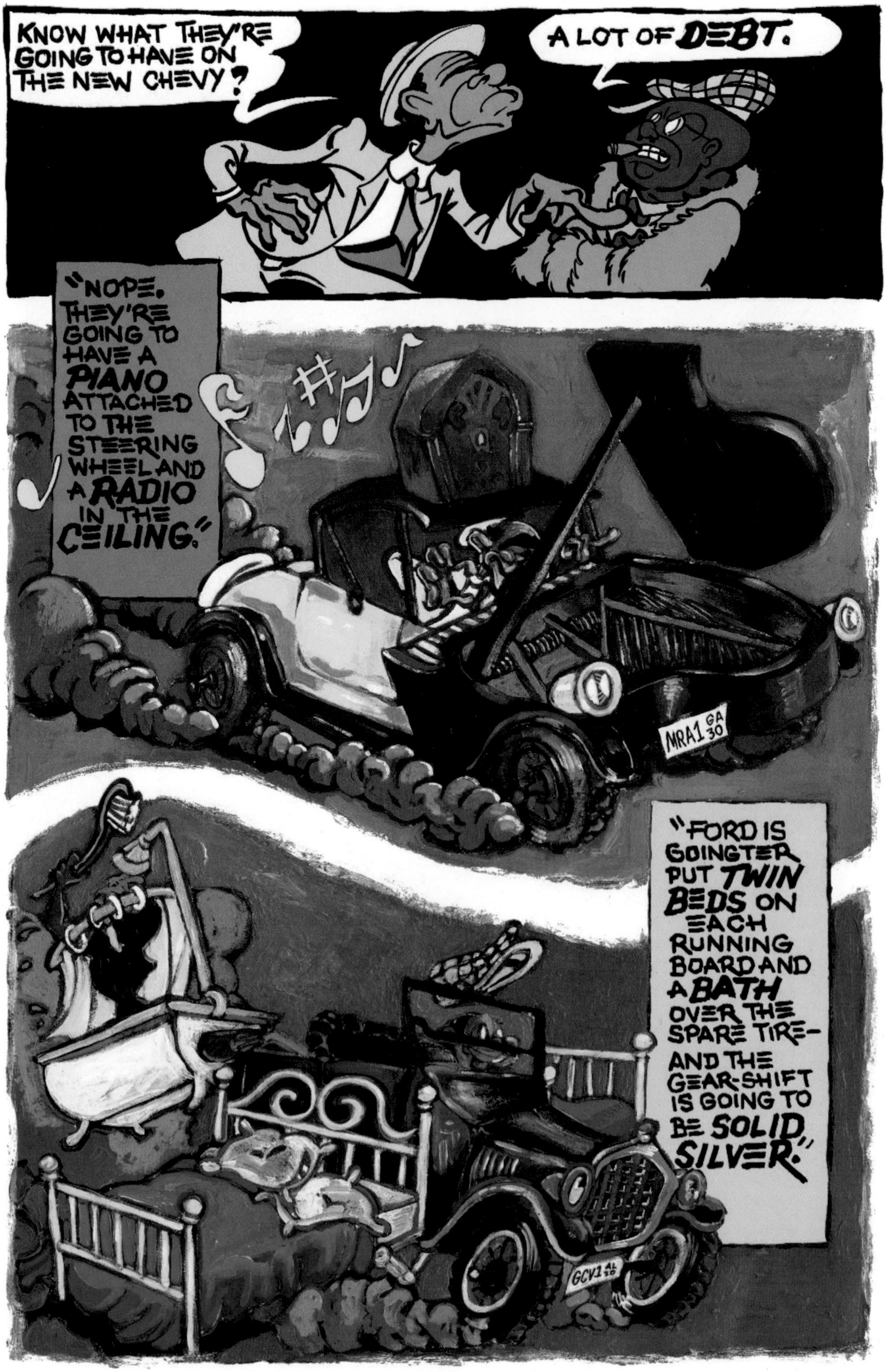
KNOW WHAT THEY'RE GOING TO HAVE ON THE NEW CHEVY?
A LOT OF DEBT.
"NOPE. THEY'RE GOING TO HAVE A PIANO ATTACHED TO THE STEERING WHEEL AND A RADIO IN THE CEILING."
MRA1 GA 30
"FORD IS GOINGTER PUT TWIN BEDS ON EACH RUNNING BOARD AND A BATH OVER THE SPARE TIRE— AND THE GEAR-SHIFT IS GOING TO BE SOLID SILVER."
GCV1

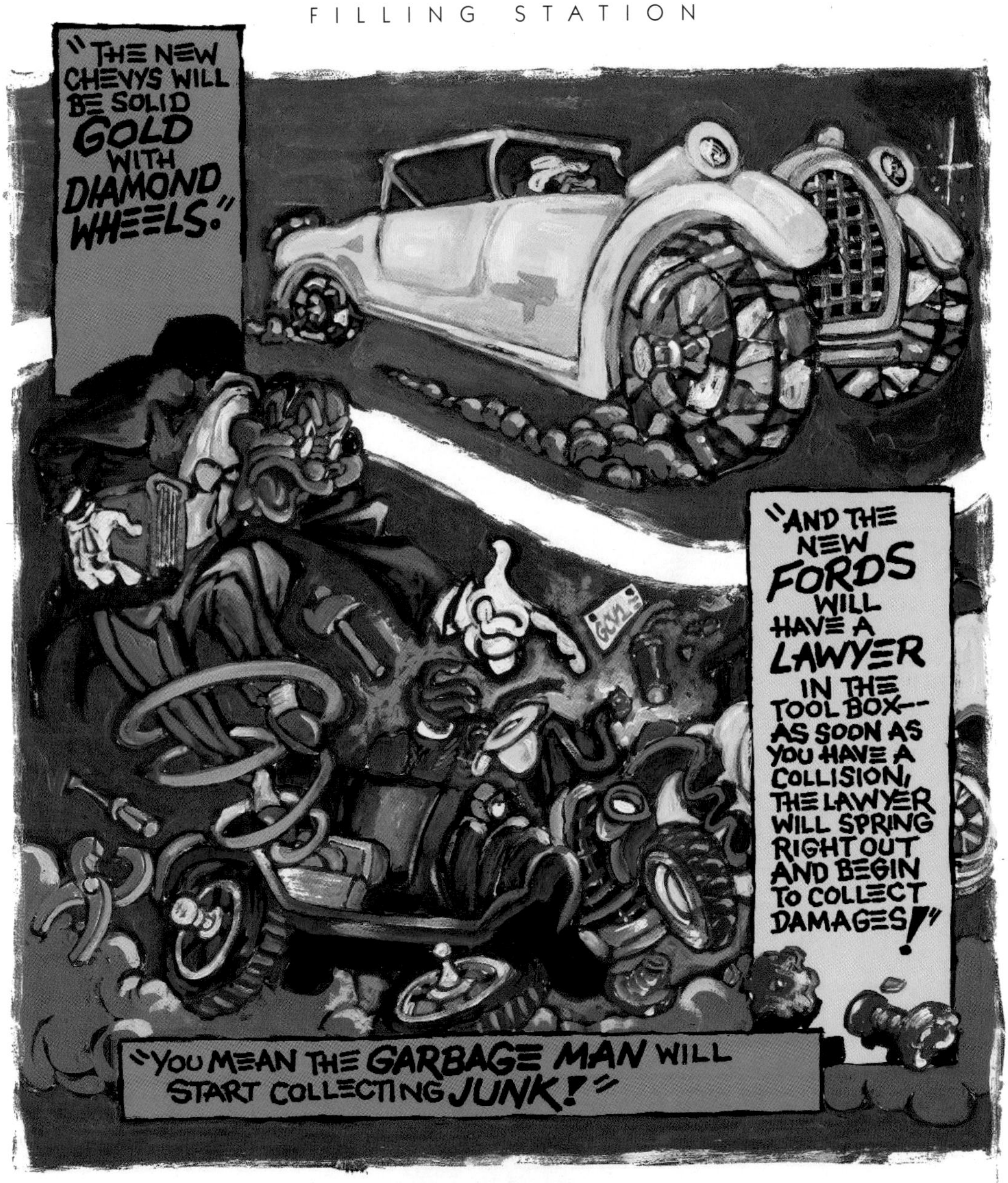
"THE NEW CHEVYS WILL BE SOLID GOLD WITH DIAMOND WHEELS."
"AND THE NEW FORDS WILL HAVE A LAWYER IN THE TOOL BOX-- AS SOON AS YOU HAVE A COLLISION, THE LAWYER WILL SPRING RIGHT OUT AND BEGIN TO COLLECT DAMAGES!"
"YOU MEAN THE GARBAGE MAN WILL START COLLECTING JUNK!"

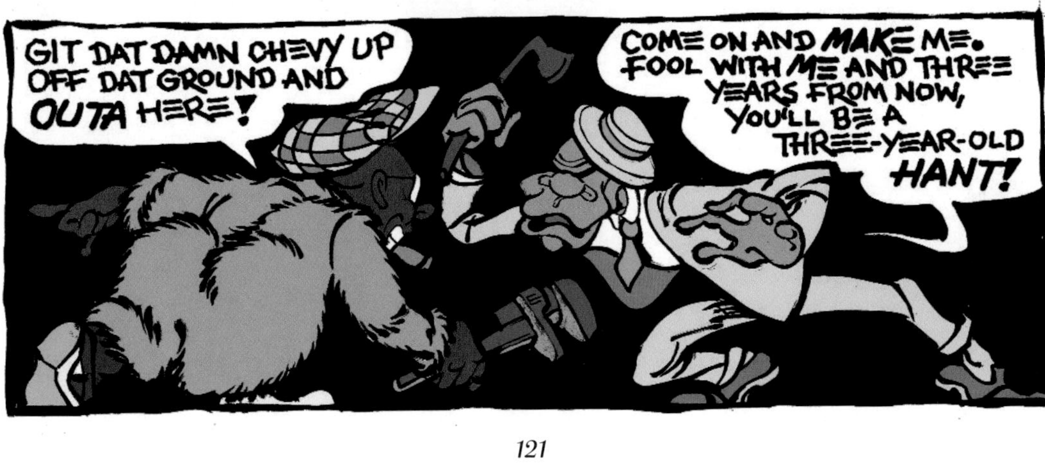
GIT DAT DAMN CHEVY UP OFF DAT GROUND AND OUTA HERE!
COME ON AND MAKE ME. FOOL WITH ME AND THREE YEARS FROM NOW, YOU'LL BE A THREE-YEAR-OLD HANT!

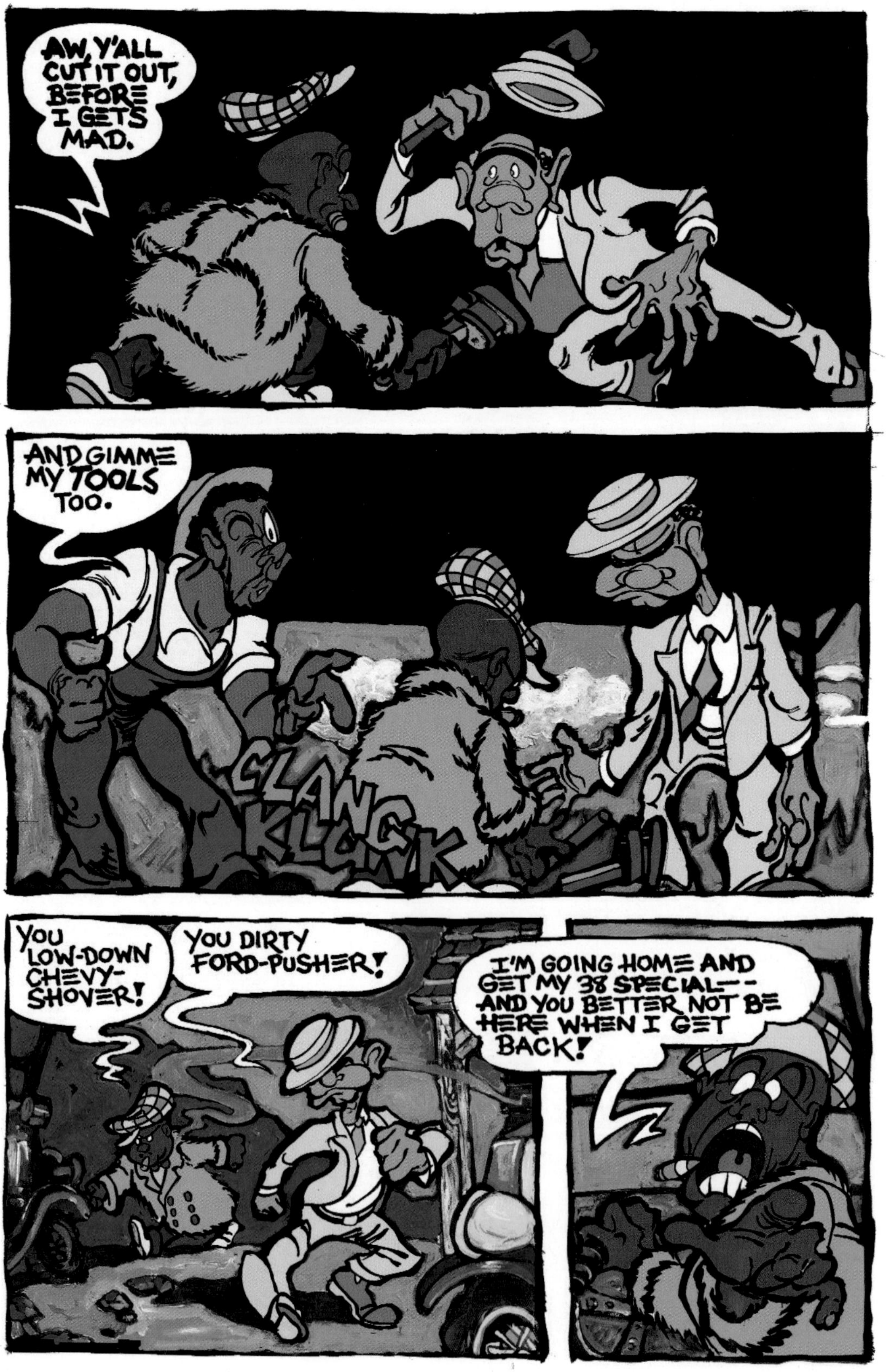
AW, Y'ALL CUT IT OUT, BEFORE I GETS MAD.
AND GIMME MY TOOLS TOO.
CLANG
KLUNK
YOU LOW-DOWN CHEVY-SHOVER!
YOU DIRTY FORD-PUSHER!
I'M GOING HOME AND GET MY 38 SPECIAL-- -AND YOU BETTER NOT BE HERE WHEN I GET BACK!

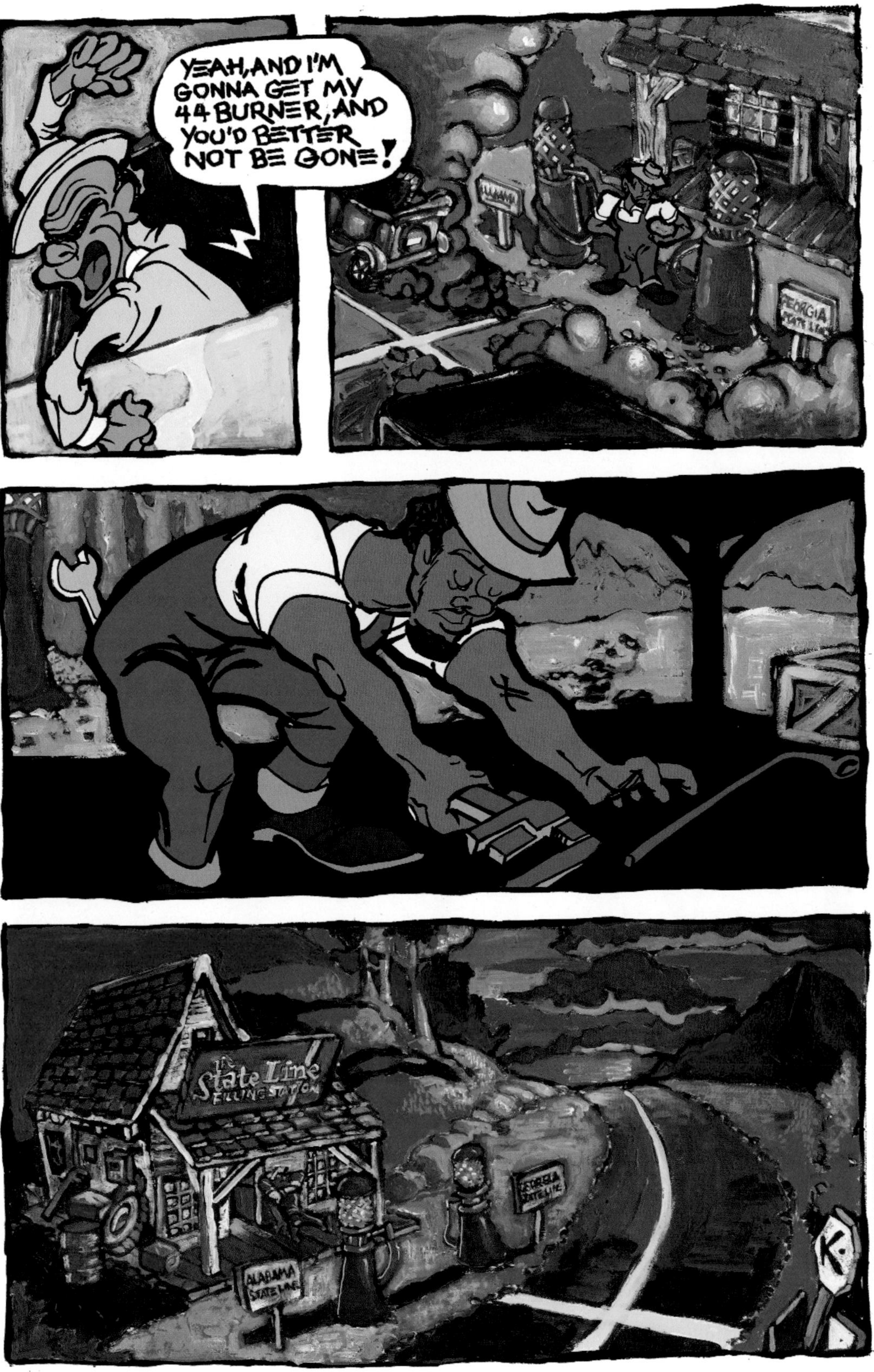
YEAH, AND I'M GONNA GET MY 44 BURNER, AND YOU'D BETTER NOT BE GONE!
State Line
FILLING STATION
ALABAMA STATE LINE

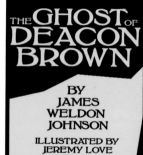

THE GHOST OF DEACON BROWN

BY
JAMES
WELDON
JOHNSON

ILLUSTRATED BY
JEREMY LOVE

1917

IN A BACKWOODS TOWN
LIVED DEACON BROWN,
AND HE WAS A MISER OLD;
HE WOULD TRUST NO BANK,
SO HE DUG, AND SANK
IN THE GROUND A BOX OF GOLD,
DOWN DEEP IN THE GROUND
A BOX OF GOLD.

HE HID HIS GOLD,
AS HAS BEEN TOLD,
HE REMEMBERED THAT HE DID IT;
BUT SAD TO SAY,
ON THE VERY NEXT DAY,
HE FORGOT JUST WHERE HE HID IT:
TO FIND HIS GOLD HE TRIED AND TRIED
TILL HE GREW FAINT AND SICK, AND DIED.

R.I.P.
DEACON
BROWN

THEN ON EACH DARK AND GLOOMY NIGHT
A FORM IN PHOSPHORESCENT WHITE,
A GENUINE HAIR-RAISING SIGHT,
WOULD WANDER THROUGH THE TOWN.
AND AS IT SLOWLY ROAMED AROUND,
WITH A SPADE IT DUG EACH FOOT OF GROUND;
SO THE FOLKS ABOUT
SAID THERE WAS NO DOUBT
'TWAS

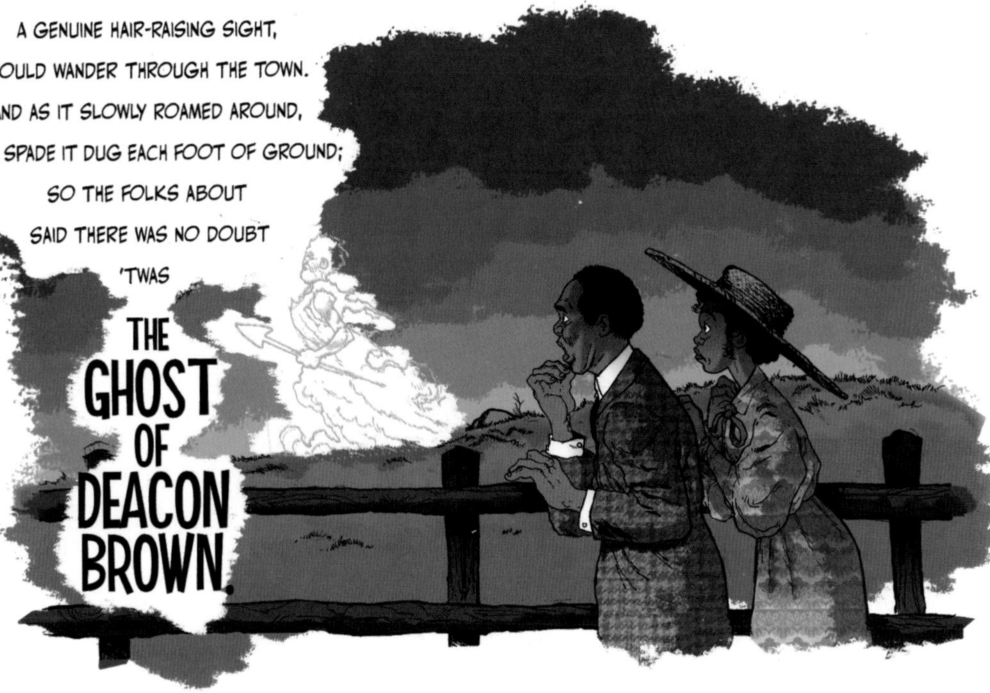

THE GHOST OF DEACON BROWN.

AROUND THE CHURCH
THIS GHOST WOULD SEARCH,
AND WHENEVER IT WOULD SEE
THE PASSERS-BY
TAKE WINGS AND FLY
IT WOULD LAUGH IN GHOSTLY GLEE,
HEE, HEE!
IT WOULD LAUGH IN GHOSTLY GLEE.

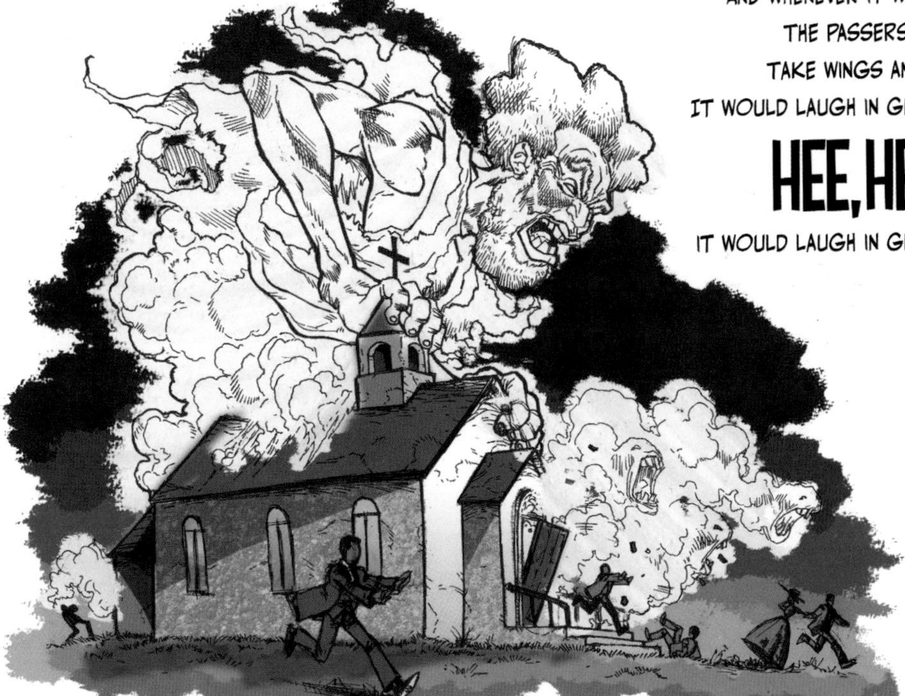

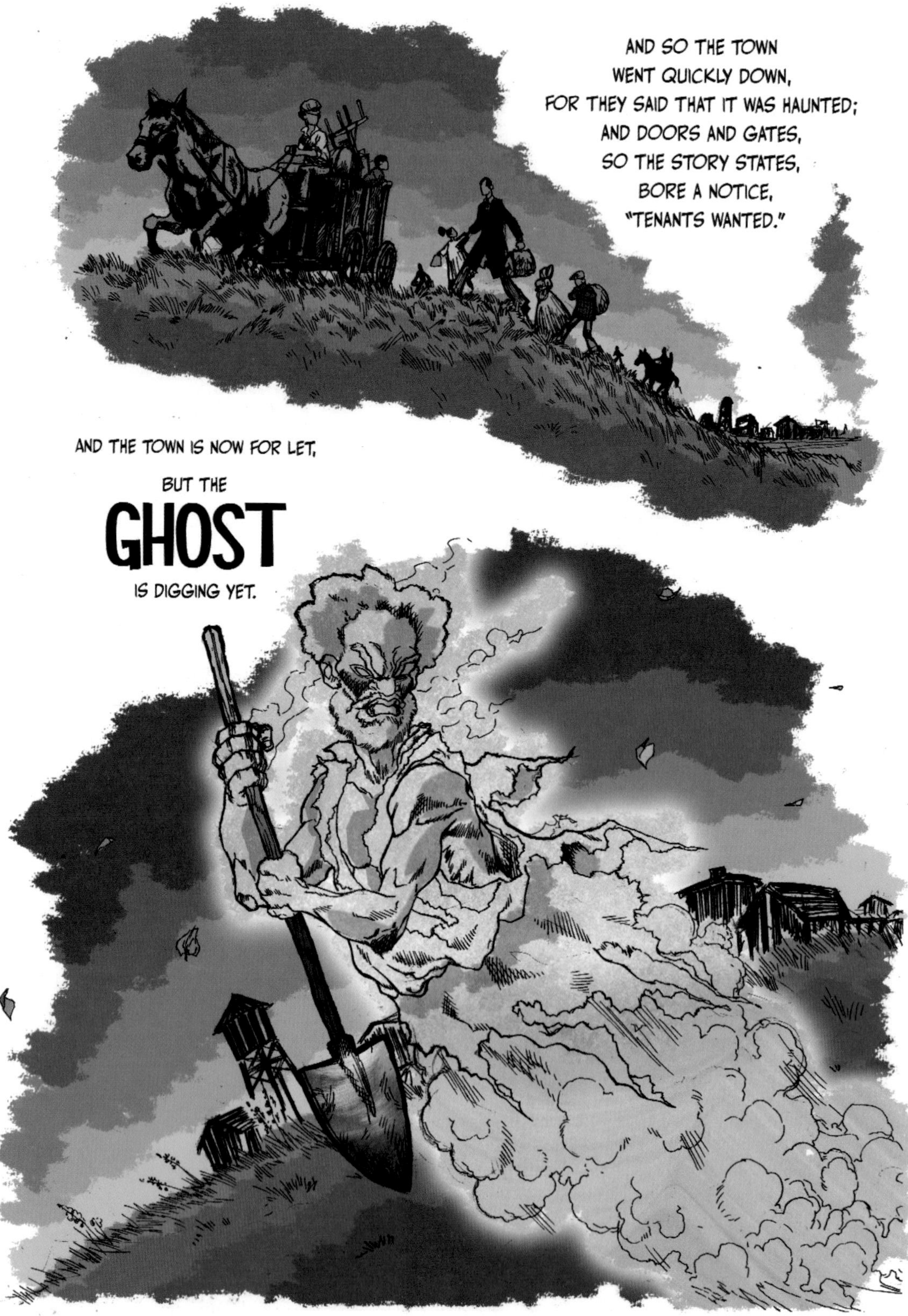
AND SO THE TOWN
WENT QUICKLY DOWN,
FOR THEY SAID THAT IT WAS HAUNTED;
AND DOORS AND GATES,
SO THE STORY STATES,
BORE A NOTICE,
"TENANTS WANTED."
AND THE TOWN IS NOW FOR LET,
BUT THE
GHOST
IS DIGGING YET.

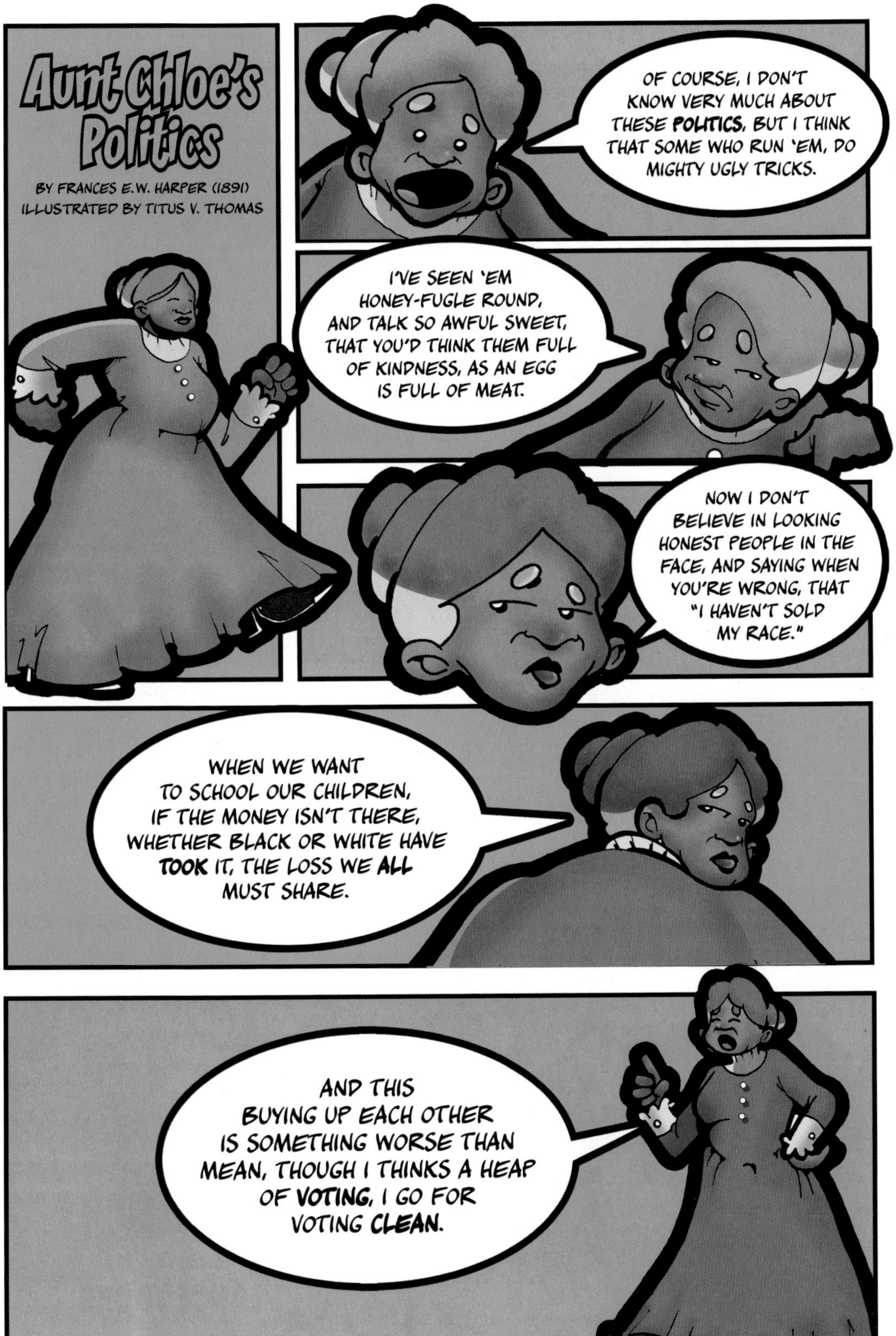
Aunt Chloe's Politics
BY FRANCES E.W. HARPER (1891)
ILLUSTRATED BY TITUS V. THOMAS
OF COURSE, I DON'T KNOW VERY MUCH ABOUT THESE POLITICS, BUT I THINK THAT SOME WHO RUN 'EM, DO MIGHTY UGLY TRICKS.
I'VE SEEN 'EM HONEY-FUGLE ROUND, AND TALK SO AWFUL SWEET, THAT YOU'D THINK THEM FULL OF KINDNESS, AS AN EGG IS FULL OF MEAT.
NOW I DON'T BELIEVE IN LOOKING HONEST PEOPLE IN THE FACE, AND SAYING WHEN YOU'RE WRONG, THAT "I HAVEN'T SOLD MY RACE."
WHEN WE WANT TO SCHOOL OUR CHILDREN, IF THE MONEY ISN'T THERE, WHETHER BLACK OR WHITE HAVE TOOK IT, THE LOSS WE ALL MUST SHARE.
AND THIS BUYING UP EACH OTHER IS SOMETHING WORSE THAN MEAN, THOUGH I THINKS A HEAP OF VOTING, I GO FOR VOTING CLEAN.

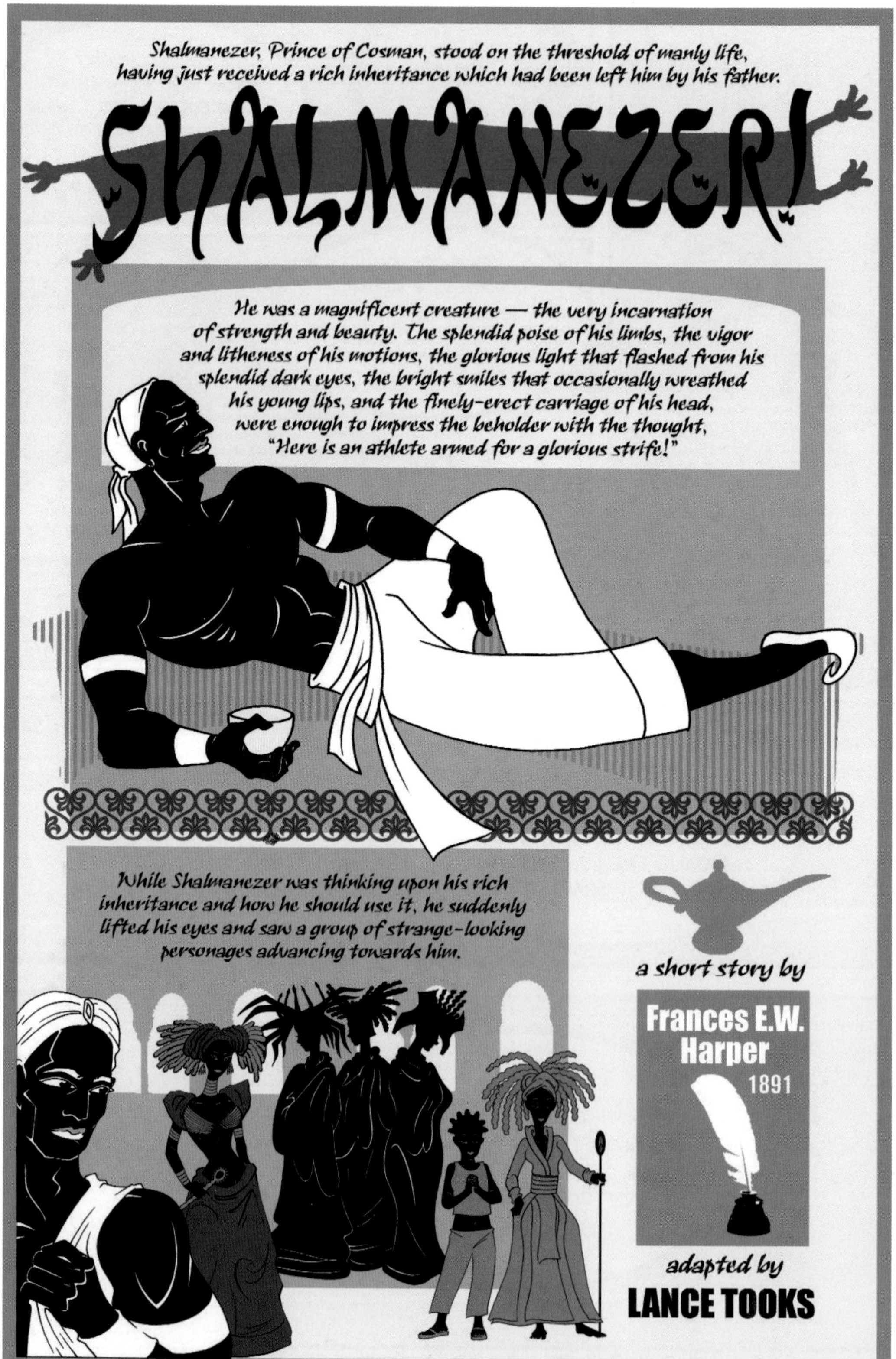
Shalmanezer, Prince of Cosman, stood on the threshold of manly life, having just received a rich inheritance which had been left him by his father.
SHALMANEZER!
He was a magnificent creature — the very incarnation of strength and beauty. The splendid poise of his limbs, the vigor and litheness of his motions, the glorious light that flashed from his splendid dark eyes, the bright smiles that occasionally wreathed his young lips, and the finely-erect carriage of his head, were enough to impress the beholder with the thought, "Here is an athlete armed for a glorious strife!"
While Shalmanezer was thinking upon his rich inheritance and how he should use it, he suddenly lifted his eyes and saw a group of strange-looking personages advancing towards him.
a short story by
Frances E.W. Harper
1891
adapted by
LANCE TOOKS

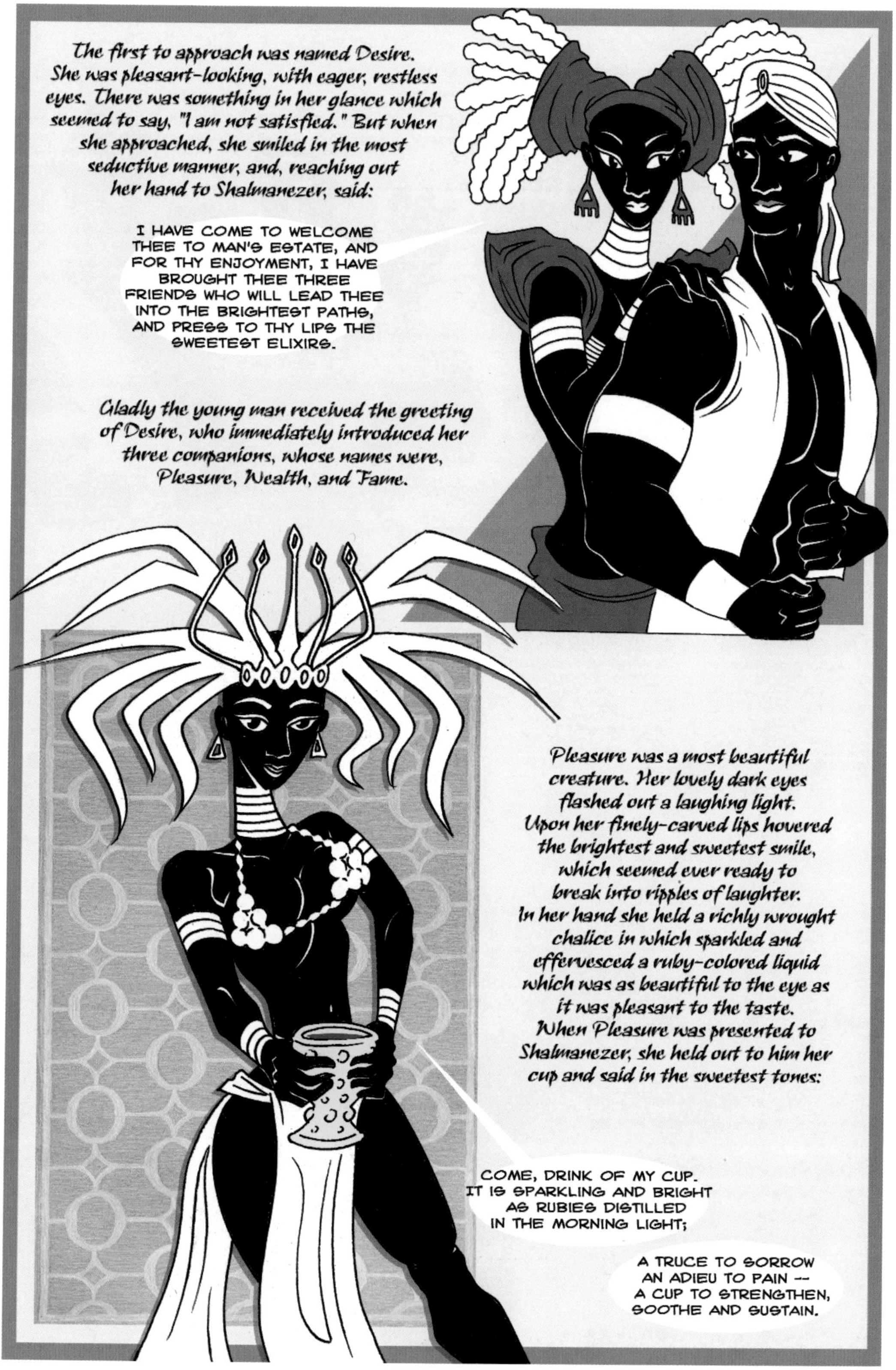
The first to approach was named Desire. She was pleasant-looking, with eager, restless eyes. There was something in her glance which seemed to say, "I am not satisfied." But when she approached, she smiled in the most seductive manner, and, reaching out her hand to Shalmanezer, said:
I HAVE COME TO WELCOME THEE TO MAN'S ESTATE, AND FOR THY ENJOYMENT, I HAVE BROUGHT THEE THREE FRIENDS WHO WILL LEAD THEE INTO THE BRIGHTEST PATHS, AND PRESS TO THY LIPS THE SWEETEST ELIXIRS.
Gladly the young man received the greeting of Desire, who immediately introduced her three companions, whose names were, Pleasure, Wealth, and Fame.
Pleasure was a most beautiful creature. Her lovely dark eyes flashed out a laughing light. Upon her finely-carved lips hovered the brightest and sweetest smile, which seemed ever ready to break into ripples of laughter. In her hand she held a richly wrought chalice in which sparkled and effervesced a ruby-colored liquid which was as beautiful to the eye as it was pleasant to the taste. When Pleasure was presented to Shalmanezer, she held out to him her cup and said in the sweetest tones:
COME, DRINK OF MY CUP. IT IS SPARKLING AND BRIGHT AS RUBIES DISTILLED IN THE MORNING LIGHT;
A TRUCE TO SORROW AN ADIEU TO PAIN -- A CUP TO STRENGTHEN, SOOTHE AND SUSTAIN.

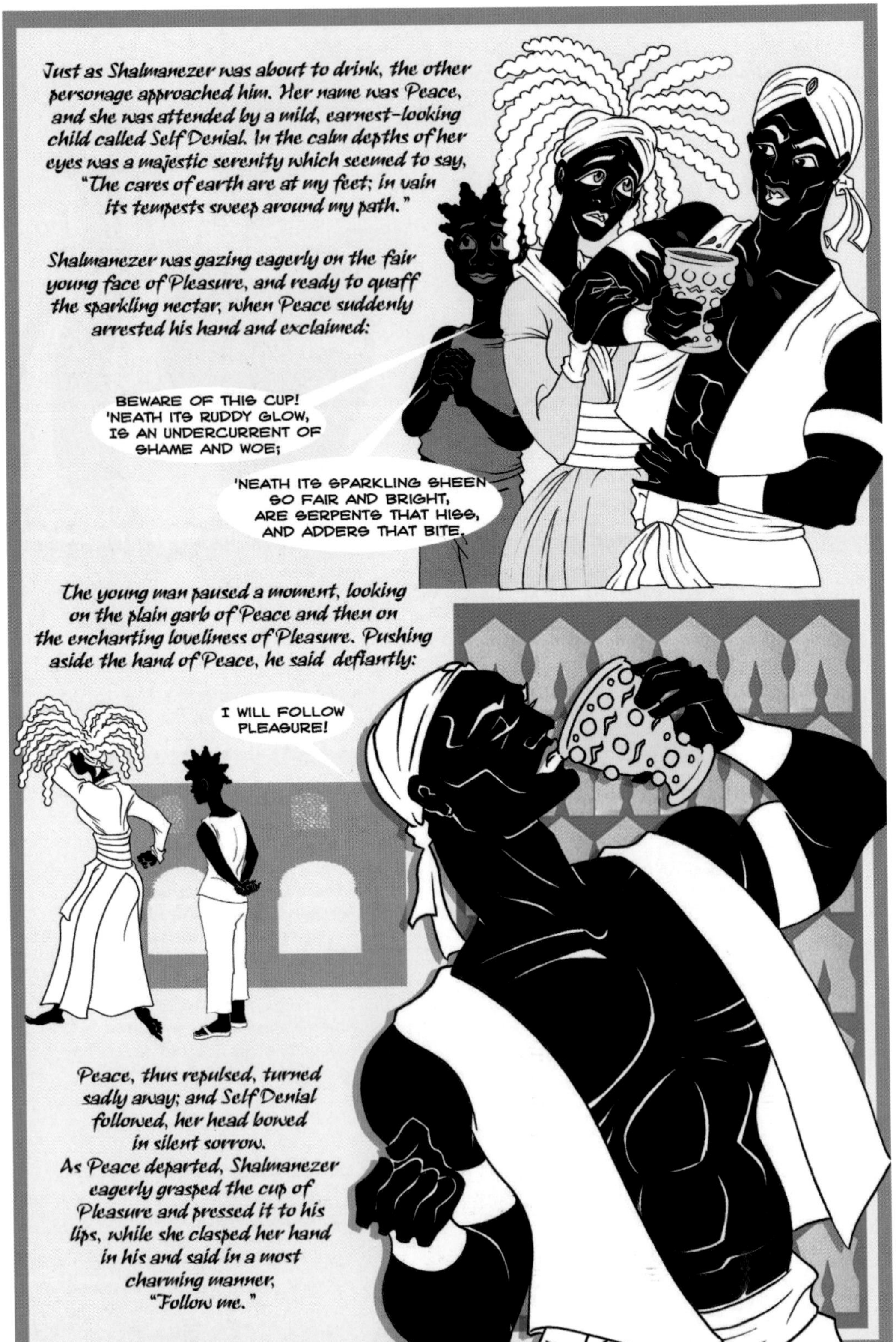
Just as Shalmanezer was about to drink, the other personage approached him. Her name was Peace, and she was attended by a mild, earnest-looking child called Self Denial. In the calm depths of her eyes was a majestic serenity which seemed to say, "The cares of earth are at my feet; in vain its tempests sweep around my path."
Shalmanezer was gazing eagerly on the fair young face of Pleasure, and ready to quaff the sparkling nectar, when Peace suddenly arrested his hand and exclaimed:
BEWARE OF THIS CUP! 'NEATH ITS RUDDY GLOW, IS AN UNDERCURRENT OF SHAME AND WOE;
'NEATH ITS SPARKLING SHEEN SO FAIR AND BRIGHT, ARE SERPENTS THAT HISS, AND ADDERS THAT BITE.
The young man paused a moment, looking on the plain garb of Peace and then on the enchanting loveliness of Pleasure. Pushing aside the hand of Peace, he said defiantly:
I WILL FOLLOW PLEASURE!
Peace, thus repulsed, turned sadly away; and Self Denial followed, her head bowed in silent sorrow.
As Peace departed, Shalmanezer eagerly grasped the cup of Pleasure and pressed it to his lips, while she clasped her hand in his and said in a most charming manner, "Follow me."

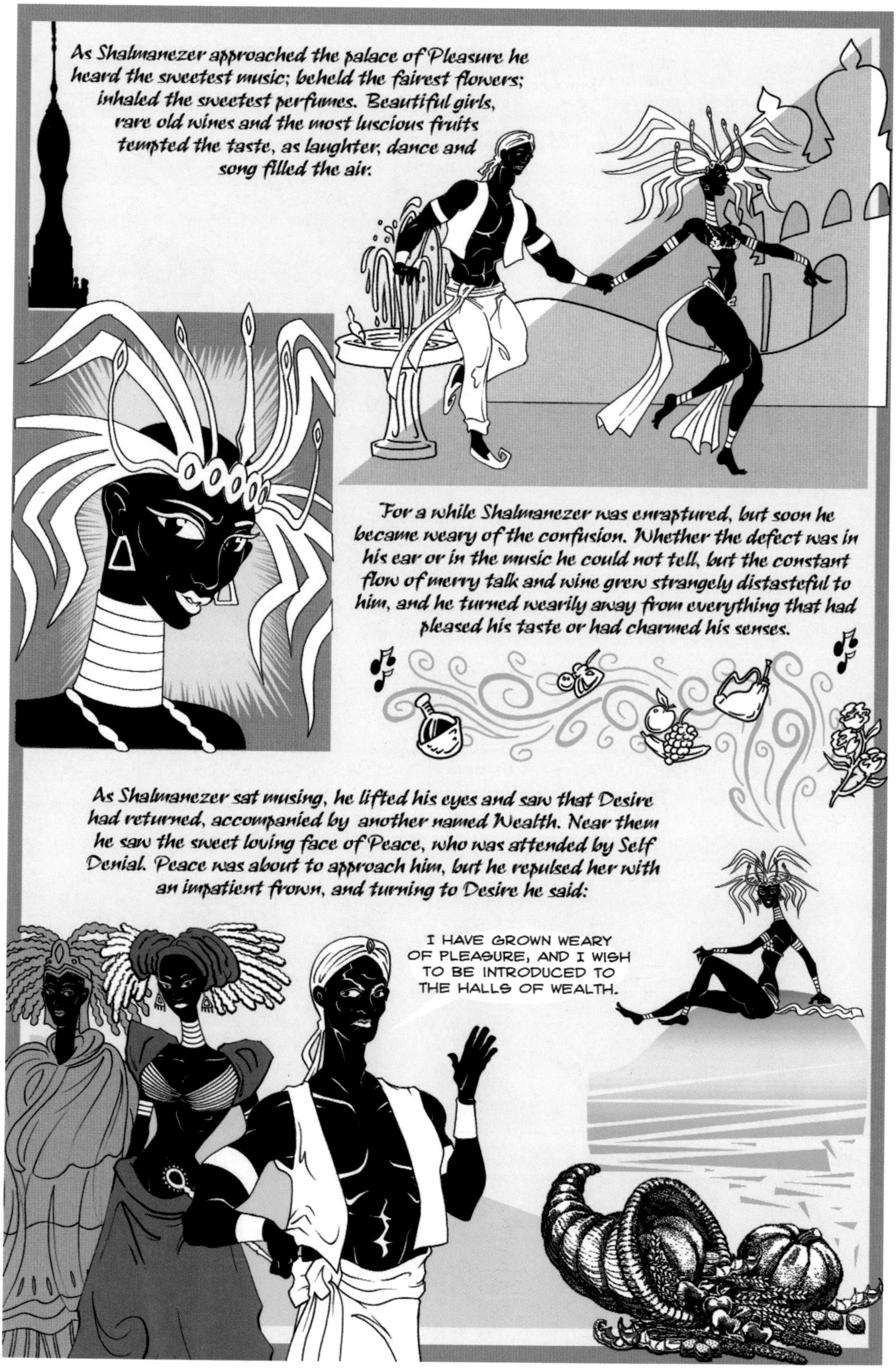
As Shalmanezer approached the palace of Pleasure he heard the sweetest music; beheld the fairest flowers; inhaled the sweetest perfumes. Beautiful girls, rare old wines and the most luscious fruits tempted the taste, as laughter, dance and song filled the air.
For a while Shalmanezer was enraptured, but soon he became weary of the confusion. Whether the defect was in his ear or in the music he could not tell, but the constant flow of merry talk and wine grew strangely distasteful to him, and he turned wearily away from everything that had pleased his taste or had charmed his senses.
As Shalmanezer sat musing, he lifted his eyes and saw that Desire had returned, accompanied by another named Wealth. Near them he saw the sweet loving face of Peace, who was attended by Self Denial. Peace was about to approach him, but he repulsed her with an impatient frown, and turning to Desire he said:
I HAVE GROWN WEARY OF PLEASURE, AND I WISH TO BE INTRODUCED TO THE HALLS OF WEALTH.

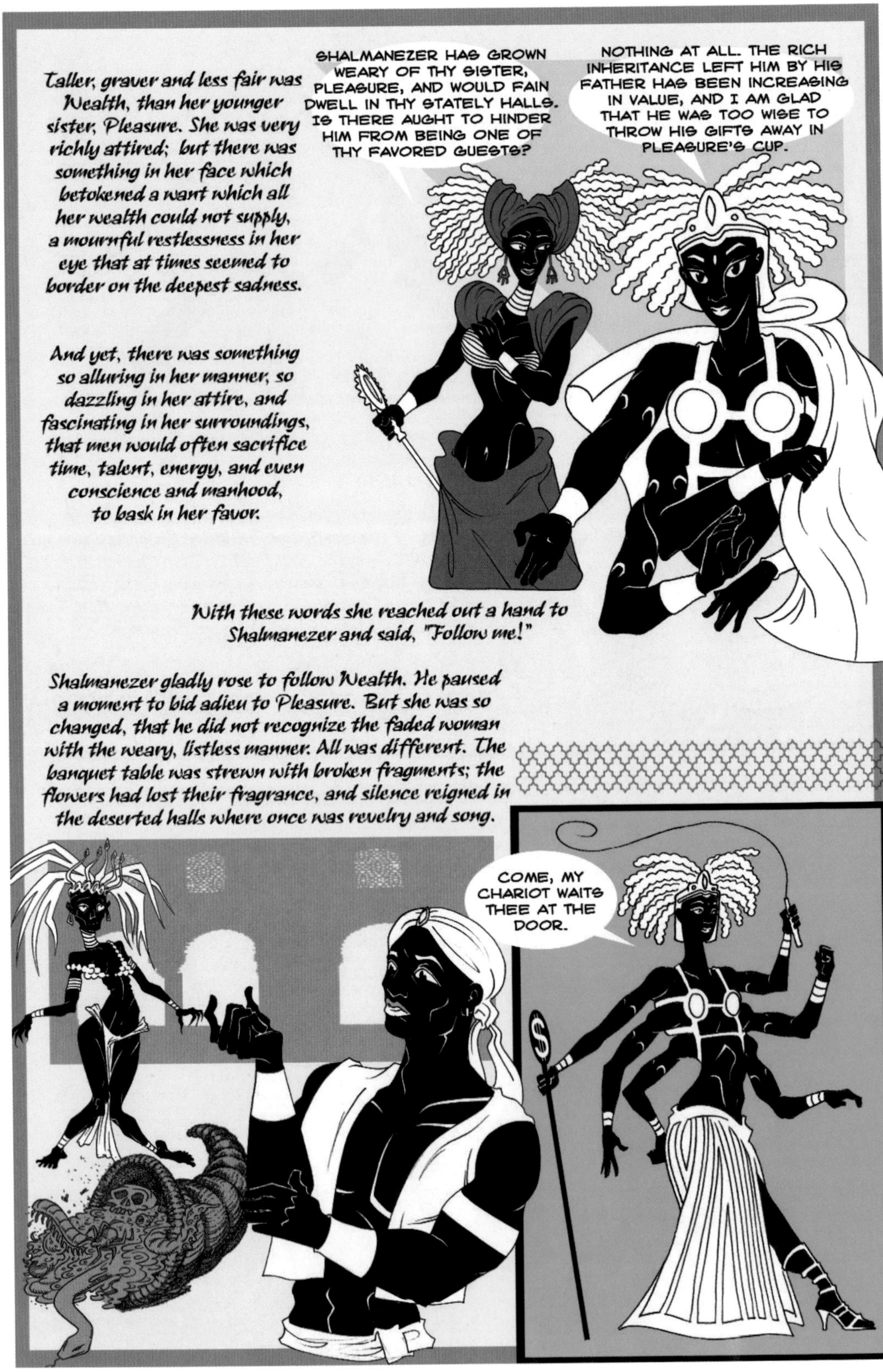
Taller, graver and less fair was Wealth, than her younger sister, Pleasure. She was very richly attired; but there was something in her face which betokened a want which all her wealth could not supply, a mournful restlessness in her eye that at times seemed to border on the deepest sadness.
SHALMANEZER HAS GROWN WEARY OF THY SISTER, PLEASURE, AND WOULD FAIN DWELL IN THY STATELY HALLS. IS THERE AUGHT TO HINDER HIM FROM BEING ONE OF THY FAVORED GUESTS?
NOTHING AT ALL. THE RICH INHERITANCE LEFT HIM BY HIS FATHER HAS BEEN INCREASING IN VALUE, AND I AM GLAD THAT HE WAS TOO WISE TO THROW HIS GIFTS AWAY IN PLEASURE'S CUP.
And yet, there was something so alluring in her manner, so dazzling in her attire, and fascinating in her surroundings, that men would often sacrifice time, talent, energy, and even conscience and manhood, to bask in her favor.
With these words she reached out a hand to Shalmanezer and said, "Follow me!"
Shalmanezer gladly rose to follow Wealth. He paused a moment to bid adieu to Pleasure. But she was so changed, that he did not recognize the faded woman with the weary, listless manner. All was different. The banquet table was strewn with broken fragments; the flowers had lost their fragrance, and silence reigned in the deserted halls where once was revelry and song.
COME, MY CHARIOT WAITS THEE AT THE DOOR.
$

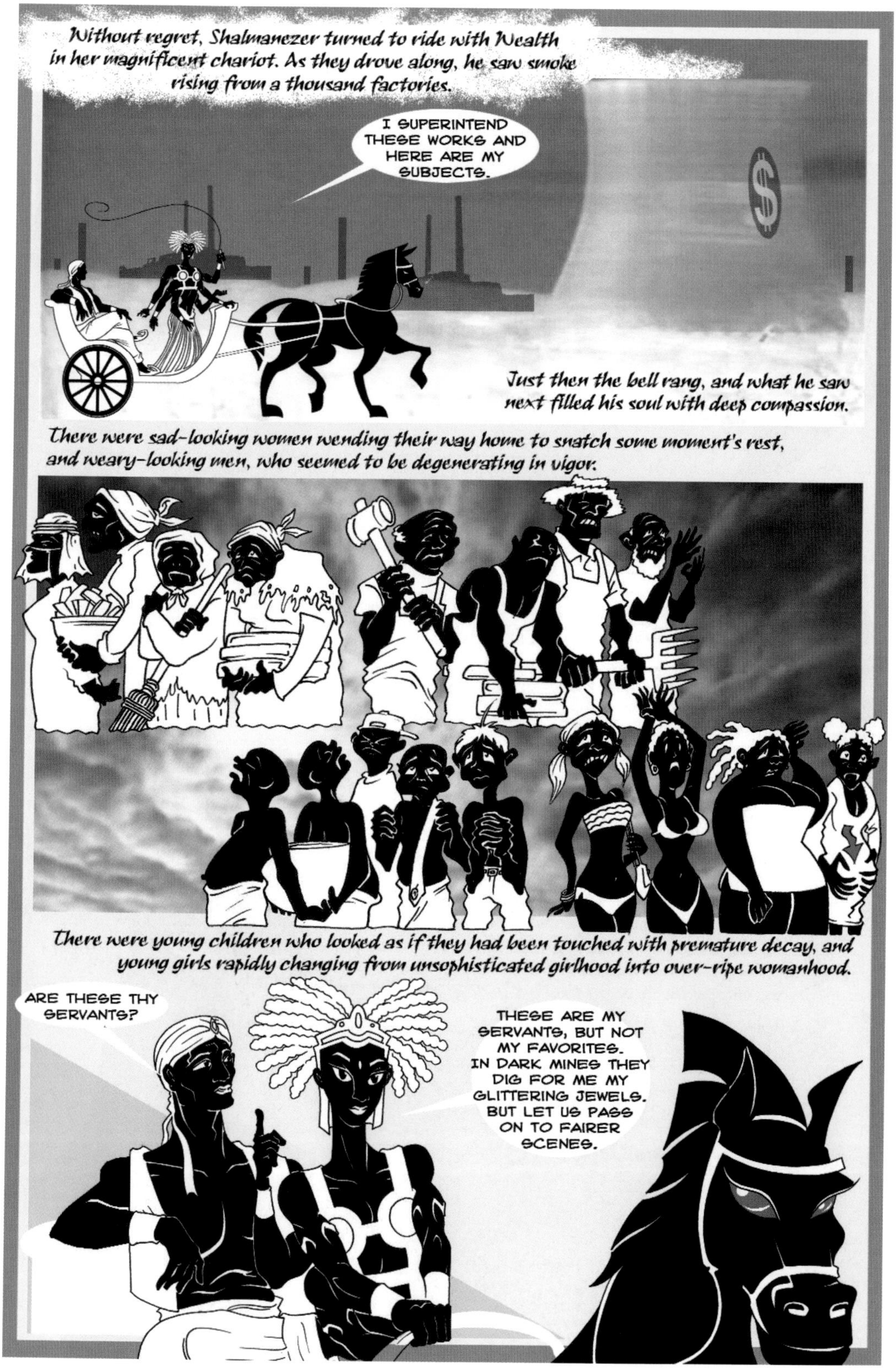
Without regret, Shalmanezer turned to ride with Wealth in her magnificent chariot. As they drove along, he saw smoke rising from a thousand factories.
I SUPERINTEND THESE WORKS AND HERE ARE MY SUBJECTS.
$
Just then the bell rang, and what he saw next filled his soul with deep compassion.
There were sad-looking women wending their way home to snatch some moment's rest, and weary-looking men, who seemed to be degenerating in vigor.
There were young children who looked as if they had been touched with premature decay, and young girls rapidly changing from unsophisticated girlhood into over-ripe womanhood.
ARE THESE THY SERVANTS?
THESE ARE MY SERVANTS, BUT NOT MY FAVORITES. IN DARK MINES THEY DIG FOR ME MY GLITTERING JEWELS. BUT LET US PASS ON TO FAIRER SCENES.

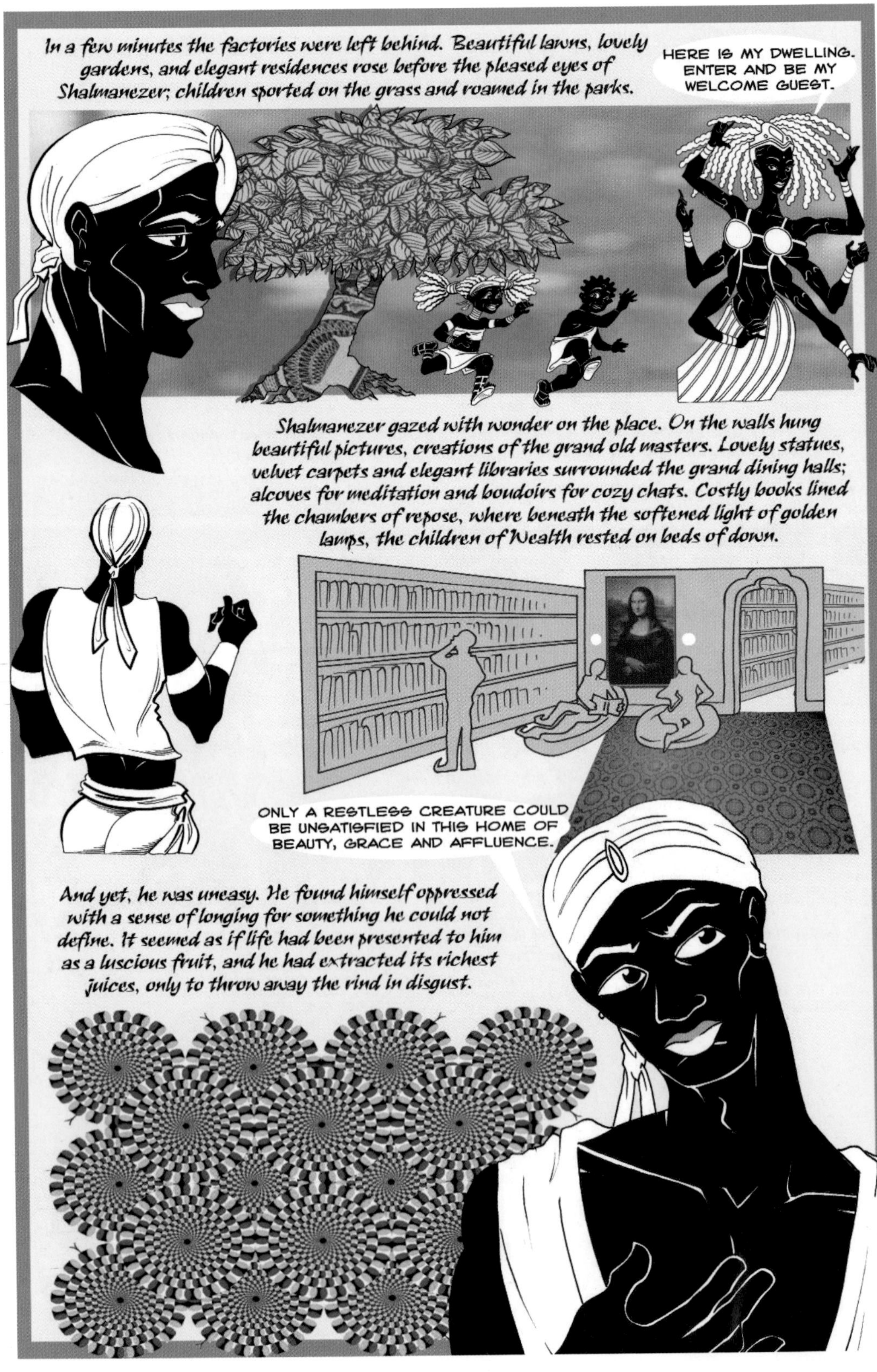
In a few minutes the factories were left behind. Beautiful lawns, lovely gardens, and elegant residences rose before the pleased eyes of Shalmanezer; children sported on the grass and roamed in the parks.
HERE IS MY DWELLING. ENTER AND BE MY WELCOME GUEST.
Shalmanezer gazed with wonder on the place. On the walls hung beautiful pictures, creations of the grand old masters. Lovely statues, velvet carpets and elegant libraries surrounded the grand dining halls; alcoves for meditation and boudoirs for cozy chats. Costly books lined the chambers of repose, where beneath the softened light of golden lamps, the children of Wealth rested on beds of down.
ONLY A RESTLESS CREATURE COULD BE UNSATISFIED IN THIS HOME OF BEAUTY, GRACE AND AFFLUENCE.
And yet, he was uneasy. He found himself oppressed with a sense of longing for something he could not define. It seemed as if life had been presented to him as a luscious fruit, and he had extracted its richest juices, only to throw away the rind in disgust.

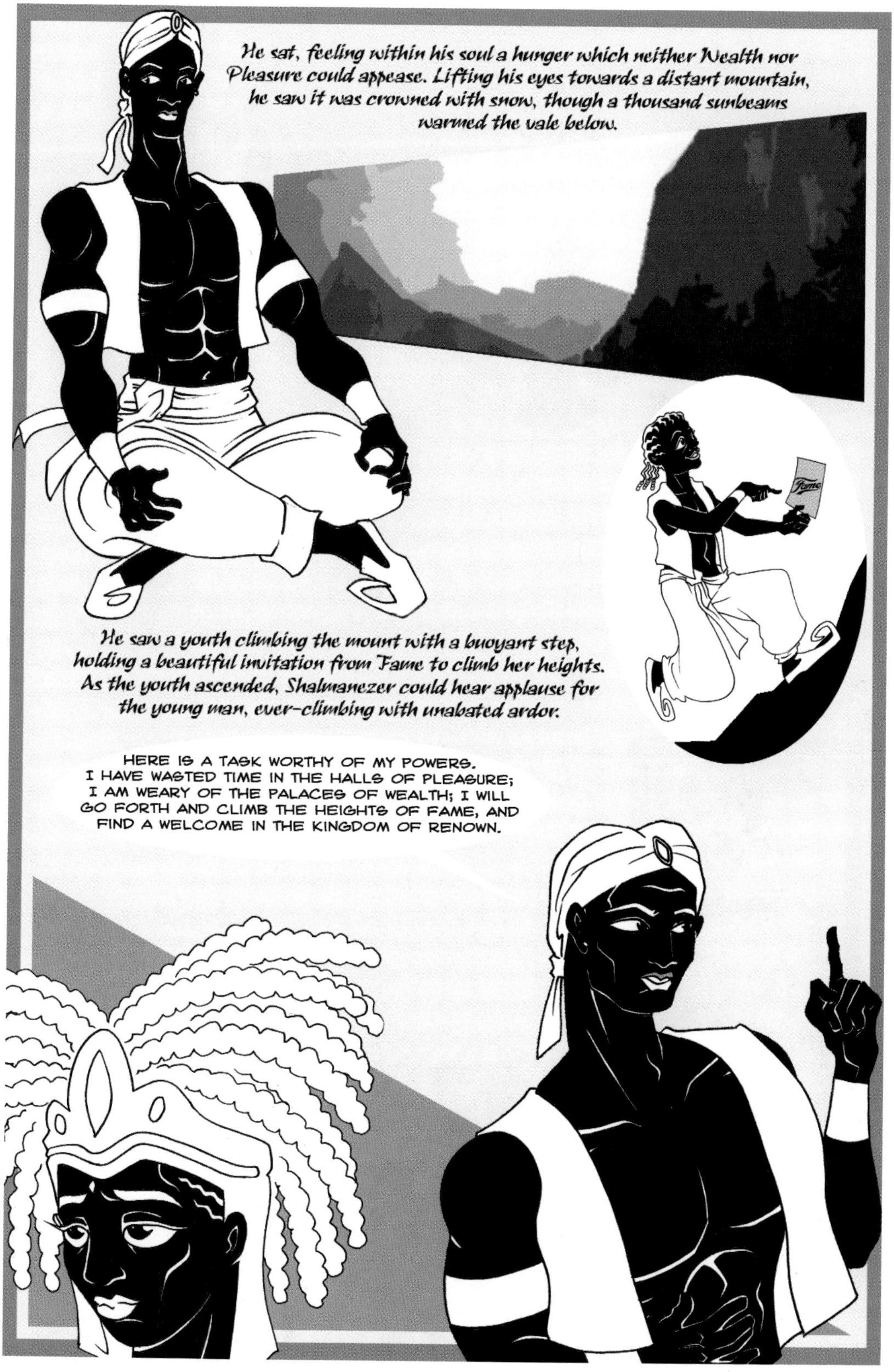
He sat, feeling within his soul a hunger which neither Wealth nor Pleasure could appease. Lifting his eyes towards a distant mountain, he saw it was crowned with snow, though a thousand sunbeams warmed the vale below.
Fame
He saw a youth climbing the mount with a buoyant step, holding a beautiful invitation from Fame to climb her heights. As the youth ascended, Shalmanezer could hear applause for the young man, ever-climbing with unabated ardor.
HERE IS A TASK WORTHY OF MY POWERS. I HAVE WASTED TIME IN THE HALLS OF PLEASURE; I AM WEARY OF THE PALACES OF WEALTH; I WILL GO FORTH AND CLIMB THE HEIGHTS OF FAME, AND FIND A WELCOME IN THE KINGDOM OF RENOWN.

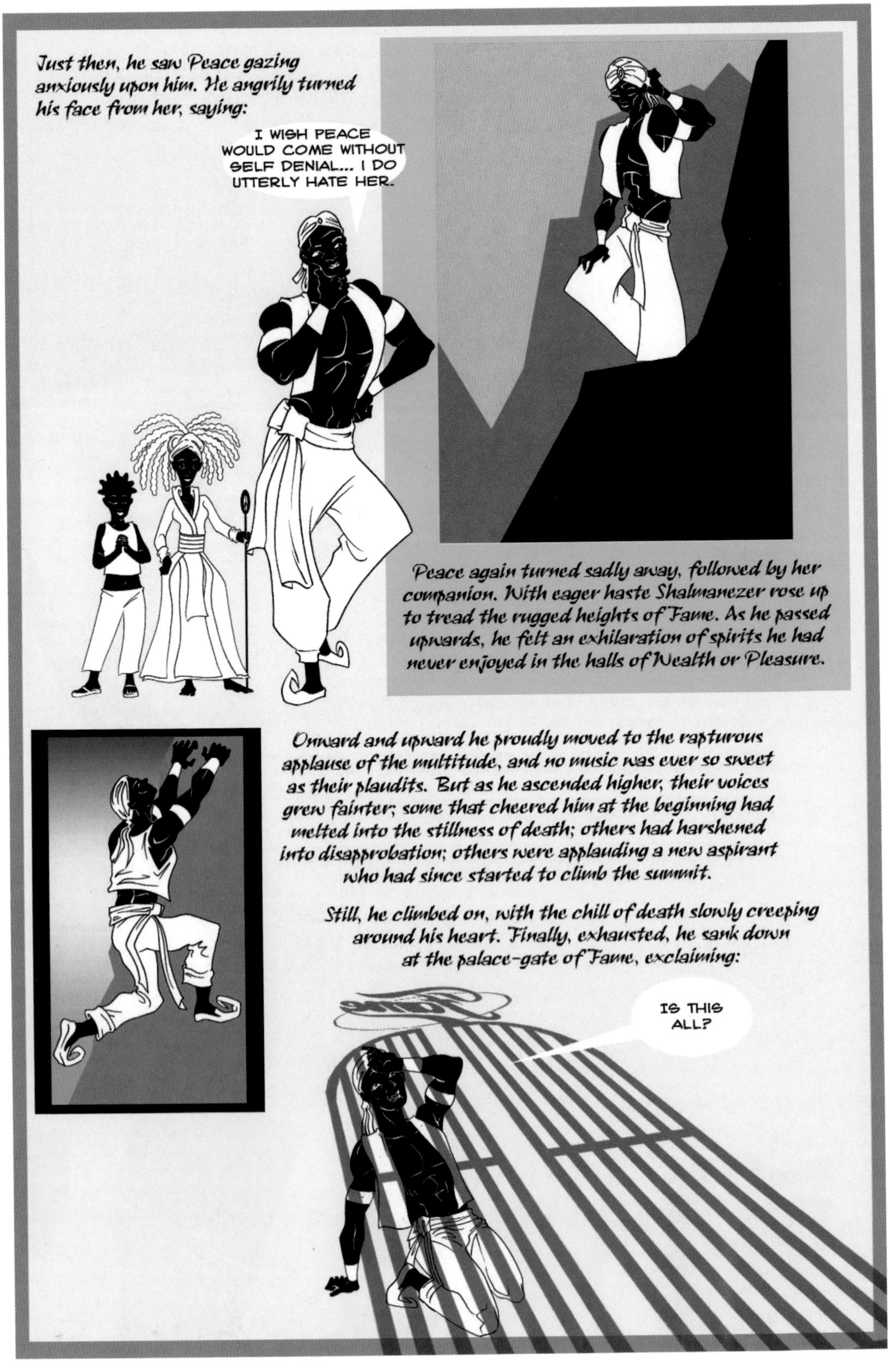
Just then, he saw Peace gazing anxiously upon him. He angrily turned his face from her, saying:
I WISH PEACE WOULD COME WITHOUT SELF DENIAL... I DO UTTERLY HATE HER.
Peace again turned sadly away, followed by her companion. With eager haste Shalmanezer rose up to tread the rugged heights of Fame. As he passed upwards, he felt an exhilaration of spirits he had never enjoyed in the halls of Wealth or Pleasure.
Onward and upward he proudly moved to the rapturous applause of the multitude, and no music was ever so sweet as their plaudits. But as he ascended higher, their voices grew fainter; some that cheered him at the beginning had melted into the stillness of death; others had harshened into disapprobation; others were applauding a new aspirant who had since started to climb the summit.
Still, he climbed on, with the chill of death slowly creeping around his heart. Finally, exhausted, he sank down at the palace-gate of Fame, exclaiming:
IS THIS ALL?

Very stately and grand was the cloud-capped palace of Fame. The pillars were engraven with the names of generals, conquerors, poets, illustrious men and celebrated women. Between them stood statues on which the tooth of Time was slowly gnawing. Those heights which had seemed so enchanting at a distance, now seemed more like barren mounds, around which the winds of Death were ever sweeping.

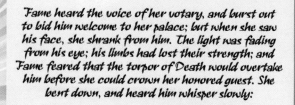

Fame heard the voice of her votary, and burst out to bid him welcome to her palace; but when she saw his face, she shrank from him. The light was fading from his eye; his limbs had lost their strength; and Fame feared that the torpor of Death would overtake him before she could crown her honored guest. She bent down, and heard him whisper slowly:

PEACE! PEACE!

137

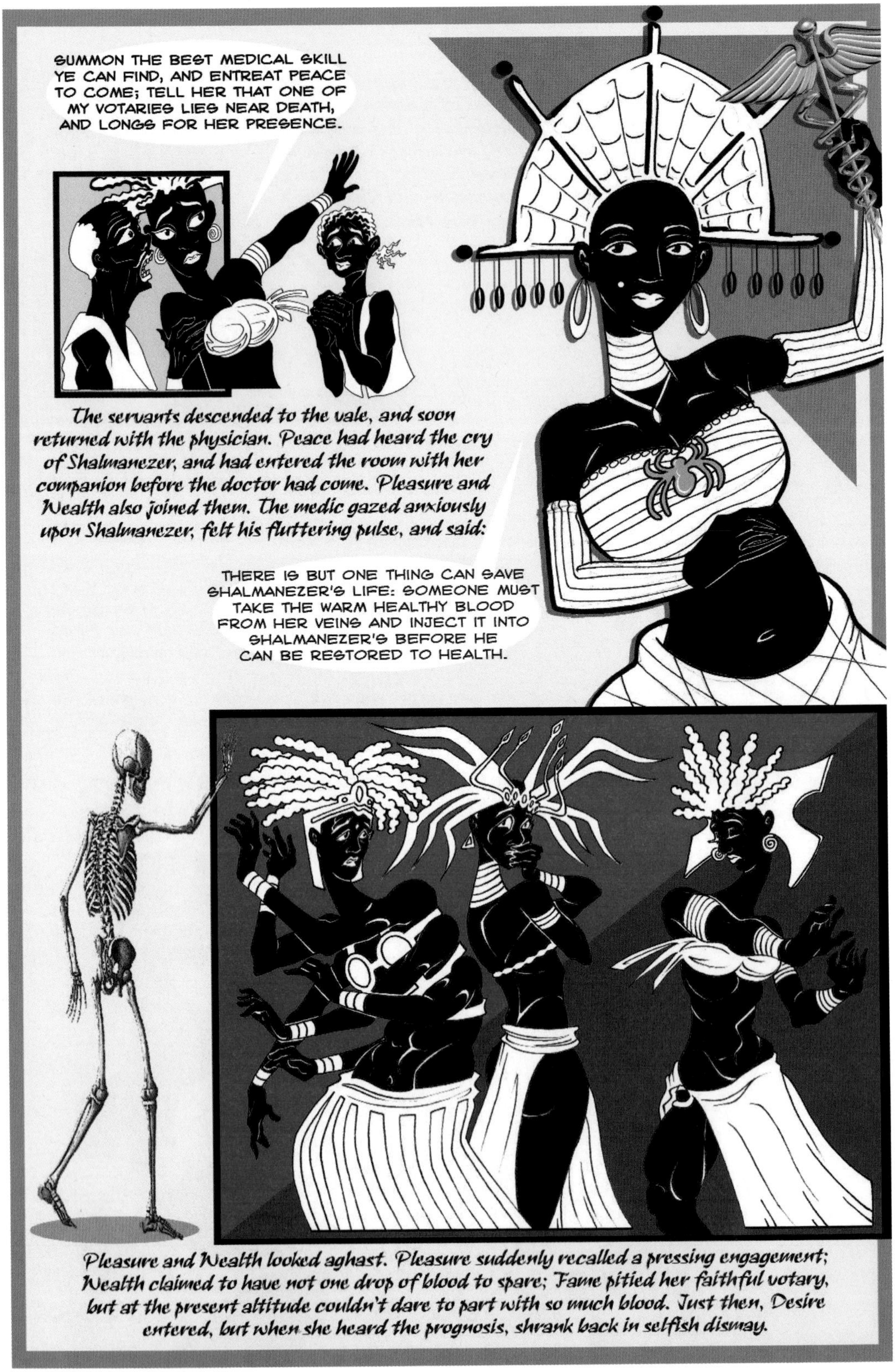
SUMMON THE BEST MEDICAL SKILL YE CAN FIND, AND ENTREAT PEACE TO COME; TELL HER THAT ONE OF MY VOTARIES LIES NEAR DEATH, AND LONGS FOR HER PRESENCE.
The servants descended to the vale, and soon returned with the physician. Peace had heard the cry of Shalmanezer, and had entered the room with her companion before the doctor had come. Pleasure and Wealth also joined them. The medic gazed anxiously upon Shalmanezer, felt his fluttering pulse, and said:
THERE IS BUT ONE THING CAN SAVE SHALMANEZER'S LIFE: SOMEONE MUST TAKE THE WARM HEALTHY BLOOD FROM HER VEINS AND INJECT IT INTO SHALMANEZER'S BEFORE HE CAN BE RESTORED TO HEALTH.
Pleasure and Wealth looked aghast. Pleasure suddenly recalled a pressing engagement; Wealth claimed to have not one drop of blood to spare; Fame pitied her faithful votary, but at the present altitude couldn't dare to part with so much blood. Just then, Desire entered, but when she heard the prognosis, shrank back in selfish dismay.

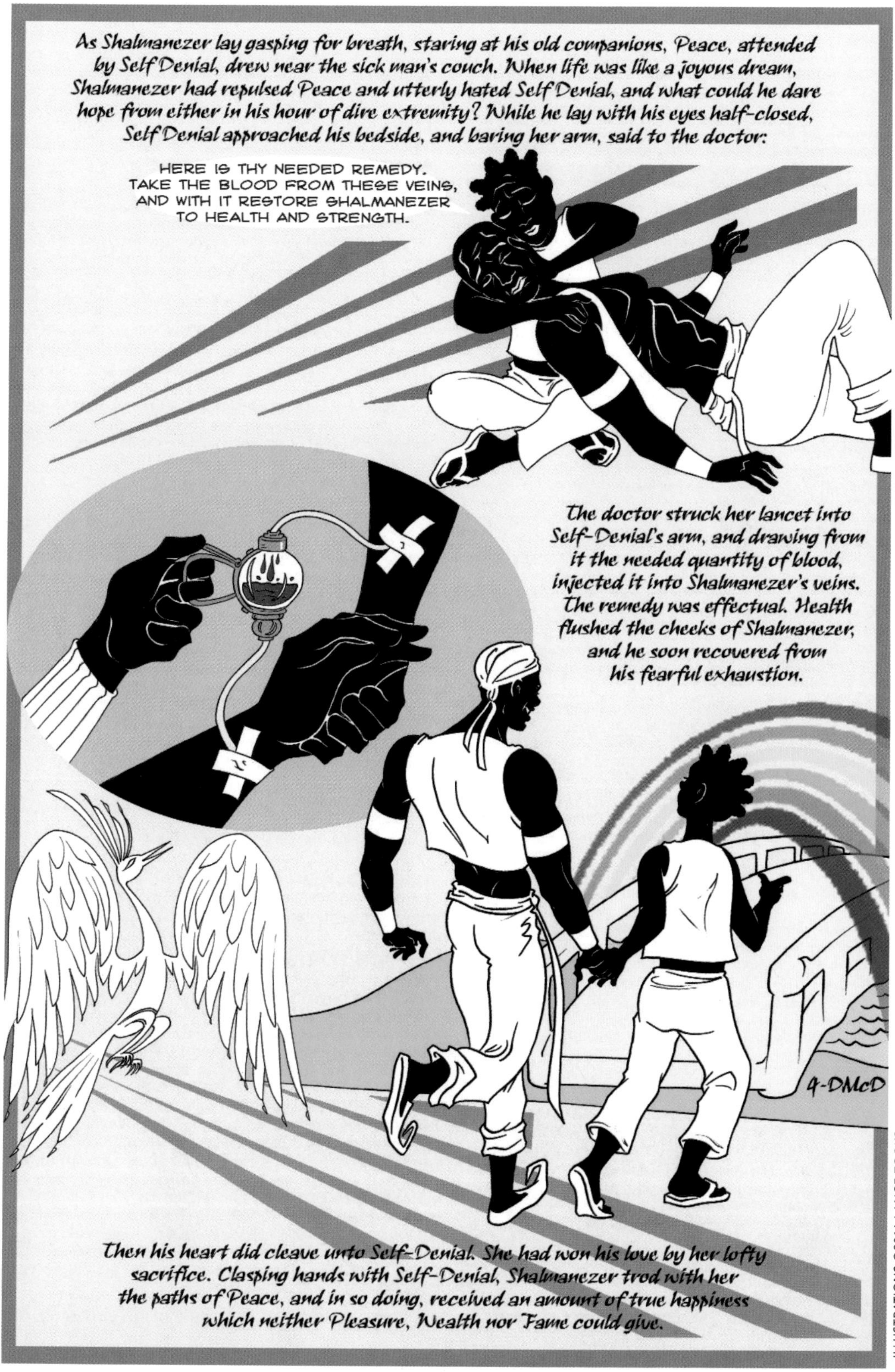

As Shalmanezer lay gasping for breath, staring at his old companions, Peace, attended by Self Denial, drew near the sick man's couch. When life was like a joyous dream, Shalmanezer had repulsed Peace and utterly hated Self Denial, and what could he dare hope from either in his hour of dire extremity? While he lay with his eyes half-closed, Self Denial approached his bedside, and baring her arm, said to the doctor:
HERE IS THY NEEDED REMEDY. TAKE THE BLOOD FROM THESE VEINS, AND WITH IT RESTORE SHALMANEZER TO HEALTH AND STRENGTH.
The doctor struck her lancet into Self-Denial's arm, and drawing from it the needed quantity of blood, injected it into Shalmanezer's veins. The remedy was effectual. Health flushed the cheeks of Shalmanezer, and he soon recovered from his fearful exhaustion.
4-DMcD
Then his heart did cleave unto Self-Denial. She had won his love by her lofty sacrifice. Clasping hands with Self-Denial, Shalmanezer trod with her the paths of Peace, and in so doing, received an amount of true happiness which neither Pleasure, Wealth nor Fame could give.

AFUA RICHARDSON (cover, page 36)

Afua Njoki Richardson, aka "Lakota Sioux" is a New York native comic book creator. She is the winner of the 2011 Nina Simone Artistic Achievement Award for being one of the few African-American female comic book creators to have worked for all the comic book giants: Marvel, DC and Image Comics. In the spirit of Nina Simone, Afua is a political activist, a classical flautist, a professional singer, songwriter, actress and human beatbox artist, sharing stages with music greats such as Parliment Funkadelic, Sheila E and Sir Melvin van Peebles. She currently illustrates *Genius* (Top Cow Productions), the winner of the 2008 Pilot Season Reader's Choice Award. Afua's EP release entitled *a.squared*, with pianist Alexa Edmonds, is due to be released in late 2011. Learn more at www.afuarichardson.com.

LANCE TOOKS (pages 1, 38, 74, 128)

The co-editor of *African-American Classics*, Lance Tooks (lancetooksjournal.blogspot.com) began his comics career as a Marvel Comics assistant editor. Lance has also worked as an animator on more than a hundred television commercials, films and music videos. He has self-published the comics *Danger Funnies*, *Divided by Infinity* and *Muthafucka*, and illustrated *The Black Panthers for Beginners*, written by Herb Boyd. His stories have appeared in *Graphic Classics: Edgar Allan Poe*, *Graphic Classics: Ambrose Bierce*, *Graphic Classics: Mark Twain* and *Graphic Classics: Robert Louis Stevenson*. Lance's first graphic novel, *Narcissa*, was named one of the year's best books by *Publisher's Weekly*, and his four-volume *Lucifer's Garden of Verses* series for NBM Comics Lit has won two Glyph Awards. He collaborated with Harvey Pekar on *The Beats: a Graphic History* and Studs Terkel's *Working*, and has recently adapted tales by Mary Shelley and W. Somerset Maugham for the upcoming *The Graphic Canon*, from Seven Stories Press. Lance moved from his native New York to Madrid, Spain, where he's hard at work on a new and very original graphic novel.

JAMES WELDON JOHNSON (page 2)

James Weldon Johnson (1871–1938) was a a poet, songwriter, teacher, and civil rights activist. In 1916 he became Field Secretary for the NAACP, and in 1920 the General Secretary, a post he held for ten years. He was one of the first African-American professors at New York University, and later a professor of creative literature and writing at Fisk University. In 1917 he published his first collection of poetry, *Fifty Years and Other Poems*, and in 1927 a second collection, *God's Trombones: Seven Negro Sermons in Verse*. He also edited three ground-breaking anthologies: *The Book of American Negro Poetry* (1922), *The Book of American Negro Spirituals* (1925), and *The Second Book of Negro Spirituals* (1926). During his later years he turned to nonfiction including *Black Manhattan* (1930), a history of the Harlem Renaissance, the autobiography *Along This Way* (1933), and *Negro Americans, What Now?* (1934), an essay on civil rights.

MAC McGILL (page 2)

Mac McGill's illustrations have appeared in *World War 3 Illustrated*, *The N.Y. Independent*, *HighTimes Magazine*, *The Guardian Radical Newsweekly*, *The Progressive Magazine*, *The City Sun*, *The Amsterdam News* and many other publications. The original art for his *IX XI MMI*, a limited edition art book published by the Brooklyn Artist Alliance (2001) is in the permanent collection of the Library of Congress. Mac has exhibited his work at BD Amadora (Portugal), Babel Festival (Greece), HU19 Underground Festival (Italy), School of Visual Arts (NYC), San Francisco Art Academy and many other venues. He has taught art at the Greenwich Village Youth Council and is currently working on *Song for Katrina*, a wordless graphic novel about the 2005 hurricane. Mac is a native New Yorker, and can be reached at mac@stealthisemail.com.

FLORENCE LEWIS BENTLEY (page 4)

Florence Lewis Bentley was the literary editor of the *Philadelphia Press*, and later a social leader in Chicago and the wife of Dr. C.E. Bentley, a prominent Chicago dentist. *Two Americans* was first published in *The Crisis* (September 1921), the official magazine of the NAACP, founded by W. E. B. Du Bois.

ALEX SIMMONS (pages 4, 82)

Alex Simmons (www.simmonshereandnow.com) is a professional freelance writer, teaching artist, and public speaker, as well as an arts and education consultant. Simmons has penned more than seventeen middle school and young adult novels, including the critically acclaimed adventure series, *Blackjack*, about an African-American soldier of fortune in the 1930s. He received the 2010 Glyph Best Writer Award for his work with Archie Comics. He has penned articles for magazines, two educational documentaries, three biographies, several stage plays, and three movie novelizations. Simmons is the founder of the annual Kids' Comic Con (a comic book convention for children, families, and educators), and the curator of the Color of Comics art exhibition, representing the portrayal of people of color in comics. This event was chosen to be part of the Fessman International Cultural Arts Festival in Senegal, Africa, in December 2010.

TREVOR VON EEDEN (page 4)

Trevor Von Eeden was born in Guyana in 1959, and moved to New York City in 1970. At age 17, he became DC Comics' first black artist – and one of the youngest they'd ever hired. He co-created *Black Lightning*, DC's first black superhero to have his own book, and is known for his work on *Batman*, *Green Arrow*, *Black Canary*, and a 1984 mini-series called *Thriller*. Since 2001, Trevor has illustrated a series of short stories, *Joe in the Future*, for *Heavy Metal Magazine*. He recently finished writing and drawing *The Original Johnson*, a biography of boxer Jack Johnson (IDW Publishing, 2010), and in 2011 designed and illustrated a series of superhero comics produced for the National Hockey League by Stan Lee. See more work on Trevor's official website at www.trevorvoneeden.com.

ADRIAN JOHNSON (page 4)

Born in Atlanta, Georgia, Adrian has worked freelance since the age of 20 under his own company, Inazuma Studios. A lifelong Georgia native, Adrian currently works and resides in Norcross, Georgia with his wife Samantha and two daughters. You can view samples of his color work and original art at www.inazumastudios.com.

W. E. B. DU BOIS (page 26)

William Edward Burghardt Du Bois (1868–1963) graduated from Fisk University, and was the first African-American to earn a Ph.D. from Harvard University. He became a professor at Atlanta University and at The New School in New York City. Du Bois published more than 4,000 articles and essays, 22 books, and established four academic journals in his career. As an advocate of Pan-Africanism, the belief that all people of African descent had common interests and should work together in the struggle for their freedom, Du Bois was the most important black leader in the U.S. during the first half of the 20th century. He was one of the founders of the National Association for the Advancement of Colored People (NAACP) in 1909, and edited *The Crisis*, its official magazine, from 1910 to 1934. As editor, he encouraged the development of black literature and art, and campaigned for increased political representation and the formation of a black intellectual elite who would work for the progress of the African-American race.

KYLE BAKER (page 26)

At age 17, Kyle Baker started as an intern and inker at Marvel Comics. In 1990 he moved to DC Comics, where he illustrated *The Shadow, Justice, Inc., The Spirit, Hawkman,* and *Plastic Man.* Baker has authored sixteen graphic novels, including *The Cowboy Wally Show, Why I Hate Saturn,* and *You Are Here.* He currently illustrates *Deadpool Max* for Marvel. Baker has won both the Harvey Award and the Eisner Award, the comics industry's highest honors. As an animator, he has worked for Disney, Warner Bothers, HBO, Dreamworks, Cartoon Network and more, on series and features including *Looney Tunes, Phineas and Ferb,* and *Shrek.* For more information, and to see more of Kyle's work, visit www.qualityjollity.com.

LANGSTON HUGHES (pages 34, 36)

James Langston Hughes (1902–1967) was a poet, novelist, playwright, columnist and social activist. He was born in Missouri, and lived briefly in Mexico, France and England. Following his graduatuion from Lincoln University in Pennsylvania in 1929, he moved to Harlem, in New York City, which became his primary home for the remainder of his life. He was one of the leaders of the Harlem Renaissance, a cultural movement that writer James Weldon Johnson referred to as "the flowering of Negro literature." Hughes was also noted for his involvement in the world of jazz, which had a strong influence on his writing. His first book of poetry, *The Weary Blues,* was published in 1926. In 1930 his first novel, *Not Without Laughter,* won the Harmon Gold Medal for Literature. His collection of short stories, *The Ways of White Folks* (1934) led to his receiving a Guggenheim Fellowship. In addition to his large body of poetry, Hughes wrote eleven plays and countless works of prose, including the well-known "Simple" books, collecting his twenty years of newspaper columns for the *Chicago Defender.*

STAN SHAW (page 34)

Stan Shaw illustrates for various clients all over the country including *The Village Voice, Esquire, Slate,* Starbucks, the Seattle Mariners, Nintendo, Rhino Records, Microsoft, BET, POV, DC Comics, ABCNEWS.com, Wizards of The Coast, *Amazing Stories, Vibe,* The Flying Karamazov Brothers and *Willamette Week.* In addition to practicing illustration, Stan teaches it, at Cornish School of the Arts, School of Visual Concepts and Pacific Lutheran University. He is now part of a group of artists advising on an illustration textbook. His work can be seen at www.drawstanley.com, and in *Graphic Classics: Ambrose Bierce, Graphic Classics: O. Henry, Graphic Classics: Rafael Sabatini, Graphic Classics: Oscar Wilde,* and *Poe's Tales of Mystery.*

ALICE DUNBAR NELSON (page 38)

Alice Dunbar Nelson (1875-1935) was born in New Orleans, and graduated from Straight University in that city. She married writer Paul Laurence Dunbar in 1898. Theirs was a stormy relationship, and they separated in 1902. She briefly married a second time to physician Henry A. Callis in 1910, divorced, and in 1916 married journalist Robert J. Nelson. After her separation from Dunbar, Alice moved to Wilmington, Delaware, where she taught for eighteen years at Howard High School, State College for Colored Students and Hampton Institute. In addition to her teaching, she was a poet, journalist, playwright, and unpublished novelist. Her first collection of stories and poems, *Violets and Other Tales,* was published in 1895. A second collection, *The Goodness of St. Rocque and Other Stories,* was released in 1899. These were the only two books that were published during her lifetime, though many of her stories and essays appeared in newspapers and journals including *The Crisis, Opportunity, Journal of Negro History,* and *The Messenger.* Alice was a social activist, and worked as a field organizer for women's suffrage, served with the Women's Commission on the Council of National Defense, as executive secretary of the American Friends Inter-Racial Peace Committee, and helped found the Industrial School for Colored Girls in Delaware.

CLAUDE McKAY (pages 44, 45)

Claude McKay (1889–1948) was born in Jamaica, and came to the U.S. in 1912 to attend Booker T. Washington's Tuskegee Institute. He objected to the "machinelike existence" at Tuskegee and the racism he encountered in South Carolina, and transferred to Kansas State University. In 1914, after reading W. E. B. Du Bois' *Souls of Black Folk,* he moved to New York City, where he became one of the most important writers of the Harlem Renaissance. McKay was already an established writer in Jamaica, with his first book of poems, *Songs of Jamaica* (1912). Many of his numerous poems written in the U.S. were reactions to the racism he encountered in this country. *Home to Harlem* (1928), the first of McKay's three novels, won the Harmon Gold Award for Literature, but caused his estrangement from Du Bois, who objected to the book's frank depictions of sexuality and nightlife in Harlem.

GLENN BREWER (page 44)

Glenn Brewer graduated with Honors and a BFA in Fine Arts from the Columbus College of Art and Design. He has created illustrations for numerous companies and publications including TSR, Inc., Visionary Entertainment Studios, *The New Orleans Tribune, Frost Illustrated,* Tygeron Graphics and Unchained Spirit Enterprises, a children's book publisher. Brewer is best known for the six-part comic series *Askari Hodari,* which he wrote, illustrated and published. *Askari Hodari* was nominated twice and eventually won the Howard E. Day Prize. Brewer also was nominated for a Glyph Award in the Best Self-Publisher category for his *Askari Hodari* series. You can see more of Glenn's work at www.glennbrewer.blogspot.com.

JOHN JENNINGS (page 45)

John Jennings is an Associate Professor of Visual Studies at the State University of New York at Buffalo. Jennings is an illustrator, curator, and visual culture scholar who studies various aspects of the "black image" in popular media. He is also an activist, visual artist, and design educator who frequently writes and lectures on race and diversity issues in the arts. Jennings is the co-author of the graphic novel *The Hole: Consumer Culture* and co-founder of J2D2 Arts with research partner Damian Duffy. The latest book from Jennings and Duffy, *Black Comix: African American Independent Comics Art and Culture,* was released in June 2010. Information on the duo's projects may be found at j2d2arts.blogspot.com and www.blackcomixbook.com.

ZORA NEALE HURSTON (pages 46, 110)

Zora Neale Hurston (1891–1960) was born in Alabama, but moved at an early age to Eatonville, Florida, the nation's first incorporated black township. Her home town life became the basis of most of her fifty stories, four novels, plays and essays. Hurston studied at Morgan Academy in Baltimore, Howard University in Washington, D.C., and in 1928 graduated with a degree in anthropology from Barnard College in New York City, where she was the only black student. In New York she met Langston Hughes, Wallace Thurman and other young black writers, and became one of the central figures of the Harlem Renaissance. While her work was originally lauded, many readers objected to the representation of black dialect in Hurston's stories, and her work slid into obscurity for decades. In 1975, *Ms. Magazine* published Alice Walker's essay, *In Search of Zora Neale Hurston,* which revived interest in the author. She is now best known for her 1937 novel *Their Eyes Were Watching God,* which was adapted for a 2005 film by Oprah Winfrey's Harpo Productions.

ARIE MONROE (page 46)

Arie Monroe is a born and raised Kansas City, Missouri native who dreamed of being a Ninja Turtle, but settled for being an animator and illustration artist instead. She attended school in New Jersey at the Joe Kubert School of Cartoon Graphics where she studied character animation and comic book illustration. She has worked as a licensing illustrator for some time and is now freelancing from her studio in her home town. You can see more of Arie's work at www.drawlikecrazy.net and mainasha.daportfolio.com/gallery/502237.

ROBERT W. BAGNALL (page 54)

Robert W. Bagnall (1883 – 1943) was a minister, civil rights activist, and a graduate of Bishop Payne Divinity School in Petersburg, Virginia. Bagnall presided over several African Methodist Episcopal congregations along the Atlantic seaboard before arriving at Detroit's St. Matthews AME Church in 1911. There he became one of the founding members of Detroit's branch of the NAACP. Bagnall went on to serve as a regional NAACP recruiter before being appointed as national Director of Branches between 1921 and 1932. The following year Bagnall returned to the ministry as rector of St. Thomas Episcopal Church in Philadelphia, where he served until his death. *Lex Talionis* first appeared in *The Crisis*, April 1922.

CHRISTOPHER PRIEST (page 54)

Christopher J. Priest (born James Christopher Owsley in 1961) grew up in New York, and now lives in Colorado. In 1978 Priest began work as an intern at Marvel Comics, and was promoted to editor (the first African-American editor in mainstream comics) in charge of *Spider-Man* books in 1984. Priest became the first black writer in modern comics with his *Falcon Limited* series. He went on to write for nearly every major comics character published, including *Power Man & Iron Fist, Conan The Barbarian, Wolverine, Green Lantern, The Ray* and *Black Panther*. In 1993 Jim Owsley legally changed his name to Christopher Priest. He never discusses the real reason behind his name change, but insists every story you may have heard about it is absolutely true. In addition to his comics writing, Priest is an ordained Baptist minister serving in Colorado Springs, and a professional music producer. You can read more about and by Priest at www.digital-priest.com.

JIM WEBB (page 54)

Jim Webb's work has crossed several borders. Besides being a storyboard and layout artist for MTV Animation and storyboarding episodes of acclaimed shows such as *The Venture Brothers* and *Teenage Mutant Ninja Turtles*, Jim has done comic book work for a variety of publishers including Harris, Mirage and Digital Webbing. He's contributed style-guide designs for DC Licensing and background inking for Marvel's *Secret Invasion* series. Most recently he created layouts for ads for TV Land's hit series *Hot in Cleveland*, and is currently working on his creator-owned comic, *The Adversary*, for Atlas Unleashed. See more at www.jimwebb.us.

JEAN TOOMER (page 64)

Jean Toomer (1894–1967) was born Nathan Eugene Toomer in New Orleans. His mother's family was wealthy and influential in Louisiana, where her father, Pickney B.S. Pinchback, had been the only African-American ever to have served as governor. Toomer's father, Nathan Toomer, Sr., was the son of a slave, and left the family before young Nathan was born. Jean was raised in his grandfather's household in affluent areas of New Orleans and Washington, D.C., where he was not exposed to racism until he entered high school in Washington. He attended various colleges, including the University of New York and the University of Wisconsin, but did not graduate, instead choosing to independently pursue his interests in literature and philosophy. In 1921 he moved to Georgia where he served as interim principal of the Sparta Agricultural and Industrial Institute. Toomer's parents were of African-American descent, but the entire family could pass for white. Living in the rural South stimulated Jean's racial consciousness, and he used this new identification with his racial past to create his most famous work, *Cane*, in 1923. The novel incorporated a number of his previously published short stories including *Becky*.

MAT JOHNSON (page 64)

Mat Johnson is a novelist who sometimes writes other things. He is the author of the novels *Pym, Drop,* and *Hunting in Harlem,* and the nonfiction novella *The Great Negro Plot*. In 2007, he was named the first USA James Baldwin Fellow by the United States Artists Foundation. He is also a recipient of the Hurston/Wright Legacy Award, the Thomas J. Watson Fellowship, and a Barnes & Noble Discover Great New Writers selection. Johnson did his first comics writing on the five-issue limited series *Hellblazer Special: Papa Midnite* (2005). In 2008, Vertigo Comics published his graphic novel *Incognegro*, a noir mystery that deals with the issue of "passing." He is currently a faculty member at the University of Houston Creative Writing Program.

RANDY DUBURKE (page 64)

Randy DuBurke (www.randyduburke.com) was born in Washington, Georgia. "I lived my first few years in rural Georgia with my mother's parents. Then my parents brought me to New York where I immediately decided I wanted to be an artist and spent the subsequent years working for that goal," says Randy. He has now been a professional illustrator for twenty years, having done comics, animation, editorial illustration, book covers and children's books. Clients include Byron Priess, DC Comics, Vertigo Comics, Marvel Comics, *The New York Times Book Review*, MTV Animation, Chronicle Books, Clarion Books, and Lee and Low Books. He was awarded the 2003 Coretta Scott King/John Steptoe award for best new talent/illustration for his first children's book *The MoonRing*. After spending most of his life in New York, Randy now lives with his wife and children in Switzerland.

JAMES D. CORROTHERS (page 69)

James David Corrothers (1869–1917) was raised by his grandfather in the predominantly white town of South Haven, Michigan. After his grandfather's death in 1885, Corrothers worked odd jobs in Indiana, Ohio, and finally Chicago. There he met journalist Henry Demarest Lloyd who, after reading Corrothers' poetry, helped him get a job at the *Chicago Tribune*. When an article he submitted was rewritten by a white reporter, Corrothers quit the paper in protest. He went on, however, to work for several other Chicago dailies. His newspaper dialect sketches were collected in *The Black Cat Club* (1902), his most popular book. Despite his literary success, Corrothers entered the ministry, serving successively in the African Methodist Episcopal, Baptist and Presbyterian churches. He continued to write stories and poetry, and became one of the most widely published African-American writers of the late nineteenth and early twentieth centuries.

KENJJI (page 69)

Kenjji Jumanne-Marshall is an award-winning Detroit illustrator whose works have been featured in *The New York Times, Orlando Weekly, Japan Times, XLR8R* and *Wired* magazines. He recently won a prize in the Grosse Pointe Artists Association's Caricature show, and regularly appears at Metro Detroit's summer festivals as a caricature artist. Kenjji's art has appeared in art galleries and exhibits worldwide, and he has taught Cartooning & Caricature at the College for Creative Studies, the Flint Institute of Arts and the YMCA. Kenjji was recently awarded a grant from the Creative Capital Foundation and previously won a grant from the Xeric foundation for his comic book, *WitchDoctor*. For more information and art visit www.kenjji.com.

PAUL LAURENCE DUNBAR (pages 74, 75)

Paul Laurence Dunbar (1872 – 1906), born the son of ex-slaves in Dayton, Ohio, became the first African-American to gain national eminence as a poet. He wrote his first poem at age six and gave his first public recital at age nine. *Oak and Ivy*, his first collection of poetry, was published in 1892. In 1893, he was invited to recite at the World's Fair. There he met abolitionist Frederick Douglass, who called Dunbar "the most promising young colored man in America." Dunbar's work appeared in magazines and journals including *Harper's Weekly*, *The Saturday Evening Post*, *The Denver Post*, and *Current Literature*. Although he lived to be only 33 years old, Dunbar ultimately produced twelve books of poetry, four collections of short stories, five novels, and a play. He also wrote lyrics for *In Dahomey*, the first musical written and performed entirely by African-Americans to appear on Broadway.

LARRY PONCHO BROWN (page 75)

Larry "Poncho" Brown (www.larryponchobrown.com) is a native of Baltimore, Maryland, and received his BFA degree from the Maryland Institute College of Art. He started his first business at the age of seventeen as a signwriter, and has been a full time artist ever since. His art, both fine and commercial, has been published nationally in *Art Trends*, *U.S. Art Gallery*, *Images*, *Upscale*, *Ebony*, *Essence*, and *Jet* magazines His work is also featured in the UCLA Fowler Museum of Cultural History Textile Series book, *Wrapped in Pride*. Poncho founded Raising The Arts, which provides fundraising opportunities for nonprofit organizations, and has created over 65 images for such organizations since 1987. He was awarded Artist of the Year by the African American Visual Arts Association in 2000, the Heritage Arts Festival Palette Award in 2003, and the Save the Arts Award as Museum's Choice in 2010.

ETHEL M. CAUTION (page 76)

Ethel Mae Caution (aka Ethel Caution-Davis) (1880 – 1981) was born in Cleveland, Ohio. Her parents died when she was very young, and she took her adoptive mother's name of Davis. She was raised in Boston, attended Girl's Latin School, and graduated from Wellesley College in 1912, the fourth black woman to do so. After teaching jobs in North Carolina and Kansas, she became Dean of Women at Talladega College in Alabama. She later moved to New York City, where she was a public assistance employee and director of a residence club for single women. Never married, Ethel died in New York City at age 101.

LEILANI HICKERSON (page 76)

Freelance illustrator Leilani Hickerson was born in New Jersey in 1983. She graduated in 2006 from The University of the Arts in Philadelphia, attaining the university's most distinguished illustration award. You can see examples of her art in the anthology *Black Comix: African American Independent Comics, Art & Culture*, and online at lanitai.deviantart.com and leilanihickerson.blogspot.com. Leilani is currently collaborating with her sister, Margarita, on an upcoming children's comic, *My Hafu*.

EFFIE LEE NEWSOME (page 81)

Mary Effie Lee Newsome (1885 – 1979) was a short fiction writer, editor, and the first well-known African-American poet whose work consisted primarily of poems for children. She was the daughter of Dr. Benjamin Franklin Lee, a president of Wilberforce University and a bishop of the African Methodist Episcopal Church. Mary attended Wilberforce, Oberlin College, and the University of Pennsylvania, and later married a minister, the Reverend Henry Nesby Newsome. A number of her poems appeared in *The Brownies' Book*, a magazine published by W. E. B. Du Bois. From 1925 to 1929 she wrote a children's column, *The Little Page*, for *The Crisis*, the official magazine of the NAACP. Her column, consisting of nature poetry, nonsense verse, and parables about being young and black in the racially biased 1920s, was an important link between *The Brownies' Book* and works for children in the 1930s by Langston Hughes and Arna Bontemps. Her poems for adult readers are included in Hughes' and Bontemps' *The Poetry of the Negro* (1949), and she collected her poems for children in *Gladiola Garden* (1940).

KEITH MALLETT (page 81)

Keith Mallett was born in Roaring Spring, Pennsylvania. He began painting at age twelve, and later studied at the Art Students League and Hunter College in New York City. While in New York, Mallett began working for the music industry, painting covers for Virgin Records and creating T-shirts for music groups. In 1980 he moved to Los Angeles and then to San Diego, where he currently resides. In California, Keith worked as a freelance artist, and for fifteen years as the in-house artist for Frontline Art Publishers. He was recently commissioned to design the official limited edition print commemorating the 50th anniversary of Jackie Robinson's breakthrough into major league baseball. His artwork can be found in many private and corporate collections, and is currently published by Canadian Art Prints, one of the largest fine art publishers in the world. A feature article on Keith appeared in *U.S. Art Magazine*, and *Décor Magazine* recently featured him in an artist's profile. You can see more of Keith's art at www.keithmallett.com.

CHARLES W. CHESNUTT (page 82)

Charles Waddell Chesnutt (1858–1932) was a teacher, lawyer, activist, and the most prominent black prose author of his time. Chesnutt was born in Cleveland, Ohio, the son of free blacks who had emigrated from Fayetteville, N.C. When he was eight years old, his parents returned to Fayetteville, where Charles worked in the family grocery store and attended a school founded by the Freedmen's Bureau. In 1880 he became principal of the Fayetteville State Normal School for Negroes. In 1883, seeking broader opportunities, he moved his family to Cleveland. There he passed the state bar examination and established his own court reporting firm. *The Goophered Grapevine* was Chesnutt's first nationally recognized work. Its publication in the August 1887 issue of the *Atlantic Monthly* marked the first time that a story by a black author had appeared in that prestigious magazine. Despite the critical acclaim resulting from his works of fiction and nonfiction, Chesnutt was unable to make a living as an author, but his successful business allowed him to keep writing, and he published two short story collections, three novels, and numerous essays. He was awarded the Spingarn Medal in 1928 by the NAACP for his pioneering literary work on behalf of the Afro-American struggle.

SHEPHERD HENDRIX (page 82)

Shepherd Hendrix began his comics career in 1991 as an inker on DC Comics' *Swamp Thing*. He also penciled and inked *Restaurant at the End of the Universe* with Steve Leialoha. In the late 1990s, he left the industry and began working as a storyboard artist, background designer, and concept artist, using both traditional and digital mediums, collaborating with LucasArts and EA Games. In 2006, he returned to comics, illustrating the Eisner Award-nominated *Stagger Lee*, written by Derek McCulloch, for Image Comics. You can find pages from *Stagger Lee* in *Black Comix: African American Independent Comics, Art & Culture*, and more examples of Shepherd's art at www.shepko.com.

LEILA AMOS PENDLETON (page 100)

Leila Amos Pendleton (1860 – 1938) was a teacher in the public schools of Washington, D.C. In 1898 she founded the Alpha Charity Club of Anacostia, and was its president for thirteen years. She was also the founder and president of the Social Purity Club of Washington, vice-president of the District of Columbia of the Northeastern Federation of Women's Clubs, secretary of the National Association of Assemblies of the order of the Golden Circle, and an auxiliary to the Scottish Rite of Freemasonry, S. J., U. S. A. In 1912 Pendleton published *A Narrative of the Negro*, a book aimed at instilling in black children an appreciation and pride in their racial heritage. *Sanctum 777 N.S.D.C.O.U. Meets Cleopatra* first appeared in *The Crisis*, May 1922.

KEVIN J. TAYLOR (page 100)

Kevin J. Taylor is a self-taught artist/painter who spent years doing set design, storyboarding, animation and, for the last 21 years, has created comics and graphic novels of his own characters, doing all of the writing and illustration. He is best known for his erotic graphic novels, including *Girl* for NBM/Eurotica. Kevin was born and raised in New York City, and now lives in Spain. You can find examples of his (for adults) work at www.kevinjtaylor.com.

JAMES EDWIN CAMPBELL (*page 108*)
James Edwin Campbell (1867–1896) was a poet, journalist, editor, short story writer and educator. Born in Pomeroy, Ohio, Campbell was an 1884 graduate of Pomeroy Academy. He worked first as a teacher in Ohio, then in 1890 moved to West Virginia, where he served as principal of Langston School in Point Pleasant, and of the Collegiate Institute in Charleston, an agricultural and mechanical arts school for African-American youths. Active in politics and a skilled public speaker, Campbell moved to Chicago after marrying and became a staff writer for the *Times-Herald*. He contributed articles and poems to several periodicals, and participated in the publication of *Four O'Clock Magazine*. Campbell published two poetry collections, *Driftings and Gleanings* (1887) and *Echoes from the Cabin and Elsewhere* (1895), which critics have judged to be the finest group of dialect poems of the nineteenth century. His promising career was cut short when he died of pneumonia in Pomeroy at age twenty-eight.

MASHEKA WOOD (*page 108*)
Masheka Wood is a cartoonist, illustrator and lettering artist who has drawn for MTV, the *Urban Voice of Comics* magazine and *Covered*, among other outlets. His art has been featured in the anthology *Black Comix: African American Independent Comics, Art & Culture* and in the exhibits *Out of Sequence* and *Other Heroes*. Currently he's working on an illustrated guide to the human body and a memoir of his temp years in the New York of the '00s. Masheka lives in Brooklyn with his wife, cartoonist Mikhaela Reid, their baby daughter and two dumb cats. See his stuff at www.whatmashekadid.com.

MILTON KNIGHT (*page 110*)
Milton Knight says he started drawing, painting and creating his own attempts at comic books and animation at age two. "I've never formed a barrier between fine art and cartooning," explains Milton. "Growing up, I treasured Chinese watercolors, Breughel, Charlie Brown and Terrytoons equally." His work has appeared in *Heavy Metal, High Times, National Lampoon* and *Nickelodeon Magazine*, and he has illustrated record covers, posters, candy packaging and T-shirts, and occasionally exhibited his paintings. Labor on *Ninja Turtles* comics allowed him to get up a grubstake to move to the West Coast in 1991, where he became an animator and director on *Felix the Cat* cartoons. Milton's comics titles include *Midnite the Rebel Skunk* and *Slug and Ginger*, and he has just finished a second Zora Neale Hurston adaptation, *Poker!*, which will appear in *The Graphic Canon*, from Seven Stories Press. More comics and illustrations by Milton Knight can be found at www.miltonknight.net and in *Graphic Classics: Edgar Allan Poe, Graphic Classics: H.G. Wells, Graphic Classics: Jack London, Graphic Classics: Ambrose Bierce, Graphic Classics: O. Henry, Graphic Classics: Rafael Sabatini, Horror Classics* and *Adventure Classics*. He currently exhibits and teaches at The Colonnade Art Gallery and Studio in Pasadena, CA.

JEREMY LOVE (*page 124*)
Jeremy Love (www.gettosake.com) is an award-winning writer, illustrator, and animator. His critically acclaimed serialized graphic novel *Bayou*, from DC/Zuda, was nominated for an Eisner Award for Best Digital Comic and won five Glyph Awards. Making his debut over a decade ago, Love has also worked on creator-owned projects for Dark Horse (*Fierce, Shadow Rock*), on established properties such as *G.I. Joe, Batman*, and *Fraggle Rock*, and on various animated projects.

FRANCES E. W. HARPER (*pages 127, 128*)
Frances Ellen Watkins Harper (1825–1911) was an author, orator, and social reformer notable for her poetry, speeches,

and essays on abolition, temperance, and women's suffrage. The daughter of free black parents, she was born in Philadelphia, and grew up in the home of an uncle whose school for black children she attended. At age thirteen Frances went to work as a domestic in a Quaker household in Baltimore, but continued her education with her employers' encouragement. Her poems appeared in newspapers, and in 1845 a collection was printed as *Autumn Leaves*. Following the passage of the Fugitive Slave Law in 1850, conditions for free blacks in Maryland deteriorated and Frances moved to Ohio, where she taught sewing at Union Seminary. She moved on to Pennsylvania in 1851, where she helped escaped slaves along the Underground Railroad to Canada. In 1859 Watkins' *The Two Offers* appeared in the *Anglo-African*, the first short story to be published by an African-American. In 1860, she married Fenton Harper and moved to Ohio, where she turned her energy to women's rights. She helped organize the National Association of Colored Women in 1896, and was elected its vice president in 1897. She also continued with her writing, and in 1892 she published *Iola Leroy, or Shadows Uplifted*, one of the first novels by an African-American woman. Although a popular writer during her lifetime, Harper was not acclaimed by literary critics and her reputation waned until recent decades, when black women and feminists in general resurrected her legacy.

TITUS V. THOMAS (*page 127*)
Titus V. Thomas is a graphic designer and cartoonist from the Bronx, NY. Titus has designed for critically acclaimed TV shows including Bill Cosby's *The Little Bill Show, Dora the Explorer*, and *Backyardigans* on Nick Jr. He has also designed for various companies including NBA Entertainment, Varcity Clothing, The Creative Kitchen, Merkury Innovations, Atlantic Studios, Sony Music, *YSB Magazine*, and ADHERE Network. A major highlight of Titus' art career was being asked to illustrate and design the multicultural children's cookbook *Everybody Eats Lunch*, written by Cricket Azima. The book won the National Parenting Publication Award in 2008. For more info on Titus and his company, TitusCanDraw, LLC, visit www.tituscandraw.com.

JIMMIE ROBINSON (*back cover*)
Jimmie Robinson is a California native, born in 1963. Raised in Oakland, he attended special art magnet programs since elementary school, starting with Mosswood Arts, Renaissance Middle School and Concordia High School. He graduated at age sixteen, and directly pursued his art career with home study and college classes. Jimmie married at 21, had a daughter and put his art career on hold while he worked for a printing company, First Western Graphics/Prep-Sat Technologies, for thirteen years. Prep-Sat was a forerunner in the digital desktop publishing era and Robinson learned the craft from the ground up. This facilitated his return to the arts and he created Jet Black Graphics, which led to his career with Image Comics as a creator of both superhero and all-ages children's comics including *Amanda & Gunn, Code Blue, Evil & Malice, Avigon* and *Bomb Queen*. See more of Jimmie's work at homepage.mac.com/jimmykitty.

TOM POMPLUN
The designer, editor and publisher of *Graphic Classics®*, Tom also designed *Rosebud*, a journal of fiction, poetry and illustration, from 1993 to 2003, and in 2001 he founded the *Graphic Classics* series, now celebrating its tenth year. Tom is currently working on a revised edition of the out-of-print *Graphic Classics: Robert Louis Stevenson*, scheduled for April 2012 release, and on an all-new volume, *Halloween Classics*, for August 2012. Tom would particularly like to thank longtime *Graphic Classics* contributor and *African-American Classics* co-editor Lance Tooks, who has been involved in every step of the creation of this book, from conception, through story, scripting and artist selections to final proofing, as well as contributing his own art. Without him, this book would not have been possible.